BRIDGET JONES

The Edge of Reason

VIKING

75 years
•

ALSO BY HELEN FIELDING

Bridget Jones's Diary

HELEN FIELDING

BRIDGET JONES

The Edge of Reason

Viking

VIKING
Published by the Penguin Group
Penguin Putnam Inc., 375 Hudson Street,
New York, New York 10014, U.S.A.
Penguin Books Ltd, 27 Wrights Lane, London W8 5TZ, England
Penguin Books Australia Ltd, Ringwood, Victoria, Australia
Penguin Books Canada Ltd, 10 Alcorn Avenue,
Toronto, Ontario, Canada M4V 3B2
Penguin Books (N.Z.) Ltd, 182–190 Wairau Road,
Auckland 10, New Zealand

Penguin Books Ltd, Registered Offices:
Harmondsworth, Middlesex, England

First American edition
Published in 2000 by Viking Penguin,
a member of Penguin Putnam Inc.

7   9   10   8

PUBLISHER'S NOTE
This is a work of fiction. Names, characters, places, and incidents
either are the product of the author's imagination or are used
fictitiously, and any resemblance to actual persons, living or dead,
business establishments, events, or locales is entirely coincidental.

CIP data available.

ISBN 0-670-89296-3

This book is printed on acid-free paper. ∞

Printed in the United States of America
Set in Bembo
Designed by Betty Lew

CONTENTS

To the other Bridgets

ACKNOWLEDGMENTS

With thanks to Gillon Aitken, Sunetra Atkinson, Peter Bennet-Jones, Frankie Bridgewood, Richard Coles, Richard Curtis, Scarlett Curtis, Pam Dorman, Ursula Doyle, Breene Farrington, Nellie Fielding, the Fielding family, First Circle Films, Colin Firth, Paula Fletcher, Piers Fletcher, Andrew Forbes, Tina Jenkins, Sara Jones, Tracey MacLeod, Sharon Maguire, Emma Parry, Henrietta Perkins, Harry Ritchie, Sarah Sands, Tom Shone, Peter Straus, Russ Warner, Working Title Films, for inspiration, feedback and support. Research by Sara Jones.

And special thanks to Kevin Curran.

BRIDGET JONES

The Edge of Reason

1

Happily Ever After

129 lbs. (total fat groove), boyfriends 1 (hurrah!), shags 3 (hurrah!), calories 2,100, calories used up by shags 600, so total calories 1,500 (exemplary).

7:15 a.m. Hurrah! The wilderness years are over. For four weeks and five days now have been in functional relationship with adult male thereby proving am not love pariah as previously feared. Feel marvelous, rather like Posh Spice or similar radiant newlywed posing with sucked-in cheeks and lip gloss while everyone imagines her in bed with David Beckham. Ooh. Mark Darcy just moved. Maybe he will wake up and talk to me about my opinions.

7:30 a.m. Mark Darcy has not woken up. I know, will get up and make him fantastic fried breakfast with sausages, scrambled eggs and mushrooms or maybe eggs Benedict or Florentine.

7:31 a.m. Depending what eggs Benedict or Florentine actually are.

7:32 a.m. Except do not have any mushrooms or sausages.

7:33 a.m. Or eggs.

7:34 a.m. Or—come to think of it—milk.

7:35 a.m. Still has not woken up. Mmmm. He is lovely. Love looking at Him asleep. V. sexy broad shoulders and hairy chest. Not that sex object or anything. Interested in brain. Mmmm.

7:37 a.m. Still has not woken up. Must not make noise, realize, but maybe could wake Him subtly by thought vibes.

7:40 a.m. Maybe will put . . . GAAAAAH!

7:50 a.m. Was Mark Darcy sitting bolt upright yelling, "Bridget, will you stop. Bloody. Staring at me when I am asleep. Go find something to do."

8:45 a.m. In Coins Café having cappuccino, chocolate croissant and cigarette. Is relief to have fag in open and not to be on best behavior. V. complicated actually having man in house as cannot freely spend requisite amount of time in bathroom or turn into gas chamber as conscious of other person late for work, desperate for pee etc.; also disturbed by Mark folding up underpants at night, rendering it strangely embarrassing now simply to keep all own clothes in pile on floor. Also he is coming round again tonight so have to go to supermarket either before or after work. Well, do not *have* to but horrifying truth is want to, in bizarre possibly genetic-throwback-style way such as could not admit to Sharon.

8:50 a.m. Mmm. Wonder what Mark Darcy would be like as father (father to own offspring, mean. Not self. That would indeed be sick in manner of Oedipus)?

8:55 a.m. Anyway, must not obsess or fantasize.

9 a.m. Wonder if Una and Geoffrey Alconbury would let us put marquee on their lawn for the recept— Gaaah!
  Was my mother, walking into my café bold as brass in a Country Casuals pleated skirt and apple-green blazer with shiny gold but-

tons, like a spaceman turning up in the House of Commons squirting slime and sitting itself down calmly on the front bench.

"Hello, darling," she trilled. "Just on my way to Debenhams and I know you always come in here for your breakfast. Thought I'd pop in and see when you want your colors done. Ooh I fancy a cup of coffee. Do you think they'll warm up the milk?"

"Mum, I've told you I don't want my colors done," I muttered, scarlet, as people stared and a sulky, rushed-off-her-feet waitress bustled up.

"Oh don't be such a stick-in-the-mud, darling. You need to make a statement about yourself! Not sitting on the fence all the time in all these fudges and slurries. Oh, hello, dear."

Mum went into her slow, kindly "Let's try to make best friends with the waiting staff and be the most special person in the café for no fathomable reason" voice.

"Now. Let. Me. See. D'you know? I think I'll have a coffee. I've had so many cups of tea this morning up in Grafton Underwood with my husband Colin that I'm sick to death of tea. But could you warm me up some milk? I can't drink cold milk in coffee. It gives me indigestion. And then my daughter Bridget will have . . ."

Grrr. Why do parents do this. Why? Is it desperate mature person's plea for attention and importance, or is it that our urban generation are too busy and suspicious of each other to be open and friendly? I remember when I first came to London I used to smile at everyone until a man on the tube escalator masturbated into the back of my coat.

"Espresso? Filter? Latte? Cap: half-fat or decaf?" snapped the waitress, sweeping all the plates off the table next to her and looking at me accusingly as if Mum was my fault.

"Half-fat decaf cap and a latte," I whispered apologetically.

"What a surly girl, doesn't she speak English?" huffed Mum at her retreating back. "This is a funny place to live, isn't it? Don't they know what they want to put on in the morning?"

I followed her gaze to the fashionable Trustafarian girls at the next table. One was tapping at her laptop and wearing Timberlands, a petticoat, a Rastafarian bonnet and a fleece, while the other, in Prada stilettos, hiking socks, surfing shorts, a floor-length llamaskin coat and a Bhutanese herdsman's woolly hat with earflaps, was yelling into her mobile headset, "I mean, he said if he found me smoking skunk again he'd take away the flat. And I'm like, 'Fucking, Daddy' "—while her six-year-old child picked miserably at a plate of chips.

"Is that girl talking to herself with that language?" said Mum. "It's a funny world you live in, isn't it? Wouldn't you do better living near normal people?"

"They are normal people," I said furiously, nodding in illustration out at the street where unfortunately a nun in a brown habit was pushing two babies along in a pram.

"You see this is why you get yourself all mixed up."

"I don't get myself mixed up."

"Yes you do," she said. "Anyway. How's it going with Mark?"

"Lovely," I said moonily, at which she gave me a hard stare.

"You're not going to you-know-what with him, are you? He won't marry you, you know."

Grrr. Grrrr. No sooner have I started going out with the man she'd been trying to force me onto for eighteen months ("Malcolm and Elaine's son, darling, divorced, terribly lonely and rich") than I feel like I'm running some kind of Territorial Army obstacle course, scrambling over walls and nets to bring her home a big silver cup with a bow on.

"You know what they say afterwards," she was going on. " 'Oh, she was easy meat.' I mean when Merle Robertshaw started going out with Percival her mother said, 'Make sure he keeps that thing just for weeing with.' "

"Mother—" I protested. I mean it was a bit rich coming from her. Not six months ago she was running around with a Portuguese tour operator with a gentleman's handbag.

"Oh, did I tell you," she interrupted, smoothly changing the subject, "Una and I are going to Kenya."

"What!" I yelled.

"We're going to Kenya! Imagine, darling! To darkest Africa!"

My mind started to whirl round and round searching through possible explanations like a slot machine before it comes to a standstill: Mother turned missionary? Mother rented *Out of Africa* again on video? Mother suddenly remembered about *Born Free* and decided to keep lions?

"Yes, darling. We want to go on safari and meet the Masai tribesmen, then stay in a beach hotel!"

The slot machine clunked to a halt on a series of lurid images of elderly German ladies having sex on the beach with local youths. I stared levelly at Mum.

"You're not going to start messing around again, are you?" I said. "Dad's only just got over all that stuff with Julio."

"Honestly, darling! I don't know what all the fuss was about! Julio was just a friend—a penfriend! We all need friends, darling. I mean even in the best of marriages one person just isn't enough: friends of all ages, races, creeds and tribes. One has to expand one's consciousness at every—"

"When are you going?"

"Oh, I don't know, darling. It's just an idea. Anyway must whizz. Byee!"

Bugger. It's 9:15. Am going to be late for morning meeting.

11 a.m. Sit Up Britain office. Was luckily only two minutes late for meeting, also managed to conceal coat by rolling it into ball to create pleasing sense of having been in for hours and merely detained on urgent transdepartmental business elsewhere in building. Made my way in composed manner through hideous open-plan office littered with the telltale remnants of bad daytime TV—here an inflatable sheep with a hole in its bottom, there a blowup of Claudia Schiffer wearing Madeleine Albright's head, there a large cardboard sign saying: "LESBIANS! Out! Out! Out!"—towards where Richard Finch, sporting sideburns and black trendy spectacles, his portly frame squeezed hideously into a '70s retro safari suit, was bellowing at the assembled twenty-something research team.

"Come on, Bridget Droopy-Drawers Late Again," he yelled, spotting my approach. "I'm not paying you to roll coats into a ball and try to look innocent, I'm paying you to turn up on time and come up with ideas."

Honestly. The lack of respect day after day is beyond human endurance.

"Right, Bridget!" he roared. "I'm thinking New Labour Women. I'm thinking image and roles. I want Color Me Beautiful in the studio. Get them to give Margaret Beckett a makeover. Highlights. Little black dress. Stockings. I want to see Margaret looking like sex on legs."

Sometimes there seems no limit to the absurdity of what Richard Finch will ask me to do. One day, I will find myself persuading Harriet Harman and Tessa Jowell to stand in a supermarket while I ask passing shoppers if they can tell which one is which, or trying to persuade a Master of the Hunt to be chased naked through the countryside by a pack of vicious foxes. Must find more-worthwhile fulfilling job of some kind. Nurse, perhaps?

11:03 a.m. At desk. Right, had better ring Labour press office. Mmmm. Keep getting shag flashbacks. Hope Mark Darcy was not really annoyed this morning. Wonder if it is too early to ring him at work?

11:05 a.m. Yes. As it says in *How to Get the Love You Want*—or maybe it was *Keeping the Love You Find?*—the blending together of man and woman is a delicate thing. Man must pursue. Will wait for him to ring me. Maybe had better read papers to brief self about New Labour policy in case actually get Margaret Beckett on end of . . . Gaaah!

11:15 a.m. Was Richard Finch yelling again. Have been put on the fox-hunting item instead of Labour Women and have got to do live insert from Leicestershire. Must not panic. Am assured, receptive, responsive woman of substance. My sense of self comes not from my worldly achievements but from within. Am assured, receptive . . . Oh God. Is pissing it down. Do not want to go out in fridge-crossed-with-swimming-pool-like world.

11:17 a.m. Actually is v.g. to get interview to do. Big responsibility—relatively speaking, obviously, not like having to decide whether to send cruise missiles to Iraq, or holding clamp on main arterial valve during surgery, but chance to grill Fox-Murderer on camera and actually make a point rather like Jeremy Paxman or similar *Newsnight* presenter with Iranian—or Iraqi—ambassador.

11:20 a.m. Might even be asked to do trial item for *Newsnight*.

11:21 a.m. Or series of short specialized reports. Hurrah! Right, better get out cuts . . . Oh. Telephone.

11:30 a.m. Was going to ignore it but thought it might be interviewee: Sir Hugo Rt. Hon. Boynton-Fox-Murderer with directions about silos, pig huts on the left, etc. so picked up: was Magda.

"Bridget, hi! I was just ringing to say in the potty! In the potty! Do it in the potty!"

There was a loud crashing noise followed by the sound of running water and screaming in manner of Muslims being massacred by Serbs with "Mummy will smack! She will smack!" as if on a loop in the background.

"Magda!" I yelled. "Come back!"

"Sorry, hon," she said, eventually returning. "I was just ringing to say . . . tuck your willy inside the potty! If you let it hang out it'll go on the floor!"

"I'm in the middle of work," I said pleadingly. "I've got to set off to Leicestershire in two minutes . . ."

"Great, fine, rub it in, you're all very glamorous and important and I'm stuck at home with two people who haven't learned to speak the English language yet. Anyway, I was just ringing to say that I've fixed for my builder to come round and do your shelves tomorrow. Sorry to have bothered you with my boring domesticity. He's called Gary Wilshaw. Bye."

Phone rang again before had time to call back. Was Jude, sobbing in a sheep's voice.

"It's OK, Jude, it's OK," I said, tucking the phone under my chin and trying to shove the cuttings into my handbag.

"It's Vile Richard heggggggggg."

Oh dear. After Christmas Shaz and I convinced Jude that if she had *just one more* mad conversation with Vile Richard about the shifting sands of his Commitment Problem she would have to be put into a mental hospital; and therefore they would not be able to have any minibreaks, relationship counseling, or future together *anyway* for years and years until she was released into Care in the Community.

In a magnificent feat of self-love she ditched him, cut her hair and started turning up to her staid job in the City wearing leather jackets and hipster jeans. Every striped-shirted Hugo, Johnny or Jerrers who had ever idly wondered what was under Jude's suit was catapulted into a state of priapic frenzy and she seems to have a different one on the phone every night. But somehow, the whole subject of Vile Richard still makes her sad.

"I was just going through all the stuff he left, ready to chuck it out, and I found this self-help book . . . book called . . . called . . ."

"It's OK. It's OK. You can tell me."

"Called *How to Date Young Women: A Guide for Men Over Thirty-five*."

Jesus.

"I just feel terrible, terrible . . ." she was saying. ". . . I can't stand being out in dating hell again. . . . It's an impenetrable sea . . . I'm going to be on my own forever. . . ."

Working towards balance between importance of friendship and impossibility of getting to Leicestershire in negative amount of time, gave merely preliminary first-aid advice in manner of holding on to sense of self: probably left it there on purpose; no you're not; etc.

"Oh, thanks, Bridge," said Jude, after a while seeming a bit calmer. "Can I see you tonight?"

"Um, well, Mark's coming round."

There was a silence.

"Fine," she said coolly. "Fine. No, you have a good time."

Oh God, feel guilty with Jude and Sharon now I have boyfriend, almost like traitorous double-crossing side-switching guerrilla. Have arranged to see Jude tomorrow night instead, with Shaz, and merely talk through everything again on phone tonight, which seemed to go down OK. Now, had better quickly ring Magda and make sure she doesn't feel boring and realizes how opposite-of-glamorous job is.

"Thanks, Bridge," said Magda after we'd talked for a bit. "I'm just feeling really low and lonely since the baby. Jeremy's working again tomorrow night. Don't suppose you'd like to come round?"

"Um, well, I'm supposed to be seeing Jude in 192."

There was a loaded pause.

"And I suppose I'm too much of a dull Smug Married to come along?"

"No, no, come. Come, that would be great!!" I overcompensated. Knew Jude would be cross as would take focus away from Vile Richard but resolved to sort out later. So now am really late and have got to go to Leicestershire without actually having read fox-hunting cuts. Maybe could read in car when at traffic lights. Wonder if should quickly ring Mark Darcy to tell him where am going?

Hmmm. No. Bad move. But then what if I'm late? Had better ring.

11:35 a.m. Humph. Conversation went like this:

Mark: Yes? Darcy here.

Me: It's Bridget.

Mark: (Pause) Right. Er. Everything OK?

Me: Yes. It was nice last night, wasn't it? I mean—you know, when we . . .

Mark: I do know, yes. Exquisite. (Pause) I'm actually with the Indonesian ambassador, the head of Amnesty International and the Under-Secretary of State for Trade and Industry just at the moment.

Me: Oh. Sorry. I'm just going to Leicestershire. I thought I'd let you know in case anything happens to me.

Mark: In case anything . . . ? What?

Me: I mean in case I'm . . . late. (I finished lamely.)

Mark: Right. Well, why not ring with an ETA when you're through? Jolly good. Bye now.

Hmmm. Don't think I should have done that. It says specifically in *Loving Your Separated Man Without Losing Your Mind* that the one thing they really do not like is being called up for no real reason when they are busy.

7 p.m. Back in flat. Nightmare rest of day. After challenging traffic and rain-blocked journey, found self in rain-swept Leicestershire, knocking on the door of a big, square house surrounded by horse boxes, with only thirty minutes to go till transmission. Suddenly the door burst open, and a tall man was standing in corduroy trousers and a quite sexy baggy sweater.

"Humph," he said, eyeing me up and down. "Better bloody well come in. Your chaps are out the back. Where have you bloody well been?"

"I have been suddenly diverted from a top political story," I said hoity-toitily, as he led me into a big kitchen full of dogs and bits of saddle. Suddenly he turned and stared at me furiously, then biffed the table.

"It's supposed to be a free country. Once they start telling us we can't even bloody hunt on a Sunday where will it end? Baaaah!"

"Well, you could say that about people keeping slaves, couldn't you?" I muttered. "Or cutting the ears off cats. It just doesn't seem very gentlemanly to me, a crowd of people and dogs careering after one frightened little creature for fun."

"Have you ever bloody seen what a fox does to a chicken?" Sir Hugo bellowed, turning red in the face. "If we don't hunt 'em the countryside will be overrun."

"Shoot them then," I said, staring at him murderously. "Humanely. And chase something else on Sundays, like in greyhound racing. Fasten a little fluffy animal impregnated with fox smell on to a wire."

"Shoot them? Have you ever tried to shoot a bloody fox? There'll be your little frightened foxes left wounded in agony all over the bloody shop. Fluffy animal. Grrrrr!"

Suddenly he grabbed the phone and dialed. "Finch, you total arse!" he bellowed. "What have you sent me . . . some bloody little pinko? If you think you're coming out with the hunt next

Sunday . . ." At which moment the cameraman put his head round the door and said huffily, "Oh you're here, are you?" Then looked at his watch. "Don't feel you have to let us know or anything."

"Finch wants to talk to you," said Sir Hugo.

Twenty minutes later, under pain of sacking, I was on a horse preparing to trot into shot and interview the Rt. Hon. Bossybottom, also on a horse.

"OK, Bridget, we're coming to you in fifteen, go, go, go," yelled Richard Finch in my earpiece from London, at which I squeezed my knees into the horse, as instructed. Unfortunately, however, the horse would not set off.

"Go, go, go, go, go!" yelled Richard. "I thought you said you could bloody ride."

"I said I had a natural seat," I hissed, digging frantically with my knees.

"OK, Leicester, tighter on Sir Hugo till fucking Bridget gets it together five, four, three, two . . . go."

At this the Hon. Purpleface launched into a bellowing prohunting advertisement as I dug frantically with my heels until the horse reared up neurotically, cantering sideways into the shot as I clung to its neck.

"Oh my fuck, wind it up, wind it up!" yelled Richard.

"Well, that's all we've got time for. Now back to the studio!" I trilled as the horse wheeled round again and started reversing at the cameraman.

After the sniggering crew had gone I went—mortified—into the house for my things, only to practically bump into the Rt. Hon. Biffing Giant.

"Hah!" he growled. "Thought that stallion might teach you what's what. Fancy a bloody one?"

"What?" I said.

"Bloody Mary?"

Fighting instinctive urge to glug at the vodka I drew myself up to my full height. "Are you saying you sabotaged my report on purpose?"

"Maybe." He smirked.

"That's absolutely disgraceful," I said. "And not worthy of a member of the aristocracy."

"Hah! Spirit. I like that in a woman," he said throatily, then lunged towards me.

"Get off!" I said, dodging out of his way. I mean, honestly. What was he thinking of? Am professional woman, not there to be made passes at. In any sense. Though, actually, just goes to prove how much men like it if they think you are not after them. Must remember for more useful occasion.

Now have just got in, having trailed round Tesco Metro and staggered upstairs with eight carrier bags. Am really tired. Humph. How come is always me who goes to supermarket? Is like having to be career woman and wife at same time. Is like living in seventeenth . . . Oooh. Answerphone light is flashing.

"Bridget"—Richard Finch—"I want to see you in my office at nine o'clock tomorrow. Before the meeting. That's nine a.m., not nine p.m. Morning. Daylight. I don't know how else to put it, really. Just bloody well make sure you're there."

He sounded really pissed off. Hope am not about to discover impossibility of having a nice flat, a nice job and a nice boyfriend. Anyway, am going to give Richard Finch what for about journalistic integrity. Right. Better start getting everything ready. Am so tired.

8:30 p.m. Have managed to get energy back using Chardonnay, shoved all mess away, lit fire and candles, had bath, washed hair and put on makeup and v. sexy black jeans and spaghetti-strap top. Not exactly comfortable, in fact crotch of trousers and spaghetti straps really digging into self, but look nice, which is important. For as Jerry Hall said, a woman must be a cook in the kitchen and a whore in the sitting room. Or some room anyway.

8:35 p.m. Hurrah! Will be lovely, cozy, sexy evening with delicious pasta—light yet nourishing—and firelight. Am marvelous career woman/girlfriend hybrid.

8:40 p.m. Where the bloody hell is he?

8:45 p.m. Grrr. What is point of self rushing round like scalded flea if he is just going to swan in whenever he feels like it?

8:50 p.m. Bloody Mark Darcy, am really . . . Doorbell. Hurrah!

He looked gorgeous in his work suit with the top buttons of his shirt undone. As soon as he came in he dropped his briefcase, took me in his arms and turned me round in a little sexy dance. "So good to see you," he murmured into my hair. "I really enjoyed your report, fantastic horsewomanship."

"Don't," I said, pulling away. "It was awful."

"It was brilliant," he said. "For centuries people have been riding horses forwards and then, with one seminal report, a lone woman changes the face—or arse—of British horsemanship forever. It was groundbreaking, a triumph." He sat down on the sofa wearily. "I'm wrecked. Bloody Indonesians. Their idea of a breakthrough in human rights is to tell a person he's under arrest while they're shooting the back of his head off."

I poured him a glass of Chardonnay and brought it to him in manner of James Bond–style hostess saying, with a calming smile, "Supper won't be long."

"Oh my God," he said, looking around terrified as if there might be Far Eastern militia hiding in the microwave. "Have you cooked?"

"Yes," I said indignantly. I mean, you would have thought he would have been pleased! Also he had not so much as mentioned the whore outfit.

"Come here," he said, patting the sofa, "I'm only teasing you. I've always wanted to go out with Martha Stewart."

Was nice having cuddle but, thing was, pasta had already been on for six minutes and was going to go floury.

"I'll just do the pasta," I said, extracting myself. Just then, the phone rang and I lunged at it out of pure habit, thinking it might be him.

"Hi. It's Sharon. How's it going with Mark?"

"He's here," I whispered keeping my teeth and mouth clenched in the same position so Mark would not lip-read.

"What?"

" 'E's 'ere," I hissed clenched-teethedly.

15

"It's all right," said Mark, nodding reassuringly. "I realize I'm here. I don't think it's the sort of thing we should be keeping from each other."

"OK. Listen to this," said Shaz excitedly. " 'We are not saying that all men cheat. But all men do think about it. Men have these desires eating at them all the time. We try to contain our sexual urges . . .' "

"Actually, Shaz, I'm just cooking pasta."

"Oooh, 'just cooking pasta,' are we? I hope you're not turning into a Smug Going-Out-with-Someone. Just listen to this and you'll want to put it on his head."

"Hang on," I said, glancing nervously at Mark. I took the pasta off the heat and went back to the phone.

"OK," said Shaz excitedly. " 'Sometimes instincts override higher-level thinking. A man will stare at, approach or bed a woman with small breasts if he is involved with a woman with large breasts. You may not think variety is the spice of life, but believe us, your boyfriend thinks so.' "

Mark was starting to drum his fingers on the arm of the sofa.

"Shaz . . ."

"Wait . . . wait. It's this book called *What Men Want*. Right . . . 'If you have a beautiful sister, or friend, rest assured that your boyfriend is HAVING THOUGHTS ABOUT SEX WITH HER.' "

There was an expectant pause. Mark had started miming throat-slitting and toilet-chain-flushing motions.

"I mean, isn't that revolting? Aren't they just . . . ?"

"Shaz, can I call you back later?"

Next thing Shaz was accusing me of being obsessed with men when I was supposed to be a feminist. So I said, if she was supposed to be so uninterested in them, why was she reading a book called *What Men Want*? It was all turning into a hideously unfeminist man-based row when we realized it was ridiculous and said we'd see each other tomorrow.

"So!" I said brightly, sitting down next to Mark on the sofa. Unfortunately had to get up again as had sat on something that turned out to be an empty yogurt carton.

"Yeees?" he said, brushing the yogurt off my bottom. Sure there cannot have been that much on or needing quite such hard brushing but was very nice. Mmm.

"Shall we have supper?" I said, trying to keep my mind on the task in hand.

Had just put pasta in bowl and poured jar of sauce on it when the phone rang again. Decided to leave it till had eaten but answerphone clicked on and Jude sheep-voiced out, "Bridge, are you there? Pick up, pick up. Come on, Bridge, pleeeeeeease."

I picked up the phone, as Mark hit himself hard on the forehead. The thing is, Jude and Shaz have been kind to me for years before I even met Mark, so obviously it would not be right to leave the answerphone on now.

"Hi, Jude."

Jude had been to the gym where she ended up reading some article calling single girls over thirty "retreads."

"The guy was arguing that the sort of girls who wouldn't go out with him in their twenties would go out with him now but he didn't want them anymore," she said sadly. "He said they were all obsessed with settling down and babies and his rule with girls now was 'Nothing over twenty-five.' "

"Oh honestly!" I laughed gaily, trying to fight a lurch of insecurity in my own stomach. "That's just complete bollocks. No one thinks you're a retread. Think of all those merchant bankers who've been ringing you up. What about Stacey and Johnny?"

"Huh," said Jude, though she was starting to sound more cheerful. "I went out with Johnny and his friends from Credit Suisse last night. Someone told a joke about this guy who drank too much in an Indian restaurant and passed out in a korma and Johnny is so literal that he went, 'Christ! How bloody awful. I knew a bloke who ate a lot of Indian food once, and he ended up with a stomach ulcer!' "

She was laughing. The crisis had clearly passed. You see there is nothing seriously wrong, she just gets a bit paranoid sometimes. Chatted a bit more and, once her confidence seemed firmly back in residence, I rejoined Mark at the table only to discover the pasta was not quite as had planned: slopping about wetly in white-colored water.

"I like it," said Mark supportively, "I like string, I like milk. Mmmm."

"Do you think we'd better call out for a pizza?" I said, feeling a failure and a retread.

We ordered pizzas and ate them in front of the fire. Mark told me all about the Indonesians. I listened carefully and gave him my opinions and advice, which he said were very interesting and very "fresh," and I told him about horrid sacking meeting with Richard Finch. He gave me very good advice about working out what I wanted from the meeting and giving Richard plenty of places to go other than sacking me. As I explained to him, it was rather like the win-win mentality as advocated in *The 7 Habits of Highly Effective People* when the phone rang again.

"Leave it," said Mark.

"Bridget. Jude. Pick up. I think I've done the wrong thing. I just called Stacey and he hasn't called back."

I picked up. "Well, maybe he's out."

"Of his mind, just like you," said Mark.

"Shut up," I hissed, while Jude ran through the scenario. "Look, I'm sure he'll ring tomorrow. But if he doesn't, just move back one of the *Mars and Venus* Stages of Dating. He's pulling away like a Martian rubber band and you have to let him feel his attraction and spring back."

When I got off the phone, Mark was watching the football.

"Rubber bands and win-win Martians," he said, smirking at me. "It's like war command in the land of gibberish here."

"Don't you talk to your friends about emotional matters?"

"Nope," he said, flicking the remote control from one football match to the other. I stared at him in fascination.

"Do you want to have sex with Shazzer?"

"I'm sorry?"

"Do you want to have sex with Shazzer and Jude?"

"I'd be delighted! Did you mean individually? Or both at the same time?"

Trying to ignore his superficial tone, I pressed on. "When you met Shazzer after Christmas did you want to sleep with her?"

"Well. The thing is, you see, I was sleeping with you."

"But has it crossed your mind ever?"

"Well, of course it's crossed my *mind*."

"What?" I exploded.

"She's a very attractive girl. It would have been odd, surely, if it hadn't?" He grinned wickedly.

"And Jude," I said indignantly. "Sleeping with Jude. Has that ever 'crossed your mind'?"

"Well, from time to time, fleetingly, I suppose it has. It's just human nature, isn't it?"

"Human nature? I've never imagined sleeping with Giles or Nigel from your office."

"No," he murmured. "I'm not sure that anyone else has either. Tragically. Except possibly José in the post room."

Just as we'd cleared away the plates and started snogging on the rug, the phone rang again.

"Leave it," said Mark. "Please—in the name of God and all his cherubim, seraphim, saints, archangels, cloud attendants and beard trimmers—leave it."

The answerphone was already clicking on. Mark crashed his head down onto the floor as a man's voice boomed out.

"Ah, hi. Giles Benwick here, friend of Mark's. Don't suppose he's there, is he? It's just . . ." Suddenly his voice cracked. "It's just my wife just told me she wants a separation and . . ."

"Good God," said Mark and grabbed the phone. An expression of pure panic spread across his face. "Giles. Christ. Steady on . . . um . . . ah . . . um, Giles, I think I'd better give you to Bridget."

Mmm. Did not know Giles but think advice was quite good. Managed to calm him down and point him in direction of one or two useful volumes. Had lovely shag with Mark afterwards and felt v. safe and cozy lying on his chest, made all the worrying theories seem irrelevant. "Am I a retread?" I said sleepily as he leaned over to blow out the candle.

"A retard? No, darling," he said, patting my bottom reassuringly. "A little strange, perhaps, but not a retard."

2

Jellyfish at Large

*128 lbs., cigarettes smoked in front of Mark 0 (v.g.), cigarettes smoked in se-
cret 7, cigarettes not smoked 47* (v.g.).*

** i.e. nearly smoked but remembered had given up so specifically did not
smoke those particular 47. Number is not therefore number of cigarettes in
entire world not smoked (would be ridiculous, overlarge-type number).*

8 a.m. Flat. Mark has gone off to his flat to change before work so
can have little cigarette and develop inner growth and win-win
mentality ready for sacking meeting. So what I am working towards
is creating a feeling of calm equilibrium and . . . Gaaah! Doorbell.

8:30 a.m. It was Magda's builder, Gary. Fuck, fuck, fucketty fuck.
Forgot he was supposed to be coming round.

"Ah! Super! Hello! Could you come back in ten minutes? I'm
just in the middle of something," I trilled, then doubled up, cring-
ing in nightie. What would I be in the middle of? Sex? A soufflé?
Making a vase on a potter's wheel that absolutely couldn't be left in
case it dried in an incomplete form?

Still had wet hair when doorbell rang again but at least had clothes
on. Felt surge of middle-class guilt as Gary smirked at decadence of
those who loll idly in bed while a whole different world of genuine

hardworking folk have been up for so long is practically time for their lunch.

"Would you care for some tea or coffee?" I said graciously.

"Yeah. Cup of tea. Four sugars but don't stir it."

I looked at him hard wondering if this was a joke or a bit like smoking cigarettes but not inhaling. "Right," I said, "right," and started making the tea at which Gary sat down at kitchen table and lit up a fag. Unfortunately, however, when came to pour out tea realized did not have any milk or sugar.

He looked at me incredulously, surveying the array of empty wine bottles. "No milk or sugar?"

"The milk's, er, just run out and actually I don't know anybody who takes sugar in tea . . . though of course it's great to . . . er . . . to take sugar," I tailed off. "I'll just pop to the shop."

When I came back, I thought somehow he might have got his tools out of the van, but he was still sitting there, and started telling a long, complicated story about carp fishing on reservoir near Hendon. Was like business lunch where everyone chats away from the subject for so long, it becomes too embarrassing to destroy fantasy of delightful purely social occasion and you never actually get to the point.

Eventually, I crashed into seamlessly incomprehensible fish anecdote with, "Right! Shall I show you what I want doing?" and instantly realized had made crass, hurtful gaffe suggesting that I was not interested in Gary as person but merely as workman so had to reenter fish anecdote to make amends.

9:15 a.m. Office. Rushed into work, hysterical at being five minutes late, to find bloody Richard Finch nowhere to be seen. Though actually is good as have time to further plan my defense. Weird thing is: office is completely empty! So, clearly most days, when I am panicking about being late and thinking everyone else is already here reading the papers they are all being late as well, though just not quite as late as me.

Right, am going to write down my key points for meeting. Get it clear in my head like Mark says.

"Richard, to compromise my journalistic integrity by . . ."

"Richard, as you know, I take my profession as a TV journalist very seriously . . ."

"Why don't you just go fucking fuck yourself, you fat . . ."

No, no. As Mark says, think what you want, and what he wants, and also think win–win as instructed in *The 7 Habits of Highly Effective People*. Gaaaaah!

11:15 a.m. Was Richard Finch clad in a crushed raspberry Galliano suit with an aquamarine lining, galloping backwards into the office as if on a horse.

"Bridget! Right. You're crap but you're off the hook. They loved it upstairs. Loved it. Loved it. We have a proposition. I'm thinking bunny girl, I'm thinking Gladiator, I'm thinking canvassing MP. I'm thinking Oprah Winfrey meets Jerry Springer meets *Teletubbies* meets *Ready Steady Life-Swap*."

"What?" I said indignantly.

Turned out they had cooked up some demeaning scheme where every week I had to try out a different profession, then fuck it up in an outfit. Naturally I told him I am a serious professional journalist and will not consider prostituting myself in such a way, with the result that he went into a foul sulk and said he was going to consider what my value was to the program, if any.

8 p.m. Had completely stupid day at work. Richard Finch was trying to order me to appear on the program wearing tiny shorts next to blowup of Fergie in gym wear. Was trying to be very win–win about the whole thing, saying was flattered but thought they might do better with a real model, when sex god Matt from graphics came in carrying the blowup and said, "Do you want us to put up an animated ring round the cellulite?"

"Yeah, yeah, if you can do the same over Fergie," said Richard Finch.

That was it. That was just about enough. Told Richard was not in the terms of my contract to be humiliated on screen and was no way going to do it.

Got home, late and exhausted, to find Gary the Builder still there and house completely taken over with burnt toast under the grill, washing up and copies of the *Angler's Mail* and *Coarse Fisherman* all over the place.

"What do you think?" said Gary, proudly nodding at his handiwork.

"They're great! They're great!" I gushed, feeling mouth going into funny tight shape. "There's just one little thing. Do you think you could make it so the supports are all in line with each other?"

Shelves, in fact were put up in mad asymmetrical manner with supports here, there and everywhere, different on each layer.

"Yeah, well, you see, the problem is it's your electric cable, because if I plug the wall here it'll short-circuit the lot," Gary began, at which point the phone rang.

"Hello?"

"Hi, is that dating war command?" Was Mark on the mobile.

"The only thing I could do is take them out and put rivets under the awlings," gibberished Gary.

"Have you got someone there?" crackled Mark above the traffic.

"No, it's just the . . ." I was about to say builder but did not want to insult Gary so changed it to "Gary—a friend of Magda's."

"What's he doing there?"

"Course you'll need a new raw-gidge," continued Gary.

"Listen, I'm in the car. Do you want to come out for supper tonight with Giles?"

"I've said I'll see the girls."

"Oh Christ. I suppose I'll be dismembered and dissected and thoroughly analyzed."

"No you won't . . ."

"Hang on. Just going under the Westway." Crackle, crackle, crackle. "I met your friend Rebecca the other day. She seemed very nice."

"I didn't know you knew Rebecca," I said, breathing very quickly.

Rebecca is not exactly a friend, except that she's always turning up in 192 with me and Jude and Shaz. But the thing about Rebecca is, she's a jellyfisher. You have a conversation with her that seems all nice and friendly, then you suddenly feel like you've been stung and you don't know where it came from. You'll be talking about jeans and she'll say "Yes, well, if you've got cellulite jodhpurs, you're best in something really well cut like Dolce and Gabbana"—she herself having thighs like a baby giraffe—then smoothly move on to DKNY chinos as if nothing has happened.

"Bridge, are you still there?"

"Where . . . where did you see Rebecca?" I said, in a high, strangled voice.

"She was at Barky Thompson's drinks last night and introduced herself."

"Last night?"

"Yes, I dropped in on my way back because you were running late."

"What did you talk about?" I said, conscious of Gary smirking at me, with a fag hanging out of his mouth.

"Oh. You know, she asked about my work and said nice things about you," said Mark casually.

"What did she say?" I hissed.

"She said you were a free spirit . . ." The line broke up for a moment.

Free spirit? Free spirit in Rebecca-speak is tantamount to saying, "Bridget sleeps around and takes hallucinatory drugs."

"I suppose I could put up an RSJ and suspend them," Gary started up again, as if the phone conversation were not going on.

"Well. I'd better let you go, hadn't I, if you've got someone there," said Mark. "Have a good time. Shall I call you later?"

"Yes, yes, talk to you later."

I put the phone down, mind reeling.

"After someone else, is he?" said Gary in a rare and extremely unwelcome moment of lucidity.

I glared at him. "What about these shelves . . . ?"

"Well. If you want them all in line, I'll have to move your leads, and that'll mean stripping the plaster off unless we rawl in a three by four of MDF. I mean if you'd told me you wanted them symmetrical before, I'd have known, wouldn't I? I suppose I could do it now." He looked round the kitchen. "Have you got any food in?"

"They're fine, absolutely lovely just like that," I gabbled.

"If you want to cook me a bowl of that pasta I'll . . ."

Have just paid Gary £120 in cash for insane shelves to get him out of the house. Oh God, am so late. Fuck, fuck, telephone again.

9:05 p.m. Was Dad—which was strange since normally he leaves telephonic communication to Mum.

"Just called to see how you're doing." He sounded very odd.

"I'm fine," I said worriedly. "How are you?"

"Jolly good, jolly good. Very busy in the garden, you know, very busy though not much to do out there in the winter of course. . . . So, how's everything?"

"Fine," I said. "And everything's fine with you?"

"Oh, yes, yes, perfectly fine. Um, and work? How's work?"

"Work's fine. Well, I mean disastrous obviously. But are you all right?"

"Me? Oh yes, fine. Of course the snowdrops will be pop, plop, ploppeeddee plopping through soon. And everything's all right with you, is it?"

"Yes, fine. How's things with you?"

After several more minutes of the impenetrable conversational loop I had a breakthrough: "How's Mum?"

"Ah. Well, she's, she's ah . . ."

There was a long, painful pause.

"She's going to Kenya. With Una."

The worst of it was, the business with Julio the Portuguese tour operator started last time she went on holiday with Una.

"Are you going too?"

"No, no," blustered Dad. "I've no desire to sit getting skin cancer in some appalling enclave sipping piña colada and watching topless tribal dancers prostitute themselves to lascivious geriatrics in front of tomorrow's breakfast buffet."

"Did she ask you to?"

"Ah. Well. You see, no. Your mother would argue that she is a person in her own right, that our money is her money, and she should be allowed to freely explore the world and her own personality at a whim."

"Well, I suppose as long as she keeps it to those two," I said. "She does love you, Dad. You saw that"—nearly said "last time" and changed it to—"at Christmas. She just needs a bit of excitement."

"I know, but, Bridget, there's something else. Something quite dreadful. Can you hold on?"

I glanced up at the clock. I was supposed to be in 192 already and hadn't got round to telling Jude and Shaz yet that Magda was coming. I mean, it is delicate at the best of times, trying to combine friends from opposite sides of the marriage divide, but Magda has just had a baby. And I feared that wouldn't be good for Jude's mind-set.

"Sorry about that: just closing the door." Dad was back. "Anyway," he went on conspiratorially. "I overheard your mother talking on the phone earlier today. I think it was to the hotel in Kenya. And she said, she said . . ."

"It's all right, it's all right. What did she say?"

"She said, 'We don't want twins and we don't want anything under five foot. We're coming here to enjoy ourselves.'"

Christ alive.

"I mean"—poor Dad, he was practically sobbing—"am I actually to stand by and allow my own wife to hire herself a gigolo on arrival?"

For a moment was at a loss. Advising one's own father on the suspected gigolo-hiring habits of one's own mother is not a subject had ever seen covered in any of my books.

In the end I plumped for trying to help Dad boost his own self-esteem, whilst suggesting a period of calm distance before discussing things with Mum in the morning: advice I realized I would be completely incapable of following myself.

By this time I was beyond late. Explained to Dad that Jude was having a bit of a crisis.

"Off you go, off you go! When you've got time. Not to worry!"

he said overcheerily. "Better get out in the garden while the rain's holding off." His voice sounded odd and thick.

"Dad," I said, "it's nine o'clock at night. It's midwinter."

"Ah, right," he said. "Jolly good. Better have a whisky, then."

Hope he is going to be OK.

⁓ WEDNESDAY 29 JANUARY

131 lbs. (gaah! But possibly due to wine bag inside self), cigarettes 1 (v.g.), jobs 1, flats 1, boyfriends 1 (continuing good work).

5 a.m. Am never, never going to drink again as long as live.

5:15 a.m. Evening keeps coming back to me disturbingly in lumps.

After panting rush through rain, arrived at 192 to find Magda not arrived yet, thank God, and Jude already in a state, allowing her thinking to get into a Snowball Effect, extrapolating huge dooms from small incidents as specifically warned against in *Don't Sweat the Small Stuff.*

"I'm never going to have any children," she was monotoning, staring straight ahead. "I'm a retread. That guy said women over thirty are just walking pulsating ovaries."

"Oh for God's sake!" snorted Shaz, reaching for the Chardonnay. "Haven't you read *Backlash*? He's just a moral-free hack, recycling woman-bashing, Middle England propaganda to keep women down like *slaves*. I hope he goes prematurely bald."

"But how likely is it I am going to meet someone new, now, and have time to form a relationship and persuade them they want to have children? Because they never do before they get them."

Wish Jude would not talk about biological clock in public. Obviously one worries about such things in private and tries to pretend whole undignified situation isn't happening. Bringing it up in 192 merely makes one panic and feel like a walking cliché.

Happily, Shazzer was off on a rant. "Far too many women are

wasting their young lives having children in their twenties, thirties and early forties when they should be concentrating on their careers," she growled. "Look at that woman in Brazil who had one at sixty."

"Hurrah!" I said. "Nobody wants never to have any children but it's the sort of thing you always want to do in two or three years' time!"

"Fat chance," said Jude darkly. "Magda said even after she and Jeremy were married, whenever she mentioned children he went all funny and said she was getting too serious."

"What, even after they were married?" said Shaz.

"Yes," said Jude, picked up her handbag and went off to the loo in a huff.

"I've had a great idea for Jude's birthday," said Shaz. "Why don't we get her one of her eggs frozen?"

"Shhh." I giggled. "Wouldn't it be a bit difficult to do as a surprise?"

Just then, Magda walked in, which was all very unfortunate as (a) had still not got round to warning the girls and (b) got shock of life as had only seen Magda once since the birth of her third baby and her stomach had not gone down yet. She was sporting a gold shirt and velvet headband, in unignorable contrast to everyone else's urban combat/sportswear outfits.

Was just pouring Magda a glass of Chardonnay when Jude reappeared, looked from Magda's stomach to me, and gave me a filthy look. "Hi, Magda," she said gruffly. "When's it due?"

"I had her five weeks ago," said Magda, chin wobbling.

Knew it was a mistake to combine different species of friends, knew it.

"Do I look that fat?" Magda whispered to me, as if Jude and Shaz were the enemy.

"No, you look great," I said. "Glowing."

"Do I?" Magda said, brightening. "It just takes a bit of time to . . . you know . . . deflate. Also, you know I had mastitis . . ."

Jude and Shaz flinched. Why do Smug Married girls do this, why?

Casually launching into anecdotes about slashings, stitchings and effusions of blood, poison, newts and God knows what as if making light and delightful social chitchat.

"Anyway," Magda was going on, glugging at the Chardonnay and beaming happily at the friends like someone let out of prison, "Woney said to put a couple of cabbage leaves in your bra—it has to be Savoy—and after about five hours it draws out the infection. Obviously it gets a bit manky, with the sweat and milk and discharge. And Jeremy got a bit annoyed about me getting into bed with all the bleeding Down There and a bra full of damp leaves but I feel so much better! I've practically used up a whole cabbage!"

There was a stunned pause. I glanced worriedly around the table but Jude seemed to have suddenly cheered up, sleeking down her Donna Karan crop top, which revealed a beguiling glimpse of pierced navel and perfectly honed flat midriff while Shazzie adjusted her Wonderbra.

"Anyway. Enough of me. How are things going with *you?*" said Magda as if she had been reading one of those books advertised in the newspapers with a drawing of a strange '50s-looking man and a headline DOES GOOD CONVERSATION ELUDE YOU? "How's Mark?"

"He's *lovely*," I said happily. "He makes me feel so . . ." Jude and Shazzer were exchanging glances. Realized I was probably sounding a bit too smug. "The only thing is . . ." I tack-changed.

"What?" said Jude, leaning forward.

"It's probably nothing. But he called me tonight, and said he'd met Rebecca."

"WHATTTT?" exploded Shazzer. "How the fuck dare he? Where?"

"At a party last night."

"What was he doing at a party last night?" yelled Jude. "With Rebecca, without you?"

Hurrah! Was suddenly just like old times again. Carefully dissected whole tone of phone call, feelings about, and possible significance of, fact that Mark must have come straight to my flat *from the party*, yet did not mention either the party or Rebecca till a full *twenty-four hours* later.

"It's Mentionitis," Jude was saying.

"What's that?" said Magda.

"Oh, you know, when someone's name keeps coming up all the time, when it's not strictly relevant: 'Rebecca says this' or 'Rebecca's got a car like that.'"

Magda went quiet. I knew exactly why. Last year she kept telling me she thought something was up with Jeremy. Then eventually she found out he'd been having an affair with a girl in the City. I handed her a Silk Cut.

"I know exactly what you mean," she said, putting it into her mouth and nodding at me appreciatively. "How come he always comes round to your place anyway? I thought he had some great big mansion in Holland Park."

"Well, he does, but he seems to prefer to—"

"Hmm," said Jude. "Have you read *Beyond Co-dependency With a Man Who Can't Commit?*"

"No."

"Come back to my place after. I'll show you."

Magda looked up at Jude like Piglet hoping to be included on an outing with Pooh and Tigger. "He's probably just trying to get out of the shopping and clearing up," she said eagerly. "I've never met a man who didn't secretly think he should be looked after like his father was by his mother no matter how evolved they pretend to be."

"Exactly," snarled Shazzer, at which Magda beamed with pride. Unfortunately things immediately swung back to the fact that Jude's American hadn't returned her call, at which Magda immediately undid all her good work.

"Honestly, Jude!" said Magda. "I can't understand how you can deal with the collapse of the ruble to a standing ovation from the entire trading floor and then get into a state like this over a stupid man."

"Well, the thing is, Mag," I explained, trying to smooth things over, "the ruble is much easier to deal with than a man. There are clear and precise rules governing its behavior."

"I think you should leave it a couple of days," said Shaz thoughtfully. "Try not to obsess and then when he does ring just be light and really busy and say you haven't got time to talk."

"Wait a minute," Magda bludgeoned in. "If you want to talk to him, what's the point of waiting three days, then saying you haven't got time to talk to him? Why don't *you* call *him*?"

Jude and Shazzer gaped at her, incredulous at the insane Smug Married suggestion. Everyone knows that Anjelica Huston never, ever rang Jack Nicholson, and that men cannot bear not to be the pursuer.

Whole scenario went from bad to worse, with Magda talking wide-eyedly about how when Jude met the right man it would be "as easy as leaves falling off a tree." At 10:30 Magda jumped to her feet and said, "Well, better go! Jeremy's back at eleven!"

"What did you have to ask Magda for?" said Jude the second she was out of earshot.

"She was lonely," I said lamely.

"Yeah, right. Because she had to spend two hours on her own without Jeremy," said Shazzer.

"She can't have it both ways. She can't be in a Smug Married Family then moan because she isn't in a Singleton Urban Family," said Jude.

"Honestly, if that girl were thrown out into the cut and thrust of the modern dating world she'd be eaten alive," muttered Shaz.

"ALERT, ALERT, REBECCA ALERT," nuclear-sirened Jude.

We followed her gaze out of the window to where a Mitsubishi urban jeep was pulling up containing Rebecca with one hand on the wheel and the other holding the phone to her ear.

Rebecca eased her long legs out, rolling her eyes at someone who had the nerve to be walking past when she was on the phone, crossed the road without paying any attention to cars so they had to screech to a halt, did a little pirouette as if to say, "Fuck off, everyone, this is my personal space," then walked smack into a tramp lady with a shopping cart and completely ignored her.

She burst into the bar, swishing her long hair over her head from her face so it immediately swished back again in a swingy, shiny curtain. "OK, must run. Love you! Byeee!" she was saying into her mobile. "Hi, hi," she said, kissing us all, sitting down and gesturing to the waiter for a glass. "How's it going? Bridge, how's it going with Mark? You must be really pleased to get a boyfriend at last."

"At last." Grrr. First jellyfish of the evening. "Are you in heaven?" she cooed. "Is he taking you to the Law Society dinner on Friday?"

Mark hadn't said anything about any Law Society dinner.

"Oh sorry, have I put my big foot in it?" said Rebecca. "I'm sure he's just forgotten. Or maybe he thinks it isn't fair on *you*. But I think you'll cope fine. They'll probably think you're really sweet."

As Shazzer said afterwards, it wasn't so much a jellyfish as a Portuguese man-of-war. The fishermen were surrounding it in their boats trying to drag it back to the beach.

Rebecca flounced off to some do or other, so the three of us ended up lurching back to Jude's flat.

" 'The Man Who Can't Commit will not want you in his own domain,' " Jude was reading out as Shaz fiddled with the *Pride and Prejudice* video to try to find the bit where Colin Firth dives into the lake.

" 'He likes to come to your tower, like a knight errant with no responsibilities. And then he goes back to his castle. He can take and make whatever phone calls he likes without you knowing about it. He can keep his place—and himself—to himself.' "

"Too right," muttered Shaz. "OK, come on, he's going to dive in."

We all fell silent then, watching Colin Firth emerging from the lake dripping wet, in the see-through white shirt. Mmm. Mmmm.

"Anyway," I said defensively, "Mark isn't a Man Who Can't Commit—he's already been married."

"Well, then it might mean he thinks you're a 'Just For Now Girl,' " hiccuped Jude.

"Bastard!" slurred Shazzer. "Blurry bastards. Fwaw, look at that!"

Eventually staggered home, lunged expectantly towards answerphone, then stopped in dismay. No red light. Mark hadn't called. Oh God, is 6 a.m. already and have got to get some more sleep.

8:30 a.m. Why hasn't he rung me? Why? Humph. Am assured, receptive, responsive woman of substance. My sense of self depends on myself and not on . . . Wait a minute. Maybe phone is not working.

8:32 a.m. Dialing tone seems normal, but will ring from mobile to check. If not working might mean everything is fine.

8:35 a.m. Humph. Phone is working. I mean he definitely said he was going to call last . . . Oh goody, telephone!

"Oh hello, m'dear. Didn't wake you up, did I?"

Was my dad. Instantly felt guilty for being horrible, selfish daughter, more interested in own four-week-old relationship than threat to parents' three-decade-long marriage from higher than five foot, nontwin Kenyan gigolos.

"What's happened?"

"It's fine." Dad laughed. "I brought the phone call up with her and—oops-a-daisy—here she comes."

"Honestly, darling!" said Mum, grabbing the phone. "I don't know where Daddy gets these silly ideas from. We were talking about the beds!"

I smiled to myself. Obviously Dad and I have minds like sewers.

"Anyway," she went on, "it's all going ahead. We're off on the eighth of Feb! Kenya! Imagine! Ooh did I tell you? Julie Enderbury's preggy again."

"Listen, I really do have to go, I—"

What is it about mothers and the phone which, immediately you say you have to go, makes them think of nineteen completely irrelevant things they have to tell you that minute?

"Yes. It's her third," she said accusingly. "Oh and the other thing is, Una and I have decided we're going to ski the net."

"I think the expression is 'surf' but I've—"

"Ski, surf, snowboard—doesn't matter, darling! Merle and Percival are on it. You know: used to be head of the burns unit at Northampton Infirmary. Anyway, the other thing is, are you and Mark coming home for Easter?"

36

"Mum, I've got to go now, I'm late for work!" I said. Finally, after about ten more minutes of irrelevance I managed to get rid of her and sank gratefully back on the pillow. Does make me feel a bit feeble though, if mother is online and I'm not. I was on it but a company called GBH sent me 677 identical junk mails by mistake and have not been able to get any sense out of it since.

⁓ **THURSDAY 30 JANUARY**

131 lbs. (emergency: lacy pants have begun to leave patterns on self), items of lovely sexy slippy underwear tried on 17, items of giant incontinence-wear-style scary unsightly underwear purchased 1, boyfriends 1 (but entirely dependent on concealing scary new underwear from same).

9 a.m. Coins Café. Having coffee. Hurrah! Everything is lovely. He just rang! Apparently he did call me last night but didn't leave a message as he was going to ring back later, but then fell asleep. Slightly suspicious, but he asked me to come to the law thing tomorrow. Also Giles from his office said how nice I'd been on the phone.

9:05 a.m. Bit scary, though, law do. Is black tie. Asked Mark about what was expected of me and he said, "Oh nothing. Don't worry about it. We'll just sit at a table and eat a meal with some people from work. They're just my friends. They'll love you."

9:11 a.m. "They'll love you." You see that, already, is tacit admission that am up on trial. So is very important to make a good impression.

9:15 a.m. Right, am going to be positive about this. Am going to be marvelous: elegant, vivacious, beautifully dressed. Oh, though. Do not have long dress. Maybe Jude or Magda will lend me one.
 Right:

Pre–Law Society Dinner Countdown
Day 1. (today)
Projected food intake:

1. Breakfast: fruit shake, comprising oranges, banana, pears, melons or other fruit in season. (NB prebreakfast cappuccino and chocolate croissant already consumed.)
2. Snack: fruit but not too near lunch as takes one hour to get enzymes down.
3. Lunch: salad with protein.
4. Snack: celery or broccoli. Will go to gym after work.
5. After-gym snack: celery.
6. Dinner: grilled chicken and steamed vegetables.

6 p.m. Just leaving office. Am going late-night underwear shopping tonight with Magda to solve figure problems in short term. Magda is going to lend me jewels and v. elegant long, dark-blue dress which, she says, needs a bit of "help" and apparently all film stars etc. wear controlling undergarments at premieres. Means cannot go to gym but sturdy undergarment much more effective in short term than gym visit.

Also, just in general, have decided against random daily gym visits in favor of whole new program beginning with fitness assessment tomorrow. Obviously cannot expect body to be significantly transformed in time for dinner, which is precisely point of underwear shopping, but at least will be invigorated. Oh, telephone.

6:15 p.m. Was Shazzer. Quickly told her about pre–law party program (including unfortunate pizza-for-lunch debacle), but when told her about fitness assessment she seemed to spit down the telephone.

"Don't do it," she warned in a sepulchral whisper.

Turns out Shaz previously endured similar assessment with enormous *Gladiators*-style woman with fierce red hair called "Carborundum" who stood her in front of a mirror in the middle of the gym and bellowed, "The fat on your bottom has slipped down, pushing the fat on your thighs round to the sides in the form of saddlebags."

Hate the idea of the *Gladiators*-style woman. Always suspect one day *Gladiators* program will get out of control, Gladiators will turn flesh-eating and producers will start tossing Christians to Carborundum and her ilk. Shaz says I should definitely cancel, but my point is if, as Carborundum suggests, fat is able to behave in this slippage-style way then clearly it ought to be possible to mold and squeeze existing fat into nicer shape—or even different shapes as occasion demands. Cannot help but wonder if was free to arrange own fat according to choice would I still wish to reduce amount? Think would have huge big breasts and hips and tiny waist. But would there be too much fat to dispose of in this way? And where could one put the excess? Would it be bad to have fat feet or ears if the rest of one's body was perfect?

"Fat lips would be all right," Shazzer said, "but not . . ."—lowering her voice to a disgusted whisper—". . . fat labia."

Ugh. Sometimes Shazzer is completely disgusting. Right. Got to go. Am meeting Magda in Marks & Sparks at 6:30.

9 p.m. Back home. Shopping experience was perhaps best described as educational. Magda insisted on waving ghastly huge scary pants at me. "Come on, Bridget: the New Corsetry! Think '70s, think Cross Your Heart, think girdle," she said, holding up a sort of Cyclist Serial Killer's outfit in black Lycra with shorts, boning and a sturdy bra.

"I'm not wearing that," I hissed out of the corner of my mouth. "Put it back."

"Why not?"

"What if someone, you know, feels it?"

"Honestly, Bridget. Underwear is there to do a job. If you're wearing a sleek little dress or a pair of trousers—for work, say—you want to create a smooth line. Nobody's going to feel you at work, are they?"

"Well, they might," I said defensively, thinking about what used to happen in the lift at work when I was "going out"—if one can describe that commitment-phobicity nightmare as such—with Daniel Cleaver.

"What about these?" I said hopefully, holding up a gorgeous set that was made out of the same material as sheer black stockings only bra- and pants-shaped.

"No! No! Totally 1980s. This is what you want," she said, waving something that looked like one of Mum's roll-ons crossed with her long johns.

"But what if someone puts their hand up your skirt?"

"Bridget, you are unbelievable," she said loudly. "Do you get up every morning with the idea that some man might randomly put his hand up your skirt during the course of the day? Don't you have any control over your sexual destiny?"

"Yes I do actually," I said defiantly, marching towards the changing room with a whole handful of sturdy pants. Ended up trying to squeeze myself into a black rubberlike sheath, which came up to just below my breasts and kept unraveling itself from both ends like an unruly condom. "What if Mark sees me in it or feels it?"

"You're not going to smooch in a club. You're going to a formal dinner where he'll be making an impression on his colleagues. He'll be concentrating on that—not trying to grope you."

Not sure Mark ever concentrates on making an impression on anyone actually, as is confident in self. But Magda is right about the underwear. One must move with the times, not becoming entrenched in narrow underwear concepts.

Right, must get early night. Gym appointment is at eight in morning. Actually really think whole personality is undergoing seismic change.

130 lbs., alcohol units 6 (2)*, cigarettes 12 (0), calories 4,284 (1,500), lies told to fitness assessor (14).

* Figures in parentheses denote data given to fitness assessor.

9:30 a.m. It is typical of the new louche health club culture that personal trainers are allowed to behave like doctors without any sort of Hippocratic oath.

"How many alcohol units do you drink a week?" said "Rebel": Brad Pitt–style whippersnapper fitness assessor as I sat trying to hold in stomach in bra and pants.

"Fourteen to twenty-one," I lied smoothly, at which he had the nerve to flinch.

"And do you smoke?"

"I've given up," I purred.

At this, Rebel glanced pointedly into my bag where, OK, there was a packet of Silk Cut Ultra, but so?

"When did you give up?" he said primly, typing something into the computer that would obviously go straight to Conservative Central Office and ensure I am sent to a boot camp next time I get a parking fine.

"Today," I said firmly.

Ended up standing having fat measured with pincers by Rebel.

"Now I'm just making these marks so I can see what I'm measuring," he said bossily, putting circles and crosses all over me with a felt tip. "They'll come off if you rub them with a bit of white spirit."

Next had to go into gym and do exercises with all sorts of unexplained eye contact and touching with Rebel—e.g., standing opposite with hands on each other's shoulders with Rebel doing squats, bouncing bottom robustly on mat and me making awkward attempts to bend knees slightly. At end of whole thing felt as though had had long and intimate sex session with Rebel and we were practically going out. Afterwards got dressed and had shower, then was unsure what to do—seemed ought at least to go back in and ask what time he'd be home for dinner. But of course am having dinner with Mark Darcy.

V. excited about dinner. Have been practicing in outfit and really it looks excellent, sleek smooth lines, all thanks to scary pants, which there is no reason he should find out about. Also really no reason why should not be v.g. escort. Am woman of world with career etc.

Midnight. When finally arrived at Guildhall, Mark was pacing up and down outside in black tie and big overcoat. Fwaw. Love when you are going out with someone and they suddenly seem like an extremely attractive stranger and all you want to do is rush home and shag them senseless as if you have only just met. (Not, of course, that that is what normally do with people have only just met.) When he saw me he looked really shocked, laughed, then composed his features and gestured me towards the doors in polite, public-school fashion.

"Sorry I'm late," I said breathlessly.

"You're not," he said, "I lied about the kickoff." He looked at me again in a strange way.

"What?" I said.

"Nothing, nothing," he said overcalmly and pleasantly, as if I were a lunatic standing on a car holding an ax in one hand and his wife's head in the other. He ushered me through the door, as a uniformed footman held it open for us.

Inside was high, dark-paneled entrance hall with many black-tied old people murmuring around. Saw woman in sequined crusty top thing looking at me in odd way. Mark nodded pleasantly at her and whispered in my ear, "Why don't you just slip into the cloakroom and look at your face."

I shot off into loo. Unfortunately, in the dark of taxi, I had applied dark gray Mac eyeshadow to my cheeks instead of blusher: the sort of thing that could happen to anyone, obviously, as packaging identical. When came out of toilets, neatly scrubbed with coat handed in, stopped dead in tracks. Mark was talking to Rebecca.

She was wearing a coffee-colored plunging, backless satin number that clung to her every fleshless bone with clearly no corset. Felt like my dad did when he put a cake into the Grafton Underwood fete and when he returned to it after the judging it had a note on saying, "Not up to Competition Standard."

"I mean it was just too funny," Rebecca was saying and laughing full in Mark's face affectionately. "Oh Bridget," Rebecca said, as I joined them. "How are you, lovely girl!" She kissed me, at which could not stop self pulling face. "Feeling nervous?"

"Nervous?" said Mark. "Why would she be nervous? She's the embodiment of inner poise, aren't you, Bridge."

For just a split second saw a look of annoyance cross Rebecca's face before she composed it again and said, "Ahhh, isn't that sweet? I'm so happy for you!" Then she glided off with a coy little backwards look at Mark.

"She seems very nice," said Mark. "Always seems extremely nice and intelligent."

Always?? I was thinking. Always? I thought he'd only met her twice. He slid his arm dangerously close to my corset so had to jump away. A couple of huffer-puffers came up to us and started congratulating Mark about something he'd done with a Mexican. He chatted pleasantly for a minute or two, then skillfully extracted us and led us through to the dining room.

Was v. glamorous: dark wood, round tables, candlelight and shimmering crystal. Trouble was, kept having to jump away from Mark every time he put his hand on my waist so he wouldn't feel the corset.

Our table was already filling up with an array of brittly confident thirty-something lawyers, bellowing with laughter and trying to outdo each other with the sort of flippant conversational sallies that are obviously tips of huge icebergs of legal and Zeitgeisty knowledge:

"How do you know if you're addicted to the Internet?"

"You realize you don't know the gender of your three best friends." Haaar Waagh. Harharhar.

"You can't write full stops any more without adding co.uk." BAAAAAAAAAAA!

"You do all your work assignments in HMTL Protocol." Blaaaaagh harhar. Braaaah. Hahah.

As the room started to settle into the meal, a woman called Louise Barton-Foster (incredibly opinionated lawyer and the sort of woman you can imagine forcing you to eat liver) started holding forth for what seemed like three months with complete bollocks.

"But in a sense," she was saying, staring ferociously at the menu, "one could argue the entire ER Emeuro Proto is a Gerbilisshew."

Was perfectly OK—just sat quietly and ate and drank things—until Mark suddenly said, "I think you're absolutely right, Louise. If I'm going to vote Tory again I want to know my views are being (a) researched and (b) represented."

I stared at him in horror. Felt like my friend Simon did once when he was playing with some children at a party when their grandfather turned up and he was Robert Maxwell—and suddenly Simon looked at toddlers and saw they were all mini–Robert Maxwells with beetling brows and huge chins.

Realize when start a relationship with a new person there will be differences between you, differences that have to be adapted to and smoothed down like rough corners, but had never, ever in a million years suspected I might have been sleeping with a man who voted Tory. Suddenly felt I didn't know Mark Darcy at all, and for all I knew, all the weeks we had been going out he had been secretly collecting limited edition miniature pottery animals wearing bonnets from the back pages of Sunday supplements, or slipping off to rugby matches on a bus and mooning at other motorists out of the back window.

Conversation was getting snootier and snootier and more and more showy-offy.

"Well, how do you know it's 4.5 to 7?" Louise was barking at a man who looked like Prince Andrew in a stripy shirt.

"Well, I did read economics at Cambridge."

"Who taught you?" snapped another girl, as if this were going to win the argument.

"Are you all right?" whispered Mark out of the corner of his mouth.

"Yes," I muttered, head down.

"You're . . . *quivering*. Come on. What is it?"

Eventually I had to tell him.

"So I vote Tory, what's wrong with that?" he said, staring at me incredulously.

"Shhhhhh," I whispered, looking nervously round the table.

"What's the problem?"

"It's just," I began, wishing Shazzer were here, "I mean, if I voted Tory I'd be a social outcast. It would be like turning up at Café Rouge on a horse with a pack of beagles in tow, or having dinner parties on shiny tables with side plates."

"Rather like this, you mean?" He laughed.

"Well, yes," I muttered.

"So what do you vote, then?"

"Labour, of course," I hissed. "Everybody votes Labour."

"Well, I think that's patently been proved not to be the case, *so far*," he said. "Why, as a matter of interest?"

"What?"

"Why do you vote Labour?"

"Well," I paused thoughtfully, "because voting Labour stands for being left wing."

"Ah." He seemed to think this was somehow hugely amusing. Everyone was listening now.

"And socialist," I added.

"Socialist. I see. Socialist meaning . . . ?"

"The workers standing together."

"Well, Blair isn't exactly going to shore up the powers of the unions, is he?" he said. "Look what he's saying about Clause Four."

"Well, the Tories are rubbish."

"Rubbish?" he said. "The economy's in better shape now than it's been in for seven years."

"No it's not," I said emphatically. "Anyway, they've probably just put it up because there's an election coming."

"Put what up?" he said. "Put the economy up?"

"How does Blair's stand on Europe compare to Major's?" Louise joined in.

"Yar. And why hasn't he matched the Tory promise to increase spending on health year by year in real terms?" said Prince Andrew.

Honestly. Off they went again all showing off to each other. Eventually could stand it no longer.

"The point is you are supposed to vote for the principle of the thing, not the itsy-bitsy detail about this percent and that percent. And it is perfectly obvious that Labour stands for the principle of sharing, kindness, gays, single mothers and Nelson Mandela as opposed to braying bossy men having affairs with everyone shag-shag-shag left, right and center and going to the Ritz in Paris then telling all the presenters off on the *Today* program."

There was a cavernous silence round the table.

"Well, I think you've got it in a nutshell there," said Mark, laughing and rubbing my knee. "We can't argue with that."

Everyone was looking at us. But then, instead of someone taking the piss—such as would have happened in the normal world—they pretended nothing had happened and went back to the clinking and braying, completely ignoring me.

Could not gauge how bad or otherwise incident was. Was like being amongst a Papua New Guinea tribe, and treading on the chief's dog and not knowing whether the murmur of conversation meant it didn't matter or that they were discussing how to make your head into a frittata.

Someone rapped on the table for the speeches, which were just really, really, crashingly, fist-eatingly boring. As soon as they were over Mark whispered, "Let's get out, shall we?"

We said our good-byes, and set off across the room. "Er . . . Bridget," he said, "I don't want to worry you. But you've got something slightly odd-looking round your waist."

Shot my hand down to check. Scary corset had somehow unraveled itself from both ends turning into bulging roll round my waist like giant spare tire.

"What is it?" said Mark, nodding and smiling to people as we made our way through the tables.

"Nothing," I muttered. As soon as we got out of the room I made a bolt for the loo. Was really difficult getting the dress off and unraveling the scary pants then putting the whole nightmare ensemble back again. Really wished I was at home wearing a pair of baggy trousers and a sweater.

When I emerged into the hallway I nearly turned straight back into the loos. Mark was talking to Rebecca. Again. She whispered something in his ear, then burst out into a horrid hooting laugh.

I walked up to them and stood there awkwardly.

"Here she is!" said Mark. "All sorted out?"

"Bridget!" said Rebecca, pretending to be pleased to see me. "I hear you've been impressing everyone with your political views!"

Wished could think of something v. amusing to say, but instead just stood there looking out under lowered eyebrows.

"Actually, it was great," said Mark. "She made the whole lot of us look like pompous arses. Anyway, must be off, nice to see you again."

Rebecca kissed us both effusively in a cloud of Gucci Envy then sashayed back into the dining room in a way that was really obvious she hoped Mark was watching.

Couldn't think what to say as we walked to the car. He and Rebecca had obviously been laughing at me behind my back and then he'd tried to cover up for it. Wished could ring up Jude and Shaz for advice.

Mark was behaving as if nothing had happened. As soon as we set off he started trying to slide his hand up my thigh. Why is it that the less you appear to want sex with men the more they do?

"Don't you want to keep your hands on the wheel?" I said, desperately trying to shrink back, to keep the edge of the rubber roll-on thing away from his fingers.

"No. I want to ravish you," he said, lunging at a traffic light.

Managed to remain intact by feigning road safety obsession.

"Oh. Rebecca said did we want to go round for dinner sometime?" he said.

I couldn't believe this. I've known Rebecca for four years and she has never once asked me round for dinner.

"She looked nice, didn't she? Nice dress thing."

It was Mentionitis. It was Mentionitis happening before my very ears.

We'd reached Notting Hill. At the lights, without asking me, he just turned in the direction of my house, and away from his. He was keeping his castle intact. It was probably full of messages from Rebecca. I was a Just For Now Girl.

"Where are we going?" I burst out.

"Your flat. Why?" he said, looking round in alarm.

"Exactly. Why?" I said furiously. "We've been going out for four weeks and six days. And we've never stayed at your house. Not once. Not ever! Why?"

Mark went completely silent. He indicated, turned left, then swung back towards Holland Park Avenue without saying a word.

"What's the matter?" I said eventually.

He stared straight ahead and flicked on the indicator. "I don't like shouting."

When we got back to his house it was awful. Walked up the steps together in silence. He opened the door, picked up the mail and flicked the lights on in the kitchen.

Kitchen is the height of a double-decker bus and one of those seamless stainless steel ones where you cannot tell which one is the fridge. Was a strange absence of things lying around and three pools of cold light in the middle of the floor.

He strode off to the other end of the room, footsteps echoing hollowly as if in underground cavern on school trip, stared worriedly at the stainless steel doors and said, "Would you like a glass of wine?"

"Yes please, thank you," I said politely. There were some modern-looking high stools at a stainless steel breakfast bar. I climbed awkwardly on to one, feeling like Andy Williams preparing to do a duet with Petula Clark.

"Right," said Mark. He opened one of the stainless steel cupboard doors, noticed it had a bin attached to it, then closed it again, opened another door and gazed down in surprise at a washing machine. I looked down, wanting to laugh.

"Red or white wine?" he said abruptly.

"White, please." Suddenly I felt really tired, my shoes hurt, my scary pants were digging into me. I just wanted to go home.

"Ah." He had located the fridge.

Glanced across and saw the answerphone on one of the counters. Stomach lurched. The red light was flashing. Looked up to find Mark standing right in front of me holding a wine bottle in Conran-esque distressed iron decanter. He looked really miserable too.

"Look, Bridget, I . . ."

I got off the stool to put my arms round him, but then immediately his hands went to my waist. I pulled away. I had to get rid of the bloody thing.

"I'm just going to go upstairs for a minute," I said.

"Why?"

"To the loo," I said wildly, then teetered off in the now agonizing shoes towards the stairs. Went into the first room I came to, which seemed to be Mark's dressing room, a whole room full of suits and shirts and lines of shoes. Got myself out of the dress and, with huge relief, started peeling off the scary pants, thinking could put on a dressing gown and maybe we could get all cozy and sort things out but suddenly Mark appeared in the doorway. I stood frozen in full scary undergarment exposure, then started to frantically pull it off while he stared, aghast.

"Wait, wait," he said, as I reached for the dressing gown, looking intently at my stomach. "Have you been drawing noughts and crosses on yourself?"

Tried to explain to Mark about Rebel and not being able to buy white spirit on a Friday night but he just looked very tired and confused.

"I'm sorry, I have no idea what you're talking about," he said. "I've got to get some sleep. Shall we just go to bed?"

He pushed open another door, turned on the light. I took one look then let out a big noise. There, in the huge white bed, was a lithe oriental boy, stark naked, smiling weirdly, and holding out two wooden balls on a string, and a baby rabbit.

3

Doooom!

129 lbs., alcohol units 6 (but mixed with tomato juice, v. nutritious), ciga-
rettes 400 (entirely understandable), rabbits, deer, pheasants or other wildlife
found in bed 0 (massive improvement on yesterday), boyfriends 0, boyfriends
of ex-boyfriend 1, no. of normal potential boyfriends remaining in world 0.

12:15 a.m. Why do these things keep happening to me? Why?
WHY? The one time someone seems a nice sensible person such as
approved of by mother and not married, mad, alcoholic or fuckwit,
they turn out to be gay bestial pervert. No wonder he didn't want
me to go to his house. Was not that he is commitment phobic or
fancies Rebecca or I am Just For Now Girl. Is because he was keeping oriental boys in bedroom together with wildlife.

Was hideous shock. Hideous. Stared at the oriental boy for about
two seconds then shot back into the dressing room, flung my dress
on, ran down the stairs hearing shouting in the bedroom behind me
in manner of American troops being massacred by Vietcong,
teetered into the street and started waving frantically at taxis like call
girl who has stumbled on a client who wanted to do a dump on her
head.

Maybe is true what Smug Marrieds say that only men left single
are single because they have massive flaw. That is why everything is
such a fucking, fucking, fucking . . . I mean not that being gay is itself a flaw, but definitely is if are girlfriend of one who pretended

53

was not. Am going to be on own on Valentine's Day for fourth year running, spend next Christmas in single bed in parents' house. Again. Doom. Doooom!

Wish could ring up Tom. Typical of him to go to San Francisco just when need advice from gay perspective, typical. He is always asking me to give him advice for hours on end about his crises with other homosexuals then when I need advice about a crisis with a homosexual, what does he do? He goes to BLOODY SAN FRAN-CISCO.

Calm, calm. Realize is wrong to avoid responsibility for mood by blaming entire incident on Tom, especially in view of fact that incident has nothing to do with Tom. Am assured, receptive, responsive woman of substance, totally complete within myself . . . Gaah! Telephone.

"Bridget. It's Mark. I'm so sorry. I'm so sorry. That was an awful thing to happen."

He sounded terrible.

"Bridget?"

"What?" I said, trying to stop my hands shaking so I could light a Silk Cut.

"I know what it must have looked like. I got as much of a shock as you. I've never seen him before in my life."

"Well, who was he then?" I burst out.

"It turns out he's my housekeeper's son. I didn't even know she had a son. Apparently he's schizophrenic."

There was shouting in the background.

"I'm coming, I'm coming. Oh God. Look, I'm going to have to go sort this out. It sounds like he's trying to strangle her. Can I call you later?"—more shouting—"Hang on, just . . . Bridget, I'll call you in the morning."

Very confused. Wish could ring Jude or Shaz to find out if excuse is valid but is middle of night. Maybe will try to sleep.

9 a.m. Gaah! Gaah! Telephone. Hurrah! No! Doom! Have just re-membered what happened.

9:30 a.m. Was not Mark but my mother.

"D'you know, darling, I'm absolutely livid."

"Mum," I interrupted resolutely. "Do you mind if I ring you back on the mobile?"

It was all coming back to me in waves. I had to get her off the phone in case Mark was trying to call.

"Mobile, darling? Don't be silly—you haven't had one of those since you were two. Do you remember? With little fishes on? Oh. Daddy wants a word but . . . Anyway, here he is."

I waited, looking frantically between the mobile and the clock.

"Hello, my dear," said Dad wearily. "She's not going to Kenya."

"Great, well done," I said, glad that at least one of us not in crisis. "What did you do?"

"Nothing. Her passport's expired."

"Hah! Brilliant. Don't tell her you can get new ones."

"Oh, she knows, she knows," he said. "The thing is, if you have a new one, you have to have a new photo. So it's not out of any respect for me, it's purely a matter of flirting with customs officials."

Mum grabbed the phone. "It's just completely ridiculous, darling. I had my photo taken and I look as old as the hills. Una said try it in a booth but it's worse. I'm keeping the old passport and that's an end of the matter. Anyway, how's Mark?"

"He's fine," I said, in a high, strangled voice, narrowly avoiding adding: he likes to sleep with oriental youths and fiddle with rabbits, isn't that fun?

"Well! Daddy and I thought you and Mark would like to come to lunch tomorrow. We haven't seen you both together. I thought I'd just stick a lasagne in the oven with some beans."

"Can I ring you back later? I'm late for . . . yoga!" I said, inspired.

Managed to get free of her after a freakishly short fifteen-minute wind-down during which it became increasingly clear that the entire might of the British Passport Office was not going to be much of a match for Mum and the old photo, then fumbled for another Silk Cut, desolate and confused. Housekeeper? I mean I know he does have a housekeeper but . . . And then all this stuff with

Rebecca. And he votes Tory. Maybe will eat some cheese. Gaah! Telephone.

Was Shazzer.

"Oh Shaz," I said miserably, and started to blurt out the story.

"Stop right there," she said, before I'd even got as far as the oriental boy. "Stop. I'm going to say this once and I want you to listen."

"What?" I said, thinking if there was one person in the world incapable of just saying something once—apart from my mother—it was Sharon.

"Get out."

"But . . ."

"Get out. You've had the warning sign, he votes Tory. Now get out before you get too involved."

"But wait, that's not . . ."

"Oh for God's sake," she growled. "He's got it every which way, hasn't he? He comes to your house, he has everything done for him. You turn up all dressed up to the nines for his ghastly Tory friends and what does he do? Flirts with Rebecca. Patronizes you. And votes Tory. It's all just manipulative, paternalistic . . ."

I glanced nervously at the clock. "Um, Shaz, can I ring you back on the mobile?"

"What! In case he rings you? No!" she exploded.

Just then the mobile actually started ringing.

"Shaz, I'm going to have to go. I'll call you later."

Pressed OK eagerly on the mobile.

Was Jude. "Oh, oh I feel so hung over. I think I'm going to throw up." She started launching into great long story about party at the Met Bar but had to stop her as really felt whole oriental youth issue was more pressing. Really felt was right about this. Was not being selfish.

"Oh God, Bridge," said Jude when I'd finished. "You poor thing. I think you've handled it really, really well. I really do. You've really come on."

Felt huge glow of pride, followed by puzzlement. "What did I do?" I said, looking round the room alternating between self-satisfied smiling and confused blinking.

"You've done exactly what it says in *Women Who Love Too Much*. You've done nothing. Just detached. We cannot solve their problems for them. We simply detach."

"Right, right," I said, nodding earnestly.

"We don't wish them ill. We don't wish them well. We do not call them. We do not see them. We simply detach. Housekeeper's son, my arse. If he's got a housekeeper how come he's always round your place getting you to wash up?"

"But what if it *was* the housekeeper's son?"

"Now, Bridget," said Jude sternly, "this is what's called Denial."

11:15 a.m. Have arranged to meet Jude and Shazzer in 192 for lunch. Right. Am not going to be in Denial.

11:16 a.m. Yes. Am completely detached. You see!

11:18 a.m. Cannot believe he still hasn't fucking, fucking, fucking well rung. Hate passive-aggressive behavior of telephone in modern dating world, using noncommunication as means of communication. Is terrible, terrible: with simple ring or nonring meaning difference between love and friendliness and happiness and being cast out into ruthless dating trench war again, exactly the same but feeling even more of a fuckup than last time.

Noon. Could not believe it. Phone actually started ringing while I was staring at it, as if I had made it ring through thought-vibe energy and this time it was Mark.

"How are you?" he said wearily.

"I'm fine," I said, trying to be detached.

"Shall I pick you up and we'll go for lunch and talk?"

"Um, I'm having lunch with the girls," I said really quite detachedly indeed.

"Oh *God.*"

"*What?*"

"Bridget. Do you have any idea what sort of night I've had? I had this boy trying to strangle his mother in the kitchen, the police and ambulance round, tranquilizer darts, drives to the hospital, hysterical Filipinos all over the house. I mean I'm really, really sorry you had to go through all that, but so did I and it was hardly my fault."

"Why didn't you call before?"

"Because every time I got a second to call, either on the phone or the mobile, you were bloody well engaged!"

Hmmm. Detachment did not go particularly well. He really has had an awful time. Have arranged to meet him for dinner and he says he's going to sleep this afternoon. Alone, I do so deeply and sincerely hope.

~ **Sunday 2 February**

128 lbs. (excellent: am turning into Oriental Boy), cigarettes 3 (v.g.), calories 2,100 (v. modest), boyfriends 1 again (hurrah!), self-help books counted out loud in dismissive incredulous manner by newly reinstated boyfriend 37 (only sensible in this day and age).

10 p.m. In flat. Everything is good again. Dinner was a bit awkward to start with but got better when decided I did believe him about story, especially as he said I should come and see the housekeeper today.

But then, when we were having our chocolate mousses, he said, "Bridge? Last night even before this happened I'd started to feel as though things weren't right."

Felt cold clunk of dread in stomach. Which was ironic really considering had been thinking things weren't right myself. But really, it is all very well you yourself thinking things aren't right in a relationship, but if the other person starts doing it is like someone else criticizing your mother. Also it starts you thinking you are about to be chucked, which, apart from pain, loss, heartbreak etc. is very humiliating.

"Bridge? Are you in a hypnotic state?"

"No. Why did you think things weren't right?" I whispered.

"Well, every time I tried to touch you, you shrank away as if I were some elderly lech."

Huge sense of relief. Explained to him about the scary pants at which he started really laughing. Ordered some dessert wine, both got a bit squiffy and ended up going back to my flat and having fantastic shag.

This morning, when we were lying around reading the papers in front of the fire, started wondering whether should bring up the Rebecca business, and why he always stays at my house. But then Jude said I shouldn't because jealousy is v. unattractive trait to opposite sex.

"Bridget," said Mark, "you seem to have gone into a trance. I was asking what was the meaning of the new shelving system. Are you meditating? Or is the shelf support system in some way Buddhist?"

"It's because of the electric wire," I said vaguely.

"What are all these books?" he said, getting up and looking at them. "*How to Date Young Women: A Guide for Men Over Thirty-five? If the Buddha Dated? Going for It* by Victor Kiam?"

"They're my self-help books!" I said protectively.

"*What Men Want? Beyond Co-dependency with a Man Who Can't Commit? Loving Your Separated Man Without Losing Your Mind?* You do realize you're building up the largest body of theoretical knowledge about the behavior of the opposite sex in the known universe. I'm starting to feel like a laboratory animal!"

"Um . . ."

He was grinning at me. "Are you supposed to read them in pairs?" he said, pulling a book off the shelves. "Cover yourself both ways? *Happy to Be Single* with *How to Find Your Perfect Partner in Thirty Days? Buddhism Made Simple* with *Going for It* by Victor Kiam?"

"No," I said indignantly. "You read them individually."

"Why on earth do you buy this stuff?"

"Well, actually I have a theory about this," I began excitedly (because actually I do have a theory about it). "If you consider other world religions such as—"

"Other world religions? Other than what?"

Grrr. Sometimes wish Mark was not so bloody legally trained.

"Other than self-help books."

"Yes, I thought you might be about to say that. Bridget, self-help books are not a religion."

"But they are! They are a new *form* of religion. It's almost as if human beings are like streams of water so when an obstacle is put in their way, they bubble up and surge around it to find another path."

"Bubble up and surge around, Bridge?"

"What I mean is if the organized religion collapses then people start trying to find another set of rules. And actually, as I was *saying*, if you look at self-help books they have a lot of ideas in common with other religions."

"Such as . . . ?" he said, waving his hand in an encouraging circle.

"Well, Buddhism and . . ."

"No. Such as what ideas?"

"Well," I began, panicking slightly as unfortunately the theory is not all that well developed as yet, "positive thinking. It says in *Emotional Intelligence* that optimism, that everything will turn out all right, is the most important thing. Then, of course, there is belief in yourself, like in *Emotional Confidence*. And if you look at Christianity . . ."

"Yeees . . . ?"

"Well, that bit they read at weddings, it's the same: 'These three things remain: faith, *hope* and love.' Then there's living in the moment—that's *The Road Less Traveled* and also Buddhist."

Mark was looking at me as if I were mad.

". . . And forgiveness: it says in *You Can Heal Your Life* that holding on to resentment is bad for you and you have to forgive people."

"So what's that then? Not Muslim, I hope. I don't think you find much forgiveness in a faith that lops people's hands off for stealing bread buns."

Mark was shaking his head and staring at me. It did not seem to me that he really understood the theory. But maybe that was because Mark's spiritual soul is not very advanced, which could actually prove to be another problem in our relationship.

" 'Forgive us our trespasses as we forgive those who trespass against us'!!" I said indignantly. Just then the phone rang.

"That'll be dating war command," said Mark. "Or maybe the Archbishop of Canterbury!"

Was my mum. "What are you doing still there? Chop, chop. I thought you and Mark were coming to lunch."

"But Mum . . ." Was sure had not said we were coming to lunch, was sure of it. Mark was rolling his eyes and turning on the football.

"Honestly, Bridget. I've made three pavlovas—though actually it's just as easy to make three pavlovas as one, and I've taken a lasagne out and . . ."

Could hear Dad going, "Leave her alone, Pam," in the background as she went on and on huffily about the dangers of refreezing meat, then he came on the phone.

"Don't worry, m'dear. I'm sure you didn't tell her you were coming. It just turned into that in her head. I'll try to calm things down. Anyway, the bad news is, she's going to Kenya."

Mum grabbed the phone. "It's all sorted out with the passport. We got a lovely photo done in that wedding shop in Kettering, you know, where Ursula Collingwood had Karen's pictures done."

"Was it air-brushed?"

"No!" she said, indignantly. "At least they may have done something with the computer but it was nothing to do with brushes. Anyway, Una and I are going next Saturday. Just for ten days. Africa! Imagine!"

"What about Dad?"

"Honestly, Bridget! Life is for living! If Daddy wants to live between golf and the potting shed, that's up to him!"

Eventually managed to get away, encouraged by Mark standing over me holding a rolled newspaper in one hand and tapping his watch with the other. Went round to his house and definitely do believe him now, because the housekeeper was there cleaning the kitchen with fifteen members of her family who all seemed to want to worship Mark as a god. Then we stayed at his house and had all candles in the bedroom. Hurrah! Think it is all right. Yes. Is definitely all right. Love Mark Darcy. Sometimes he seems a bit scary but underneath he is very kind and sweet. Which is good. I think.

Particularly as is Valentine's Day in twelve days' time.

127 lbs. (v.g.), alcohol units 3, cigarettes 12, no. of days to Valentine's Day 11, no. of minutes spent obsessing about feminist wrongness of obsessing re: Valentine's Day 162 approx. (bad).

8:30 a.m. Hope Dad is going to be OK. If Mum is going on Saturday that means she will be leaving him on his own for Valentine's Day, which is not very nice. Maybe I will send him a card, as if from a mystery admirer.

Wonder what Mark will do? Sure he will send a card, at least.

I mean definitely, he will.

And maybe we will go out for dinner or other treat. Mmmm. V. nice to have boyfriend on Valentine's Day for once. Ah, telephone.

8:45 a.m. Was Mark. He is going to New York tomorrow for two weeks. He sounded a bit unfriendly actually, and said he was too busy to meet up tonight because he had to get all his papers and everything together.

Managed to be nice about it and just said, "Oh that's nice," waiting till had put phone down to yell "But it's Valentine's Day a week on Friday, it's Valentine's Day. Baaaaaaah!"

Anyway. That is just immature. Thing that matters is the relationship, not cynical marketing ploys.

8 a.m. In café having cappuccino and chocolate croissant. There, you see! Have got self out of negative thought bog, and actually is probably very good that Mark is going away. Will give him chance to spring away like a Martian rubber band, as it says in *Mars and Venus on a Date*, and really feel his attraction. Also will give me chance to work on myself and catch up with own life.

Plan for When Mark Is Away

1. Go to gym every day.
2. Have lots of lovely evenings with Jude and Shazzer.
3. Do continuing good work sorting out flat.
4. Spend time with Dad when Mum is away.
5. Really work hard at work to improve position.

Noon. Office. Peaceful morning. Was given an item to do on green cars. "That's environmentally green, Bridget," said Richard Finch, "not green colored."

Became clear early on green car item would never make it, leaving self free to fantasize re: Mark Darcy and design new headed stationery for self using different fonts and hues while thinking up new item ideas that would really bring me to the forefront of . . . Gaaah!

12:15 p.m. Was bloody Richard Finch yelling: "Bridget. This isn't arseing Care in the Community. It is a television production office meeting. If you must stare out of the window, at least try to do it without sliding that pen in and out of your mouth. So can you do that?"

"Yes," I said sulkily, putting the pen down on the table.

"No, not can you take the pen out of your mouth, can you find me a Middle England, middle-class voter, fifty plus, own home, who is in favor?"

"Yes, no problem," I breathed airily, thinking I could ask Patchouli in favor of what later.

"In favor of what?" said Richard Finch.

I gave him a really quite enigmatic smile. "I think you might find you've answered your own question there," I said. "Male or female?"

"Both," said Richard sadistically, "one of each."

"Straight or gay?" I exoceted back.

"I said Middle England," he snarled witheringly. "Now get on the bloody phone, and try to remember to put a skirt on in future, you're distracting my team."

Honestly, as if they would take any bloody notice as they are all obsessed with their careers and it is not that short, it had just ridden up.

Patchouli says it is in favor of the European or single currency. Which she thinks means either. Oh fuck, oh fuck. Right. Ah, telephone. That'll be the Shadow Treasury press office.

12:25 p.m. "Oh, hello, darling." Grrr. Was my mother. "Listen, have you got a tube top?"

"Mum, I've told you not to ring me at work unless it's an emergency," I hissed.

"Oh I know, but you see the problem is we're going on Saturday and the shops are still full of their winter things."

Suddenly, I had an idea. It took a while to get it through.

"Honestly, Bridget," she said after I explained. "We don't want lorries coming from Germany taking all our gold away in the night."

"But Mum, you'd be on TV again! Think of your public."

Silence.

"It will help the currency of the African people." Not sure if this was strictly true but never mind.

"Well, that may well be, but I haven't got time for TV appearances when I'm trying to pack."

"Listen," I hissed, "do you want the tube top or not?"

12:40 p.m. Hurrah! Have managed to get not one, not two, but three Middle England voters. Una wants to come up with Mum so they can go through my wardrobe and pop into Dickens and Jones, and Geoffrey wants to be on the television. Am top-flight researcher.

"So! Busy, are we?" Richard Finch was looking all postluncheon sweaty and swaggery. "Planning the Jones version of the really effective single currency plan, are we?"

"Well, not quite," I murmured with a cool self-deprecating smile. "But I have got you your Middle-England voters who are pro. Three of them, actually," I added casually while rifling through my "notes."

"Oh, didn't anyone tell you?" he said, smirking evilly. "We've dropped it. We're doing bomb scares now. Can you get me a couple of Tory commuters from Middle England who can see the IRA's argument?"

8 p.m. Ugh. Spent three hours in wind-whipped Victoria trying to manipulate commuters' opinions in direction of IRA to point where began to fear immediate arrest and transfer to Maze Prison. Got back to office, worrying what Mum and Una would find in my wardrobe, to guffawing conversation with Richard Finch along lines of "You didn't really think you were going to find anyone, did you? Sucker!"

Have got to, got to find another job. Ooh goody, telephone.

Was Tom. Hurrah! He is back!

"Bridget! You've lost so much weight!"

"Have I?" I said delighted, before remembering observation was being made down telephonic line.

Tom then went into great long enthuse about his trip to San Francisco.

"The boy on customs was completely divine. He said, 'Anything to declare?' I said, 'Only this outrageous tan!' Anyway, he gave me his number and I shagged him in a bathhouse!"

Felt familiar flash of envy at ease of gay sex, where people seem to shag each other immediately just because they both feel like it and nobody worries about having three dates first or how long to leave it before phoning afterwards.

After forty-five minutes outlining increasingly outrageous escapades he went, "Anyway, you know how I hate talking about me. How are *you*? How's that Mark guy, with his firm little buttocks?"

Told him Mark was in New York but decided to leave Rabbitboy till later for fear of overarousing him. Chose instead to bore on about work.

"I've got to find another job, it's really undermining my sense of personal dignity and self-esteem. I need something that will allow me to make serious use of my talents and abilities."

"Hmmm. I see what you mean. Have you thought about soliciting?"

"Oh very funny."

"Why don't you do some journalism on the side? Do some interviews in your spare time?"

Was really brilliant idea. Tom said he was going to talk to his friend Adam on the *Independent* about giving me an interview or a review to do or something!

Am going to be top-flight journalist and gradually build up more and more work and extra money so can give up job and merely sit on sofa with laptop on knee. Hurrah!

~ **WEDNESDAY 5 FEBRUARY**

Just called Dad to see how he was and if he would like to do something nice on Valentine's Day.

"Oh you are good, m'dear. But your mother said I need to expand my consciousness."

"So?"

"I'm going up to Scarborough to play golf with Geoffrey."

Goody. Glad he's feeling OK.

~ **THURSDAY 13 FEBRUARY**

129 lbs., alcohol units 4, cigarettes 19, gym visits 0, early Valentines 0, mentions of Valentine's Day by boyfriend 0, point of Valentine's Day if boyfriend does not even mention it 0.

V. fed up. Is Valentine's Day tomorrow and Mark has not even mentioned it. Do not understand why he has to stay in New York all weekend anyway. Surely the legal offices are closed.

Goals achieved in Mark's absence:

No. of gym visits 0.

Evenings spent with Jude and Shazzer 6 (and another one tomorrow night, looks like).

Minutes spent with Dad 0. Minutes spent talking to Dad about his feelings 0. Minutes spent talking to Dad about golf with Geoffrey bellowing in the background 287. Journalistic articles written 0. Pounds lost 0. Pounds gained 2.

Have sent Mark Valentine anyway. Chocolate heart. Sent it to hotel before he went saying "not to open till Feb 14th." Think he will know it is from me.

⌒ FRIDAY 14 FEBRUARY

130 lbs., gym visits 0, Valentines 0, flowers, trinkets, Valentine's gifts 0, point of Valentine's Day 0, difference between Valentine's Day and any other day 0, point of living: uncertain, possibility of overreaction to disaster of Non-Valentine's Day: slight.

8 a.m. Really beyond caring about things like Valentine's Day. Is just so not important in general scheme of things.

8:20 a.m. Will just go downstairs and see if post has come.

8:22 a.m. Post has not come.

8:27 a.m. Post has still not come.

8:30 a.m. Post has come! Hurrah!

8:35 a.m. Was bank statement. Nothing from Mark, nothing, nothing, nothing, nothing, nothing. Nothing.

8:40 a.m. Cannot believe am spending Valentine's Day alone again. Worst was two years ago when went to Gambia with Jude and Shaz and had to go one day early because of flights. When went down to dinner was all hearts in trees. Every single table contained couple holding hands and had to sit there on own reading *Learning to Love Yourself.*

Feel v. sad. He can't have not known. He just doesn't care. It must mean I am a Just For Now Girl because, as it says in *Mars and Venus on a Date*, I think if a man is seriously interested in you he always buys you presents like lingerie and jewels and not books or vacuums. Maybe is his way of saying it is all over and is going to tell me when he gets back.

8:43 a.m. Maybe Jude and Shaz were right and should have just got out when warning signs came. You see with Daniel last year if first time he stood me up on our first date with a pathetic excuse I had got out and detached, instead of going into Denial, would never have ended up finding a naked woman on a sun lounger on his roof terrace. Actually come to think of it, Daniel is anagram of Denial!

Is a pattern. Keep on finding naked people in boyfriends' houses. Am repeating patterns.

8:45 a.m. Oh my God. Am £200 overdrawn. How? How? How?

8:50 a.m. You see. Something good comes out of everything. Have found weird check on statement for £149, which do not recognize. Convinced it is check that wrote out to dry cleaner's for £14.90 or similar.

9 a.m. Rang up bank to see who it was to, and it was a "Monsieur S. F. S." Dry cleaners are fraudsters. Will ring Jude, Shazzer, Rebecca, Tom and Simon telling them not to go to Duraclean anymore.

9:30 a.m. Hah. Just went into Duraclean to check out "Monsieur S. F. S." under guise of taking little black silk nightie in to be cleaned. Could not help remarking that staff of dry cleaner's seemed to be not so much French but Indian. Maybe Indo-French, though.

"Could you tell me your name, please?" I said to the man as I handed in my nightie.

"Salwani," he said, smiling suspiciously nicely.

S. Hah!

"And your name?" he asked.

"Bridget."

"Bridget. You write your address here, please, Bridget."

You see that was very suspicious. Decided to put Mark Darcy's address as he has staff and burglar alarms.

"Do you know a Monsieur S. F. S.?" I said, at which the man became almost playful.

"No, but I think I am knowing you from somewhere," he said.

"Don't think I don't know what's going on," I said, then shot out of the shop. You see. Am taking things into own hands.

10 p.m. Cannot believe what has happened. At half past eleven, youth came into office bearing enormous bunch of red roses and brought them to my desk. Me! You should have seen the faces of Patchouli and Horrible Harold. Even Richard Finch was stunned into silence, only managing a pathetic "Sent them to ourself, did we?"

Opened the card and this is what it said:

Happy Valentine's Day to the light of my dreary old life.
Be at Heathrow, Terminal 1, at 8:30 a.m. tomorrow to
pick up ticket from British Airways desk (ref: P23/R55)
for magical mystery minibreak. Return Monday a.m. in
time for work. Will meet you at the other end.
    (Try to borrow a ski suit and some sensible shoes.)

Cannot believe it. Just cannot believe it. Mark is taking me on Valentine ski surprise. Is a miracle. Hurrah! Will be v. romantic in Christmas-card village amongst twinkling lights etc. sashaying down slopes hand in hand like Snow King and Queen.

Feel awful for getting into negative thought bog obsession, but was sort of thing that could happen to anyone. Definitely.

Just called Jude, has lent me ski outfit: black all-in-one in manner of Michelle Pfeiffer as Catwoman or similar. Only slight problem have only been skiing once when at school and sprained ankle on first day. Never mind. Sure it will be easy.

168 lbs. (feels like—giant inflatable ball full of fondue, hot dogs, hot chocolate etc.), grappas 5, cigarettes 32, hot chocolates 6, calories 8,257, feet 3, near-death experiences 8.

1 p.m. Edge of precipice. Cannot believe situation am in. When got to top of mountain felt paralyzed by fear so encouraged Mark Darcy to go ahead, while I put skis on watching him going "whoosh, fzzzzzz, fzzzz" down slope in manner of exocet missile, banned killer firework. Whilst v. much grateful for being brought skiing, could not believe nightmare of getting up on to hill in first place, baffled by what was point of clunking through giant concrete edifices full of grilles and chains like something out of concentration camp, with half-bent knees and equivalent of plaster casts on each foot, carrying unwieldy skis, which kept separating, being shoved through automated turnstile in manner of sheep heading for sheep dip when could have been all cozy in bed. Worst of it is hair has gone mad in altitude, forming itself into weird peaks and horns like bag of Cadbury's Misshapes, and Catwoman suit is designed exclusively for long thin people like Jude with result that look like pantomime aunt. Also three-year-olds keep whizzing by without using any poles, standing on one leg performing somersaults etc.

Skiing really is v. dangerous sport, am not imagining it. People get paralyzed, buried by avalanches etc., etc. Shazzer told me about when friend of hers had gone on very scary off-piste skiing mission and lost nerve so pisteurs had to come and take him down on a stretcher then *let go of the stretcher.*

2:30 p.m. Mountain café. Mark came whizzing up "whooosh fzzzzzzz" and asked me if I was ready to come down now.

70

Explained in whisper, had made mistake by coming on slope as skiing actually is v. dangerous sport—so much so that holiday insurance won't even insure it. Is one thing having accident that you could not foresee; quite another willingly putting yourself in an extremely dangerous situation, knowingly dicing with death or maiming, like doing bungee jumping, climbing Everest, letting people shoot apples off head etc.

Mark listened quietly and thoughtfully. "I take your point, Bridget," he said. "But this is the nursery slope. It's practically horizontal."

Told Mark I wanted to go back down on the lift thing but he said it was a button lift and you can't go downhill on a button. Forty-five minutes later Mark had got me downslope by pushing me along a bit then running round to catch me. When got to bottom thought fit to broach question of perhaps popping down cable car back to village again in order to have a little rest and a cappuccino.

"The thing is, Bridget," he said, "skiing is like everything else in life. It's just a question of confidence. Come on. I think you need a grappa."

2:45 p.m. Mmm. Love the delicious grappa.

3 p.m. Grappa is really v.g. top beverage. Mark is right. Am probably marvelous natural at skiing. Only thing need to get blurry confidence up.

3:15 p.m. Top of nursery slope. Oh gor! This blurry easy-peasy. Off go. Wheeeee!

4 p.m. Am marvelous, am fantastic skier. Just came downslope perfect with Mark: "whoosh fzzzzzz," whole body swaying, moving in perfect harmony as if instinctive. Wild elation! Have discovered whole new lease on life. Am sportswoman in manner of Princess Anne! Filled with new vigor and positive thought! Confidence! Hurrah! New confident life ahead! Grappa! Hurrah!

5 p.m. Went for rest to mountain café and Mark was suddenly greeted by a whole bunch of lawyery-banker-type people amongst whom tall, thin, blond girl standing with back to me in white ski suit, fluffy earmuffs and Versace shades. She was hooting with laughter. As if in slow motion, she flicked her hair back off her face, and as it swooshed forward in a soft curtain, I began to realize I recognized her laugh, then watched her turn her face towards us. It was Rebecca.

"Bridget!" she said, clinking over and kissing me. "Gorgeous girl! How fantastic to see you! What a coincidence!"

I looked at Mark, who was all perplexed, running his hand through his hair.

"Um, it's not really a coincidence, is it?" he said awkwardly. "You did suggest that I bring Bridget here. I mean, delightful to see you all of course, but I'd no idea you were all going to be here too."

One thing that is really good about Mark is that I do always believe him, but when did she suggest it? When?

Rebecca looked flustered for a moment, then smiled winningly. "I know, it just reminded me how gorgeous it is in Courcheval, and all the others were coming so . . . Oooh!" Conveniently, she "wobbled over" and had to be "caught" by one of the waiting admirers.

"Hmmm," said Mark. He didn't look very happy at all. I stood head down trying to work out what was going on.

Eventually could stand the strain of trying to be normal no longer, so whispered to Mark that was just going to have another little go on the nursery slope. Got self in queue for button lift much more easily than usual, just so grateful to be away from weird scenario. Missed first couple of buttons through inaccurate grabbing but managed to get next one.

Trouble was once set off, nothing seemed to be quite right, all bumpy and nonsmooth almost as if was scampering. Suddenly was aware of child waving at me from sidelines and yelling something in French. Looked across in horror to café balcony to see all Mark's friends shouting and waving as well. What going on? Next thing saw Mark running towards me frantically from direction of café.

"Bridget," he yelled as he got within earshot, "you've forgotten to put your skis on."

"Bloody fool," roared Nigel as we returned to the café. "Stupidest thing I've seen for years."

"Do you want me to stay with her?" said Rebecca to Mark, all wide-eyed concern—as if I were a troublesome toddler. "Then you can have a good ski before dinner."

"No, no, we're fine," he said, but I could see from his face he wanted to go off and have a ski, and I really wanted him to because he loves skiing. But simply could not face the thought of a skiing lesson from bloody Rebecca.

"Actually, I think I need a rest," I said. "I'll just have a hot chocolate and recover my composure."

Drinking chocolate in the café was fantastic, like drinking huge cup of chocolate sauce, which was good because distracted me from sight of Mark and Rebecca traveling up on the chair lift together. Could see her being all gay and tinkly touching his arm.

Eventually they reappeared whizzing down like the Snow King and Queen—him in black and her in white—looking like a couple out of an upmarket chalet brochure in the picture that implies that—as well as eight black runs, four hundred lifts and half board—you can have great sex like these two are just about to have.

"Oh, it's so exhilarating," said Rebecca, putting her goggles on her head and laughing into Mark's face. "Listen, do you both want to have supper with us tonight? We're going to have a fondue up the mountain, then a torchlight ski down—oh sorry, Bridget, but you could come down in the cable car."

"No," Mark said abruptly. "I missed Valentine's Day so I'm taking Bridget for a Valentine's dinner."

The good thing about Rebecca is there is always a split second when she gives herself away by looking really pissed off.

"Okey-dokey, whatever, have a fun time," she said, flashed the toothpaste advert smile, then put her goggles on and skied off with a flourish towards the town.

"When did you see her?" I said. "When did she suggest Courcheval?"

He frowned. "She was in New York."

I reeled, dropping one of my ski poles. Mark burst out laughing, picked it up and gave me a big hug.

"Don't look like that," he said against my cheek. "She was there with a crowd, I had one ten-minute conversation with her. I said I wanted to do something nice to make up for missing Valentine's Day and she suggested here."

A small indeterminate noise came out of me.

"Bridget," he said, "I love you."

⌒ SUNDAY 16 FEBRUARY

Weight: do not care (actually, no scales), number of times replayed sublime L-word moment in head: exorbitant black-hole-type number.

Am just so happy. Do not feel angry about Rebecca but generous and accepting. She is a perfectly pleasant, posey stick insect/cow. Me and Mark had lovely v. good fun dinner with lots of laughing and said how much we had missed each other. Gave him a present, which was a little key chain with Newcastle United on it, and Newcastle United boxer shorts, which he really, really liked. He gave me a Valentine gift of a red silk nightie, which was a bit on the small side but he didn't seem to mind, rather the opposite if perfectly honest about it. Also afterwards he told me about all the work things that had happened in New York and I gave him my opinions about it all, which he said were very reassuring and "unique"!

P.S. No one must read this bit as is shameful. Was so excited about him saying the L-word so early on in the relationship that accidentally rang up Jude and Shaz and left messages telling them. But realize now this was shallow and wrong.

132 lbs. (gaah! Gaah! Bloody hot chocolate), alcohol units 4 (but including airplane flight so v.g.), cigarettes 12, embarrassing neocolonialist acts committed by mother 1 extremely large one.

Minibreak was fantastic, apart from Rebecca, but had a bit of a shock at Heathrow this morning. Were just standing in the arrivals hall looking for the taxi sign when voice said: "Darling! You shouldn't have come to meet me, you silly billy. Geoffrey and Daddy are waiting for us outside. We've just come to get Daddy a present. Come and meet Wellington!"

Was my mother, tanned bright orange, with her hair in Bo Derek braids with beads on the ends and wearing a voluminous orange batik outfit like Winnie Mandela.

"I know you're going to think he's a Masai but he's a Kikuyu! A Kikuyu! Imagine!"

I followed her gaze to where Una Alconbury, also orange and dressed in head-to-toe batik but wearing her reading glasses and carrying a green leather handbag with a big gold clasp, was standing at the counter in Sock Shop with her purse open. She was gazing up delightedly at an enormous black youth with a loop of flesh hanging from each ear with a film canister in one of them and dressed in a bright blue checked cloak.

"*Hakuna Matata.* Don't worry, be happy! Swahili. Isn't it smashing? Una and I have had the most super time and Wellington's come back to stay! Hello, Mark," she said, perfunctorily acknowledging his presence. "Come along, darling, why don't you say *Jambo* to Wellington!"

"Shut up, Mother, shut up," I hissed out of the corner of my mouth, looking from side to side nervously. "You can't have an African tribesman to stay. It's neocolonialist and Daddy's only just got over Julio."

"Wellington is not," said my mum, drawing herself up to her full height, "a tribesman. Well, at least he is, darling, a proper tribesman!

I mean he lives in a dung hut! But he wanted to come! He wants to do worldwide travel just like Una and I!"

Mark was a bit uncommunicative in taxi home. Bloody Mother. Wish I had a normal round mum like other people, with gray hair, who would just make lovely stews.

Right, am going to call Dad.

9 p.m. Dad has retreated into his worst suppressed Middle English emotional state and sounded completely plastered again.

"How's things?" I ventured when I eventually got an excitable Mum off the phone and him on.

"Oh fine, fine, you know. Zulu warriors in the rockery. Primroses coming through. Everything fine with you?"

Oh God. I don't know if he can cope with all the craziness again. Have said to call me any time but is v. hard when he is being all stiff upper lip.

~ **TUESDAY 18 FEBRUARY**

132 lbs. (serious emergency now), cigarettes 13, masochistic fantasies about Mark being in love with Rebecca 42.

7 p.m. In turmoil. Got back from another nightmare day at work in a rush (Shaz has inexplicably decided she is into football, so me and Jude are going round there to watch Germans beat Turks, Belgians, or similar) to two answerphone messages, neither from Dad.

First was from Tom saying his friend Adam on the *Independent* says he wouldn't mind giving me a go at interviewing someone as long as I find somebody really famous to interview and I don't expect to be paid.

I mean surely that is not what happens in newspapers? How does everybody pay for their mortgages and drink problems?

Second was from Mark. Said he was out with Amnesty and the Indonesians tonight and could he ring me at Shazzer's to see what happened in the match. Then there was a sort of pause and he said,

"Oh and, er, Rebecca has invited us and all the 'gang' to her parents' house in Gloucestershire for a house party next weekend. What do you think? I'll call you later."

Know exactly what I think. Think I would rather sit in a little hole in Mum and Dad's rockery making friends with all the worms all weekend than go to Rebecca's house party and watch her flirting with Mark. I mean why didn't she ring me up to invite us? It's Mentionitis. It's just complete Mentionitis. There's no question about it. Telephone. Bet it's Mark. What shall I say?

"Bridget, pick up, put it down, put it down. PUT IT DOWN."

I picked up confusedly. "Magda?"

"Oh Bridget! Hi! How was the skiing?"

"It was great but . . ." Told her the whole story about Rebecca and New York and the house party. "I don't know whether I should go or not."

"Of course you've got to go, Bridge," said Magda. "If Mark wanted to go out with Rebecca he'd be going out with Rebecca, just say—get off, get off, Harry get off the back of that chair now or Mummy will smack. You're two very different kinds of people."

"Hmmm. You see, I *think* Jude and Shazzer would argue—"

Jeremy grabbed the phone. "Listen, Bridge, taking advice on dating from Jude and Shazzer is like taking advice from a diet consultant who weighs two hundred pounds."

"Jeremy!" bellowed Magda. "He's just playing devil's advocate, Bridge. Ignore him. Every woman has her aura. He's chosen you. Just go along, be gorgeous, and keep an eye on her. Nooo! Not on the floor!"

She's right. Am going to be assured, receptive, responsive woman of substance and have a lovely time emanating aura. Hurrah! Will just call Dad then go to football.

Midnight. Back in flat. Once out in freezing cold assured woman of substance evaporated into insecurity. Had to walk past workmen working under bright lights on gas main. Was wearing v. short coat and boots so braced myself to deal with lewd catcalls and embarrassing remarks then felt complete arse when none came.

Reminded me of when was fifteen and walking along lonely backstreet into town and man started following me then grabbed my arm. Turned to look at attacker in alarm. At time was v. thin in tight jeans. Also, however, had winged spectacles and brace on teeth. Man took one look at my face and ran off.

On arrival confided feelings re: workmen to Jude and Sharon. "That's the whole point, Bridget," Shazzer exploded. "These men are treating women as objects, as if our only function is physical attractiveness."

"But they weren't," said Jude.

"That's exactly why the whole thing is so objectionable. Now come on, we're supposed to be watching the match."

"Mmm. They've got lovely big thighs, haven't they?" said Jude.

"Mmmm," I agreed, distractedly wondering if Shaz would go mad if brought up Rebecca during the match.

"I knew someone who slept with a Turk once," said Jude. "And he had a penis that was so enormous he couldn't sleep with anyone."

"What? I thought you said she slept with him," said Shazzer, keeping one eye on the television.

"She slept with him but she didn't do it," explained Jude.

"Because she couldn't because his thing was too big," I said supportively of Jude's anecdote. "What a terrible thing. Do you think it goes by nationality? I mean do you think the Turks . . . ?"

"Look, shut up," said Shazzer.

For a while we all fell silent, imagining the many penises tucked neatly into shorts and thinking of all the games of many different nationalities in the past. Was just about to open my mouth, but then Jude, who seemed to have become rather fixated for some reason, piped up, "It must be very weird having a penis."

"Yes," I agreed, "very weird to have an active appendage. If I had one I would think about it all the time."

"Well, yes, you'd worry about what it would do next," said Jude.

"Well, exactly," I agreed. "You might suddenly get a gigantic erection in the middle of a football match."

"Oh for God's sake!" yelled Sharon.

"OK, keep your hair on," said Jude. "Bridge? Are you all right? You seem a bit down about something."

I looked nervously at Shaz, then decided this was too important to let lie. I cleared my throat for attention and announced: "Rebecca rang Mark up and asked us on a minibreak this weekend."

"WHAT?" Jude and Shaz exploded simultaneously.

Was really glad the seriousness of the situation was fully appreciated. Jude got up for the Milk Tray and Shaz fetched another bottle from the fridge.

"The thing is," Sharon was summing up, "we've known Rebecca for four years. Has she ever once in all that time invited you, me or Jude on one of her posh house party weekends?"

"No." I shook my head solemnly.

"But the thing is," said Jude, "if you don't go then what if he goes on his own? You can't let Rebecca get him in her clutches. And also it's obviously important to someone in his position to have someone who's a good social partner."

"Hgumph," snorted Shazzer. "That's just retrospective bollocks. If Bridget says she doesn't want to go and he goes without her and he gets off with Rebecca then he's a second-rate charlatan and not worth having. Social partner—pah. We're not in the 1950s now. She's not cleaning the house all day in a pointy bra, then entertaining his colleagues like some trophy Stepford wife. Tell him you know Rebecca's after him and that's why you don't want to go."

"But then he'll be flattered," said Jude. "There's nothing a man finds more attractive than a woman who is in love with him."

"Says who?" said Shaz.

"The baroness in *The Sound of Music*," said Jude sheepishly.

Unfortunately, by the time we turned our attention back to it the game appeared to be over.

Next thing Mark rang.

"What happened?" he said excitedly.

"Um . . ." I said, gesturing wildly at Jude and Shazzer, who looked completely blank.

"You did watch it, didn't you?"

"Yes, of course, *football's coming home, it's coming . . .*" I sang, vaguely remembering this was something to do with Germany.

"So why don't you know what happened then? I don't believe you."

"We did. But we were . . ."

"What?"

"Talking," I finished lamely.

"Oh God." There was a long silence. "Listen, do you want to go to Rebecca's?"

I looked from Jude to Shaz, frantically. One yes. One no. And a yes from Magda.

"Yes," I said.

"Oh great. It'll be fun, I think. She said to bring a swimsuit."

A swimsuit! Doom. Dooooooooom.

On way home, discovered same lot of workmen tumbling pissed out of pub. Put nose in air and decided did not care whether they whistled or not but just as walked past was huge cacophony of appreciative noises. Turned round, pleased to give them a filthy look only to find they were all looking the other way and one of them had just thrown a brick through the window of a Volkswagen.

⌒ **SATURDAY 22 FEBRUARY**

131 lbs. (horrifying), alcohol units 3 (best behavior), cigarettes 2 (huh), calories 10,000 (probably: suspected Rebecca sabotage), dogs up skirt 1 (constantly).

Gloucestershire. Turns out Rebecca's parents' "country cottage" has stable blocks, outbuildings, pool, full staff and its own church in the "garden." As we scrunched across the gravel, Rebecca— snooker-ball-bottomed in jeans in manner of Ralph Lauren ad— was playing with a dog, sunlight dappling her hair, amongst an array of Saab and BMW convertibles.

"Emma! Get down! Hiiiii!" she cried, at which dog broke free and put its nose straight up my coat.

"Mwah, come and have a drink," she said welcoming Mark as I wrestled with the dog's head.

Mark rescued me, shouting, "Emma! Here!" and chucking the stick, so the dog brought it back, tail wagging.

"Oh, she adores you, don't you, darling, don't you, don't you, don't you?" Rebecca cooed, fussing the dog's head like it was her and Mark's firstborn baby.

My mobile rang. Tried to ignore it.

"I think that's yours, Bridget," said Mark.

I took it out and pressed the button.

"Oh, hello, darling, guess what?"

"Mother, what are you ringing me on my mobile for?" I hissed, watching Rebecca leading Mark away.

"We're all going to *Miss Saigon* next Friday! Una and Geoffrey and Daddy and I and Wellington. He's never been to a musical before. A Kikuyu at *Miss Saigon*. Isn't that fun? And we've got tickets for you and Mark to join us!"

Gaah! Musicals! Strange men standing with their legs apart bellowing songs straight ahead.

By the time I got into house Mark and Rebecca had disappeared and was nobody around except the dog, which put its nose up my coat again.

4 p.m. Just back from walk round "garden." Rebecca kept installing me in conversations with men, then dragging Mark off miles ahead of everyone else. Ended up walking along with Rebecca's nephew: sub–Leonardo DiCaprio look-alike, hunted-looking in an Oxfam overcoat, whom everyone referred to as "Johnny's boy."

"I mean, like, I do have a name," he muttered.

"Oh don't be absuuuuuuuuuurd!" I said, pretending to be Rebecca. "What is it?"

He paused, looking embarrassed. "St. John."

"Oh." I sympathized.

He laughed and offered me a fag.

"Better not," I said, nodding in Mark's direction.

"Is he your boyfriend or your father?"

He steered me off the path towards a minilake and lit me a cigarette.

Was v. nice smoking and giggling naughtily. "We'd better go back," I said, stubbing cigarette out under my welly.

Others were miles ahead, so we had to run: young and wild and free, in manner of Calvin Klein adverts. When we caught up Mark put his arms round me. "What have you been doing?" he said into my hair. "Smoking like a naughty schoolgirl?"

"I haven't had a cigarette for five years!" tinkled Rebecca.

7 p.m. Mmm. Mmm. Mark just got all horny before supper. Mmmmm.

Midnight. Rebecca made a great fuss of putting me next to "Johnny's boy" at dinner—"You two are getting on sooooooo well!!"—and herself next to Mark.

They looked perfect together in their black tie. Black tie! As Jude said, was only because Rebecca wanted to show off her figure in Country Casuals gear and evening wear like Miss World entrant. Right on cue she went, "Shall we change into our swimwear now?" and tripped off to change, reappearing minutes later in an immaculately cut black swimsuit, legs up to the chandelier.

"Mark," she said, "would you give me a hand? I need to take the cover off the pool."

Mark looked from her to me worriedly.

"Of course. Yes," he said awkwardly and disappeared after her.

"Are you going to swim?" said the whippersnapper.

"Well," I began, "I wouldn't want you to think I'm not a determined and keenly motivated sportswoman, but eleven o'clock at night after a five-course dinner is not my most swimmy time."

We chatted for a while, then I noticed the last of our fellow diners were leaving the room.

"Shall we go and have coffee?" I said, getting up.

"Bridget." Suddenly, he lurched drunkenly forward, and started trying to kiss me. The door burst open. Was Rebecca and Mark.

"Oops! Sorry!" said Rebecca, and shut the door.

"What do you think you're doing!" I hissed, horrified, at the whippersnapper.

"But . . . Rebecca said you told her you really fancied me, and, and . . ."

"And what?"

"She said you and Mark were in the process of splitting up."

I grabbed the table for support. "Who told her that?"

"She said"—he looked so mortified I felt really sorry for him—"she said Mark did."

⌁ SUNDAY 23 FEBRUARY

172 lbs. (probably), alcohol units 3 (since midnight and is only 7 a.m.), cigarettes 100,000 (feels like), calories 3,275, positive thoughts 0, boyfriends: extremely uncertain figure.

When I got back to room, Mark was in the bath so I sat in nightie, planning my defense.

"It was not what you think," I said with tremendous originality, as he emerged.

"No?" he said, whisky in hand. He started striding around in his barrister mode, clad only in a towel. Was unnerving, but unbelievably sexy. "Had you a marble stuck in your throat, perhaps?" he said. "Was 'Sinjun' being, rather than the trust-funded teenage layabout he appears, actually a top ear, nose and throat surgeon attempting to extract it with his tongue?"

"No," I said, carefully and thoughtfully. "That is not what it was either."

"Then were you hyperventilating? Was 'Sinjun'—having garnered the rudiments of first aid into his marijuana-addled brain, perhaps from a poster on the wall of the many drug rehab units he has visited in his short and otherwise uneventful life—trying to administer the kiss of life? Or did he simply mistake you for a choice morsel of 'skunk' and find himself unable to . . ."

I started to laugh. Then he started laughing too, then we started kissing and one thing led to another and afterwards we fell asleep in each other's arms.

In the morning, woke up all rosy thinking everything was OK but then looked around and saw him already dressed, and knew was not anywhere near OK.

"I can explain," I said, dramatically sitting bolt upright. For a moment we looked at each other and started laughing. But then he turned serious.

"Go on, then."

"It was Rebecca," I said. "St. John told me Rebecca told him that I told her I fancied him and . . ."

"And you believed this bewildering catalogue of Chinese whispers?"

"And that you told her we were—"

"Yes?"

"Splitting up," I said.

Mark sat down and started rubbing his fingers very slowly across his forehead.

"Did you?" I whispered. "Did you say that to Rebecca?"

"No," he said eventually. "I didn't say that to Rebecca, but . . ."

I daren't look at him.

"But maybe we . . ." he began.

The room started to go blotchy. Hate this about dating. One minute you're closer to someone than anyone in the whole world, next minute they only need to say the words "time apart," "serious talk" or "maybe you . . ." and you're never going to see them again and will have to spend the next six months having imaginary conversations in which they beg to come back, and bursting into tears at the sight of their toothbrush.

"Do you want to split up . . . ?"

There was a knock at the door. Was Rebecca radiant in dusky pink cashmere. "Last call for breakfast, folks!" she cooed and didn't go.

84

Ended up breakfasting with mad unwashed hair, while Rebecca swung her shiny mane and served kedgeree.

On the way home we drove in silence while I struggled not to show how I felt or say anything wet. Know from experience how awful it is trying to persuade someone you shouldn't split up when they have already made up their mind, and then you think back over what you said. And feel such an idiot.

"Don't do this!" I wanted to yell when we stopped outside my house. "She's trying to pinch you and it's all a plot. I didn't kiss St. John. I love you."

"Well, bye then," I said dignifiedly, and forced myself to get out of the car.

"Bye," he muttered, not looking at me.

Watched him turn the car round really fast and screechily. As he drove off, I saw him angrily brush his cheek as if he was wiping something away.

4

Persuasion

210 lbs. (combined weight of self and unhappiness), alcohol units 1—i.e. me, cigarettes 200,000, calories 8,477 (not counting chocolate), theories as to what's going on 447, no. of times changed mind about what to do 448.

3 a.m. Don't know what I would have done without the girls yesterday. Called them instantly after Mark drove off, and they were round within fifteen minutes, never once saying "I told you so."

When Shazzer bustled in with armfuls of bottles and carrier bags, barking, "Has he rung?" was like being in *ER* when Dr. Greene arrives.

"No," said Jude, popping a cigarette in my mouth as if it were a thermometer.

"Only a matter of time," said Shaz brightly, unpacking a bottle of Chardonnay, three pizzas, two tubs of Häagen-Dazs Pralines and Cream and a packet of fun-sized Twixes.

"Yup," said Jude, putting the *Pride and Prejudice* tape on top of the video, together with *Through Love and Loss to Self-Esteem, The Five Stages of Dating Workbook* and *How to Heal the Hurt by Hating.* "He'll be back."

"Do you think I should call him?" I said.

"No!" yelled Shaz.

"Have you gone out of your mind?" bellowed Jude. "He's being a Martian rubber band. The *last* thing you must do is call him."

"I know," I said huffily. I mean surely she didn't think I was *that* badly read.

"You *let* him go back to his cave and feel his attraction, and you move back from Exclusivity to Uncertainty."

"But what if he . . . ?"

"You'd better unplug it, Shaz," sighed Jude. "Otherwise she'll spend the whole night waiting for him to ring instead of working on her self-esteem."

"Noooo!" I cried, feeling like they were going to cut my ear off.

"Anyway," said Shaz brightly, pulling the phone out of the wall with a click, "it'll do him good."

Two hours later was feeling quite confused.

"'The more a man likes a woman the more he will avoid getting involved'!" said Jude triumphantly, reading from *Mars and Venus on a Date.*

"Sounds like masculine logic to me!" said Shaz.

"So chucking me could actually be a sign that he's really serious about the relationship?" I said excitedly.

"Wait, wait." Jude was staring hard at *Emotional Intelligence.* "Was his wife unfaithful to him?"

"Yes," I mumbled through a mouthful of Twix. "A week after their wedding. With Daniel."

"Hmmm. You see it sounds to me that he was *also* having an Emotional Hijacking, probably because of an earlier emotional 'bruise' that you have inadvertently hit. Of course! Of course! That's it! That's why he overreacted to you snogging the boy. So don't worry, once the bruise has stopped sending his whole nervous system into disarray he'll realize his mistake."

"And realize he ought to go out with someone else because he likes you so much!" said Sharon, merrily lighting up a Silk Cut.

"Shut up, Shaz," hissed Jude. "Shut up."

It was too late. The specter of Rebecca loomed up, filling the room like an inflatable monster.

"Oh, oh, oh," I said, screwing up my eyes.

"Quick, get her a drink, get her a drink," yelled Jude.

"I'm sorry, I'm sorry. Put *Pride and Prejudice* on," gabbled Shaz, pouring neat brandy into my mouth. "Find the wet shirt. Shall we have the pizzas?"

Was a bit like Christmas, or more like when somebody dies and with funeral and all the fuss nothing is normal so people do not notice the loss because they are so distracted. It is when life goes back to what it was without the person that the trouble starts. Like now for example.

7 p.m. Wild joy! Got home to find answerphone light flashing.

"Bridget, hi, it's Mark. I don't know where you were last night but anyway, just checking in. I'll try you again later."

Try me again later. Hmmm. So presumably that means not to ring him.

7:13 p.m. He hasn't rung. Unsure what is correct procedure now. Better ring Shaz.

On top of everything else, hair has gone mad as if in sympathy. Bizarre the way that hair is normal for weeks on end then suddenly in space of five minutes goes berserk, announcing it is time to cut in manner of baby starting yelling to be fed.

7:30 p.m. Played the message over the phone to Shaz and said, "Should I call him back?"

"No! Let him suffer. If he's chucked you and changed his mind he's got to prove he bloody well deserves you."

Shaz is right. Yes. Am in v. assertive mood re: Mark Darcy.

8:35 p.m. Oh, though. Maybe he is sad. Hate thinking of him sitting in his Newcastle United T-shirt being sad. Maybe I should just ring him and get to the bottom of it.

8:50 p.m. Was just about to ring Mark and blurt out how much I liked him and it was all just misunderstandings but fortunately Jude rang before I had time to pick up the phone. Told her about the brief but worryingly positive mood.

"So you mean you're in Denial again?"

"Yes," I said uncertainly. "Should I ring him tomorrow maybe?"

"No, if you want to get back together, you've got to leave it unsullied by scenes. So wait four or five days till you've recovered your composure, then, yes, there's nothing wrong with giving him a light, friendly call just to let him know everything's OK."

11 p.m. He hasn't rung. Oh fuck. Am so confused. Whole dating world is like hideous game of bluff and double bluff with men and women firing at each other from opposite lines of sandbags. Is as if there is a set of rules that you are supposed to be sticking to, but no one knows what they are so everyone just makes up their own. Then you end up getting chucked because you didn't follow the rules correctly, but how could you be expected to, when you didn't know what they were in the first place?

⌒ **TUESDAY 25 FEBRUARY**

No. of times driven past Mark Darcy's house to see if there are any lights on 2 (or 4 if count both ways). No. of times dialed 141 (so cannot trace my number if he 1471s) then rang his answerphone just to hear his voice 5 (bad) (v.g. for not leaving message though). No. of times looked Mark Darcy's number up in phone book just to prove to self he still exists 2 (v. restrained), percentage of outgoing calls made from mobile to keep line clear in case he rings 100. Percentage of incoming callers creating angry resentment for not being Mark Darcy—unless ringing to talk about Mark Darcy—and urged to get off the phone as quickly as possible in case blocking call from Mark Darcy 100.

8 p.m. Magda just called to ask how the weekend went. Ended up blurting out the whole story.

"Listen, if you take it from him one more time you're going in the naughty chair! Harry! Sorry, Bridge. So what does he say about it?"

"I haven't spoken to him."

"What? Why not?"

Explained about the answerphone message and the whole rubber band/emotional bruise/liking me too much theory.

"Bridget, you are literally unbelievable. There's nothing in the entire story to suggest he's chucked you at all. He just got in a bad mood because he caught you snogging someone."

"I wasn't snogging someone. I was being happened upon against my will!"

"But he's not a mind reader. How's he supposed to know what you feel? You have to communicate. Take that out of his mouth now! You're coming with me. You're coming upstairs with me to the naughty chair."

8:45 p.m. Maybe Magda is right. Maybe I just assumed that he was chucking me and he didn't mean that at all. Maybe in the car he was just upset about the whole snogging thing and wanted *me* to say something and now he thinks I am avoiding him!! Am going to ring. That is the trouble with modern (or ex) relationships, there just isn't enough *communication*.

9 p.m. Right, am going to do it.

9:01 p.m. Here goes.

9:10 p.m. Mark Darcy answered by barking "Yesssss?" in incredibly impatient voice with all noise in background.

Crestfallen, I whispered, "It's me, it's Bridget."

"Bridget! Are you mad? Don't you know what's going on? You haven't called me for two days and now you ring me in the middle of the most important, the most crucial—Noooooo! Nooooo! You stupid, bloody . . . Jesus Christ. You stupid—right beside the ref. That was a foul! You'll be . . . he's booking him. He's going off. Oh Jesus—look, I'll call you back when it's over."

9:15 p.m. Of course knew it was some kind of Trans-Universe final or whatever it is, had just forgotten owing to emotional thought bog. Sort of thing that could happen to anyone.

9:30 p.m. How could I be so stupid? How? How?

9:35 p.m. Oh goody—telephone! Mark Darcy!

Was Jude. "What?" she said. "He didn't talk to you because he was in the middle of a *football match*? Go out. Go out immediately. Don't be in when he calls back. How dare he!"

Immediately realized Jude was right and if Mark really cared about me football would not have been more important. Shaz was even more emphatic.

"The only reason men are so obsessed with football is that they're bone idle," she exploded. "They think by supporting some team or other and making a lot of noise they've actually won the match themselves and deserve to have cheering and clapping and a great fuss made of them."

"Yes. So are you coming round to Jude's?"

"Er, no . . ."

"Why not?"

"I'm watching the match with Simon."

Simon? Shazzer and Simon? But Simon is just one of our mates.

"But I thought you just said . . . ?"

"That's different. The reason I like football is it's a very interesting game."

Hmm. Was just leaving the house when phone rang again.

"Oh, hello, darling. It's Mum. We're having the most marvelous time. Everyone adores Wellington! We took him to the Rotary and—"

"Mother," I hissed. "You can't parade Wellington around like some sort of exhibit."

"Do you know, darling," she said icily, "if there's one thing I really don't like it's racism and bigotry."

"What?"

"Well. When the Robertsons were up from Amersham we took them to the Rotary and you didn't say anything about that, did you?"

I gawped, trying to untangle the web of warped logic.

"Always putting everyone in little boxes, aren't you, with your

'Smug Marrieds' and 'Singletons' and colored people and homos. Anyway, I was just ringing about *Miss Saigon* on Friday. It starts at seven thirty."

Oh Christ. "Er . . . !" I said wildly. Sure I didn't say yes, sure of it.

"Now come along, Bridget. We've bought the tickets."

Resignedly agreed to bizarre jaunt, making gabbling excuse about Mark working, which completely set her off.

"Working, durrr! What's he doing working on a Friday night? Are you sure he's not working too hard? I really don't think work-ing—"

"Mum, I've really got to go, I'm late for Jude," I said firmly.

"Oh, always rushing about. Jude, Sharon, yoga. I'm surprised you and Mark have got any time to see each other at all!"

Once round at Jude's flat, the conversation moved naturally to Shazzer and Simon.

"But, actually"—Jude leaned forward confidentially, even though no one else was there—"I bumped into them in the Conran Shop on Saturday. And they were giggling together over cutlery like a pair of Smug Marrieds."

What is it about modern Singletons that only way they can have a normal relationship is if it isn't supposed to be a relationship? There's Shaz who isn't going out with Simon doing what couples are sup-posed to do, and me and Mark who are supposed to be going out not seeing each other at all.

"If you ask me people should not say 'just good friends' but 'just going out with each other,' " I said darkly.

"Yup," said Jude. "Maybe the answer is platonic friends combined with a vibrator."

Got back to remorseful message from Mark saying he had tried to ring straight after the match but phone was permanently engaged and now I was out. Was just wondering whether to call him back when he rang.

"Sorry about earlier," he said. "I'm just really down about it, aren't you?"

"I know," I said tenderly, "I feel exactly the same."

"I just keep thinking: why?"

95

"Exactly!" I beamed, huge rush of love and relief washing over me.

"So stupid and unnecessary," he said, anguished. "A pointless outburst with devastating consequences."

"I know," I nodded, thinking, blimey, he's taking it even more dramatically than me.

"How can a man live with that?"

"Well, everyone's only human," I said thoughtfully. "People have to forgive each other and . . . themselves."

"Chuh! It's easy to say that," he said. "But if he hadn't been sent off we'd never have been subjected to the tyranny of the penalty shoot-out. We fought like kings amongst lions, but it cost us the game!"

I gave a strangled cry, mind reeling. Surely it cannot be true that men have football instead of emotions? Realize football is exciting and binds nations together with common goals and hatreds but surely wholesale anguish, depression and mourning hours later is taking—

"Bridget, what's the matter? It's only a game. Even I can see that. When you called me during the match I was so caught up in my own feelings that . . . But it's only a game."

"Right, right," I said, staring around the room crazily.

"Anyway, what's going on? I haven't heard a peep from you for days. Hope you haven't been snogging any more teenage . . . Oh hang on, hang on, they're playing it back. Shall I come round tomorrow, no, wait, I'm playing five-a-side—Thursday?"

"Er . . . yes," I said.

"Great, see you about eight o clock."

∼ WEDNESDAY 26 FEBRUARY

130 lbs., alcohol units 2 (v.g.), cigarettes 3 (v.g.), calories 3,845 (poor), minutes not spent obsessing re: Mark Darcy 24 (excellent progress), variations on twin-horned sculpture dreamed up by hair 13 (alarming).

8:30 a.m. Right. Everything is probably fine (apart, obviously, from hair) though it is possible that Mark was avoiding issue as did not want to talk about emotions on the phone. So tomorrow night is crucial.

Important thing is to be assured, receptive, responsive, not complain about anything, move back a Stage and . . . er, look really sexy. Will see if can get hair cut in lunch hour. And will go to gym before work. Maybe have a steam bath so will be all glowing.

8:45 a.m. Letter has come for me! Hurrah! Maybe late Valentine card from secret admirer, which has been misdirected owing to incorrect post code.

9 a.m. Was letter from bank about overdraft. Also enclosing check to "M. S. F. S." Hah! Had forgotten about that. Dry-cleaner fraud is about to be exposed and I will get £149 back. Ooh, note just fluttered out.

Note said: "This check is to Marks & Spencer's Financial Services."

Was for Christmas payment on M&S card. Oh. Oh dear. Feel bit bad now for mentally accusing innocent dry cleaner's and being all funny with the boy. Hmm. Too late to go to gym now, also too generally upset. Will go after work.

2 p.m. Office. In loos. Total, total disaster. Just got back from hairdresser's. Told Paolo about just wanting tiny trim to turn hair from mad chaos into that of Rachel from *Friends*. He started running his hands through it and I instantly felt in care of genius who understood self's inner beauty. Paolo seemed marvelously in control, throwing the hair this way and that, then blowing it about into huge bouff, giving me knowing looks as if to say "I'm gonna make you into one *hot* chick."

Then suddenly he stopped. Hair looked totally insane—like schoolteacher who has had perm followed by pudding-basin cut. He looked at me with an expectant, confident smirk and his assistant came up and started gushing, "Oh it's *heaven*." Panicked, staring at self in horror but had established such a bond of mutual admiration with Paolo that to say I hated hair would make whole thing collapse like impossibly embarrassing house of cards. Ended up joining in mad gushing about monster hair and giving Paolo £5 tip. When got back to work, Richard Finch said I looked like Mr. Spock from *Star Trek*.

7 p.m. Back home. Hair is complete fright wig with hideous short fringe. Just spent forty-five minutes staring in mirror with brows raised trying to make fringe look longer but cannot spend whole of tomorrow night looking like Roger Moore when the baddy with the cat has threatened to blow up him, the world and the tiny box full of MI5 vital computers.

7:15 p.m. Attempt to mimic early Linda Evangelista by arranging fringe into diagonal line using gel has turned self into Donald Trump.

Incensed with rage at stupid Paolo. Why would someone do that to another person? Why? Hate sadistic megalomaniac hairdressers. Am going to sue Paolo. Am going to report Paolo to Amnesty International and expose him on national television.

Far too depressed to go to gym.

7:30 p.m. Called Tom to tell him of trauma who said I should not be so superficial but to think of Irish Secretary Mo Mowlam and cancer-treated bald head. V. ashamed. Not going to obsess anymore. Also Tom said had I thought up anyone to interview yet.

"Well, I've been a bit busy," I said guiltily.

"You know what? You gotta get your ass in gear"—oh God, don't know what has come over him in California—"Who are you really interested in?" he went on. "Isn't there a celebrity you'd really like to interview?"

Thought about this then suddenly realized. "Mr. Darcy!" I said.

"What? Colin Firth?"

"Yes! Yes! Mr. Darcy! Mr. Darcy!"

So now have got project. Hurrah! Am going to get to work and set up interview using his agent. Will be marvelous, can get out all cuttings and really bring out unique perspective on . . . Oh, though. Had better wait till fringe has grown. Gaaah! Doorbell. Had better not be Mark. But he definitely said tomorrow! Calm, calm.

"It's Gary," went the entry phone.

"Oh hi, hi. Gareeeee!" I overcompensated without a blind idea who he was. "How are you?" I said, thinking, and come to mention it, who?

"Cold. Are you gonna let me in?"

Suddenly recognized the voice—"Oh *Gary*," I gushed even more crazily overcompensatorily. "Come on up!!!"

Hit self hard on head. What was he doing here?

He came in wearing paint-smeared, builder-type jeans, an orange T-shirt and strange checked jacket with pretend sheepskin collar.

"Hi," he said, sitting down at the kitchen table as if he were my husband. Was unsure how to deal with two-people-in-room-with-totally-different-concept-of-reality scenario.

"Now, Gary," I said. "I'm in a bit of a rush!"

He said nothing and started rolling a cigarette. Suddenly started to feel scared. Maybe he was a mad rapist. But he never tried to rape Magda, at least as far as I know.

"Was there something you'd forgotten?" I said nervously.

"Nope," he said, still rolling the cigarette. I glanced at the door wondering if I should make a run for it. "Where's your soil pipe?"

"Gareeeeeeeee!" I wanted to yell. "Go away. Just go away. I'm seeing Mark tomorrow night, and I've got to do something with my fringe and work out on the floor."

He put the cigarette in his mouth and stood up. "Let's have a look in the bathroom."

"Noooo!" I yelled, remembering there was an open tub of Jolene bleach and a copy of *What Men Want* on the side of the washbasin. "Look, can you come back another . . . ?"

But he was already poking about, opening the door and peering down the stairs and heading towards the bedroom.

"Have you got a back window in here?"

"Yes."

"Let's have a look."

I stood nervously in the bedroom doorway, while he opened the window and looked out. He did seem more interested in pipes than actually attacking me.

"Thought so!" he said triumphantly, bringing his head back in and closing the window. "You've got room for an infill extension out there."

"I'm afraid you're going to have to go away," I said, drawing myself up to my full height and moving back into the living room. "I've got to go somewhere."

But he was already heading past me to the stairs again.

"Yup, you've got room for an infill. Mind you, you'll have to move the soil pipe."

"Gary . . ."

"You could have a second bedroom—little roof terrace on top. Sweet."

Roof terrace? Second bedroom? I could make it into an office and start my new career.

"How much would it cost?"

"Oooh." He started shaking his head sorrowfully. "Tell you what, let's go down to the pub and have a think."

"I can't," I said firmly. "I'm going out."

"All right. Well, I'll have a think and give you a ring."

"Jolly good. Well! Best get going!"

He picked up his coat, tobacco and cigarette papers, opened his bag and laid a magazine down reverentially on the kitchen table.

As he reached the door, he turned and gave me a knowing look. "Page seventy-one," he said. "Ciao."

Picked up the magazine, thinking it was going to be *Architectural Digest* and found myself looking at *Coarse Fisherman*, with a man holding a gigantic slimy gray fish on the front. Leafed through an enormous number of pages all containing many pictures of men holding up gigantic slimy gray fish. Reached page 71 and there opposite an article on "BAC Predator Lures," sporting a denim hat with badges on and a proud, beaming smile was Gary, holding up a gigantic slimy gray fish.

129 lbs. (lost 1 lb. was hair), cigarettes 17 (due to hair), calories 625 (off food due to hair), imaginary letters to solicitors, consumer programs, Dept. of Health etc. complaining about Paolo's massacring of hair 22, visits to mirror to check growth of hair 72, millimeters grown by hair in spite of all hard work 0.

7:45 p.m. Fifteen minutes to go. Just checked fringe again. Hair has gone from fright wig to horrified, screaming, full-blown terror wig.

7:47 p.m. Still Leonard Nimoy. Why did this have to happen on most important night of relationship so far with Mark Darcy? Why? At least, though, makes change from checking thighs in mirror to see if they have shrunk.

Midnight. When Mark Darcy appeared at door lungs got in throat.

He walked in purposefully without saying hello, took a card-shaped envelope out of his pocket and handed it to me. It had my name on it but Mark's address. It had already been opened.

"It's been in the in-tray since I got back," he said, slumping down on the sofa. "I opened it this morning by mistake. Sorry. But it's probably all for the best."

Trembling I took the card from the envelope.

It depicted two cartoon hedgehogs watching a bra entwined with a pair of underpants going round in a washing machine.

"Who's it from?" he said pleasantly.

"I don't know."

"Yes you do," he said, in the sort of calm, smiley way that suggests someone is about to pull out a meat hatchet and cut your nose off. "Who is it from?"

"I told you," I muttered. "I don't know."

"Read what it says."

I opened it up. Inside, in spidery red writing it said: "Be Mine Valentine—I'll see you when you come to pick up your nightie—love—Sxxxxxxxx"

I stared at it in shock. Just then the phone rang.

Baaah! I thought, it'll be Jude or Shazzer with some hideous advice about Mark. I started to spring towards it but Mark put his hand on my arm.

"Hi, doll, Gary here." Oh God. How dare he be so overfamiliar? "Right, what we were talking about in the bedroom—I've got some ideas so give me a ring and I'll come round."

Mark looked down blinking very fast. Then he sniffed, and rubbed the back of his hand across his face as if to pull himself together. "OK?" he said. "Do you want to explain?"

"It's the builder." I wanted to put my arms round him. "Magda's builder, Gary. The one that put the crap shelves up. He wants to put an infill extension between the bedroom and the stairs."

"I see," he said. "And is the card from Gary as well? Or is it St. John? Or some other . . ."

Just then the fax started grunting. Something was coming through.

While I was staring Mark pulled the piece of paper off the fax, looked at it and handed it over. It was a scrawled note from Jude saying, "Who needs Mark Darcy when £9.99 plus P&P will buy you one of these," on top of an advert for a vibrator with a tongue.

~ **FRIDAY 28 FEBRUARY**

128 lbs. (only bright spot on horizon), reasons why people like going to musicals: mysterious unfathomable number, reasons Rebecca allowed to be alive 0, reasons for Mark, Rebecca, Mum, Una and Geoffrey Alconbury and Andrew Lloyd Webber or similar to ruin life: unclear.

Must keep calm. Must be positive. Was very bad luck all those things happening at once, no question about it. Completely understandable that Mark would just leave after all that and he did say he was going to call when he calmed down and . . . Hah! I've just realized who that bloody card was from. It must have been the dry cleaner.

When I was trying to get it out of him about the fraud and saying, "Don't think I don't know what's going on," I was dropping off my nightie. And I gave him Mark's address in case he was dodgy. The world is full of lunatics and madmen and I've got to go see *Miss Saifuckinggon* tonight.

Midnight. Initially, it wasn't too bad. It was a relief to get away from the prison of my own thoughts and the hell of dialing 1471 every time I went to the loo.

Wellington, far from being a tragic victim of cultural imperialism, looked coolly at home in one of Dad's 1950s suits as if he might have been one of the waiters from the Met Bar on his night off, responding with dignified graciousness while Mum and Una twittered around him like groupies. I turned up late so managed to exchange only the briefest of apologetic words with him at the interval.

"Is it strange being in England?" I said, then felt stupid because obviously it would be strange.

"It is interesting," he said, looking at me searchingly. "Do you find it strange?"

"So!" burst in Una. "Where's Mark? I thought he was supposed to be coming too!"

"He's working," I muttered as Uncle Geoffrey lurched up, pissed, with Dad.

"That's what the last one said, didn't he!" roared Geoffrey. "Always the same with my little Bridget," he said, patting me dangerously near my bottom. "Off they go. Weeeeeeeh!"

"Geoffrey!" said Una, adding as if making light conversation, "Do you have older women who can't get married off in your tribe, Wellington?"

"I am not an older woman," I hissed.

"That is the responsibility of the elders of the tribe," said Wellington.

"Well, I've always said that was the best way, haven't I, Colin?" said Mum smugly. "I mean, didn't I tell Bridget she should go out with Mark?"

"But when she is older, with or without husband, a woman has the respect of the tribe," said Wellington with a twinkle in my direction.

"Can I move there?" I said glumly.

"I am not sure you would be liking the smell of the walls." He laughed.

Managed to get Dad on one side and whisper, "How's it going?"

"Oh, not so bad, you know," he said. "Seems a nice-enough feller. Can we take our drinks in with us?"

Second half was a nightmare. Whole hideous jamboree on stage passed in a blur as mind went into a horrifying snowball-effect roll with images of Rebecca, Gary, vibrators and nighties getting more and more lurid as they spun past.

Fortunately the crush of people spewing out of the foyer and yelling with—presumably—joy prevented conversation till we all piled into Geoffrey and Una's Range Rover. We were going along with Una driving, Geoffrey in the front, Dad giggling merrily in the boot and me sandwiched between Mum and Wellington in the back when incident happened, horrifying and incredible.

Mum had just plonked a pair of enormous, gold-rimmed glasses on her nose.

"I didn't know you'd started wearing glasses," I was saying, startled by this uncharacteristic nod in the direction of acknowledging the aging process.

"I haven't started wearing glasses," she said gaily. "Mind that pedestrian crossing, Una."

"But," I said, "you are."

"No, no, no! I only wear them for driving."

"But you're not."

"Yes she is." Dad grinned ruefully as Mum yelled, "Mind that Fiesta, Una! He's indicating!"

"Isn't that Mark?" said Una suddenly. "I thought he was working."

"Where!" said Mum bossily.

"Over there," said Una. "Ooh, by the way, did I tell you Olive and Roger have gone to the Himalayas? Littered with toilet paper, apparently. The whole of Mount Everest."

I followed Una's pointing finger to where Mark, dressed in his dark blue overcoat and a very white, semiundone shirt, was getting out of a taxi. As if in slow motion, I saw a figure emerging from the back of the cab: tall, slim, with long blond hair, laughing up into his face. It was Rebecca.

The level of torture unleashed in the Range Rover was unbelievable: Mum and Una crazed with indignation on my behalf—"Well, I think it's absolutely disgusting! With another woman on a Friday night when he said he was working! I've a good mind to ring Elaine and give her what for"; Geoffrey drunkenly saying "Off they go! Weeh!" and Dad trying to quieten the whole thing down. The only silent people were me and Wellington, who took my hand and held it, very still and strong, without saying a word.

When we reached my flat he climbed out of the Range Rover to let me out, with the babble of "Well! I mean his first wife left him, didn't she?" "Well exactly. No smoke without fire," in the background.

"In darkness the stone becomes the buffalo," Wellington said. "In sunlight all is as it is."

"Thanks," I said gratefully, then stumbled back to the flat wondering if I could turn Rebecca into a buffalo and set her on fire without creating enough smoke to alert Scotland Yard.

∼ SATURDAY 1 MARCH

10 p.m. My flat. Very black day. Jude, Shaz and I went emergency shopping and have all come back here to get ready for night on town, designed by the girls to keep my mind off things. By 8 p.m. things were already getting squiffy. "Mark Darcy's gay," Jude was declaring.

"Of course he's gay," snarled Shazzer, pouring out more Bloody Marys.

"Do you really think so?" I said, momentarily relieved by the depressing yet ego-comforting theory.

"Well, you did find a boy in his bed, didn't you?" said Shaz.

"Why else would he go off with someone freakishly tall like Rebecca, with no sense of girlfriend-hood, no tits and no bottom— i.e., a virtual man?" said Jude.

"Bridge," said Shaz, looking up at me drunkenly. "God, d'you know? When I look at you from this angle, you've got a real double chin."

"Thanks," I said wryly, pouring myself another glass of wine and pressing ANSWER PLAY again, at which Jude and Shazzer put their hands over their ears.

"Hi, Bridget. It's Mark. You don't seem to be returning my calls. I really think, whatever, I . . . I'm really . . . We—at least I feel—I owe it to you to be friends, so I hope you'll . . . we'll. Oh God, anyway, give me a ring sometime soon. If you want to."

"Seems to have totally lost touch," grumbled Jude. "As if it's nothing to do with him when he's run off with Rebecca. You've really got to detach now. Look, are we going to this party or not?"

"Yurrr. Who's 'e bloody think he is?" said Shaz. "Owe it to you! Hggnah! You shoulssay, 'Honey, I don't need anyone in my life be-causeey *owe* it to me.' "

At that moment the phone rang.

"Hi." It was Mark. Heart was inconveniently overtaken with great wave of love.

"Hi," I said eagerly, mouthing "It's him" at the others.

"Did you get your message? I mean my message?" said Mark.

Shazzer was jabbing my leg, frantically hissing, "Give it to him, go on."

"Yes," I said, hoity-toitily. "But as I got it minutes after I saw you emerging from the taxi with Rebecca at eleven o'clock at night, I wasn't in the most amenable of humors."

Shaz stuck her fist in the air going "Yesss!!!" and Jude put her hand over Shazzer's mouth, gave me a thumbs-up and reached for the Chardonnay.

There was silence on the end of the phone.

"Bridge, why do you always have to jump to conclusions?"

I paused, hand over mouthpiece. "He says I'm jumping to conclusions," I hissed, at which Shaz, furious, made a lunge for it.

"Jump to conclusions?" I said. "Rebecca's been making a play for you for a month, you chuck me for things I haven't done, then next thing I see you getting out of a taxi with Rebecca . . ."

"But it wasn't my fault, I can explain, and I had just called you."

"Yes—to say you owed it to me to be my friend."

"But . . ."

"Go on!" hissed Shaz.

I took a big breath. "Owed it to me? Honey . . ." At this Jude and Shaz collapsed on each other in ecstasy. Honey! Was practically being Linda Fiorentino in *The Last Seduction*. "I don't need anyone in my life because they owe it to me," I went on determinedly. "I have got the best, most loyal, wise, witty, caring, supportive friends in the world. And if I *were* to be your friend after the way you've treated me . . ."

"But . . . What way?" He sounded anguished.

"If I was still to be your friend . . ." I was flagging.

"Go on," hissed Shaz.

". . . You would be *really* lucky."

"All right, you've said enough," said Mark. "If you don't want me to explain, I won't pester you with phone calls. Good-bye, Bridget."

I replaced the handset, stunned, and looked round at the friends. Sharon was lying on the rug, waving a fag triumphantly in the air and Jude was swigging straight out of the bottle of Chardonnay. Suddenly I had an awful feeling I had made the most terrible mistake.

Ten minutes later the doorbell rang. I ran at it.

"Can I come in?" said a muffled man's voice. Mark!

"Of course," I said, relieved, turning to Jude and Shaz saying, "Do you think you could, like, go in the bedroom?"

They were just disgruntledly picking themselves up from the floor when the door to the flat opened, only it wasn't Mark but Tom.

"Bridget! You're looking so thin!" he said. "Oh God." He

slumped at the kitchen table. "Oh God. Life is shite, life is a tale told by a cynical—"

"Tom," said Shazzer. "We were having a conversation."

"And none of us 'ave seen you for blurry weeks," slurred Jude resentfully.

"A conversation? Not about me? Whatever can it have been about? Oh God—fucking Jerome, fucking, fucking Jerome."

"Jerome?" I said, horrified. "Pretentious Jerome? I thought you'd banished him from your life forever."

"He left all these messages when I went to San Francisco," said Tom sheepishly. "So we started seeing each other and then tonight I just hinted at us getting back together, well, tried to snog him, and Jerome said, he said . . ." Tom brushed angrily at one eye. "He just didn't fancy me."

There was a stunned silence. Pretentious Jerome had committed a vicious, selfish, unforgivable, ego-destroying crime against all the laws of dating decency.

"I'm not attractive," said Tom despairingly. "I'm a confirmed love pariah."

Instantly we swung into action, Jude grabbing Chardonnay while Shaz put her arm round him and I brought a chair gabbling, "You're not, you're not!"

"Then why did he say that? Why? WHYYYYYYYYY?"

"It'ss perfickly obvious," said Jude, handing him a glass. "Iss because Pretentious Jerome is straight."

"Straight as a die," said Shaz. "I've known that boy wasn't gay since first time I blurry sawim."

"Straight." Jude giggled in agreement. "Straight as a very straight, straight . . . penis."

5

Mr. Darcy, Mr. Darcy

5 a.m. Aaargh. Have just remembered what happened.

5:03 a.m. Why did I do that? Why? Why? Wish could get back to sleep or up.

5:30 a.m. Weird how quickly time goes when you have a hangover. Is because you have so few thoughts: exactly opposite to when people are drowning, entire life flashes past and moment seems to last forever because they are having so many thoughts.

6 a.m. You see half an hour just went like that, because I did not have any thoughts. Oof. Actually head hurts quite a lot. Oh God. Hope was not sick on coat.

7 a.m. Trouble is, they never tell you what will happen if you drink more than two units a day or, more to point, entire week's worth of alcohol units in one night. Does it mean you will get a magenta face and gnarled nose in manner of gnome, or that you are an alcoholic? But in that case everybody at the party we went on to last night must have been an alcoholic. Except that the only people who weren't drinking were the alcoholics. Hmm.

7:30 a.m. Maybe am pregnant and will have harmed child with alcohol. Oh, though. Cannot be pregnant as just finished period and will never have sex with Mark again. Never. Never.

8 a.m. Worst of it is, being alone in middle of night without anyone to talk to or ask how drunk I was. Keep remembering increasingly hideous things that I said. Oh no. Have just remembered giving beggar 50p who, instead of "Thank you," said, "You look really pissed."

Suddenly also remember childhood mother saying: "There is nothing worse than a woman drunk." Am Yates Wine Lodge–style easy meat gutter floozy. Must go back to sleep.

10:15 a.m. Feel bit better for sleep. Maybe hangover has gone. Think will open curtains. GAAAAAAAAAAAAH! Surely is not natural for sun to be that bloody bright in the morning.

10:30 a.m. Anyway. Am going to gym in a minute and am never going to drink again, therefore is perfect moment to start Scarsdale diet. So actually what happened last night was v.g. because this is start of totally new life. Hurrah! People will say . . . Oooh, telephone.

11:15 a.m. Was Shazzer. "Bridge, was I really pissed and awful last night?"

For a moment could not remember her at all. "No, of course not," I said nicely to cheer Shazzer up, as sure if she had been really drunk I would have remembered. I gathered all my courage together and asked, "Was I?" There was silence.

"No, you were lovely, you were really sweet."

There, you see, was just hungover paranoia. Ooh, telephone. Maybe him.

Was my mother.

"Bridget, what on earth are you doing still at home? You're supposed to be here in an hour. Daddy's whizzing the baked Alaska!"

11:30 a.m. Fuck, oh fuck. She asked me for lunch on Friday night and was too weak to argue, then too pissed to remember. I can't not go again. Can I? Right. The thing to do is stay calm and eat fruit because the enzymes clear the toxicity and it will be fine. I'll just eat a tiny bit and try not to vomit and then I'll ring Mum back when I've emerged from Land of Indecision.

Pros of Going

Will be able to check that Wellington is being treated in a manner that would not offend Commission for Racial Equality.

Will be able to talk to Dad.

Will be good daughter.

Will not have to take on Mum.

Cons of Going

Will have to face torture and torment over Mark/Rebecca incident.

May be sick on table.

Phone again. Had better not be her.

"So how's your head today?" It was Tom.

"Fine," I trilled gaily, blushing. "Why?"

"Well, you were pretty far gone last night."

"Shazzer said I wasn't."

"Bridget," said Tom, "Shazzer wasn't there. She went to the Met Bar to meet Simon and from what I gather she was in much the same state as you."

⌒ **MONDAY 3 MARCH**

131 lbs. (hideous instant fat production after lard-smeared parental Sunday lunch), cigarettes 17 (emergency), incidents during parental lunch suggesting there is any sanity or reality remaining in life 0.

8 a.m. Hangover is at last beginning to clear. Massive relief to be back in own home where am adult lord of castle instead of pawn in other people's games. Decided was no real way out of Mum's lunch yesterday, but all the way up the motorway to Grafton Underwood could feel sick coming up in my throat. Village looked surreally idyllic, trimmed with daffodils, conservatories, ducks, etc. and people clipping hedges for all the world as if life were easy and peaceful, disaster had not happened, and there was such a thing as God.

"Oh hello, darling! *Hakuna Matata.* Just back from the Co-op," Mum said bustling me through into the kitchen. "Short of peas! I'm just going to play this answering-phone back."

Sat down nauseously while the answerphone boomed out, and Mum crashed around turning on gadgets, which ground and screamed in already painful head.

"Pam," went the answerphone. "Penny here. You know that chap who lives up round the corner from the garage? Well, he's committed suicide because of the noise from the clay-pigeon shooting. It's in the *Kettering Examiner.* Oh and I meant to say, can Merle put a couple of dozen mince pies in your freezer while they've got the gas board in?"

"Hello, Pam! Margo! On the scrounge! Have you got a six-inch Swiss roll tin I can borrow for Alison's twenty-first?"

I stared wildly round the kitchen, crazed at the thought of the different worlds that would be revealed by playing back people's answerphone tapes. Maybe someone should do it as an installation at the Saatchi Gallery. Mum was clattering about in the cupboards, then dialed a number. "Margo. Pam. I've got a sponge *ring* tin if that's any good? Well, why don't you use a Yorkshire pudding tin and just line the bottom with a bit of greaseproof paper?"

"Hello, hello, bomdibombom," said Dad, pottering into the kitchen. "Does anybody know the post code for Barton Seagrave? Do you think it's KT4 HS or L? Ah, Bridget, welcome to the trenches, World War Three in the kitchen, Mau Mau in the garden."

"Colin, will you tip that oil out of the chip pan?" said Mum. "Geoffrey says when you've brought it up to a high temperature ten times it should be thrown away. By the way, Bridget, I've bought you some talc." She handed me a lilac Yardley's bottle with a gold top.

"Er, why?" I said, taking hold of it gingerly.

"Well! It keeps you nice and fresh, doesn't it?"

Grrr. Grrrr. The whole thought groove was just so transparent. Mark had gone out with Rebecca because . . .

"Are you saying I smell?" I said.

"No, darling." She paused. "It's always nice to keep nice and fresh, though, isn't it?"

"Afternoon, Bridget!" It was Una appearing as if from nowhere with a plate of boiled eggs. "Pam! I forgot to tell you, Bill's trying to get the council to skim his drive because they didn't grate the top off it and that's why they've got potholes, so Eileen said will you tell them the water used to run down from your drive until they put a grate in?"

Was all gibberish. Gibberish. Felt like a patient in a coma whom nobody thought could hear anything.

"Come on, Colin, where's that Spam? They're going to be here in a moment."

"Who?" I said suspiciously.

"The Darcys. Una, pop some salad cream and paprika on those eggs, will you?"

"The Darcys? Mark's parents? Now? Why?"

Just then, the doorbell—which plays the entire tune of a town hall clock—started chiming out.

"We are the elders of the tribe!" twinkled Mum, taking off her apron. "Come on, everyone, galvanize!"

"Where's Wellington?" I hissed at Mum.

"Oh, he's out in the garden practicing his football! He doesn't like these sit-down lunches having to yaketty-yak to us all."

Mum and Una dashed off and Dad patted my arm. "Forward to the breach," he said.

Followed him into the swirly-carpet-and-ornament-land of the lounge, wondering whether I had the strength and control of my limbs to bolt and deciding I didn't. Mark's mum and dad and Una and Geoffrey were standing in an awkward circle each holding a glass of sherry. "OK, love," said Dad. "Let's get you a drink."

"Have you met . . . ?" He gestured to Elaine. "Do you know, my dear, I am sorry, I've known you for thirty years and I've completely forgotten your name."

"So how's that son of yours?" Una bludgeoned in.

"My son! Well, he's getting married, you know!" said Admiral Darcy, a genial bellower. The room suddenly went blotchy. Getting married?

"Getting married?" said Dad, holding my arm, as I tried to control my breathing.

"Oh I know, I know," said Admiral Darcy cheerily. "There's no keeping up with any of these young ones anymore: married to someone one minute, off with someone else the next! Isn't that right, m'dear?" he said, patting Mark's mother on the bottom.

"I think Una was asking about Mark, not Peter, darling," she said, with a flash of understanding in my direction. "Peter is our other son out in Hong Kong. He's getting married in June. Now come along, can't one of you chaps find Bridget a drink? They're all mouth and no trousers, aren't they?" she said, with a sympathetic look.

Somebody get me out of here, I thought. I don't want to be tortured. I want to lie on the bathroom floor with my head near the toilet bowl like normal people.

"Would you like one of these?" said Elaine, holding out a silver case full of Black Sobranies. "I'm sure they're death on a stick but I'm still here at sixty-five."

"Right, come along and sit down, everyone!" said Mum, swirling in with a plate of liver sausage. "Oof." She made a great show of coughing and fanning the air and said icily, "No smoking at table, Elaine."

I followed her into the dining room where beyond the French windows Wellington was playing an astonishingly accomplished game of keepy-uppy in a sweatshirt and a pair of blue silky shorts.

"There he goes. Keep it up, lad," chortled Geoffrey, looking out of the window, jiggling his hands up and down in his pockets. "Keep it up."

We all sat down and stared at each other awkwardly. It was like a prewedding get-together for the happy couple and both sets of parents except that the groom had run off with someone else two nights before.

"So!" said Mum. "Salmon, Elaine?"

"Thank you," said Elaine.

"We went to *Miss Saigon* the other night!" Mum began with dangerous brightness.

"Baah! Musicals. Can't bloody stand 'em, load of bloody ponces," muttered Admiral Darcy as Elaine served him a piece of salmon.

"Well, we enjoyed it!" said Mum. "Anyway . . ."

I looked frantically out of the window for some sort of inspiration and saw Wellington looking at me. "Help," I mouthed. He nodded towards the kitchen and disappeared.

"Standing around with their legs apart bellowing," roared the admiral, a man after my own heart. "Now Gilbert and Sullivan. *HMS Pinafore*, that's a different thing."

"Excuse me a moment," I said, and slipped out, ignoring Mum's furious stare.

Dashed into the kitchen to find Wellington already there. I slumped against the fridge freezer.

"What?" he said, looking at my eyes intently. "What is wrong?"

"She thinks she's one of the elders of the tribe," I whispered. "She's taking on Mark's parents, you know Mark, who we saw . . ."

He nodded. "I know all about this."

"What have you been saying to her? She's trying to engineer some powwow about him seeing Rebecca as if—"

Just then the kitchen door burst open.

"Bridget! What are you doing in here? Oh." Spotting Wellington, Mum rather stopped in her tracks.

"Pamela?" said Wellington. "What is happening?"

"Well, I just thought after what you said, we adults could . . . could sort something out!" she said, recovering her confidence and almost managing a beam.

"You were adopting the behaviors of our tribe?" said Wellington.

"Well . . . I . . ."

"Pamela. Your culture has evolved over many centuries. When outside influence appears you must not allow it to infect and dilute your birthright. As we discussed, worldwide travel brings a responsibility to observe, not to destroy." Could not help wondering how Wellington's brand-new CD Walkman fitted into all this, but Mum was nodding penitently. Had never seen her so under anyone's spell before.

"Now. Return to your guests and leave Bridget's courtship be, as is the time-old tradition of your tribe."

"Well, I suppose you're right," she said, patting her hair.

"Enjoy your lunch," said Wellington, giving me the slightest of winks.

Back in the dining room, it seemed that Mark's mother had already deftly deflected the showdown. "It's a total mystery to me how anyone gets married to anyone these days," she was saying. "If I hadn't married so young I'd never have done it."

"Oh, I quite agree!" said Dad, rather too heartily.

"What I don't understand," said Uncle Geoffrey, "is how a woman manages to get to Bridget's age without hooking anyone. New York, Outer Space, off they go! Wheee!"

"Oh, just shut up! Shut up!" I felt like yelling.

"It's very hard for young people now," Elaine interrupted again, looking hard at me. "One can marry anyone when one is eighteen. But when one's character is formed, taking on the reality of a man must seem insufferable. Present company excepted, of course."

"I should hope so," roared Mark's father merrily, patting her arm. "Otherwise, I'm going to have to swap you for two thirty-somethings. Why should my son have all the fun!" He gave a gallant nod in my direction at which my heart lurched again. Did he think we were still together? Or did he know about Rebecca and think Mark was going out with us both?

Thankfully the conversation then steamed back to *HMS Pinafore*, bounced on to Wellington's football skills, swung out on to Geoffrey and Dad's golfing holiday, fluttered over herbaceous borders, skimmed Bill's drive and then it was 3:45 and the whole nightmare was over.

Elaine pressed a couple of Sobranies into my hand as they left— "I think you might need these for the drive back. I do hope we see you again"—which seemed encouraging but not enough to build one's life on. It was Mark I wanted to go out with again not, unfortunately, his parents.

"Right, darling," said Mum, bustling out of the kitchen with a Tupperware box. "Where've you put your bag?"

"Mum," I said through clenched teeth. "I don't want any food."

"Are you all right, darling?"

"As all right as I can be under the circumstances," I muttered.

She gave me a hug. Which was nice but startling. "I know it's hard," she said. "But don't take any nonsense from Mark. It'll all work out for you. I know it will." Just as I was enjoying the unaccustomed mummy-comfort she said, "So you see! *Hakuna Matata!* Don't worry. Be happy! Now. D'you want to take a couple of packets of minestrone back with you when you go? How about some cheese slices? Can I just get past you into that drawer? Ooh, I'll tell you what. I've got a couple of pieces of fillet steak."

Why does she think food is better than love? If I'd stayed in the kitchen a minute longer I swear I would have thrown up.

"Where's Dad?"

"Oh, he'll be out in his shed."

"What?"

"His shed. He spends hours in there and then comes out smelling of—"

"Of what?"

"Nothing, darling. Off you go and say good-bye if you want to."

Outside, Wellington was reading the *Sunday Telegraph* on the bench. "Thanks," I said.

"No problem," he said, then added, "She is a good woman. A woman of strong mind, good heart and enthusiasm, but maybe . . ."

". . . about four hundred times too much, sometimes?"

"Yeah," he said, laughing. Oh my God, I hope it was just enthusiasm for life he was on about.

As I approached the shed, Dad came out looking rather red in the face and shifty. His Nat King Cole tape was playing inside.

"Ah, off back to the big, big, smokeedeesmoke of London?" he said, stumbling slightly and grabbing hold of the shed. "You a bit down, old love?" he slurred gently.

I nodded. "You too?" I said.

He folded me up in his arms and gave me a big squeeze like he used to do when I was little. It was nice: my dad.

"How have you managed to stay married so long to Mum?" I whispered, wondering what that vaguely sweet smell was. Whisky?

"Sssnot so complicated really," he said, lurching against the shed again. He cocked his head on one side, listening to Nat King Cole.

"*The greatest thing,*" he started to croon, "*you'll ever learn is how to love and be loved in return.* Just hope she still loves me not the Mau Mau."

Then he leaned over and gave me a kiss.

~ **WEDNESDAY 5 MARCH**

128 lbs. (good), alcohol units 0 (excellent), cigarettes 5 (a pleasant, healthy number), no. times driven past Mark Darcy's house 2 (v.g.), no. of times looked up Mark Darcy's name in phone book to prove still exists 18 (v.g.), 1471 calls 12 (better), no. of phone calls from Mark 0 (tragic).

8:30 a.m. My flat. Very sad. I miss Mark. Heard nothing all day Sunday and Monday then got back from work last night to message saying he was going to New York for a few weeks. "So I guess it really is good-bye."

Am trying best to keep spirits up. Have found that if when wake up in morning, immediately before feeling first stab of pain, put on Radio 4 *Today* program—even if program does appear to consist of hours and hours of *Just a Minute*–type game with politicians trying not to say "Yes" or "No" or answer any of the questions—then I can actually avoid getting caught in obsessive "if only" thought cycles and imaginary Mark Darcy conversational loops that only increase sadness and inability to get out of bed.

Must say Gordon Brown was v.g. on program this morning, managing to go on about European currency without hesitating, pausing or actually saying anything, but all the time talking calmly and fluently with news presenter shouting, "Yes or No? Yes or No?" like game show host in the background. So . . . well, could be worse. I suppose.

Wonder if European currency is the same as single currency? In some ways am in favor of this as presumably we would have different coins, which might be quite European and chic. Also they could get rid of the brown ones, which are too heavy and the 5ps and 20ps, which are too tiny and insignificant to be pleasurable. Hmm. We should hang on to the £1s though, which are fantastic, like sovereigns, and you suddenly find you have £8 in your purse when you thought you had run out. But then they would have to alter all the slot machines and . . . Gaaaaaah! Doorbell. Maybe Mark coming to say good-bye.

Was just bloody Gary. Eventually managed to get out of him that he had come to tell me that the infill extension would "only" cost £7,000.

"Where am I going to get £7,000?"

"You could get a second mortgage," he said. "It would only cost you another hundred a month."

Fortunately even he could see I was late for work so managed to get him out of the house. £7,000. Honestly.

7 p.m. Back home. Surely it is not normal to be treating my answerphone like an old-fashioned human partner: rushing home to it from work to see what mood it is in, whether it will tinklingly confirm that I am lovable and an acceptable member of society or be empty and distant, like now for example. Not only is there no message from Mark for the forty-second day running, but also no message from anyone else. Maybe should read a bit of *The Road Less Traveled*.

7:06 p.m. Yes, you see love is not something that happens to you but something you do. So what didn't I do?

7:08 p.m. Am assured, receptive, responsive woman of substance. My sense of self comes not from other people but from . . . from . . . myself? That can't be right.

7:09 p.m. Anyway. Good thing is am not obsessing about Mark Darcy. Am starting to detach.

7:15 p.m. Goody, telephone! Maybe Mark Darcy!

"Bridget, you're looking so thin!" Tom. "How are you doing, my baby?"

"Crap," I said, taking my Nicorette gum out of my mouth and starting to mold it into a sculpture. "Obviously."

"Oh come on, Bridgelene! Men! Ten a penny. How's the new interviewing career?"

"Well, I rang Colin Firth's agent and got out all the cuts. I really thought he might do it because *Fever Pitch* is coming out soon and I thought they might want the publicity."

"And?"

"They rang back and said he was too busy."

"Hah! Well, actually that's exactly what I'm ringing about. Jerome says he knows—"

"Tom," I said dangerously, "would this be Mentionitis by any chance?"

"No, no . . . I'm not going to go back with him," he lied transparently. "But anyway, Jerome knows this guy who worked on the last film with Colin Firth and he said do you want him to put in a good word for you?"

"Yes!" I said excitedly.

Realize is just another excuse for Tom to keep in touch with Pretentious Jerome but then all kind acts are a mixture of altruism and self-interest, and maybe Colin Firth will say yes!

Hurrah! Will be perfect job for me! Can go all over the world interviewing famous celebrities. Also with all the extra money could get the second mortgage for the office and roof terrace then give up hateful Sit Up Britain job and work at home. Yes! Everything is falling into place! Am going to ring up Gary. You cannot expect anything to change unless you change. Am taking things into my own hands!

Right, am not going to lie in bed being sad. Am going to get up and do something useful. Like. Um. Have a fag? Oh God. Cannot bear the thought of Mark calling up Rebecca, going through all the little details of the day like he used to do with me. Mustn't, mustn't be negative. Maybe Mark is not going out with Rebecca and will come back and be with me! You see? Hurrah!

128 lbs., alcohol units 4 (but am journalist now so obviously must be drunk), cigarettes 5, calories 1,845 (g.), lights at end of tunnel 1 (v. tiny).

4 p.m. Tom just called me at work.

"It's on!"

"What?"

"The Colin Firth thing!"

I sat straight up in my chair, quivering.

"Yes! Jerome's friend called up and Colin Firth was really nice and said if you can place it in the *Independent* he'll do it. And I'm going out for dinner with Pretentious Jerome!"

"Tom, you're a saint, a God and an archangel. So what do I have to do?"

"Just ring up Colin Firth's agent and then call Adam at the *Independent*. Oh, by the way, I told them you'd done loads of stuff before."

"But I haven't."

"Oh, don't be so bloody *literal*, Bridgelene, just tell him you have."

129 lbs. (v. unfair crimeless punishment), calories 1,200 (rest my case), mortgages 2 (hurrah!), number of bedrooms in flat: about to be 2 (hurrah!).

Have rung up bank and is fine about the second mortgage! All I have to do is fill in a few forms and stuff and then I can have £7,000 and it is only £120 a month! Cannot believe have not thought of this before. Could have been answer to all my overdraft problems!

130 lbs., calories 998 (bizarre calorie/fat inverse relationship seems to render food restraint pointless), miracles: multiple, newfound joy: infinite.

5 p.m. Something strange is going on. Not only is Colin Firth interview happening but it is going to be in Rome! Next thing they will say interview is to take place naked in sea off Caribbean island in manner of *Blind Date*. Can understand God granting one favor to make up for everything but this, surely, is beyond all normal religious reason. Suggests life is peaking in some terrifying final way followed by rapid rush downhill towards untimely death. Maybe is belated April Fool.

Just called Tom who said stop always thinking there is a trick to everything and reason interview is taking place in Rome is that Colin Firth lives there—he is right—and to try to concentrate on fact that there are other things about Colin Firth apart from playing Mr. Darcy. Like his new film *Fever Pitch* for example.

"Yup, yup, yup," I said, then told Tom was v. grateful for all his help in setting this up. "You see this is exactly what I needed!" I said excitedly. "I feel so much better now I'm concentrating on my career instead of obsessing about men."

"Er, Bridget," said Tom. "You do realize Colin Firth has a girlfriend, don't you?"

Humph.

128 lbs., alcohol units 5 (journalism training), cigarettes 22, calories 3,844 (you see? You see? Am never going to diet again).

6 p.m. A wonderful thing has happened! Just spoke to PR lady and Colin Firth is going to call me at home over the weekend to arrange things! Cannot believe it. Obviously will not be able to go out of house all weekend but that is good as will be able to do research by watching *Pride and Prejudice* video, though obviously realize must talk about other projects as well. Yes. Actually this could be real turning point in career. You see ironically enough, in a spooky sixth-sense meant-to-be-type way, Mr. Darcy has made me forget obsession with Mark Darcy. . . . Telephone! Maybe Mr. or Mark Darcy, must quickly put impressive jazz or classical record on.

Huh. Was bloody bossy man called Michael from *Independent*. "Now listen. We haven't used you before. I don't want any messing about with this. You come back on the plane we have booked for you on Monday night, you sit down with it on Tuesday morning and you hand it in by four o'clock or it won't go in. And you're asking him about the film *Fever Pitch*. *Fever Pitch*, in which, as you know, he plays a character who is not Mr. Darcy."

Actually that is quite right. Ooh, telephone.

Was Jude. She and Shazzer are coming round. Fear they will make me laugh when Mr. Darcy rings but on other hand need something to take mind off it or will burst.

~ SATURDAY 12 APRIL

129 lbs. (but can definitely lose 3 lbs. before tomorrow using hospital frankfurter diet), alcohol units 3 (v.g.), cigarettes 2 (perfect saint-style person), frankfurters 12, 1471 calls to see if not heard Colin Firth ring owing to sudden unnoticed deafness 7, sq. ft. of floor space not covered in pizza boxes, outfit choices, ashtrays etc. 2 (under sofa), no. of times watched Pride and Prejudice *video where Colin Firth dives into lake 15 (topflight researcher), calls from Colin Firth 0 (so far).*

10 a.m. Colin Firth hasn't rung.

10:03 a.m. Still hasn't rung.

10:07 a.m. Still hasn't rung. Wonder if is too early to wake Jude and Shazzer up? Maybe he is waiting till his girlfriend has gone out shopping to ring me.

5 p.m. Flat looks like bomb has hit it, due to Mr. Darcy stakeout: all sprawled all over sitting room like in *Thelma and Louise* when Thelma's house is taken over by police and Harvey Keitel is waiting for them to ring with tape recorders whirring in background. Really appreciate Jude and Shazzer's support and everything, but means have not been able to get on with preparation, apart from physical.

6 p.m. Mr. Darcy still has not rung.

6:05 p.m. Still has not rung. What am I supposed to do? Do not even know where am meeting him.

6:15 p.m. Still has not rung. Maybe girlfriend has just *refused* to go out shopping. Maybe they have just been having sex all weekend and sending out for Italian ice cream and just laughing at me behind my back.

6:30 p.m. Jude suddenly woke up and put her fingertips on her forehead.

"We must go out," she said in a strange, TV-clairvoyant-style voice.

"Are you mad?" hissed Sharon. "Go out? Have you gone out of your *mind?*"

"No," said Jude coldly. "The reason the phone isn't ringing is there is too much energy focused on it."

"Phwnaw," snorted Sharon.

"Apart from anything else it has started to stink in here. We need to clean up, let the energy flow, then go out and have a Bloody Mary," she said, looking at me temptingly.

Minutes later we were outside, blinking in the unexpectedly springlike not-dark-yet air. I made a sudden bolt back towards the door but Shazzer grabbed me.

"We are going. For. A. Bloody. Mary," she hissed, marching me along the road like a big policeman.

Fourteen minutes later we were back. I flung myself across the room and froze. The light was flashing on the answerphone.

"You see," said Jude in a horrible smug voice. "You see."

Tremulously, as if it were an unexploded bomb, Shazzer reached forward and pressed ANSWER PLAY.

"Hello, Bridget, this is Colin Firth." We all jumped a foot backwards. It was Mr. Darcy. The same posh, deep, can't-be-bothered voice that he proposed to Elizabeth Bennet in on the BBC. Bridget. Me. Mr. Darcy said Bridget. On my answerphone.

"I gather you're coming to Rome to interview me on Monday," he went on. "I was calling to arrange somewhere to meet. There's a square called the Piazza Navona, sort of easy place to find in a taxi. I'll meet you about four-thirty by the fountain. Have a safe journey."

"1471, 1471," gabbled Jude, "1471, quick, quick. No, rewind, rewind. Play it again!"

"Call him back," screamed Sharon like an SS torturer. "Call him back and ask him to meet you *in* the fountain. OhmyGod."

Just as we'd rewound, the phone had rung again. We stood there rigid, mouths open. Then Tom's voice boomed out, "Hello, you pretty little things, it's Mr. Darcy here just calling to see if anyone could help me out of this wet shirt."

Shazzer suddenly detranced. "Stop him, stop him," she screamed, flinging herself at the receiver. "Shut up, Tom, shut up, shut up, shut up."

But it was too late. My answerphone recording of Mr. Darcy saying the word "Bridget" and asking me to meet him in Rome by a fountain has been lost forever. And there is nothing anyone in the world will ever be able to do about it. Nothing. Nothing.

6

Italian Job

*125 lbs. (fat consumed by excitement and fear), alcohol units 0: excellent
(but is only 7:30 in morning), cigarettes 4 (v.g.).*

7:30 a.m. Really it is a marvelous step forward to be setting off on
journey with so much time to spare. It just goes to show, as it says in
The Road Less Traveled, that human beings have capacity to change
and grow. Tom came round last night and went through questions
with me. So am pretty much all prepared with clear brief though
was tiny bit on pissed side, to be perfectly honest.

9:15 a.m. Actually have loads of time. Everyone knows when busi-
nessmen whizz between European airports they turn up forty minutes before liftoff, with just a briefcase with nylon shirts in. Plane is
at 11:45. Must be at Gatwick at 11, so 10:30 train from Victoria and
tube at 10. Perfect.

9:30 a.m. What if it all gets too much and I just, like, burst out and
kiss him? Also trousers are too tight and will show stomach. Think
will just change into something else. Also maybe need to take sponge
bag to freshen up before interview.

9:40 a.m. Cannot believe have wasted time on packing sponge bag, when most important thing, surely, is to look nice on arrival. Hair is completely mad. Will have to wet it again. Where is passport?

9:45 a.m. Have got passport, and hair is calm, so better go.

9:49 a.m. Only problem being: cannot lift bag. Maybe had better reduce sponge bag contents to toothbrush, paste, mouthwash, cleanser and moisturizer. Oh and must take £3,500 out of microwave and leave for Gary so he can start getting materials and stuff for new office and roof terrace! Hurrah!

9:50 a.m. Goody. Have ordered minicab. Will be here in two mins.

10 a.m. Where is minicab?

10:05 a.m. Where the fuck is minicab?

10:06 a.m. Have just rung up minicab firm who say silver Cavalier is outside.

10:07 a.m. Silver Cavalier is not outside or anywhere in street.

10:08 a.m. Minicab man says silver Cavalier is definitely turning into my street at this moment.

10:10 a.m. Still no minicab. Fucking fucking minicab and all it's . . . Gaah. Is here. Oh fuck, where are keys?

10:15 a.m. In minicab now. Have definitely done journey in fifteen mins. before.

10:18 a.m. Aargh. Minicab is suddenly on Marylebone Road—inexplicably deciding on scenic tour of London instead of route to Victoria. Fight instinct to attack, kill and eat minicab driver.

10:20 a.m. Back on course now i.e. no longer heading for Newcastle, but traffic is solid. There is no occasion now in London when is not rush hour.

10:27 a.m. Wonder if is possible to get from Marble Arch to Gatwick Express in one minute?

10:35 a.m. Victoria. OK. Calm, calm. Train has gone without self. Still if get 10:45 will have clear thirty minutes before plane goes. Also plane will probably be delayed.

10:40 a.m. Wonder if there will be time to get new trousers at airport? Actually am not going to be neurotic about this. Marvelous thing about traveling alone is you can really start to develop a new character, and be quite elegant and Zen-like and no one knows you.

10:50 a.m. Wish did not keep thinking passport has jumped out of bag and gone back home.

11:10 a.m. Train has inexplicably stopped. Suddenly all extra things did, e.g. putting extra polish coat on toenails, seem unimportant alongside not actually turning up.

11:45 a.m. Cannot believe it. Plane has gone without me.

Noon. Thank God, Mr. Darcy, and all angels in heaven. Turns out can go on another plane in one hour forty minutes. Just called publicist who said no problem, she would get him to meet me two hours later. Goody, can do airport shopping.

1 p.m. V. keen on floaty-chiffon-with-roses-on-style fashions for spring but do not think they should design them so they will not fit over people's arses. Love the lovely airport shopping area. Top architect Sir Richard Rogers, Terence Conran and similar are always complaining that airports have turned into great big shopping malls but I consider that to be good. Possibly will incorporate that into next major profile possibly with Sir Richard himself if not Bill Clinton. Maybe will just try bikini on.

1:30 p.m. Right. Will just post letters and get Body Shop necessities, then go through.

1:31 p.m. Was announcement: "Will Passenger Jones, the last remaining passenger for flight BA one-seventy-five to Rome, please make her way immediately to Gate Twelve where the plane is waiting to depart."

⁓ **TUESDAY 22 APRIL**

128 lbs., alcohol units 2, cigarettes 22, calls from bossy Michael at Independent to "see how we're getting along": about 30, no. of times listened to tape of interview 17, words of interview written 0.

9 a.m. Back in flat in London after heaven-sent trip. Right, am going to write up interview. You see is amazing way that concentrating on work and career completely takes mind off romantic sadness. Was just so fantastic. Taxi dropped me off in Roman square and thought was going to faint: just fantastic—golden sunshine and huge massive square full of high-up ruins and in the middle of it all Mr. . . . Ooh, telephone.

It was Michael from the *Independent*.

"So did you do it, then?"

"Yes," I said hoity-toitily.

"And you remembered to take your tape recorder, not your Sony Walkman?"

Honestly. Do not know what Tom has told him about me but something in his tone suggests may not have been particularly respectful.

"Well, you've got till four o'clock. So get on with it."

Lala. That is ages. Will just relive day for a bit. Mmm. He looked exactly like Mr. Darcy: all smoldery and lean. And he even took me round a church with a hole in and some Adrian's tomb or other and a statue of Moses and was incredibly masterful preventing me from being knocked over by cars and kept talking Italian. Mmm.

Noon. Morning has not gone particularly well, though obviously needed some time to absorb what happened, and discuss impressions with peers so probably has been highly productive.

2 p.m. Telephone again. You see this is what it is like when you are major profile writer: phones ringing incessantly.

Was bloody bossy Michael again: "How are we coming along?"

Bloody nerve. Is not even my deadline till 4 p.m., which obviously means the end of the day. Actually really pleased with tape. Did really good thing of starting him off with easy questions before going into Tom's meaty questions, which I had written down night before despite being a little on squiffy side. Think he was really quite impressed with my line of questioning, actually.

2:30 p.m. Will just have quick cup of coffee and fag.

3 p.m. Better just listen to tape again.

Dingdong! Will just ring Shaz and play her this last bit.

Aargh, aargh. Is 3:30 and have not started. Anyway, no need to panic. They are not going to be back from lunch for ages and then will be drunk as, as . . . as journalists. Wait till they see my scoops.

How to start? Obviously interview must include my impressions of Mr. Darcy as well as skillfully weaving in stuff about new film *Fever Pitch*, theater, film, etc. They will probably give me a regular interview spot every week: the Bridget Jones Profile. Jones meets Darcy. Jones meets Blair. Jones meets Marcos except dead.

4 p.m. How can I be expected to create if bloody Michael keeps ringing up all the time saying what I must and must not put in? Grrr. If that is him again . . . They have no respect for journalists in that office. None whatsoever.

5:15 p.m. Harhar. "I. Am. Do. Ing. It," I said. That has shut him up.

6 p.m. Anyway is OK. All top journalists have deadline crises.

7 p.m. Oh fuck, oh fuck. Oh fuck, oh fuck.

129 lbs. (really seem to be stuck in some kind of fat groove), congratulatory calls from friends, relatives and colleagues about Colin Firth interview 0, congratulatory calls from Independent *staff about Colin Firth interview 0, congratulatory calls from Colin Firth about Colin Firth interview 0 (odd, surely?).*

8 a.m. Article is coming out today. Was a bit rushed but probably not that bad. Might be quite good actually. Wish paper would hurry up and come.

8:10 a.m. Paper has still not come.

8:20 a.m. Hurrah! Paper is here.
Have just seen interview. *Independent* have completely ignored what wrote. Realize was bit on late side but this is intolerable. Here is what was published:

> *Due to insuperable technical difficulties it has been necessary to print Bridget Jones's interview with Colin Firth as a direct transcript of the recording.*

BJ: Right. I'm going to start the interview now.
CF: *(Slightly hysterical sounding)* Good, good.
(Very long pause)
BJ: What is your favorite color?
CF: I'm sorry?
BJ: What is your favorite color?

CF: Blue.

(Long pause)

BJ: What is your favorite pudding?

CF: Er. Crème brûlée.

BJ: You know the oncoming film *Fever Pitch* by Nick Hornby?

CF: I do know it, yes.

BJ: *(Pause. Rustling paper)* Do . . . Oh. *(More rustling paper)* Do you think the book of *Fever Pitch* has spored a confessional gender?

CF: Excuse me?

BJ: Has. Spored. A. Confessional. Gender.

CF: *Spored* a confessional gender?

BJ: Yes.

CF: Well. Certainly Nick Hornby's style has been very much imitated and I think it's a very appealing, er, gender whether or not he actually, um . . . *spored* it.

BJ: You know in the BBC *Pride and Prejudice?*

CF: I do know it, yes.

BJ: When you had to dive into the lake?

CF: Yes.

BJ: When they had to do another take, did you have to take the wet shirt off and then put a dry one on?

CF: Yes, I, I probably did have to, yes. *Scusi. Ha vinto. É troppo forte. Sì, grazie.*

BJ: *(Breathing unsteadily)* How many takes diving into the lake did you have to do?

CF: *(Coughs)* Well. The underwater shots were a tank in Ealing Studios.

BJ: Oh no.

CF: I'm afraid so. The, um, *moment* of being airborne—ex-tremely brief—was a stuntman.

BJ: But it looked like Mr. Darcy.

CF: That was because he had stuck-on sideburns and a Mr. Darcy outfit on top of a wet suit, which actually made him look like Elvis as you last saw him. He could only do it once for insurance reasons and then he had to be checked for abrasions for about six weeks afterwards. All the other wet-shirt shots were me.

BJ: And did the shirt have to keep being rewet?

CF: Yes. They'd spray it down. They'd spray it down and then—

BJ: What with?

CF: I'm sorry?

BJ: What with?

CF: A squirter thing. Look can we . . . ?

BJ: Yes, but what I mean is did you ever have to take the shirt off and . . . and put another one on?

CF: Yes.

BJ: To be wet again?

CF: Yes.

BJ: (*Pause*) You know the oncoming film *Fever Pitch*?

CF: Yes.

BJ: What do you see as the main differences and similarities between the character Paul from *Fever Pitch* and . . . ?

CF: And?

BJ: (*Sheepishly*) Mr. Darcy.

CF: No one's ever asked me that.

BJ: Haven't they?

CF: No. I think the main differences are—

BJ: Do you mean it's a really obvious question?

CF: No. I mean no one's ever asked me that.

BJ: Don't people ask you that all the time?

CF: No, no. I can assure you.

BJ: So it's a—

CF: It's a totally brand-new, newborn question, yes.

BJ: Oh goody.

CF: Shall we get on now?

BJ: Yes.

CF: Mr. Darcy's not an Arsenal supporter.

BJ: No.

CF: He's not a schoolteacher.

BJ: No.

CF: He lived nearly two hundred years ago.

BJ: Yes.

CF: Paul in *Fever Pitch* loves being in a football crowd.

BJ: Yes.

CF: Whereas Mr. Darcy can't even tolerate a country dance. Now. Can we talk about something that isn't to do with Mr. Darcy?

BJ: Yes.

(*Pause. Rustling papers*)

BJ: Are you still going out with your girlfriend?

CF: Yes.

BJ: Oh.

(*Long pause*)

CF: Is everything all right?

BJ: (*Almost inaudible*) Do you think small British movies are the way forward?

CF: I can't hear.

BJ: (*Miserably*) Do you think small British movies are the way forward?

CF: The way forward to . . . (*Encouragingly*) . . . to what?

BJ: (*Very long thoughtful pause*) The future.

CF: Right. They seem to be getting us along step by step, I think. I quite like small movies but I do also like big movies and it would be nice if we made more of those as well.

BJ: But don't you find it a problem her being Italian and everything?

CF: No.

(*Very long silence*)

BJ: (*Sulkily*) Do you think that Mr. Darcy has a political dimension?

CF: I did speculate on what his politics might be, if he had any. And I don't think that they would be very appealing to a reader of the *Independent*. It's that pre-Victorian or

Victorian idea of being the rich social benefactor, which would be very Thatcherite probably. I mean the thought of socialism obviously hadn't entered the . . .

BJ: No.

CF: . . . entered his sphere. And it is clearly stated by way of showing what a good chap he is that he is very nice towards his tenants. But I think that he'd be closer to a sort of Nietzschean figure, a—

BJ: What is neacher?

CF: You know, the idea of the, er, human being as superman.

BJ: Superman?

CF: Not Superman himself, no. No. (*Slight groaning noise*) I don't think he wore his underpants over his breeches, no. Look, I'd *really* like to get off this subject now.

BJ: What will be your next project?

CF: It's called *The World of Moss*.

BJ: Is it a nature program?

CF: No. No, no. No. It's um, it's, er, about an eccentric family in the thirties, the father of which owns a moss factory.

BJ: Doesn't moss grow naturally?

CF: Well, no, he makes something called sphagnum moss, which was used to dress World War One wounds and, er, it's, er, quite a light, er, comic . . .

BJ: (*Very unconvincingly*) It sounds very good.

CF: I very much hope it will be.

BJ: Could I just check something about the shirt?

CF: Yes.

BJ: How many times altogether exactly did you have to take it off and put it on again?

CF: Precisely . . . I don't know. Um. Let me see . . . there was the bit where I was walking towards Pemberley. That was shot once. One take. Then there was the bit where I give my horse to somebody . . . I think there was a change.

BJ: (*Brightening*) There was a change?

CF: (*Strictly*) There was. One change.

BJ: So it was mainly just the one wet shirt, though?

CF: The one wet shirt, which they kept respraying, yes. All right?

BJ: Yes. What is your favorite color?

CF: We've had that.

BJ: Um. (*Paper rustling*) Do you think the film *Fever Pitch* was in reality all about emotional fuckwittage?

CF: Emotional what?

BJ: Fuckwittage. You know: men being mad alcoholic commitment phobics and just being interested in football all the time.

CF: No, I don't really. I think in some ways Paul is much more at ease with his emotions and has much more liberty with them than his girlfriend. I think that, in fact, in the final analysis, is what's so appealing about what Nick Hornby's trying to say on his behalf: that, in a rather mundane, everyday world he has found something where you have access to emotional experiences that—

BJ: Excuse me.

CF: (*Sighs*) Yes?

BJ: Don't you find the language barrier a problem with your girlfriend?

CF: Well, she speaks very good English.

BJ: But don't you think you'd be better off with someone who *was* English and more your own age?

CF: We seem to be doing all right.

BJ: Humph. (*Darkly*) So far. Do you ever prefer doing the theater?

CF: Um. I don't subscribe to the view that the theater's where the real acting is, that film's not really acting. But I find I do prefer the theater when I'm doing it, yes.

BJ: But don't you think the theater's a bit unrealistic and embarrassing and also you have to sit through the acting for hours before you have anything to eat and you can't talk or—

CF: Unrealistic? Embarrassing and unrealistic?

BJ: Yes.

CF: Do you mean unrealistic in the sense that it . . . ?

BJ: You can tell it isn't real.

CF: That sort of unrealistic, yes. (*Slight moaning sound*) Um. I think it shouldn't be if it's good. It's much more . . . It feels more artificial to make a film.

BJ: Does it? I suppose it doesn't go all the way through, does it?

CF: Well, no. It doesn't. No. Yes. A film doesn't go all the way through. It's shot in little bits and pieces. (*Louder groaning noise*) Little bits and pieces.

BJ: I see. Do you think Mr. Darcy would have slept with Elizabeth Bennet before the wedding?

CF: Yes, I do think he might have.

BJ: *Do* you?

CF: Yes. I think it's entirely possible. Yes.

BJ: (*Breathlessly*) Really?

CF: I think it's possible, yes.

BJ: *How* would it be possible?

CF: Don't know if Jane Austen would agree with me on this but—

BJ: We can't know because she's dead.

CF: No, we can't . . . but I think Andrew Davies's Mr. Darcy would have done.

BJ: *Why* do you think that, though. Why? Why?

CF: Because I think it was very important to Andrew Davies that Mr. Darcy had the most enormous sex drive.

BJ: (*Gasps*)

CF: And, um . . .

BJ: I think that came across really, really well with the acting. I really think it did.

CF: Thank you. At one point Andrew even wrote as a stage direction: "Imagine that Darcy has an erection."

(*V. large crashing noise*)

BJ: Which bit was that?

CF: It's when Elizabeth's been walking across the country and bumps into him in the grounds in the early stages.

BJ: The bit where she's all muddy?

CF: And disheveled.

BJ: And sweaty?

CF: Exactly.

BJ: Was that a difficult bit to act?

CF: You mean the erection?

BJ: (*Awed whisper*) Yes.

CF: Um, well, Andrew also wrote that I don't propose that we should focus on it, and therefore no acting required in that department at least.

BJ: Mmm.

(*Long pause*)

CF: Yes.

(*More pause*)

BJ: Mmm.

CF: Is that it, then?

BJ: No. What was it like with your friends when you started being Mr. Darcy?

CF: There were a lot of jokes about it: growling, "Mr. Darcy" over breakfast and so on. There was a brief period when they had to work quite hard to hide their knowledge of who I really was and—

BJ: Hide it from who?

CF: Well, from anyone who suspected that perhaps I was like Mr. Darcy.

BJ: But do you think you're not like Mr. Darcy?

CF: I do think I'm not like Mr. Darcy, yes.

BJ: I think you're exactly like Mr. Darcy.

CF: In what way?

BJ: You talk the same way as him.

CF: Oh, do I?

BJ: You look exactly like him, and I, oh, oh . . .

(*Protracted crashing noises followed by sounds of struggle*)

7

~

Mood-Swinging Singletons

126 lbs. (yesss! yesss!), alcohol units 4, cigarettes 4, spiritual realizations as joint result of Road Less Traveled *and alcohol units 4, flats without holes in 0, no. of pounds in bank 0, boyfriends 0, people to go out with tonight 0, election parties invited to 0.*

5:30 p.m. Office. Challenging two days at work with Richard Finch reading out bits of the interview then bellowing with deep, gurgling laughter in manner of Dracula, but at least has got me out of myself. Also Jude said the interview was quite good and really gave an excellent sense of the atmosphere of the whole thing. Hurrah! Have not heard anything back from Adam or Michael at *Independent* but sure they will ring soon and maybe ask me to do another one, then can be freelance in home office, typing on roof terrace with herbs in terra-cotta pots! Also is only one week to election when everything is going to change! Will stop smoking, and Mark will come back and find new professional me with large indoor/outdoor living flat.

5:45 p.m. Humph. Just rang in for messages. One only, from Tom saying he had spoken to Adam and everyone at the *Independent* is really annoyed. Left him urgent message to call me back and explain.

5:50 p.m. Oh dear. Worried about arranging second mortgage now. Will not have any extra money and what if lose job? Maybe had better tell Gary do not want the infill extension and get the £3,500 back. Lucky thing is, Gary was supposed to start yesterday but he just came and left all his tools then went away again. Seemed annoying at the time, but maybe, as it turns out, was message from God. Yes. Will call him when get home then go to gym.

6:30 p.m. Back home. Gaaah! Gaaah! Gaaah! Is bloody great hole in side of flat! Is left open to outside world in manner of gaping precipice and all the houses at the other side can see in. Is entire weekend stretching ahead with giant hole in wall, all bricks everywhere and nothing to do! Nothing! Nothing!

6:45 p.m. Ooh, telephone—maybe someone inviting me to an election party! Or Mark!

"Oh, hello, darling, guess what?" My mother. Obviously I had to get a cigarette.

"Oh, hello, darling, guess what?" she said again. Sometimes I wonder how long she would carry on like this, in manner of a parrot. It is one thing to say "Hello? Hello?" if there is silence on the other end, but "Oh, hello, darling, guess what? Oh, hello, darling, guess what?" is surely not normal.

"What?" I said sulkily.

"Don't speak to me in that tone of voice."

"What?" I said again in a lovely appreciative daughter voice.

"Don't say 'What?' Bridget, say 'Pardon?'"

I took a puff on my kind normal friend the Silk Cut Ultra.

"Bridget, are you smoking?"

"No, no," I said, panicking, stubbing out the cigarette and hiding the ashtray.

"Anyway, guess what? Una and I are holding a Kikuyu election party for Wellington behind the rockery!"

I breathed deeply through my nose and thought about Inner Poise.

"Don't you think that's super? Wellington's going to leap over a bonfire as a full warrior! Imagine! Right over! Dress is tribal. And we're all going to drink red wine and pretend it's cow's blood! Cow's blood! That's why Wellington's got such strong thighs."

"Er, does Wellington know about this?"

"Not yet, darling, but he's bound to want to celebrate the election. Wellington's very keen on the free market and we don't want the Thin Red Wedge back under the bed. I mean we'll end up with what's-his-name and the miners back. You won't remember the power cuts when you were at school, but Una was giving the speech at the Ladies' Luncheon and she couldn't plug her curling tongs in."

7:15 p.m. Eventually managed to get Mum off the phone, at which it rang again immediately on ringback. Was Shaz. Told her how fed up I was feeling, and she was really sweet: "Come on, Bridge. We simply can't define ourselves in terms of being with another person! We should celebrate how fantastic it is being free! And there'll be the election soon and the whole mood of the nation is going to change!"

"Hurrah!" I said. "Singletons! Tony Blair! Hurrah!"

"Yes!" enthused Shazzer. "Many people in relationships have a terrible time at weekends, forced to slave for ungrateful children and being beaten by their own spouses."

"You're right! You're right!" I said. "We can go out whenever we like and have fun. Shall we go out tonight?"

Humph. Sharon is going to a dinner party with Simon in manner of Smug Married.

7:40 p.m. Jude just rang in a spirit of highly charged sexual overconfidence. "It's on again with Stacey!" she said. "I saw him last night and he was talking about his family!"

There was an expectant pause.

"Talking about his family!" she said again. "Which means he's thinking seriously about me. And we snogged. And I'm seeing him tonight and it's the fourth date so . . . doobeedoobeedoo. Bridge? Are you still there?"

"Yes," I said in a small voice.

"What's the matter?"

Mumbled something about the hole in the wall and Mark.

"The thing is, Bridge. You've got to Attain Closure on that one and move on," she said, seemingly not noticing that her last lot of advice had completely failed, which might just invalidate this.

"You've got to start working on Loving Yourself. Come on, Bridge! It's fantastic. We can shag whoever we want."

"Singletons hurrah!" I said. So why am I depressed?

Am going to call Tom again.

8 p.m. Out. Everyone is out enjoying themselves except me.

9 p.m. Just read a bit of *You Can Heal Your Life* and now see exactly where have been going wrong. As Sondra Ray, the great rebirther, said, or maybe it wasn't her. Anyway, this is it: "Love is never outside ourselves, love is within us."

Yes!

"What may be keeping love away? . . . Unreasonable standards? Movie Star Images? Feelings of unworthiness? A belief that you are unlovable?"

Huh. Is not belief is fact. Am going to open bottle of Chardonnay and watch *Friends*.

11 p.m. *Road Less Traveled* blurry good. Is cathexis or similar. "Unitary division of loveinclud self love if love for another." Sblurry good. Ooof. Tumbled over.

⌇ **SATURDAY 26 APRIL**

130 lbs., alcohol units 7 (hurrah!), cigarettes 27 (hurrah!), calories 4,248 (hurrah!), gym visits 0 (hurrah!).

7 a.m. Aargh. Who set that bloody thing off?

7:05 a.m. Today I will take responsibility for my own life and start loving myself. I am lovely. I am marvelous. Oh God. Where's the Silk Cut?

7:10 a.m. Right. Going to get up and go to gym.

7:15 a.m. Actually, though, it is probably quite dangerous to work out before you have properly woken up. Will jar joints. Will go tonight before *Blind Date*. Is stupid to go in the daytime on Saturday when there is so much to do e.g. shopping. Must not mind that Jude and Shaz are both probably in bed shagging wildly, shag, shag, shag.

7:30 a.m. Shag.

7:45 a.m. Obviously it is too early for anyone to ring. Just because I am awake does not mean anyone else is. Must learn to have more empathy with others.

8 a.m. Jude just rang but practically impossible to tell as total sheep-voice sobbing, gulping experience.

"Jude, what's wrong?" I said, devastated.

"I'm having a breakdown," she sobbed. "Everything seems black, black. I can't see any way out I can't . . ."

"It's all right. It's going to be all right," I said, staring wildly out of the window to see if there was a psychiatrist passing. "Does it feel serious or is it just PMT?"

"It's very, very bad," she said in a zombielike voice. "It's been building up in me for about eleven years." She broke down again. "The whole weekend stretching ahead alone, alone. I just don't want to carry on living."

"Good, that's good," I said reassuringly, wondering whether I should ring the police or the Samaritans.

Turned out Stacey had inexplicably just dropped her off after dinner last night and not mentioned seeing her again. So now she felt she'd failed at Thursday's snog.

"I'm so depressed. The whole weekend stretching ahead. Alone alone, I could die and—"

"Do you want to come round tonight?"

"Oooh, yes please!! Shall we go to 192? I can wear my new Voyage cardi."

Next thing Tom rang.

"Why didn't you call me back last night?" I said.

"What?" he said in a strange, dull monotone.

"You didn't call me back."

"Oh," he said wearily. "I didn't think it was fair to talk to anyone."

"Why?" I said, puzzled.

"Oh. Because I have lost my former personality and become a manic-depressive."

It turned out Tom has been working alone at home all week, obsessing about Jerome. Eventually helped Tom to realize that the phantom madness was quite funny, given that if he hadn't informed me he was clinically insane I wouldn't have noticed any difference.

I reminded Tom of when Sharon once didn't come out of the house for three days because she thought her face was collapsing from sun damage like a movie aging special effect and didn't want to face anyone or expose herself to UVP rays till she'd privately come to terms with it. Then when she came to Café Rouge she looked exactly like she did the week before. Managed, finally, to get off the subject of Tom and on to my career as a major celebrity interviewer which unfortunately seems to be over, for the time being at least.

"Don't worry, babe," said Tom. "They'll have forgotten all about it in ten minutes, you'll see. You can make a comeback."

2:45 p.m. Feeling much better now. Have realized answer is not to obsess about own problems but help others. Have just spent an hour and fifteen minutes on phone cheering up Simon who was clearly not in bed with Shazzer. Turns out he was supposed to see this girl called Georgie tonight, who he has been intermittently secretly shagging on Saturday nights, but now Georgie says she doesn't think Saturday night is a good idea because it seems too much like they are an "item."

"I'm a love pariah doomed by the gods always to be alone," Simon raged. "Always, always. The whole of Sunday stretching ahead."

As I told him, it is great being single because we are free! Free! (Somehow hope Shaz does not find out exactly how free Simon is, though.)

3 p.m. Am marvelous: have been almost like therapist all day. As I said to Jude and Tom, any time day or night they can call me, not just be sad on their own. So you see I am very wise and well balanced almost in manner of the Mother Superior in *The Sound of Music*. In fact can easily imagine self singing "Climb Ev'ry Mountain" at wall in middle of 192 with Jude kneeling appreciatively behind.

4 p.m. Phone just rang. Was Shazzer on verge of tears but trying to pretend she wasn't. Turns out Simon just called her with the Georgie scenario (v. annoying as obviously own Mother Superior act was not sufficient for the, now realize, emotionally greedy Simon).

"But I thought you were 'just good friends'?" I said.

"So did I," she said. "But I now realize I was just secretly fantasizing that we were in a higher form of love. It's just awful being single," she burst out. "No one to put their arm round you at the end of the day, no one to help you mend the boiler. The whole weekend stretching ahead! Alone! Completely alone!"

4:30 p.m. Hurrah! Everyone is coming round, Shaz, Jude and Tom (though not Simon as in disgrace for Mixed Messages), and we are going to get an Indian takeaway and watch videos of *ER*. Love being single as you can have fun with all different people and life is full of freedom and potential.

6 p.m. A terrible thing has happened. Magda just called.

"Put it back in the potty. Put it back in! Listen, I don't know if I should tell you this, Bridge, but put it back. Put the ploppy BACK IN!"

"Magda . . ." I said dangerously.

"Sorry, hon. Look, I just rang to tell you that Rebecca . . . now look that's really nasty, isn't it? Yakky! Yakky! Say yakky."

"WHAT?"

"Mark's coming home next week. She's invited us to a postelection welcome-back dinner for him and . . . NOOOOOOO! OK, OK, put it in my hand."

I slumped dizzily at the kitchen table fumbling for a cigarette.

"All right. Put it in Daddy's hand, then. The thing is, Bridge, would you rather we said yes or are you doing another one? Well, do it in the potty, then. In the potty!"

"Oh God," I said. "Oh God."

6:30 p.m. Am going out for fags.

7 p.m. Whole of London is full of couples holding hands in spring, shagging each other shag, shag, shag, and planning lovely minibreaks. Am going to be alone for rest of life. Alone!

8 p.m. Everything is turning out fantastic. Jude and Tom came round first with wine and magazines and were taking piss out of me for not knowing what a pashmina was. Jude decided Stacey had a big bum and also kept putting his hand on hers and saying "Happee?," which she had not revealed before and definitely meant he was out of the window.

Also, everyone agreed it was good that Magda should go to the hateful Rebecca's dinner party as a spy, and that if Mark really *is* going out with Rebecca then he is definitely gay, which is good—especially for Tom, who was really cheered up. Also, Jude is going to have election party and not ask Rebecca. HA!

AHAHAHAHAHAHHAHAHAHAHAHAHHAHAHAHAH-HAHAHAHAHAHA!

Next thing, Shaz turned up in tears, which was really nice in a way because usually she does not show that she minds about anything.

"Bloodybloodys," she got out eventually. "It's just been an entire year of emotional fuckups, and I'm so confused."

All rushed to first aid with *Vogue*, sparkling wine, cigarettes etc. and Tom announced there was no such thing as platonic friendship.

"Of course there blurry is," slurred Jude. "You jus obsessed with sex."

"No, no," said Tom. "It's just a fin-de-millennium way of dealing with the nightmare of relationships. All friendships between men and women are based on the sexual dynamic. The mistake people make is ignoring this, then getting upset when their friend doesn't shag them."

"I'm not getting upset," muttered Shazzer.

"What about friends when neither fancies the other?" said Jude.

"Doesn't happen. Sex is what drives it. 'Friends' is a bad definition."

"Pashminas," I slurred, slurping on my Chardonnay.

"That's it!" said Tom excitedly. "It's fin-de-millennium pashminaism. Shazzer is Simon's 'pashmina' because she wants to shag him most so he diminishes her and Simon is Shazzer's 'pashmaster.'"

At this, Sharon burst into tears, which took twenty minutes to sort out with another bottle of Chardonnay and packet of fags until we could come up with a list of further definitions, as follows:

Pashmincer.   A friend who you really fancy who's actually gay. ("Me, me, me," Tom said.)

Pashmarried.   A friend who you used to go out with and is now married with children who likes having you around as memory of old life but makes you feel like mad barren pod-womb imagining vicar is in love with self.

Ex-pashspurt.   An ex-partner who wants to get back with you but pretends just to want to be friends then keeps making passes and getting cross.

"What about 'pash-hurts'?" said Shaz sulkily. "Friends who turn your own private emotional disaster into a sociological study at the expense of your feelings."

At this point I decided I'd better go out for cigarettes. Was just standing in sordid pub on corner, waiting for change for cigarette machine when nearly jumped out of skin. Across the bar was a man who looked exactly like Geoffrey Alconbury, only instead of a yellow diamond-patterned sweater and golfing slacks, he was wearing pale blue jeans, ironed with a crease down the front and a leather jacket over a black nylon string vest. Tried to compose self by staring furiously at a bottle of vodka. It couldn't be Uncle Geoffrey. Glanced up and realized he was talking to a boy who looked about seventeen. It was Uncle Geoffrey. It definitely was!

Hesitated, unsure what to do. Briefly considered abandoning cigarettes and departing to spare Geoffrey's feelings. But then some Tyson-esque inner angriness reminded me of all the times Geoffrey has totally humiliated me in his environment, bellowing at the top of his voice. Ha! Ahahahaha! Uncle Geoffrey was on my territory now.

Was just about to go over and bellow "Who's this then? Durr! Got yourself a young whippersnapper!" at the top of my voice, when felt a tap on my shoulder. Turned round to see no one there and felt a tap on my other shoulder. This was Uncle Geoffrey's favorite trick.

"Ahahahaha, what's my little Bridget doing in here, looking for a fellah?" he roared.

I couldn't believe it. He'd put a yellow sweater with a cougar on over the vest, the boy was nowhere to be seen, and he was trying to brazen it out.

"You're not going to find one in here, Bridget, they all look like woofters to me. Bent as a ten-bob note! Ahahaha. I've just come in for a packet of slim panatellas."

At that moment the boy reappeared holding the leather jacket and looking all twitchy and disturbed.

"Bridget," said Geoffrey as if with the full weight of Kettering Rotary behind him, then ran out of steam, and turned to the barman. "Come on, lad! Have you got those slim panatellas I asked you for? I've been waiting twenty minutes."

"What are you doing in London?" I said suspiciously.

"London? I've been up at the AGM for the Rotarians. It doesn't belong to you, you know, London."

"Hi, I'm Bridget," I said pointedly to the boy.

"Oh yes. This is, er, Steven. He's wanting to put himself up for treasurer, aren't you, Steven? Just giving him a spot of advice. Right. Better be off. Be good! And if you can't be good be careful!! Ahahaha!" And he shot out of the pub, followed by the boy, looking back at me resentfully.

Back at the flat Jude and Shazzer could not believe I had let such an opportunity for revenge go by.

"Think what you could have said," said Shaz, screwing her eyes up with disbelieving regret.

"Well! Glad to see you've got yourself a feller at last, Uncle GeoffrEEEEEY! We'll see how long this one lasts, won't we? Off they go—weeeeh!"

Tom, though, had a really annoying expression of pompous concern on his face.

"It's tragic, tragic," he burst out. "So many men up and down the country living a lie! Imagine all the secret thoughts, shames and desires eating away within the walls of suburbia, between the sofa and the French window of Lies! He probably goes to Hampstead Heath. He's probably taking terrible, terrible risks. You should talk to him, Bridget."

"Look," said Shaz. "Shut up. You're drunk."

"I feel sort of justified," I said thoughtfully and carefully. Started to explain that have long suspected Smug Married world of Geoffrey and Una was not all it seemed and that therefore am not freak and that living together in normal heterosexual couple is not God-instructed only way.

"Bridge, shut up. You're drunk as well," said Shaz.

"Hurrah! Let's bring it back to ourselves. There's nothing more annoying than being distracted from our own self-obsession by others," said Tom.

All got really plastered after that. Was completely fantastic evening. As Tom said, if Miss Havisham had had some jolly flatmates to take the piss out of her she would never have stayed so long in her wedding dress.

128 lbs., alcohol units 0, cigarettes 0, boyfriends 0, calls from Gary the Builder 0, possibilities of new job 0 (promising), gym visits 0, no. of gym visits so far this year 1, cost of gym membership per year £370; cost of single gym visit £123 (v. bad economy).

Right. Am definitely going to start gym program today so can go round saying smugly "Yes it hurt. Yes it worked," in manner of Conservative Party, and—in sharp contrast to them—everyone will believe me and think I am marvelous. Oh dear, though, is nine o'clock. Will go tonight instead. Where the fuck is Gary?

Later. In office. Haha! Aahahahaha! Was marvelous at work today.

"So," said Richard Finch, when we were all assembled round the table. "Bridget. Tony Blair. Women's committees. New policies with Women in Mind, any suggestions? Nothing to do with Colin Firth if you can possibly manage it."

I smiled beatifically, glancing down at my notes, then looked up with poise and confidence.

"Tony Blair should introduce a code of Dating Practice for Singletons," I said eventually.

There was a jealous pause from all the other researchers round the table.

"That's it, is it?" said Richard Finch.

"Yup," I said confidently.

"You don't think," he said, "that our potential new prime minister might have better things to do with his time?"

"Just think of the number of working hours lost through distraction, sulks, discussions to interpret situations and waiting for the phone to ring," I said. "It must be easily on a par with back pain. Also, all other cultures have specific dating rituals, but we are operating in an ill-defined sea with men and women increasingly alienated from each other."

At this, Horrid Harold let out a snort of derision.

"Oh God," drawled Patchouli, lounging with her Lycra cycle-shorted legs all over the table. "You can't proscribe people's emotional behavior. That's fascism."

"No, no, Patchouli, you haven't been listening," I said strictly. "These would be just guidelines for sexual good manners. Since a quarter of all households are single, it would significantly help the nation's mental well-being."

"I really think, in the run-up to the election—" Horrid Harold sneerily began.

"No, wait," said Richard Finch chewing, twitching his leg up and down and looking at us oddly. "How many of you are married?"

Everyone stared foolishly at the table.

"So it's just me, is it?" he said. "Just me who's holding together the tattered shreds of the fabric of British society?"

Everyone tried not to look at Saskia, the researcher Richard had been shagging all summer till he abruptly lost interest and started on the sandwich girl.

"Mind you, I'm not surprised," he went on. "Who'd marry any of you? You're incapable of committing to fetching the cappuccinos let alone to one person for the rest of your lives." At this Saskia let out a strange noise and shot out of the office.

Did a great deal of research all morning, making phone calls and talking to people. Was actually quite interesting that even those researchers who had pooh-poohed whole thing kept on coming out with suggestions.

"OK, Bridget," said Richard Finch just before lunch. "Let's hear this groundbreaking, great *oeuvre*."

Explained that Rome was not built in a day, and obviously had not completed whole work yet but these were lines was working along. I cleared my throat and began:

"Code of Dating Practice

1. If citizens know they do not want to go out with someone else they must not egg them on in the first place.
2. When a man and woman decide they would like to sleep together, if either party knows they just want a 'fling' this should be clearly stated beforehand.

3. If citizens snog or shag other citizens they must not pretend nothing is going on.

4. Citizens must not go out with other citizens for years and years but keep on saying they don't want to get too serious.

5. After sexual relations it is definitely bad manners not to stay the night."

"But what if——" rudely interrupted Patchouli.

"*Could* I just finish?" I said graciously and authoritatively. I then ran through the rest of the list adding, "Also, if governments are going to go on about family values then they have to do something more positive for Singletons than slagging them off." I paused, shuffling my papers pleasantly. "Here are my proposals:

Smug Marriage Promotional Suggestions

1. Teach *Men Are from Mars, Women Are from Venus* in schools so both sides of opposing armies understand each other.

2. Teach all boy children that sharing the housework does not mean twiddling one fork under the tap.

3. Form giant Government Matchmaking Agency for Singletons, with strict Code of Dating Practice, Mate-Seekers Allowance for drinks, phone calls, cosmetics etc., penalties for Emotional Fuckwittage and rule that you have to go on at least twelve government-arranged dates before you can declare yourself a Singleton; and only then if have reasonable grounds for rejecting all twelve.

4. If grounds are deemed unreasonable, then you have to declare yourself a Fuckwit."

"Oh Christ," said Horrid Harold. "I mean I really do think the issue is the Euro."

"No, this is good, this is ver-y good," said Richard, staring fixedly at me, at which Harold looked as though he'd eaten a pigeon. "I'm thinking live studio discussion. I'm thinking Harriet Harman, I'm thinking Robin Cook. I'm maybe even thinking Blair. Right, Bridget. Move. Set this up. Get Harman's office on the phone and get her in tomorrow, then try Blair."

Hurrah. Am head researcher on lead item. Everything is going to change for me and for the nation!

7 p.m. Humph. Harriet Harman has never rung back. And neither has Tony Blair. Item is cancelled.

⁓ TUESDAY 29 APRIL

Cannot believe Gary the Builder. Have left him a message every day this week and nothing. No reply. Maybe he's sick or something. Also keep getting whiff of really horrible smell on stairs.

⁓ WEDNESDAY 30 APRIL

Hmm. Just got home from work and hole has been covered up with big sheet of polythene but no note, no message, nothing about giving me the £3,500 back. Nothing. Wish Mark would ring.

8

Oh Baby

128 lbs., alcohol units 5 (but celebrating New Labour victory), contribution to New Labour victory—other than alcohol units—0.

6:30 p.m. Hurrah! Really there is a fantastic atmosphere today: election days are one of the few occasions when you realize it is we, the people, who are in charge and the government are just our mutatedly bloated, arrogant pawns and now our time has come to stand together and wield our power.

7:30 p.m. Just got back from shop. Is amazing out there. Everyone spilling out of the pubs completely drunk. Really feel part of something. It is not just that people want a change. No. It is a great rising up of we, the nation, against all the greed, lack of principles and of respect for real people and their problems and . . . Oh goody, telephone.

7:45 p.m. Humph. Was Tom.
"Have you voted yet?"
"Actually I was just on my way," I said.
"Oh yes. To which voting station?"
"The one round the corner."
Hate it when Tom gets like this. Just because he used to be a member of trendy lefty groups and go round singing "Sing If You're

Glad to Be Gay" in a morbid voice, there is no need for him to behave like the Spanish Inquisition.

"And which candidate will you be voting for?"

"Um," I said, looking frantically out of the window for red signs
on the lampposts. "Buck!"

"Go on then," he said. "Remember Mrs. Pankhurst."

Honestly, who does he think he is? Obviously I am going to vote.
Better get changed, though. I do not look very lefty in this.

8:45 p.m. Just back from polling station. "Do you have your voting
card?" bossy whippersnapper asked. What voting card? That's what I
want to know. Turned out I was not registered on any of their lists
even though I have been paying poll tax for bloody years so have to
go to another voting station. Just come back for *A–Z*.

9:30 p.m. Humph. Was not bloody well registered there either.
Have to go to some library or other miles away. Mind you, is great
being out on the streets tonight. We, the people, uniting for change.
Yesssss! Wish had not worn platforms though. Wish, also, did not
keep getting whiff of horrible smell on stairs every time I go out.

10:30 p.m. Cannot believe what has happened. I have let down
Tony Blair and my country through no fault of my own. Turned
out, although flat was on list, am not registered to vote, even though
I had Community Charge book with me. Honestly, all that fuss
about not having the vote if you don't pay your poll tax and turns
out you do not have vote even if you do.

"Did you fill the form in last October?" said self-important bag-
gage in ruffly-collared shirt and brooch, enjoying crazed moment of
glory just because she happened to be in charge of table in voting
station.

"Yes!" I lied. Obviously people who live in flats cannot be expected to open every boring brown envelope addressed "To the
Occupant" which plops through the door. What if Buck loses by
one vote then entire election lost by one seat? Will be my fault, my

fault. Walk to Shazzer's from polling station was hideous walk of shame. Also cannot wear platforms now as feet too crippled so will look short.

2:30 a.m. Was blurbrill party. Tories. Out! Out! Out! Oops.

129 lbs. (hurrah! Newborn New Labour pound first of new era).

8 a.m. Hurrah! Could not be more pleased about landslide. That will be one in eye for shaming Tory Party Member mother and ex-boyfriend. Har har. Cannot wait to gloat. Cherie Blair is fantastic. You see, she too would probably not fit into tiny bikinis in communal changing rooms. She too has not got snooker-ball bottom yet somehow is able to obtain clothes that encompass bottom and still make her look like role model. Maybe Cherie will now use her influence over new prime minister, who will order all clothes shops to start producing clothes that will fit attractively over everyone's arses.

Worry, though, that New Labour will be like having a crush on someone, finally being able to go out with them and then when you have your first row it is cataclysmically awful. But then Tony Blair is the first prime minister I can completely imagine having voluntary sex with. Actually Shaz had a theory last night that the reason he and Cherie were always touching each other was not the spin doctors but that Cherie was becoming increasingly aroused as the landslides came in—the aphrodisiac of power or . . . Ooh, telephone.

"Oh, hello, darling, guess what?" My mother.

"What?" I said smugly, preparing to gloat.

"We've won, darling. Isn't that marvelous! A landslide! Imagine!"

A cold shudder suddenly went over me. When we went to bed Peter Snow was striding marvelously but incomprehensibly about and it seemed pretty clear the swingometer was to Labour but . . .

Oh-oh. Maybe we misunderstood. We were a bit squiffy and nothing made any particular sense other than all the blue Tory buildings on the map of Britain being blown up. Or maybe something happened in the night and turned it back Tory.

"And guess what?"

Is all my fault. Labour has lost and is all my fault. I and people like me who, as Tony Blair warned, had become complacent. Am not fit to call myself British citizen or woman. Doom. Dooooom.

"Bridget, are you listening to me?"

"Yes," I whispered, mortified.

"We're having a Tony and Gordon Ladies' Night at the Rotary! Everyone's going to call each other by their first names and wear casual wear instead of ties. Merle Robertshaw's trying to put the kibosh on it because she says no one wants to come in slacks except the vicar, but actually Una and I think it's just because Percival's furious about the handguns. Then Wellington's going to give a speech. A black man speaking at the Rotary! Imagine! But you see that's the whole spirit of Labour, darling. Colors and ethical like Nelson Mandela. Geoffrey's been taking Wellington on little drives and showing him the pubs in Kettering. The other day they got stuck behind a Nelson Myers lorry full of scaffolding planks and we thought they'd had an accident!"

Trying not to think about the possible motivation behind Uncle Geoffrey's "little drives" with Wellington, I said, "I thought you'd just had an election party with Wellington?"

"Oh no, actually, darling, Wellington decided he didn't want to do that. He said he didn't want to pollute our culture and have Una and I jumping over fires at parties instead of handing out vol-au-vents." I burst out laughing. "So anyway he wants to do this speech and raise some money for his jet ski bike."

"What?"

"A jet ski, darling, you know? He wants to set up a little business on the beach instead of selling shells. He says the Rotary are bound to go for it because they're supporters of business. Anyway, must whizz! Una and I are taking him to get his colors done!"

Am assured, receptive, responsive woman of substance who does not take responsibility for others' behavior. Only for own. Yes.

128 lbs., alcohol units 2 (standard health issue to avoid heart attacks), cigarettes 5 (v.g.), calories 1,800 (v.g.), positive thoughts 4 (excellent).

8 p.m. Whole new positive mood. Sure everyone is being more courteous and giving under new Blair regime. Is surely clean sweep with broom sweeping out evils of Tory rule. Even feel different about Mark and Rebecca. Just because she is having a dinner party does not mean they are going out, does it? She is just being manipulative. Really, it is marvelous when one feels one has reached a plateau and everything just seems lovely. All things I used to think about not being attractive beyond a certain age are not true. Look at Helen Mirren and Francesca Annis.

8:30 p.m. Hmm, though. Is not very nice thought that dinner party is actually tonight. Think will read a bit of *Buddhism: The Drama of the Moneyed Monk*. Is good to calm down. Cannot expect life always to turn out well and everyone needs to nourish their soul.

8:45 p.m. Yes! You see problem is have been living in fantasy world, constantly turning to past or future instead of enjoying present moment. Am just going to sit here and enjoy present moment.

9 p.m. Not enjoying present moment at all. Is hole in wall, stink on stairs, growing overdraft in bank and Mark is at dinner party with Rebecca. Maybe will open bottle of wine and watch *ER*.

10 p.m. Wonder if Magda is back yet. She promised to call me the second she got in with full report. Sure she will say Mark is not going out with Rebecca and he was asking about me.

11:30 p.m. Have just rung Magda's baby-sitter. They are not back yet. Have left message to remind her to ring.

11:35 p.m. Still hasn't rung. Maybe Rebecca's dinner party is fantastic triumph and they are all still there having riotous time climaxing with Mark Darcy standing on table announcing engagement to Rebecca. . . . Ooh, telephone.

"Hi, Bridge, it's Magda."

"So how was it?" I said, too quickly.

"Oh, it was quite nice actually."

I flinched. Totally wrong thing to say, totally.

"She'd done grilled goat's cheese on a green salad and then penne carbonara only with asparagus instead of pancetta, which was lovely and then peaches baked in Marsala with mascarpone."

This was terrible.

"It was obviously Delia Smith but she denied it."

"Did she?" I said eagerly. This at least was good. He does not like people being pretentious. "And how was Mark?"

"Oh fine. He's a really nice chap, isn't he? Terribly attractive." Magda has no idea. No idea, none. Not to praise ex-boyfriends who have chucked one. "Oh and then she did orange peel coated in chocolate."

"Right," I said patiently. I mean honestly, if this were Jude or Shazzer they would have every nuance, ready and deconstructed. "And do you think he's going out with Rebecca?"

"Hmmm, I'm not sure. She was very flirty with him."

Tried to remember about Buddhism and that at least have own spirit.

"Was he already there when you got there?" I said slowly and understandingly as if talking to a very confused two-year-old.

"Yes."

"And did he leave when everyone else did?"

"Jeremy!" she suddenly yelled at the top of her voice. "Was Mark Darcy still there when we left?"

Oh *God*.

"Mark Darcy what?" I heard Jeremy bellow, and then something else.

"Has he done it in the bed?" Magda yelled. "A wee or a poo? IS IT A WEE OR A POO? Sorry, Bridge, I'm going to have to go."

"Just one more thing," I gabbled. "Did he mention me?"

"Take it out of the bed—with your hands! Well, you can wash them, can't you? Oh for God's sake grow up. Sorry, Bridge, what was that?"

"Did he mention me?"

"Um. Um. Oh fuck off, Jeremy."

"Well?"

"To be honest, Bridge, I don't think he did."

~ **SUNDAY 4 MAY**

128 lbs., alcohol units 5, cigarettes 9 (must stop slide into decadence), hatred poison plans to kill Rebecca 14, Buddhist shame at homicidal thoughts: extensive, Catholic guilt (even though not Catholic): growing.

My flat. Very bad day. Went round to Jude's earlier in zomboid state. She and Shaz were going on and on saying I had to get back on some kind of horse and started—frankly insultingly—leafing through the *Time Out* Lonely Hearts.

"I don't want to look at Lonely Hearts," I said indignantly. "It's not that bad."

"Er, Bridget," said Sharon coldly. "Weren't you the one that wanted Tony Blair to set up dating agencies for Singletons? I thought we agreed that political integrity was important."

"Oh my God, this is outrageous." Jude was reading out loud, shoving large pieces of a leftover Crunchie Easter Egg into her mouth. "'Genuine tall attractive male fifty-seven, GSOH, WLTM civilized, married luscious lady twenty to twenty-five, for discreet uninhibited no-commitment relationship.' Who do they think they are, these creeps?"

"What's GSOH and WLTM?" I said.

"Giant sore on head. Willy limp, thin mollusc?" suggested Sharon.

"Great sex on horse with little tiny mouse?" I wondered.

"It means: Good Sense of Humor, Would Like to Meet," said Jude, suspiciously suggesting she might have done this before.

"I suppose you'd have to have a sense of humor to be too mean to fork out enough to say so in genuine words," sniggered Sharon.

Talking Hearts turned out to be v. entertaining. You can actually ring up and *hear* the people advertising themselves like contestants on *Blind Date*.

"Right. My name's Barret and if you'll be my sugar and spice, I'll give *you* champers on ice."

Is not very cool to start message saying "Right" thereby giving impression of huge buildup to scary message-leaving, even though obviously is scary.

"My work is thoughtful, fulfilling and rewarding and I'm interested in all the usual kind of things—magic, occult, paganism."

"I'm handsome, I'm very passionate. I'm a writer and I'm looking for a very special leading laydee. She'll take pleasure in having a good body, I'll be at least ten years older than her and she'll like that."

"Pah!" said Shazzer. "I'm going to ring some of these sexist bastards up."

Shazzer was in seventh heaven putting them on speaker phone then murmuring sexily, "Hello, is that 'First Time Advertised' on the line? Well, get off it quickly there's a train coming." Not very mature admittedly, but seemed amusing with all Chardonnay in selves.

" 'Hi, I'm Wild Boy. I'm tall, I'm Spanish with long black hair, dark eyes, long black lashes and a lean, wild body . . .' " I read out in a stupid voice.

"Ooh!" said Jude brightly. "He sounds rather nice."

"Well, why don't you call him then?" I said.

"No!" said Jude.

"So why are you trying to get me to ring someone?"

Jude went all coy then. Turned out whole Stacey, Singleton Depression weekend thing had catapulted her into returning one of Vile Richard's calls.

"Oh God," said Shazzer and I simultaneously.

"I'm not going back out with him or anything. It's just . . . nice," she finished lamely, trying to avoid my and Shazzer's accusing stares. Got back home to hear answerphone clicking on. "Hello, Bridget," said deep, sexy, foreign *young-sounding* voice. "This is Wild Boy . . ." Bloody girls must have given him my number. Horrified by sense of danger implied by total stranger having phone number, did not pick up but merely listened while Wild Boy explained he will be in 192 tomorrow night holding a red rose.

Then immediately called Shazzer and told her off.

"Oh come on," said Shaz. "Let's all go. It'll be a laugh."

So plan is, we are all going tomorrow night. Ho hum. What am I going to do about hole in wall and stench on stairs? Bloody Gary! He's got £3,500 of mine. Right. Am going to bloody well ring him up.

⌒ Monday 5 May

127 lbs. (hurrah!), progress on hole in wall by Gary: none, progress on getting over Mark Darcy by fantasizing about Wild Boy: medium (hampered by eyelashes).

Got back to message from Gary. Said he got caught up on another job and as I was having second thoughts he thought there was no hurry. Claims he is going to sort everything out and come round tomorrow night. So you see, was worrying unnecessarily. Mmmm. Wild Boy. Maybe Jude and Shazzer are right. Have just to move on, not keep imagining Mark and Rebecca in different loving scenarios. Worry about lashes, though. How long, exactly? Fantasies of Wild Boy's lean, wild, devil body slightly spoilt by image of Wild Boy blinking under the weight of lengthy lashes like Walt Disney Bambi.

9 p.m. Got to 192 at 8:05, with Jude and Shaz in tow to sit at other table and keep eye on self. No sign of Wild Boy. Only man on own was horrible old creep in denim shirt, ponytail and sunglasses who kept staring at me. Where was Wild Boy? Gave creep filthy look.

Eventually creep was staring so much decided to move. Started to get up then nearly jumped out of skin. Creep was holding up red rose. Stared at him aghast as he removed ridiculous sunglasses, smirking, to reveal Barbara Cartland–like pair of false eyelashes. Creep was Wild Boy. Rushed out in horror followed by Jude and Shazzer collapsing in giggles.

⁓ TUESDAY 6 MAY

128 lbs. (1 lb. phantom baby?), Mark thoughts: better, progress on hole in wall by Gary: static i.e. none.

7 p.m. V. depressed. Just left message for Tom to ask if he is mad too. Realize have to learn to love self and live in moment, not obsess but think of others and be complete in self but just feel awful. Really miss Mark so much. Cannot believe he is going to go out with Rebecca. What did I do? Obviously there is something wrong with me. Just getting older and older and is clear nothing is ever going to work out so might as well just accept am always going to be alone and never have any children. Oh look, must pull self together. Gary will be here soon.

7:30 p.m. Gary is late.

7:45 p.m. Still no sign of bloody Gary.

8 p.m. Still no Gary.

8:15 p.m. Gary has not bloody well turned up. Ooh, telephone, must be him.

8:30 p.m. Was Tom saying that he was very mad and so was the cat, which had started pooing on the carpet. Then he said something rather surprising.

"Bridge?" he said. "Do you want to have a baby with me?"

"What?"

"A baby."

"Why?" I said, suddenly getting alarming image of having sex with Tom.

"Well . . ." He thought for a minute. "I'd quite like to have a baby and see my line extended but, one, I'm too selfish to look after it and, two: I'm a pouf. But you'd be good at looking after it if you didn't leave it in a shop."

Love Tom. Is as if he sort of sensed the way I'm feeling. Anyway, he said to think about it. Is just an idea.

8:45 p.m. I mean why not? Could keep it at home in a little basket. Yes! Just imagine waking up in the morning with a lovely little creature next to me to snuggle up to and love. And we could do all things together like going to the swings and Woolworth's to look at the Barbie things and home would become a lovely peaceful baby-powder-smelling haven. And if Gary turns up baby could sleep in spare bedroom. Maybe if Jude and Shazzer had babies too we could live in a community together and . . . Oh shit. Have set wastebin on fire with fag end.

~ **SATURDAY 10 MAY**

129 lbs. (phantom baby already gigantic, given age), cigarettes 7 (not necessary to stop for phantom pregnancy, surely?), calories 3,255 (eating for one plus tiny phantom), positive thoughts 4, progress on hole in wall by Gary: none.

11 a.m. Just been out for fags. Is suddenly, freakishly, really, really hot. Is fantastic! Some men are actually wandering round the streets in swimming trunks!

11:15 a.m. Just because it is summer is no reason life should fall into disarray with flat chaotic, in-tray ranging out of control, bad smells everywhere. (Ugh. Is really bad on stairs now.) Am going to change all this by spending today clearing up flat and doing in-tray. Must get things ordered ready to welcome new life into world.

11:30 a.m. Right. Will start by moving all piles of newspapers into one central pile.

11:40 a.m. Ugh, though.

12:15 p.m. Maybe will do in-tray first.

12:20 p.m. Clearly impossible without getting properly dressed.

12:25 p.m. Not keen on look in shorts. Too sporty somehow. Need little slippy dress thing.

12:35 p.m. Now where is it?

12:40 p.m. Just needs washing through and hanging out to dry. Then can get on.

12:55 p.m. Hurrah! Am going swimming to Hampstead Ponds with Jude and Shazzer! Have not done legs but Jude says pond is ladies only and teeming with lesbians who consider it mark of gay pride to be as hairy as yetis. Hurrah!

Midnight. Was fantastic at ponds, like painting of sixteenth-century nymphs only rather more of them than would expect in uplift bikinis. V. old-fashioned, with wooden decking and lifeguards. Swimming in natural environment with mud on bottom* totally new sensation.

Told them what Tom had said about the Babyfather idea.

"My God!" said Shaz. "Well, I think it's a good idea. Except that on top of 'Why aren't you married?' you'd have 'Who's the father?' to contend with."

---

* Bottom of pond, not own bottom.

"I could say it was an immaculate conception," I suggested.

"I think all this would be extremely selfish," said Jude coldly.

There was a stunned pause. We peered at her, trying to work out what was going on.

"Why?" said Shaz eventually.

"Because a child needs two parents. You would be doing it to satisfy yourself when actually you're just too selfish to have a relationship."

Blimey. I could see Shaz taking out a submachine gun and gunning her down. Next thing Shaz was off on one, ranting away with a no-holds-barred sphere of eclectic cultural reference.

"Look at the Caribbean," she ranted while the other girls looked round in alarm and I thought, mmm. Caribbean. Lovely luxury hotel and white sand.

"The womenfolk bring the children up in compounds," Shaz declared. "And the men just turn up sometimes and shag them, and now the women are getting economic power and there are pamphlets saying 'Men at Risk' because they're losing their role just like they are ALL OVER THE FUCKING WORLD."

Sometimes wonder if Sharon really is quite such a Ph.D.-style authority on, well, everything, as she pretends to be.

"A child needs two parents," said Jude doggedly.

"Oh for God's sake that's a completely narrow, paternalistic, unrealistic, partisan Smug-Middle-Class-Married-Parent view," hissed Shaz. "Everyone knows a third of all marriages end in divorce."

"Yes!" I said. "Being with one mother who loves you is bound to be better than being the product of a bitter divorce. Children need relationships and life and people around but it doesn't have to be a husband." Then suddenly remembering something my—ironically enough—mother always comes out with I said, "You can't spoil a child by loving it."

"Well, there's no need to gang up on me about it," said Jude huffily, "I'm only giving my view. Anyway, I've got something to tell you."

"Oh yeah? What?" said Shaz. "You believe in keeping human slaves?"

"Vile Richard and I are getting married."

Shazzer and I gawped in mute horror as Jude looked down, blushing winningly.

"I know, isn't it wonderful? I think when I chucked him the last time he realized you don't know what you've got till it's gone—and that finally jerked him into being able to commit!"

"Finally jerked him into realizing he'd have to get a bloody job if he couldn't live off you anymore, more like," muttered Shaz.

"Er, Jude," I said. "Did you just say you were going to marry Vile Richard?"

"Yes," said Jude. "And I wondered—will you two be bridesmaids?"

⁓ SUNDAY 11 MAY

128 lbs. (phantom baby departed in horror at impending wedding), alcohol units 3, cigarettes 15 (may as well smoke and drink freely now), Mark fantasies 2 only (excellent).

Shaz just called and both agreed that whole thing is doom. Doom. And that Jude must not marry Vile Richard because:

a. He is mad.

b. He is vile: Vile by name and vile by nature.

c. Is intolerable to have to dress up as pink puffballs and walk down aisle with everybody watching.

Am going to call Magda and tell her.

"What do you think?" I said.

"Hmm. It doesn't seem like a very promising idea. But you know, people's relationships are quite mysterious," she said enigmatically. "No one from the outside ever really understands what makes them work."

Conversation then moved on to the Babymother idea at which Magda unaccountably seemed to brighten.

"You know what, Bridge? I think you should try it out first, I really do."

"What do you mean?"

"Well, why don't you look after Constance and Harry for an afternoon and see how it goes. I mean I've often thought time-share was the answer for modern womanhood."

Blimey. Have promised to have Harry, Constance and the baby next Saturday while she has her highlights done. Also she and Jeremy are having a garden party in six weeks' time for Constance's birthday and she asked if I wanted her to invite Mark. I said yes. You see he has not seen me since February and it will be really good for him to see how I have changed and how calm and poised and full of inner strength I am now.

~ MONDAY 12 MAY

Got into work to find Richard Finch in a foul hyperactive mood, jumping around the room chewing and shouting at everyone. (Sexy Matt, who was looking particularly like a DKNY model this morning, told Horrid Harold he thought that Richard Finch was on cocaine.)

Anyway, it turned out the channel controller had turned down Richard's idea to replace the breakfast news slot with live "warts and all" coverage of the Sit Up Britain team's morning meeting. Considering the Sit Up Britain's last morning "meeting" consisted of an argument about which of our presenters was going to cover the lead story; and the lead story was about which presenters were going to be presenting the BBC and ITV news, I don't think it would have been a very interesting program; but Richard was really pissed off about it.

"Do you know what's the trouble with the news?" he was saying, taking his gum out of his mouth and flinging it in the vague direction of the bin. "It's boring. Boring, boring, bloody boring."

"Boring?" I said. "But we're just seeing the launch of the first Labour government for . . . for several years!"

"My God," he said, whipping off his glasses. "Have we got a new Labour government? Have we really? Everyone! Everyone! Gather round. Bridget's got a scoop!"

"And what about the Bosnian Serbs?"

"Oh wake up and smell the decaf cap," whined Patchouli. "So they want to carry on shooting at each other behind bushes? So? It's just so, like, five minutes ago."

"Yeah, yeah, yeah," said Richard with mounting excitement. "People don't want dead Albanians in head scarves, they want people. I'm thinking *Nationwide*. I'm thinking beer-drinking snails, I'm thinking skateboarding ducks."

So now we all have to think up Human Interest like snails that get drunk or old people going bungee jumping. I mean how are we supposed to organize a geriatric bungee jump by . . . Ah, telephone! That'll be the Mollusc and Small Amphibian Association.

"Oh, hello, darling, guess what?"

"Mum," I said dangerously, "I've told you—"

"Oh I know, darling. I just rang to tell you something very sad."

"What?" I said sulkily.

"Wellington's going home. His speech at the Rotary was fantastic. Absolutely fantastic. Do you know, when he talked about the conditions the children in his tribe live in Merle Robertshaw was actually crying! Crying!"

"But I thought he was raising money for a jet ski bike."

"Oh he is, darling. But he came up with this marvelous scheme which is right up the Rotary's street. He said if they donated money he'd not only give the Kettering branch a ten percent share in the profits, but if they'd give half of that to his village school he'd match it with another five percent of his profits. Charity and small business—isn't that clever? Anyway they raised four hundred pounds and he's going back to Kenya! He's going to build a new school! Imagine! Just because of us! He did a lovely slide show with Nat King Cole's 'Nature Boy' underneath it. And at the end he said '*Hakuna Matata!*,' and we've adopted it as our motto!"

"That's great!" I said, then saw Richard Finch staring crossly in my direction.

"Anyway, darling, we thought you—"

"Mum," I interrupted, "do you know any old people who do interesting things?"

"Honestly, what a silly question. All old people do interesting things. Look at Archie Garside—you know Archie—who used to be deputy spokesman on the governors. He's a parachute jumper. In actual fact I think he's doing a sponsored parachute jump for the Rotary tomorrow and he's ninety-two. A ninety-two-year-old parachute jumper! Imagine!"

Half an hour later I set off towards Richard Finch's desk, a smug smile playing about my lips.

6 p.m. Hurrah! Everything is lovely! Am completely back in Richard Finch's good books and am going off to Kettering to film parachute jump. And not only that, but I am going to direct it, and it is going to be the lead item.

⌒ TUESDAY 13 MAY

Do not want to be stupid TV career woman anymore. Is heartless profession. Had forgotten the nightmare of TV crews when allowed to interact freely with trusting media-virgin members of the public. Was not allowed to direct the item as deemed too complex, so was left on the ground while bossy career-crazed Greg was sent up in the plane to do it. Turned out Archie did not want to jump as could not see a good landing spot. But Greg went on and on saying, "Come on, mate, we're losing the light," and eventually pressurized him to jump towards a soft-looking ploughed field. Unfortunately, however, it wasn't a ploughed field, it was a sewerage works.

⌒ SATURDAY 17 MAY

129 lbs., alcohol units 1, cigarettes 0, dashed baby-fantasies 1, dashed Mark Darcy fantasies: all the ones about him seeing self again realizing how changed, poised i.e. thin, well-dressed, etc. am, and falling in love with self again 472.

Completely exhausted by working week. Almost too drained to get out of bed. Wish could get someone to go downstairs and fetch paper, also chocolate croissant and cappuccino. Think will stay in bed, read *Marie Claire*, and do nails, then maybe see if Jude and Shazzer fancy going to Jigsaw. Would really like to get something new for when see Mark again next week, as if to stress am changed . . . Gaaah! Doorbell. Who in their right mind would ring on someone's doorbell at ten o'clock on Saturday morning? Are they completely insane?

Later. Staggered to entry phone. It was Magda, who shouted chirpily, "Say hello to Auntie Bridget!"

Lurched in horror, dimly remembering offer to spend Saturday taking Magda's infants to the swings while she spends day having hair done and lunching with Jude and Shazzer like single girl.

Panicking, I pressed the buzzer, flung on only dressing gown could find—unsuitable, v. short, translucent—and started running round the flat to remove ashtrays, mugs of vodka, broken glass etc., etc.

"Fwoff. Here we are! I'm afraid Harry's got a bit of a snuffle, haven't we?" crooned Magda, clunking up the stairs, festooned with prams and bags like a homeless person. "Ooof. What's that smell?"

Constance, my goddaughter, who is three next week, said she had brought me a present. She seemed very pleased indeed with her gift choice and sure that I would like it. Unwrapped it excitedly. It was a fireplace catalogue.

"I think she thought it was a magazine," whispered Magda.

Demonstrated massive delight. Constance beamed smugly and gave me a kiss, which I liked, then sat down happily in front of the *Pingu* video.

"Sorry. I'm going to have to dump and dash, I'm late for my highlights," said Magda. "There's everything you need in the bag under the pram. Don't let them fall out of the hole in the wall."

It all seemed fine. The baby was asleep, Harry, who is nearly one, was sitting in the double pram next to him, holding a very battered rabbit and looking as if he was about to fall asleep too. But the second the door slammed downstairs, Harry and the baby began to scream blue murder, writhing and kicking when I tried to pick them up, like violent deportees.

Found self trying to do anything (though obviously not gagging with tape) to make them stop: dancing, waving and pretending to blow imaginary trumpet to no avail.

Constance looked up solemnly from the video, removing her own bottle from her mouth. "They're probably thirsty," she said. "You can see through your nightie."

Humiliated at being out-earth-mothered by someone not quite three, I found the bottles in the bag, handed them over and sure enough both babies stopped crying and sat there sucking, busily watching me from beneath lowered brows as if I were someone very nasty from the Home Office.

I tried to slip next door to put some clothes on, at which they took the bottles out and started yelling again. Finally, I ended up dressing in the sitting room while they watched intently as if I were a bizarre reverse striptease artist.

After forty-five minutes of Gulf War–style operation to get them, plus the prams and bags, downstairs, we reached the street. Was very nice when we got to the swings. Harry, as Magda says, has not mastered the human language yet but Constance developed a very sweet, all-adults-together confidential tone with me, saying, "I think he wants to go on the swing," when he talked gibberish, and when I bought a packet of Minstrels saying solemnly, "I don't think we'd better tell people about this."

Unfortunately, for some reason when we got to the front door, Harry started sneezing and a huge web of projectile green snot seemed to fly into the air then flop back over his face like something from *Dr. Who*. Constance then gagged in horror and threw up on my hair and the baby started screaming, which set the other two off. Desperately trying to calm the situation, I bent down, wiped the snot off Harry, and put his dummy back into his mouth while beginning a soothing rendition of "I Will Always Love You."

For a miraculous second, there was silence. Thrilled with my gifts as a natural mother, I launched into a second verse, beaming into Harry's face, at which he abruptly pulled the dummy out of his mouth and shoved it into mine.

"Hello again," said a manly voice as Harry started to scream once more. I turned round, dummy in mouth and sick all over hair to find Mark Darcy looking extremely puzzled.

"They're Magda's," I said eventually.

"Ah, I thought it was all a bit quick. Or a very well-kept secret."

"Who's that?" Constance put her hand in mine, looking up at him suspiciously.

"I'm Mark," he said. "I'm Bridget's friend."

"Oh," she said, still looking suspicious.

"She's got the same expression as you anyway," he said, looking at me in a way I couldn't fathom. "Can I give you a hand upstairs?"

Ended up with me carrying the baby and holding Constance's hand and Mark bringing the pram and holding Harry's hand. For some reason neither of us could speak, except to the children. But then I was aware of voices on the stairs. Rounded the corner and there were two policemen emptying the hall cupboard. They'd had a complaint from next door about the smell.

"You take the children upstairs, I'll deal with this," said Mark quietly. Felt like Maria in *The Sound of Music* when they've been singing in the concert and she has to get the children into the car while Captain Von Trapp confronts the Gestapo.

Talking in a cheery, fraudulently confident whisper, I put the *Pingu* video back on, gave them all some sugar-free juice in their bottles and sat on the floor between them, which they seemed more than contented about.

Then policeman appeared clutching a holdall I recognized as mine. He pulled a polythene bag of stinking blood-smeared flesh accusingly from the zip pocket with his gloved hand and said, "Is this yours, miss? It was in the hall cupboard. Could we ask you a few questions?"

I got up, leaving the children staring rapt at *Pingu* as Mark appeared in the doorway.

"As I said, I'm a lawyer," he said pleasantly to the young policemen, with just the merest steely hint of "so you'd better watch what you're doing" in his voice.

Just then the phone rang.

"Shall I get that for you, miss?" said one of the officers suspiciously, as if it might be my bits-of-dead-person supplier. I just couldn't work out how bloodstained flesh had got in my bag. The policeman put the phone to his ear, looked completely terrified for a moment, then shoved the phone at me.

"Oh, hello, darling, who's that? Have you got a man in the house?"

Suddenly the penny dropped. The last time I used that bag was when I went to Mum and Dad's for lunch.

"Mother," I said, "when I came down for lunch, did you put anything in my bag?"

"Yes, in actual fact I did, come to mention it. Two pieces of fillet steak. And you never said thank you. In the zip pocket. I mean as I was saying to Una, it's not cheap isn't fillet steak."

"Why didn't you tell me?" I hissed.

Finally managed to get a totally unpenitent mother to confess to the policemen. Even then they started saying they wanted to take the fillet steak off for analysis and maybe hold me for questioning at which Constance started crying, I picked her up, and she put her arm round my neck, holding on to my jumper as if I were about to be wrested from her and thrown in a pit with bears.

Mark just laughed, put his hand on one of the policemen's shoulder and said, "Come on, boys. It's a couple of pieces of fillet steak from her mother. I'm sure there's better things you could be doing with your time."

The policemen looked at each other, and nodded, then they started closing their notebooks and picking their helmets up. Then the main one said, "OK, Miss Jones, just keep an eye on what your mother puts in your bag in future. Thanks for your help, sir. Have a good evening. Have a good evening, miss."

There was a second's pause when Mark stared at the hole in the wall, looking unsure what to do, then he suddenly said, "Enjoy *Pingu*," and bolted off down the stairs after the policemen.

127 lbs., alcohol units 3 (v.g.), cigarettes 12 (excellent), calories 3,425 (off food), progress of hole in wall by Gary 0, positive thoughts about furnishing fabric as special-occasion-wear look 0.

Jude has gone completely mad. Just went round to her house to find entire place strewn with bridal magazines, lace swatches, gold-sprayed raspberries, tureen and grapefruit-knife brochures, terra-cotta pots with weeds in and bits of straw.

"I want a gurd," she was saying. "Or is it a yurd? Instead of a marquee. It's like a nomad's tent in Afghanistan with rugs on the floor, and I want long-stemmed patinated oil burners."

"What are you wearing?" I said, leafing through pictures of embroidered stick-thin models with flower arrangements on their heads and wondering whether to call an ambulance.

"I'm having it made. Abe Hamilton! Lace and lots of cleavage."

"What cleavage?" muttered Shaz murderously.

"That's what they should call *Loaded* magazine."

"I'm sorry?" said Jude coldly.

"'What Cleavage?'" I explained. "Like *What Car?*"

"It's not *What Car?* It's *Which Car?*" said Shaz.

"Girls," said Jude, over-pleasantly, like a gym mistress about to make us stand in the corridor in our gym knickers, "can we get on?"

Interesting how "we" had crept in. Suddenly was not Jude's wedding but our wedding and we were having to do all these lunatic tasks like tying straw round 150 patinated oil burners and going away to a health farm to give Jude a shower.

"Can I just say something?" said Shaz.

"Yes," said Jude.

"DON'T BLOODY MARRY VILE RICHARD. He's an unreliable, selfish, idle, unfaithful fuckwit from hell. If you marry him, he'll take half your money and run off with a bimbo. I know they have the prenuptial agreements but . . ."

Jude went all quiet. Suddenly realized—feeling her shoe hit my shin—I was supposed to back Shazzie up.

"Listen to this," I said hopefully, reading from the *Bride's Wedding Guide*. "'Best Man: the groom should ideally choose a level-headed responsible person . . .'"

I looked round smugly as if to prove Shaz's point but the response was chilly. "Also," said Shaz, "don't you think a wedding puts too much pressure on a relationship? I mean it's not exactly playing hard to get, is it?"

Jude breathed in deeply through her nose while we watched, on tenterhooks.

"Now!" she said eventually, looking up with a brave smile. "The bridesmaids' duties!"

Shaz lit a Silk Cut. "What are we wearing?"

"Well!" gushed Jude. "I think we should have them made. And look at this!" It was an article entitled "50 Ways to Save Money on the Big Day." "'For bridesmaids, furnishing fabrics can work surprisingly well'!"

Furnishing fabrics?

"You see," Jude was going on, "with the guest list it says, don't feel you have to invite guest's new partners—but the minute I mentioned it she said, 'Oh *we'd* love to come.'"

"Who?" I said.

"Rebecca."

I looked at Jude, dumbstruck. She wouldn't. She wouldn't expect me to walk down the aisle dressed as a sofa while Mark Darcy sat with Rebecca, would she?

"And I mean they have asked me to go on holiday with them. Not that I would go, of course. But I think Rebecca was a bit hurt that I hadn't told her before."

"What?" exploded Shazzer. "Have you no concept of the meaning of the word 'girlfriend'? Bridget's your best friend joint with me, and Rebecca has shamelessly stolen Mark, and instead of being tactful about it, she's trying to hoover everyone into her revolting social web so he's so woven in he'll never get away. And you're not taking a bloody stand. That's the trouble with the modern world— everything's forgivable. Well, it makes me sick, Jude. If that's the sort of friend you are you can walk down the aisle with Rebecca behind you wearing Ikea curtains and not us. And then see how you like it. And you can stuff your yurd, gurd, turd or whatever it is up your bum!"

So now Sharon and I are not speaking to Jude. Oh dear. Oh dear.

9

Social Hell

129 lbs., alcohol units 6 (felt I owed it to Constance), cigarettes 5 (v.g.), calories 2,455 (but mainly items covered in orange icing), escaped barn animals 1, attacks on self by children 2.

Yesterday was Constance's birthday party. Arrived about an hour late and made my way through Magda's house, following the sound of screaming into the garden where a scene of unbridled carnage was under way with adults chasing after children, children chasing rabbits and, in the corner, a little fence behind which were two rabbits, a gerbil, an ill-looking sheep and a pot-bellied pig.

I paused at the French windows, looking around nervously. Heart lurched when located him, standing on his own, in traditional Mark Darcy party mode, looking detached and distant. He glanced towards the door where I was standing and for a second we were locked in each other's gaze before he gave me a confused nod, then looked away. Then I noticed Rebecca crouched down beside him with Constance.

"Constance! Constance! Constance!" Rebecca was cooing, waving a Japanese fan in her face at which Constance was glowering and blinking crossly.

"Look who's come!" said Magda, bending down to Constance and pointing across at me.

A surreptitious smile crept across Constance's face and she set off determinedly, if slightly wobbly, towards me, leaving Rebecca look-ing foolish with the fan. I bent down when she got near and she put her arm round my neck and pressed her little hot face against mine.

"Have you brought me a present?" she whispered.

Relieved that this blatant example of cupboard love was inaudible to anyone but me I whispered, "Might have done."

"Where is it?"

"In my bag."

"Shall we go and get it?"

"Oh, isn't that sweet?" I heard Rebecca coo and looked up to see her and Mark watching as Constance took me by the hand and led me into the cool of the house.

Was quite pleased with Constance's present actually, a packet of Minstrels and a pink Barbie tutu with a gold and pink net sticking-out skirt, which had had to trawl two branches of Woolworth's to find. She liked it very much and naturally—as would any woman—wished to put it on immediately.

"Constance," I said when we had admired it from every angle, "were you pleased to see me because of me or because of the present?"

She looked at me under lowered brows. "The present."

"Right," I said.

"Bridget?"

"Yes."

"You know in your house?"

"Yes."

"Why haven't you got any toys?"

"Well, because I don't really play with that *sort* of toy."

"Oh. Why haven't you got a playroom?"

"Because I don't do that sort of playing."

"Why haven't you got a man?"

Couldn't believe it. Had only just walked into the party and was being Smug Marrieded by someone who was three.

Had long quite serious conversation then, sitting on the stairs, about everyone being different and some people being Singletons, then heard a noise and looked up to see Mark Darcy looking down at us.

"Just, er. The loo is upstairs, I assume?" he said uninterestedly.

"Hello, Constance. How's Pingu?"

"He isn't real," she said, glowering at him.

"Right, right," he said. "Sorry. Stupid of me to be so"—he looked straight into my eyes—"gullible. Happy birthday, anyway." Then he made his way past us without even giving me a kiss hello or anything. "Gullible." Did he still think I was unfaithful with Gary the Builder and the dry-cleaning man? Anyway, I thought, I don't care. It doesn't matter. Everything's fine and I'm completely over him.

"You look sad," said Constance. She thought for a moment, then took a half-sucked Minstrel out of her mouth and put it in mine. We decided to go back outside to show off the tutu, and Constance was immediately swept up by a maniacal Rebecca.

"Ooh, look, it's a fairy. Are you a fairy? What kind of fairy are you? Where's your wand?" she gabbled.

"Great present, Bridge," said Magda. "Let me get you a drink. You know Cosmo, don't you?"

"Yes," I said, heart sinking, taking in the quivering jowls of the enormous merchant banker.

"So! Bridget, great to see you!" bellowed Cosmo, eyeing me up and down leerily. "How's work?"

"Oh, great actually," I lied, relieved that he wasn't launching straight into my love life. How things had moved on! "I'm working in TV now."

"TV? Marvelous! Bloody marvelous! Are you in front of the camera?"

"Only occasionally," I said in the sort of modest tone that suggested I was practically Kate Winslet but didn't want anyone to know.

"Oh! A celebrity, eh? And"—he leaned forward in a concerned manner—"are you getting the rest of your life sorted out?"

Unfortunately at that moment Sharon happened to be passing.

She stared at Cosmo, looking like Clint Eastwood when he thinks somebody is trying to double-cross him.

"What kind of question is that?" she growled.

"What?" said Cosmo, looking round at her, startled.

"'Are you getting the rest of your life sorted out?' What do you mean by that exactly?"

"Well, ah, you know . . . when is she going to get . . . you know . . ."

"Married? So basically just because her life isn't exactly like yours you think it isn't sorted out, do you? And are you getting the rest of your life sorted out, Cosmo? How are things going with Woney?"

"Well I . . . well," huffed Cosmo, going bright red in the face.

"Oh, I am sorry. We've obviously hit a sore spot. Come on, Bridget, before I put my big foot in it again!"

"Shazzer!" I said, when we were at a safe distance.

"Oh, come on," she said. "Enough, already. They just can't go around randomly patronizing people and insulting their lifestyles. Cosmo probably wishes Woney would lose thirty pounds and stop doing that shrieking laugh all day but we don't just assume that the minute we've met him, and decide it's our business to rub it in, do we?" An evil gleam came into her eye. "Or maybe we should," she said, grabbing hold of my arm and changing direction back towards Cosmo, only to be confronted by Mark and Rebecca and Constance again. Oh Christ.

"Who do you think is older, me or Mark?" Rebecca was saying.

"Mark," said Constance sulkily, looking from side to side as if planning to bolt.

"Who do you think is older, me or Mummy?" Rebecca went on playfully.

"Mummy," said Constance disloyally, at which Rebecca gave a tinkly little laugh.

"Who do you think is older, me or Bridget?" said Rebecca, giving me a wink.

Constance looked up at me doubtfully while Rebecca beamed at her. I nodded quickly at Rebecca.

"You," said Constance.

Mark Darcy let out a burst of laughter.

"Shall we play fairies?" Rebecca trilled, changing tack, trying to take Constance by the hand. "Do you live in a fairy castle? Is Harry a fairy too? Where are your fairy-wairy friends?"

"Bridget," said Constance, looking at me levelly, "I think you'd better tell this lady I'm not really a fairy."

Later on, as I was recounting this to Shaz, she said darkly, "Oh God. Look who's here."

Across the garden was Jude, radiant in turquoise, chatting to Magda but without Vile Richard.

"The girls are here!" said Magda gaily. "Look! Over there!"

Shaz and I stared down studiously into our glasses as if we hadn't noticed. When we looked up, Rebecca was bearing down on Jude and Magda mwah-mwahing like a social-climbing literary wife who's just spotted Martin Amis talking to Gore Vidal.

"Oh Jude, I'm so happy for you, it's wonderful!" she gushed.

"I don't know what that woman's on but I want some of it," muttered Sharon.

"Oh, you and Jeremy must come, no you must. You absolutely must," Rebecca was going now. "Well, bring them! Bring the children! I love children! Second weekend in July. It's my parents' place in Gloucestershire. They'll love the pool. All sorts of lovely, lovely people are coming! I've got Louise Barton-Foster, Woney and Cosmo . . ." Snow White's stepmother, Fred and Rosemary West and Caligula, I thought she might go on.

". . . Jude and Richard, and Mark'll be there of course, Giles and Nigel from Mark's office . . ."

I saw Jude glance in our direction. "And Bridget and Sharon?" she said.

"What?" said Rebecca.

"You've invited Bridget and Sharon?"

"Oh." Rebecca looked flustered. "Well, of course, I'm not sure we've got enough bedrooms but I suppose we could use the cottage." Everyone stared at her. "Yes, I have!" She looked round wildly. "Oh, there you two are! You're coming on the twelfth, aren't you?"

"Where?" said Sharon.

"To Gloucestershire."

"We didn't know anything about it," said Sharon loudly.

"Well. You do now! Second weekend in July. It's just outside Woodstock. You've been before, haven't you, Bridget?"

"Yes," I said, coloring, remembering that hideous weekend.

"So! That's great! And you're coming, Magda, so . . ."

"Um . . ." I began.

"We'd love to come," said Sharon firmly, treading on my foot.

"What? What?" I said when Rebecca had whinnied off.

"Of course we're bloody well going," she said. "You're not letting her hijack all your friends just like that. She's trying to bludgeon everyone into some ridiculous social circle of suddenly needed, nearly friends of Mark's ready for the two of them to plop into like King and Queen Buzzy-bee."

"Bridget?" said a posh voice. I turned to see a shortish sandy-haired guy in glasses. "It's Giles, Giles Benwick. I work with Mark. Do you remember? You were terribly helpful on the phone that night when my wife said she was leaving."

"Oh, yes, Giles. How are you?" I said. "How's everything going?"

"Oh, not very good, I'm afraid," said Giles. Sharon disappeared with a backwards look, at which Giles launched into a long, detailed, and thorough account of his marital breakup.

"I so much appreciated your advice," he said, looking at me very earnestly. "And I did buy *Men Are from Mars, Women Are from Venus*. I thought it was very, very, very good, though it didn't seem to alter Veronica's point of view."

"Well, it's more dealing with dating than divorce," I loyally-to-the-Mars-and-Venus-concept said.

"Very true, very true," conceded Giles. "Tell me: have you read *You Can Heal Your Life* by Louise Hay?"

"Yes!" I said delightedly. Giles Benwick really did seem to have an extensive knowledge of the self-help book world and I was very happy to discuss the various works with him, though he did go on a bit. Eventually Magda came over with Constance.

"Giles, you really must come and meet my friend Cosmo!" she

said, rolling her eyes discreetly at me. "Bridge, would you mind looking after Constance for a mo?"

I knelt down to talk to Constance, who seemed to be worried about the aesthetic effect of chocolate smears on a tutu. Just as we had both firmly convinced ourselves that chocolate smears on pink were attractive, unusual and a positive design asset, Magda reappeared. "I think poor old Giles's got a bit of a crush on you," she said wryly and took Constance off for a poo. Before I'd got up again someone started smacking my bottom.

I turned round—thinking, I confess, maybe Mark Darcy!—to see Woney's son William and his friend, giggling evilly.

"Do it again," said William and his small friend started smacking again. Tried to get up but William—who's about six and big for his age—launched himself on to my back and wrested his arms around my neck.

"Stoppit, William," I said with an attempt at authority but at that moment there was a commotion at the other side of the garden. The pot-bellied pig had broken free and was rushing backwards and forwards letting out a high-pitched noise. There was mayhem as parents rushed for their offspring but William was still clinging tight to my back and the boy was still smacking my bottom and shrieking with *Exorcist*-style laughter. I tried to get William off, but he was surprisingly strong and clung on. My back was really hurting.

Then suddenly William's arms were released from round my neck. I felt him being lifted away and then the smacking stopped. For a moment I just hung my head, trying to get my breath back and recover my composure. Then I turned to see Mark Darcy walking away with a writhing six-year-old boy under each arm.

For a while the party was entirely taken over by the recapturing of the pig, and Jeremy giving the petting zookeeper a bollocking. The next I saw of Mark, he was wearing his jacket and saying good-bye to Magda at which Rebecca rushed over and started saying good-bye as well. I looked away quickly and tried not to think about it. Then suddenly Mark was coming over to me.

"I'm, er, off now, Bridget," he said. Could swear I saw him glance down at my tits. "Don't leave with any pieces of meat in your hand-bag, will you?"

"No," I said. For a moment we just looked at each other. "Oh, thank you, thank you for . . ." I nodded to where the incident had happened.

"Not at all," he said softly. "Any time you want me to get a boy off your back." And as if on cue, bloody Giles Benwick reappeared carrying two drinks.

"Oh, are you off, old boy?" he said. "I was just about to pump Bridget for some more of her seasoned advice."

Mark looked quickly from one of us to the other.

"I'm sure you'll be in very good hands," he said abruptly. "See you in the office on Monday."

Fuck, fuck, fuck. How come nobody ever flirts with me except when Mark is around?

"Back in the old torture chambers, eh?" Giles was saying, clapping him on the back. "On it goes. On it goes. Off you go then."

Head was in a whirl while Giles went on and on about sending me a copy of *Feel the Fear and Do It Anyway*. He was very keen to know if Sharon and I were going to Gloucestershire on the twelfth. But the sun seemed to have gone in, there was a lot of crying and "Mummy will smack"ing going on and everyone seemed to be leaving.

"Bridget." It was Jude. "Do you want to come to 192 for a—"

"No we don't," snapped Sharon. "We're going for a postmortem." Which was a lie as Sharon was meeting Simon. Jude looked stricken. Oh God. Bloody Rebecca has ruined bloody everything. Though must remember not to blame others but take responsibility for everything that happens to self.

~ **TUESDAY 1 JULY**

127 lbs. (is working!), progress on hole in wall by Gary 0.

I think I had better accept it now. Mark and Rebecca are an item. Is nothing I can do about it. Have been reading *The Road Less Traveled* some more and realize you can't have everything you want in life. Some of what you want but not everything you want. Is not what happens to you in life that counts but how you play the cards you are dealt. Am not going to think about the past and procession of disasters with men. Am going to think about the future. Oooh goody, telephone! Hurrah! You see!

Was Tom just ringing up for a moan. Which seemed nice. Until he said, "Oh, by the way, I saw Daniel Cleaver earlier on tonight."

"Oh really, where?" I trilled, in a gay yet strangled voice. Realize am new me and dating embarrassments of past—e.g., just to pluck an example out of the air, finding a naked woman on Daniel's roof last summer when was supposed to be going out with him—would never happen to new me. Even so, however, did not want specter of Daniel humiliation rearing up alarmingly in manner of Loch Ness monster, or erection.

"In the Groucho Club," said Tom.

"Did you talk to him?"

"Yes."

"What did you say?" I asked dangerously. Whole point about exes is that friends should punish and ignore them, not try to get on with both sides in manner of Tony and Cherie with Charles and Diana.

"Oof. I can't remember now, exactly. I said, um: 'Why were you so horrible to Bridget when she is so nice?'"

There was something about the way he said this in manner of a parrot that suggested he may not have been quoting himself strictly word for word.

"Good," I said, "very good." I paused, determined to leave it at that and change the subject. I mean what do I care what Daniel said?

"So what did he say?" I hissed.

"He said," said Tom, then started laughing. "He said . . ."

"What?"

"He said . . ." He was practically crying with laughter now.

"What? What? WHAAAAAAAAT?"

"'How can you go out with someone who doesn't know where Germany is?'"

I let out a high-pitched hyena laugh, almost as one does when one hears one's grandmother has died and believes it to be a joke. Then the reality hit me. I clutched the side of the kitchen table, mind reeling.

"Bridge?" said Tom. "Are you all right? I was only laughing because it's so . . . ridiculous. I mean of course you know where Germany is . . . Bridge? Don't you?"

"Yes," I whispered weakly.

There was a long, awkward pause while I tried to come to terms with what had happened, i.e. Daniel had chucked me because he thought I was stupid.

"So, then," said Tom brightly. "Where is it . . . Germany?"

"Europe."

"Yeah, but, like, where in Europe?"

Honestly. In the modern age it is not necessary to know where countries actually are since all that is required is to purchase a plane ticket to one. They do not exactly ask you at the travel agent's which countries you will be flying over before they will give you the ticket, do they?

"Just give us a ballpark position."

"Er," I stalled, head down, eyes flicking round the room to see if there might be an atlas at large.

"Which countries do you think Germany might be near?" he pressed on.

I thought about it carefully. "France."

"France. I see. So Germany is 'near France,' is it?"

Something about the way Tom said this made me feel I'd made some cataclysmic gaffe. Then it occurred to me that Germany is of course connected to Eastern Germany and therefore it is far more likely to be close to Hungary, Russia or Prague.

"Prague," I said. At which Tom burst out laughing.

"Anyway, there's no such thing as general knowledge anymore," I said indignantly. "It has been proved by articles that the media has created such a great sea of knowledge that everyone cannot possibly have the same selection of it."

"Never mind, Bridge," said Tom. "Don't worry about it. Do you want to see a movie tomorrow?"

11 p.m. Yes, am just going to go to movies now and read books. What Daniel may or may not have said is a matter of supreme indifference to me.

11:15 p.m. How dare Daniel go round bad-mouthing me! How did he know I don't know where Germany is? We never even went near it. Furthest we got to was the outskirts of Brighton. Huh.

11:20 p.m. Anyway, I am really nice. So there.

11:30 p.m. Am horrible. Am stupid. Am going to start studying *The Economist* and also go to evening classes and read *Money* by Martin Amis.

11:35 p.m. Harhar. Have found atlas now.

11:40 p.m. Hah! Right. I am going to ring up that bastard.

11:45 p.m. Just dialed Daniel's number.
"Bridget?" he said, before I had time to say anything.
"How did you know it was me?"
"Some surreal sixth sense," he drawled amusedly. "Hang on." I heard him lighting a fag. "So go on then." He inhaled deeply.
"What?" I muttered.
"Tell me where Germany is."
"It is next to France," I said. "And also Holland, Belgium, Poland, Czechoslovakia, Switzerland, Austria and Denmark. And it has a sea coast."
"Which sea?"
"North Sea."
"And?"
I stared at the atlas furiously. It didn't say the other sea.
"OK," he said. "One sea out of two is fine. So do you want to come round?"
"No!" I said. Honestly. Daniel is absolutely the limit. Am not going to get involved with all that again.

292 lbs. (feel like, compared to Rebecca), no. of pains in back from vile foam mattress 9, no. of thoughts involving Rebecca and natural disasters, electrical fires, floods, and professional killers: large, but proportionate.

Rebecca's house, Gloucestershire. In horrible guest cottage. Why did I come here? Why? Why? Sharon and I left it quite late and so arrived ten minutes before dinner. This did not go down very well with Rebecca, who trilled, "Oh, we'd almost given you up for lost!" in manner of Mum or Una Alconbury.

We were staying in a servants' cottage, which I decided was good as no danger of bumping into Mark in corridors, until we got into it: is all painted green with foam rubber single beds and Formica headboards, in sharp contrast to last time was here, staying in lovely hotel-style room with own bathroom.

"Typical Rebecca," grumbled Sharon. "Singletons are second-class citizens. Rub it in."

We teetered in late for dinner, feeling like a pair of garish divorcées because we'd put our makeup on so quickly. Dining room looked as breathtakingly grand as ever, with a huge inglenook fireplace at the end and twenty people sitting round an ancient oak dining table lit by silver candelabras and festooned with flower arrangements.

Mark was at the head of the table, sitting between Rebecca and Louise Barton-Foster and deep in conversation.

Rebecca appeared not to notice we'd come in. We stood staring awkwardly at the table till Giles Benwick bellowed, "Bridget! Over here!"

I was put between Giles and Magda's Jeremy, who seemed to have forgotten I ever went out with Mark Darcy and launched things off by going, "So! Looks like Darcy's gone for your friend Rebecca, then. Funny because there was this bit of totty, Heather someone, friend of Barky Thompson's, who seemed to be fancying a bit of a crack at the old bugger."

The fact that Mark and Rebecca were in earshot had clearly escaped Jeremy, but not me. I was trying to concentrate on his conversation and not listen to theirs, which had turned to a villa holiday Rebecca was organizing in Tuscany in August with Mark—as seemed to be the assumption—to which everybody simply *must* come, except presumably me and Shaz.

"What's that, Rebecca?" bellowed some terrible hooray I vaguely remembered from the skiing. Everyone looked at the fireplace where a new-looking family crest was engraved with the motto "*Per Determinam ad Victoriam*." It was quite strange to have a crest since Rebecca's family are not members of the aristocracy but something big in estate agents Knight, Frank and Rutley.

"*Per Determinam ad Victoriam?*" roared the hooray. "Through ruthlessness to victory. That's our Rebecca for you."

There was a huge roar of laughter and Shazzer and I exchanged a gleeful little look.

"Actually it's through determination to success," said Rebecca icily. Glanced up at Mark, a trace of a smile just disappearing behind his hand.

Somehow got through the meal, listening to Giles talking very slowly and analytically about his wife and tried to keep my mind away from Mark's end of the table by sharing my self-help book knowledge.

Was desperate to get off to bed and escape the whole painful nightmare, but we all had to go through to the big room for dancing.

I started looking through the CD collection to distract me from the sight of Rebecca slowly rotating Mark round the floor, her arms round his neck, eyes darting contentedly round the room. I felt sick, but I wasn't going to show it.

"Oh, for God's sake, Bridget. Have some common sense," said Sharon, barging up to the CDs, removing "Jesus to a Child" and putting some frenetic garage acid medley on instead. She strode on to the floor, swept Mark away from Rebecca and started dancing with him. Actually Mark was quite funny, laughing at Shazzer's attempts to make him trendy. Rebecca looked as though she had eaten a tiramisù and only just checked the fat units.

Suddenly Giles Benwick grabbed hold of me and started to rock and roll me wildly, so I found myself being flung around the room with a fixed grin on my face, head bouncing up and down like a rag doll being shagged.

After that I literally couldn't stand it any longer.

"I'm going to have to go," I whispered to Giles.

"I know," he said conspiratorially. "Shall I walk you back to the cottage?"

Managed to put him off and ended up teetering across the gravel in my Pied à Terre slingbacks and sinking gratefully into even this ludicrously uncomfortable bed. Mark is probably at this moment getting into bed with Rebecca. Wish I was anywhere else but here: the Kettering Rotary summer fete, the Sit Up Britain morning meeting, the gym. But is own fault. I decided to come.

⁓ SUNDAY 13 JULY

318 lbs., alcohol units 0, cigarettes 12 (all secret), people rescued from water accidents 1, people who shouldn't have been rescued from said water accidents but left in water to go all wrinkly 1.

Bizarre, thought-provoking day.

After breakfast, I decided to escape and wandered round the water garden, which was quite pretty, with shallow rivulets between grassy banks and under little stone bridges, surrounded by a hedge with all the fields beyond. I sat down on a stone bridge, looking at the stream, and thinking how it all didn't matter because there would always be nature, and then I heard voices approaching behind the hedge.

"... Worst driver in the world ... Mother's constantly ... correct him but ... no concept ... of steering accuracy. He lost his no-claims bonus forty-five years ago and never got it back since." It was Mark. "If I was my mother I'd refuse to go in the car with him, but they won't be parted. It's rather endearing."

"Oh, I love that!" Rebecca. "If I were married to someone I really loved I would want to be with them constantly."

"Would you?" he said eagerly. Then he went on. "I think, as you get older, then . . . the danger is if you've been single for a time, you get so locked into a network of friends—this is particularly true of women—that it hardly leaves room for a man in their lives, emotionally as much as anything because their friends and their views are their first point of reference."

"Oh, I quite agree. For me, of course I love my friends, but they're not top of my list of priorities."

You're telling me, I thought. There was silence, then Mark burst out again.

"This self-help book nonsense—all these mythical rules of conduct you're presumed to be following. And you just know every move you make is being dissected by a committee of girlfriends according to some breathtakingly arbitrary code made up of *Buddhism Today, Venus and Buddha Have a Shag* and the *Koran*. You end up feeling like some laboratory mouse with an ear on its back!"

I clutched my book, heart pounding. Surely this couldn't be how he saw what had happened with me?

But Rebecca was off on one again. "Oh, I quite agree," she gushed. "I have no time for all that stuff. If I decide I love someone then nothing will stand in my way. Nothing. Not friends, not theories. I just follow my instincts, follow my heart," she said in new simpery voice, like a flower girl-child of nature.

"I respect you for that," said Mark quietly. "A woman must know what she believes in, otherwise how can you believe in her yourself?"

"And trust her man above all else," said Rebecca in yet another voice, resonant and breath-controlled, like an affected actress doing Shakespeare.

Then there was an excruciating silence. I was dying, dying frozen to the spot, assuming they were kissing.

"Of course I said all this to Jude," Rebecca started up again. "She was so concerned about everything Bridget and Sharon had told her about not marrying Richard—he's such a great guy—and I just said, 'Jude, follow your heart.'"

I gawped, looking to a passing bee for reassurance. Surely Mark couldn't be slaveringly respectful of this?

"Ye-es," he said doubtfully. "Well I'm not sure . . ."

"Giles seems to be very keen on Bridget!" Rebecca burst in, obviously sensing she had veered off course.

There was a pause. Then Mark said, in an unusually high-pitched voice, "Oh really. And is . . . is this reciprocated?"

"Oh, you know Bridget," said Rebecca airily. "I mean Jude says she's got all these guys after her"—good old Jude, I started to think—"but she's so screwed up she won't—well, as you say, she can't get it together with any of them."

"Really?" Mark jumped in. "So have there been . . ."

"Oh, I think—you know—but she's so bogged down in her rules of dating or whatever it is that no one's good enough."

Could not work out what was going on. Maybe Rebecca was trying to make him stop feeling guilty about me.

"Really?" said Mark again. "So she isn't . . ."

"Oh, look, there's a duckling! Oh, look, a whole brood of ducklings! And there's the mother and father. Oh, what a perfect, perfect moment! Oh, let's go look!"

And off they went, and I was left, breathless, mind racing.

After lunch, it was boiling hot and everyone decamped under a tree at the edge of the lake. It was an idyllic, pastoral scene: an ancient stone bridge over the water, willows overhanging the grassy banks. Rebecca was triumphant. "Oh, this is such fun!! Isn't it, everyone? Isn't it fun?"

Fat Nigel from Mark's office was fooling about heading a football to one of the hoorays, huge stomach quivering in the bright sunlight. He made a lunge, missed and plunged headfirst into the water, displacing a giant wave.

"Yesss!" said Mark, laughing. "Breathtaking incompetence."

"It's lovely, isn't it?" I said vaguely to Shaz. "You expect to see lions lying down with lambs."

"Lions, Bridget?" said Mark. I started. He was sitting right at the other side of the group, looking at me through a gap in the other people, raising one eyebrow.

"I mean like in psalm whatsit," I explained.

"Right," he said. There was a familiar teasing look in his eye. "Do you think you might be thinking of the Lions of Longleat?"

Rebecca suddenly leaped to her feet. "I'm going to jump off the bridge!"

She looked round beaming expectantly. Everyone else was in shorts or little dresses, but she was naked except for a tiny sliver of Calvin Klein brown nylon.

"Why?" said Mark.

"Because attention was diverted from her for five minutes," breathed Sharon.

"We used to do it when we were little! It's heaven!"

"But the water's very low," said Mark.

It was true, there was a foot and a half of baked earth all the way round the waterline.

"No, no. I'm good at this, I'm very brave."

"I really don't think you should, Rebecca," said Jude.

"I have made up my mind. I am resolute!" she twinkled archly, slipped on a pair of Prada mules, and sashayed off towards the bridge. Happily, there was a bit of mud and grass attached to her upper right-hand buttock, which greatly added to the effect. As we watched, she took off the mules, held them in her hand and climbed on to the edge of the parapet.

Mark had got to his feet, looking worriedly at the water and up at the bridge.

"Rebecca!" he said. "I really don't think . . ."

"It's all right, I trust my own judgment," she said playfully, tossing her hair. Then she looked upwards, raised her arms, paused dramatically and jumped.

Everyone stared as she hit the water. The moment came when she should have reappeared. She didn't. Mark started towards the lake just as she broke the surface screaming.

He ploughed off towards her as did the other two boys. I reached in my bag for my mobile.

They pulled her to the shallows and eventually, after much writing and crying, Rebecca came limping to shore, supported between Mark and Nigel. It was clear that nothing too terrible could have happened.

I got up and handed her my towel. "Shall I dial 999?" I said as a sort of joke.

"Yes . . . yes."

Everyone gathered round staring at the injured hostess's foot. She could move her toes, daintily and professionally painted in Rouge Noir, so that was a blessing.

In the end I got the number of her doctor, took the out-of-surgery hours number from the answerphone, dialed it and handed the phone to Rebecca.

She spoke at length to the doctor, moving her foot according to his instructions and making a great range of noises, but in the end it was agreed there was no breakage, not really a sprain, just a slight jar.

"Where's Benwick?" said Nigel, as he dried himself and helped himself to a big slug of chilled white wine.

"Yes, where is Giles?" said Louise Barton-Foster. "I haven't seen him all morning."

"I'll go and see," I said, grateful to get away from the hellish sight of Mark rubbing Rebecca's delicate ankle.

It was nice to get into the cool of the entrance hall with its sweeping staircase. There was a line of statues on marble plinths, Oriental rugs on the flagstone floor, and another of the giant garish crests above the door. I stood for a moment, relishing the peace. "Giles?" I said and my voice echoed round and round. "Giles?"

There was no reply. I had no idea where his room was, so set off up the magnificent staircase.

"Giles!"

I peeked into one of the rooms and saw a gigantic carved-oak four-poster bed. The whole room was red and it looked out over the scene with the lake. The red dress Rebecca had been wearing at dinner was hanging over the mirror. I looked at the bed and felt as though I had been punched in the stomach. The Newcastle United boxer shorts I bought Mark for Valentine's Day were neatly folded on the bedspread.

I shot out of the room and stood with my back to the door, breathing unsteadily. Then I heard a moan.

"Giles?" I said. Nothing. "Giles? It's Bridget."

The moaning noise came again.

I walked along the corridor. "Where are you?"

"Here."

I pushed open the door. This room was lurid green and hideous with huge lumps of dark wood furniture everywhere. Giles was lying on his back with his head turned to one side, moaning slightly, the telephone off the hook beside him.

I sat on the bed and he opened his eyes slightly and closed them again. His glasses were skew-whiff on his face. I took them off.

"Bridget." He was holding a bottle of pills.

I took them from him. Temazepam.

"How many have you taken?" I said, taking his hand.

"Six . . . or four?"

"When?"

"Not long . . . about . . . not long."

"Make yourself sick," I said, thinking that they always pumped overdosed people's stomachs.

We went together into the bathroom. It wasn't attractive, frankly, but then I gave him lots of water and he flopped back on the bed and started to sob quietly, holding my hand. He had called Veronica, his wife, it emerged groaningly, as I stroked his head. And he had lost all sense of himself and self-respect by begging her to come back, thereby undoing all his good dignified work of the last two months. At this, she'd announced she definitely wanted a divorce and he felt desperate, which I could totally relate to. As I told him, it was enough to drive anyone to the Temazepam.

There were footsteps in the corridor, a knock, and then Mark appeared in the doorway.

"Will you ring the doctor again?" I said.

"What's he taken?"

"Temazepam. About half a dozen. He's been sick."

He stepped out in the corridor. There were more voices. I heard Rebecca go "Oh, for God's sake!" and Mark trying to quieten her down, then more low mumbling.

"I just want everything to stop. I don't want to feel like this. I want it all just to stop," moaned Giles.

"No, no," I said. "You have to have hope and confidence that everything will turn out all right, and it will."

There were more footsteps and voices in the house. Then Mark reappeared.

He gave a half smile. "Sorry about that." Then he looked serious again. "You're going to be all right, Giles. You're in good hands here. The doctor'll be round in fifteen minutes but he said nothing to worry about."

"Are you OK?" he said to me.

I nodded.

"You're being great," he said. "A rather more attractive version of George Clooney. Will you stay with him till the doctor comes?"

When the doctor had finally sorted Giles out half the people seemed to have left. Rebecca was sitting tearfully in the baronial hall with her foot up, talking to Mark, and Shaz was standing at the front door, smoking a cigarette, with both our bags packed.

"It's just so inconsiderate," Rebecca was saying. "It's ruined the whole weekend! People should be strong and resolute, it's so . . . self-indulgent and self-obsessed. Don't just say nothing, don't you think I'm right?"

"I think we should . . . talk about it later," said Mark.

After Shaz and I had said our good-byes and were putting our bags in the car, Mark came out to us.

"Well done," he barked. "Sorry. God, I sound like a sergeant major. The surroundings are getting to me. You were great, back there, with . . . with . . . well, with both of them."

"Mark!" Rebecca yelled. "I've dropped my walking stick."

"Fetch!" said Sharon.

For a split second a look of pure embarrassment flashed across

Mark's face, then he recovered himself and said, "Well, nice to see you, girls, drive safely."

As we drove away, Shaz was giggling gleefully at the idea of Mark spending the rest of his life forced to run around after Rebecca, following her orders and fetching sticks like a puppy, but my mind was turning round and round the conversation I'd overheard behind the hedge.

10

Mars and Venus in the Dustbin

130 lbs., alcohol units 4, cigarettes 12 (no longer priority), calories 3,752 (pre-diet), self-help books scheduled for dustbin 47.

8 a.m. In turmoil. Surely it cannot be that reading self-help books to improve my relationship has destroyed the whole relationship? Feel like entire life's work has been a failure. But if is one thing have learned from self-help books is how to let go of the past and move on.

About to be thrown out:
What Men Want
How Men Think and What They Feel
Why Men Feel They Want What They Think They Want
The Rules
Ignoring the Rules
Not Now Honey, I'm Watching the Game
How to Seek and Find the Love You Want
How to Find the Love You Want Without Seeking It
How to Find You Want the Love You Didn't Seek
Happy to Be Single
How Not to Be Single
If the Buddha Dated
If Mohammed Dated
If Jesus Dated Aphrodite

The Famished Road by Ben Okri (not strictly self-help book, as far as know, but will never read the bloody thing anyway)

Right. All going in the bin plus the other thirty-two. Oh God, though. Cannot bear to throw out *The Road Less Traveled* and *You Can Heal Your Life*. Where else is one to turn for spiritual guidance to deal with problems of modern age if not self-help books? Also maybe should give to Oxfam? But no. Must not ruin relationships of others, especially in Third World. Would be worse than behavior of tobacco giants.

Problems

Hole in wall of flat.

Finances in negative position owing to second mortgage for hole in wall of flat.

Boyfriend going out with Other Woman.

Not speaking to joint best friend as is going on holiday with boyfriend and Other Woman.

Work crap but necessary owing to second mortgage for hole in wall of flat.

Badly need holiday owing to boyfriend/friends/hole in wall of flat/professional and financial crises but no one to go on holiday with. Tom is going back to San Francisco. Magda and Jeremy are going to Tuscany with Mark and fucking Rebecca and probably Jude and Vile Richard too for all I know. Shazzer being evasive presumably waiting to see if Simon will agree to go somewhere with her if sleep in twin beds (not under five foot), hoping he will get into hers.

Also no money to go on holiday owing to financial crisis owing to hole in wall of flat.

No. Am not going to weaken. Have been too swayed this way and that by everyone else's ideas. They are going. In. The. Bin. I am Going. To stand on. Own. Two. Feet.

8:30 a.m. Flat is purged of all self-help books. Feel empty and spiritually at sea. But surely some of information will have stayed in head?

Spiritual principles have garnered from self-help book
study (nondating based):
1. Importance of positive thought cf.: *Emotional Intelligence, Emotional Confidence, The Road Less Traveled, How to Rid Your Thighs of Cellulite in 30 Days,* Gospel according to St. Luke, Ch. 13.
2. Importance of forgiveness.
3. Importance of going with flow and instincts rather than trying to squeeze everything into shape and organize everything.
4. Importance of confidence in self.
5. Importance of honesty.
6. Importance of enjoying present moment and not fantasizing or regretting things.
7. Importance of not being obsessed with self-help books.

So solution is to:
1. Think what a nice time am having writing lists of problems and spiritual solutions instead of planning ahead and . . .

Gaaah! Gaaah! Is 8:45! Am going to miss morning meeting and not have time for cappuccino.

10 a.m. In work. Thank God have got cappuccino to help self through aftermath of hell of buying cappuccino when late. Is bizarre how cappuccino queue thing gives whole areas of London appearance of war- or communism-torn culture with people standing patiently in huge queues for hours as if waiting for bread in Sarajevo while others sweat, roasting and grinding, banging metal things full of gunge around, with steam hissing. Is odd when people generally show less and less willingness to wait for anything that should be prepared to do so for this one thing: as if in cruel modern world is only thing one can really trust and hold on to . . . Gaaah!

10:30 a.m. Loos, work. Was Richard Finch bellowing at self. "Come on, Bridget. Don't be coy," the great lump roared in front of everyone, twitching and chewing in now-obvious post-cocaine-binge frenzy. "When are you going?"

"Er . . ." I said, hoping I could ask Patchouli, "Where?" later.

"You have no idea what I'm talking about, do you? It is literally unbelievable. When are you going on holiday? If you don't fill it in on the chart now you won't be going."

"Oh, um, yar," I said airily.

"No charto no departo."

"Sure, sure, yar, just need to check out the dates," I said clenching my teeth. As soon as the meeting was over, shot in here to loos for cheering cigarette. Does not matter if am only person in whole office not going on holiday. It does not. Does not mean am social outcast. Definitely. All is well in my world. Even if do have to do item on surrogacy, again.

6 p.m. Nightmare day trying to get women in to talk about quease-inducing egg-hatching permutations. Cannot face thought of going straight home to building site. Is gorgeous, soft sunny evening. Maybe will go for a walk on Hampstead Heath.

9 p.m. Unbelievable. Unbelievable. Just shows if you stop struggling to work everything out, and go with Flow in Zen-like positive way, solutions appear.

Was just walking along path towards the top of Hampstead Heath thinking how fantastic London is in the summer with people loosening their ties after work and spreading out shaggily in the sunshine when eye was caught by a happy-looking couple: she on her back with her head on his stomach, him smiling, and stroking her hair while he talked. Something about them looked familiar. As I got closer, I saw that it was Jude and Vile Richard.

Realized had never seen them alone together before—well, obviously because if I'd been there they wouldn't have been. Suddenly Jude burst out laughing at something Vile Richard had said. She looked really happy. I hesitated, wondering whether to walk past or go back, then Vile Richard said, "Bridget?"

I paused, frozen, and Jude looked up and gawped unattractively. Vile Richard got to his feet brushing the grass off him.

"Hey, good to see you, Bridget," he said with a grin. Realized had always seen him before in Jude-based social situations, when I'd been flanked by Shazzer and Tom and he'd been chippily resentful. "I'm just going off for some wine, you sit down with Jude. Oh, come on, she won't eat you. She won't touch anything with dairy."

When he'd gone, Jude smiled sheepishly. "I'm not pleased to see you or anything."

"Not pleased to see you either," I said gruffly.

"So do you want to sit down?"

"All right," I said, kneeling down on the rug at which she biffed me awkwardly on the shoulder nearly knocking me over.

"I missed you," she said.

"Shut-urrrrp," I said out of the corner of my mouth. For a moment, thought I was going to cry.

Jude apologized for being insensitive about Rebecca. She said she'd just got carried away by the thought of anyone who was pleased she was marrying Vile Richard. Turns out she and Vile Richard are not going to Tuscany with Mark and Rebecca, even though they were invited, because Vile Richard said he didn't want to be bossed around by a deranged social engineer and he'd rather they just went on their own. Found self unaccountably warming to Vile Richard. I said I was sorry for falling out over something so stupid as whole Rebecca thing.

"It wasn't stupid. You were really hurt," said Jude. Then she said they were delaying the wedding because it had all got so complicated but she still wanted me and Shaz to be bridesmaids. "If you want to," she said shyly. "But I know you don't like him."

"You really love him, don't you?"

"Yes," she said happily. Then she looked anxious. "But I don't know if I'm doing the right thing. It says in *The Road Less Traveled* that love isn't something you feel but something you decide to do. And also in *How to Get the Love You Want* that if you go out with someone who doesn't properly earn their own living and accepts help from his parents then they haven't deparented and it'll never work."

What was going through my head was the Nat King Cole song my dad was playing in the shed. *"The greatest thing . . . you'll ever learn . . ."*

"Also I think he's an addict because he smokes dope and addicts can't form relationships. My shrink says . . ."

". . . is how to love and be loved in return."

". . . I shouldn't have a relationship for at least a year because I'm a relationship addict," Jude went on. "And you and Shaz just think he's a fuckwit. Bridge? Are you listening to me?"

"Yes, yes, sorry. If it feels right I think you should go with it."

"Exactly," said Vile Richard, towering above us like Bacchus with a bottle of Chardonnay and two packets of Silk Cut.

Had fantastic time with Jude and Vile Richard and all piled into taxi and went back together. Once home, immediately called Shazzer to tell her the news.

"Oh," she said when I'd fully explained the Zen-like miracle workings of Flow. "Er, Bridge?"

"What?"

"Do you want to go on holiday?"

"I thought you didn't want to go with me."

"Well, I just thought I'd wait till . . ."

"Till what?"

"Oh, nothing. But anyway . . ."

"Shaz?" I prodded.

"Simon's going to Madrid to see some girl he met on the Internet."

Was torn between sorriness for Sharon, huge excitement about having someone to go on holiday with, and feelings of inadequacy for not being six-foot architect with penis when could not be further from same.

"Baaah. It's just pashmina-ism. She'll probably turn out to be a man," I said to make Shazzie feel better.

"But anyway," she said lightly, after a pause which sent huge pain vibes down the phone, "I've found these fantastic flights to Thailand for only £249 and we could go to Koh Samui and be hippies and it would hardly cost us anything!"

"Hurrah!" I said. "Thailand! We can study Buddhism and have a spiritual epiphany."

"Yes!" said Shaz. "Yes! And we're not having anything to do with any BLOODY MEN."

So, you see . . . Oh, telephone. Maybe Mark Darcy!

Midnight. Phone call was from Daniel, sounding different from usual, though still, obviously, drunk. He said he was really down because things were going badly at work, and he was sorry about the Germany thing. He accepted that I was actually very good on geography and could we have dinner on Friday? Just to talk. So said yes. Feel v.g. about same. Why should I not be friend to Daniel in his hour of need? One must not harbor resentment as that only holds one back but must forgive.

Also as Jude and Vile Richard shows—people can change and I *was* really crazy about him.

And am v. lonely.

And is just dinner.

Am definitely not going to sleep with him though.

⌒ FRIDAY 18 JULY

127 lbs. (excellent omen), condoms attempted to purchase 84, condoms purchased 36, usable condoms purchased 12 (should be plenty, think. Especially as not intended for actual use).

2 p.m. Am going out in lunch hour to buy some condoms. Not going to sleep with Daniel or anything. Is just to be on safe side.

3 p.m. Condom expedition proved total failure. Initially was totally enjoying sudden feeling of being condom consumer. When do not have sex life always feel sad when passing condom section as whole side of life that is denied to me. However, when got to counter found bewildering range of varied condoms: Ultra Safe "for extra sensitivity," Variety Pack "for extra choice" (alluring Kellogg's-style suggestion), Ultra Fine "spermicidally lubricated," Gossamer, "lubricated with a gentle lubricant without" (horrible repulsive word coming up) "spermicide," Natural styled for Extra Comfort (does that mean bigger—then what if too big?). Stared downwards furiously looking under eyelashes at condom array. Surely what one would want is Extra Sensitivity and Extra Comfort and Ultra Fine so why does one have to choose between?

"Can I help you?" said nosy chemist with knowing smirk. Obviously could not say I wanted condoms, as tantamount to announcing "Am about to have sex": almost as when people are walking round obviously pregnant and is like saying "Look, everyone, I have had sex." Cannot believe condom industry whose very existence is virtual admission that everyone has sex all the time (apart from me), instead of continuing pretense that no one does, which is surely more normal in our land.

Anyway. Just bought some throat lozenges.

6:10 p.m. Irritatingly detained at work till 6 p.m. and now chemist's is shut and have not got condoms. I know: will go to Tesco Metro. Will surely have as is store designed for impulsive Singletons.

6:40 p.m. Wandered surreptitiously up and down toothpaste aisle. Zilch. Eventually, in desperation, sidled up to supervisor-style lady and whispered, with an attempt at all-lads-together, one-eyebrow-raised smirk, "Where are your condoms?"

"We are going to do them," she said thoughtfully. "Maybe in a couple of weeks."

"Fat lot of good that is to me!" I felt like yelling. "What about tonight?" Though am not going to sleep with him, obviously!

Huh. *Soi-disant* modern, urban, Singleton-directed store. Humph.

7 p.m. Just went to local stinky double-price corner shop. Could see condoms behind counter with cigarettes and vile tights but decided against as whole setting too sordid. Wish to purchase condom product in pleasant clean Boots-style environment. Also parlous choice. Just Premium Quality Teat-Ended.

7:15 p.m. Have had brain wave. Will go to petrol station, wait in queue whilst secretly looking at condoms then . . . Actually must not conform to outdated male stereotypes feeling forward or sluttish for carrying condoms. All clean girls have condoms. Is hygiene.

7:30 p.m. Lalala. Have dunnit. Was easy. Actually managed to grab two packets: one Variety Pack (spice of life) and Improved Ultra Lightweight Latex Teat Ended for Even Greater Sensitivity. Assistant looked startled at range and quantity of condom choice yet strangely respectful: probably thought was biology teacher or similar purchasing condoms to teach early developing school pupils.

7:40 p.m. Startled by frank drawings in instruction leaflet, which disturbingly made me think about not Daniel but Mark Darcy. Hmmm. Hmmm.

7:50 p.m. Bet they had a difficult time deciding on sizing of pictures not to make anyone feel crestfallen or over-arrogant. Variety Pack is insane. "Mates colored condoms are vibrantly colored for extra fun." Extra fun? Suddenly get garish image of couples with vibrantly colored rude bits wearing paper hats, hooting with gay sexy laughter and hitting each other with balloons. Think will throw mad Variety Pack away. Right, better get ready. Oh God, telephone.

8:15 p.m. Oh bloody hell. Was Tom moaning that he'd lost his mobile and thought he left it round here. Forced me to look all over for it, even though was really late, but could not find it and eventually suspected might have thrown it away with the self-help books and newspapers.

"Well, can you go and get it?" he said eagerly.

"I'm really late. Can't I do it tomorrow?"

"But what if they empty the bins? What day do they come?"

"Tomorrow morning," I said with a sinking, bitter heart. "But the thing is, they're those big communal dustbins and I don't know which one it's in."

Ended up flinging long leather jacket on top of bra and knickers and going out into street to wait till Tom rang the phone so could find out which it was in. Was just standing on wall peering into the dustbins when a familiar voice said, "Hello."

Turned round and there was Mark Darcy.

He glanced down and I realized was standing with—fortunately coordinated—underwear on full display.

"What are you doing?" he said.

"I'm waiting for the dustbin to ring," I replied with dignity, pulling jacket around self.

"I see." There was a pause. "Have you been waiting . . . long?"

"No," I said carefully. "A normal amount of time."

Just then one of the dustbins started to ring. "Ah, that'll be for me," I said and started to try to reach into it.

"Please, allow me," said Mark, put down his briefcase, leapt, rather agilely, on to the wall, reached into the dustbin and picked out the phone.

"Bridget Jones's phone," he said. "Yes of course, I'll put her on." He handed it to me. "It's for you."

"Who's that?" hissed Tom, hysterical with excitement. "Sexy voice—who is it?"

I put my hand over the earpiece. "Thank you so much," I said to Mark Darcy who had picked a handful of self-help books out of the bin and was looking at them with a puzzled expression.

"Not at all," he said, putting the self-help books back. "Er . . ." He paused, looking at my leather jacket.

"What?" I said, heart racing.

"Oh, nothing, er, just, um, well, nice to see you." He hesitated. "Well . . . nice to see you again." Then he gave an attempt at a smile, turned and started to walk off.

"Tom, I'll call you back," I said into the protesting mobile. My heart was beating wildly. By all the laws of dating etiquette I should just let him go but I was thinking about the overheard conversation behind the hedge. "Mark?"

He turned round looking full of emotion. For a moment we just stared at each other.

"Hey! Bridge! Are you coming out for dinner without a skirt?"

It was Daniel, walking up, early, behind me.

I saw Mark take him in. He gave me a long, painful look then turned on his heel and strode away.

11 p.m. Daniel had not spotted Mark Darcy—both fortunately and unfortunately because on the one hand did not need to explain what he was doing there but on other hand could not explain why was feeling so churned up. The minute we got in the flat Daniel started trying to kiss me. It felt very strange not to want him to after all the time I spent last year desperately wanting him to and wondering why he wasn't.

"OK, OK," he said, holding out his hands, palms towards me. "No problem." He poured us both a glass of wine and sat down on the sofa, long lean legs all sexy in his jeans. "Look. I know I hurt you, and I'm sorry. I know you're feeling defensive but I'm different now, I really am. Come and sit down here."

"I'll just go put my clothes on."

"No. No. Come here," he said, patting the sofa beside him. "Come on, Bridge. I won't lay a finger on you, I promise."

I sat down gingerly, pulling my jacket around me, hands folded primly on my knee.

"There, there," he said. "Now come on, have a drink of this and just relax."

He put his arm gently round my shoulders.

"I'm haunted by the way I treated you. It was unforgivable." It was so lovely to be held again. "Jones," he whispered tenderly. "My little Jones."

He pulled me to him, laying my head against his chest. "You didn't deserve it." The old familiar scent of him wafted over me. "There. Just have a bit of a cuddle. You're all right now."

He was stroking my hair, stroking my neck, stroking my back, he started slipping my jacket off my shoulders, his hand reached down and with one flick, he'd undone my bra.

"Stoppit!" I said trying to pull the coat back round me. "Honestly, Daniel." I was half laughing. I suddenly saw his face. He wasn't laughing.

"Why?" he said, pulling the jacket roughly off my shoulders again. "Why not? Come on."

"No!" I said. "Daniel, we're just going out for dinner. I don't want to kiss you."

He dropped his head forward, breathing unsteadily, then sat up, head back, eyes closed.

I got to my feet, pulling my coat around me, and walked to the table. When I looked back, Daniel had his head in his hands. I realized he was sobbing.

"I'm sorry, Bridge. I've been promoted downstairs. Perpetua's got my job. I feel redundant, and now you don't want me. No girls will want me. Nobody wants a man at my age without a career."

I stared at him in astonishment. "And how do you think I felt last year? When I was bottom of the pile in that office and you were messing me around and making me feel like a retread?"

"Retread, Bridge?"

Was going to explain about the retread theory, but something made me decide I just wouldn't bother.

"I think it'd be best if you go now," I said.

"Oh, come on, Bridge."

"Just go," I said.

Hmm. Anyway. Will just detach from whole thing. Glad am going away. Will be able to free self's head of all men issues in Thailand and concentrate on self.

129 lbs. (why? On bikini-purchase day, why?), confusing thoughts about Daniel: too many, bikini bottoms fitted into 1, bikini tops fitted into: half, rude thoughts about Prince William 22, no. of times wrote "Prince William and his lovely date Miss Bridget Jones at Ascot" on Hello! *magazine 7.*

6:30 p.m. Bloody, bloody, bloody. Have spent all day in changing rooms of Oxford Street trying to squeeze my breasts into bikini tops designed for people with breasts either arranged one on top of the other in the center of their chests or one under each arm, with the harsh downlighting making me look like River Café frittata. Obvious solution is one-piece but then will return with already squashily textured stomach highlighted against rest of body by whiteness.

Urgent bikini diet weight-loss target program: week 1

Sun. 20 July	129 lbs.
Mon. 21 July	128 lbs.
Tues. 22 July	127 lbs.
Wed. 23 July	126 lbs.
Thurs. 24 July	125 lbs.
Fri. 25 July	124 lbs.
Sat. 26 July	123 lbs.

Hurray! So by a week today will be almost down to target weight so then, with body bulk thus adjusted, all will need to do is alter texture and arrangement of fat through exercise.

Oh fuck. Will never work. Am only sharing a room and probably bed with Shaz. Will concentrate instead on my spirit. Anyway Jude and Shaz are coming round soon. Hurrah!

Midnight. Lovely evening. V. nice to be back with girls again, though Shaz whipped herself up into such a frenzy of indignation about Daniel was all I could do to stop her ringing the police and having him arrested for date rape.

"Redundant? You see?" she was ranting. "Daniel's an absolute archetype of fin-de-millennium male. It's becoming clear to him that women are the superior race. He's realizing he has no role or function so what does he do? He turns to violence."

"Well, he only tried to kiss her," said Jude mildly, flicking idly through the pages of *What Marquee*.

"Pah! That's exactly the point. She's bloody lucky he didn't burst into her bank dressed as an Urban Warrior and kill seventeen people with a submachine gun."

Just then the phone rang. It was Tom, not, unaccountably, ringing to thank me for sending his mobile back after all the bloody trouble the pesky item has caused but wanting my mum's phone number. Tom seems to be quite pally with Mum, seeing her in what I suspect is a Judy Garland/Ivana Trump kitsch sort of way (which is odd since only last year I remember Mum lecturing me on how gayness was "just laziness, darling, they simply can't be bothered to relate to the opposite sex"—but then that was last year). Suddenly feared that Tom was going to ask my mother to perform "Non, Je Ne Regrette Rien" in a sequined dress in a club called Pump, which she would—naively yet egomaniacally—agree to, thinking it was something to do with ancient machinery in Cotswold Mill Houses.

"What do you want it for?" I said suspiciously.

"Isn't she in a book club?"

"Dunno. Anything's possible. Why?"

"Jerome's sensing his poems are ready, so I'm finding him book club venues. He did one last week in Stoke Newington and it was awesome."

"Awesome?" I said, doing a bulging-cheeked vomit face at Jude and Shaz. Ended up giving Tom the number in spite of reservations, as suspect Mum might be needing another diversion now Wellington has gone.

"What is it about book clubs?" I said when I'd put the phone down. "Is it just me, or have they suddenly sprung up from nowhere? Should we be in one or do you have to be Smug Married?"

"You have to be Smug Married," said Shaz definitively. "That's because they fear their minds are being sucked dry by the paternalistic demands of . . . Oh my God, look at Prince William."

"Let me look," interrupted Jude, snatching the copy of *Hello!* with its photo of the lithe young royal whippersnapper. Tried not to snatch it myself. Although, clearly, wish to admire as many pictures of Prince William as possible, preferably in a range of outfits, realize urge is both intrusive and wrong. Cannot, though, ignore impression of great things fermenting around in young royal brain, and sense that, at maturity, will rise up like ancient knight of Round Table thrusting sword in air and creating dazzling new order, which will make President Clinton and Tony Blair look like passé elderly gentlemen.

"How young is too young, would you say?" said Jude dreamily.

"Too young to be your legal son," said Shaz definitively as if was already part of government statute: which suppose it is, come to think of it, depending how old you are. Just then the phone rang again.

"Oh, hello, darling. Guess what?" My mother. "Your friend Tom—you know the 'homo'—well, he's bringing a poet to read at the Lifeboat Book Club! He's going to read us romantic poems. Like Lord Byron! Isn't that fun?"

"Er . . . yes?" I floundered.

"Actually, it's nothing special," she sniffed airily. "We often have visiting authors."

"Really? Like who?"

"Oh, lots of them, darling. Penny's *very* good friends with Salman Rushdie. Anyway, you will be coming, darling, won't you?"

"When is it?"

"A week on Friday. Una and I are doing vol-au-vents hot with Chunky Chicken."

A sudden fear convulsed me. "Are Admiral and Elaine Darcy coming?"

"Durr! No boys allowed, silly. Elaine's coming but the chaps are turning up later."

"But Tom and Jerome are coming."

"Oh, they're not boys, darling."

"Are you sure Jerome's poems will be the sort of thing that . . ."

"Bridget. I don't know what you're trying to say. We weren't born yesterday, you know. And the whole point about literature is free expression. Ooh, and I think Mark's coming along later. He's up doing Malcolm's will with him—you never know!"

129 lbs. (total failure of bikini diet), cigarettes 19 (diet aid), calories 625 (not too late, surely).

6:30 p.m. Grr. Grrr. Leaving for Thailand tomorrow, nothing is packed and had failed to realize that "a week on Friday" for book club is to-bloody-night. Really, really do not want to drive all way to Grafton Underwood. Is hot steamy evening and Jude and Shaz are going to lovely party at River Café. Obviously, though, is important to support Mum, Tom's love life, Art etc. Is respecting self by respecting others. Also does not matter if tired tomorrow when get on plane as going on holiday. Sure trip preparation will not take long as only need capsule wardrobe (just a couple of bodies and a sarong!) and packing always expands to fill the time available so best use of time, surely, is to make time available v. short. Yes! You see! So will do everything!

Midnight. Just back. Arrived v. late owing to typical motorway signpost debacle (if war today, better, surely, to confuse Germans by leaving signposts up?). Was greeted by Mum, wearing a very strange maroon velvet kaftan which presume she intended to be literary.

"How's Salman?" I said as she tut-tutted about my lateness.

"Oh, we decided to do chicken instead," she said sniffily, leading me through the ripply-glassed French doors, into the lounge where the first thing I noticed was a garish new "family crest" above the fake stone fireplace saying *"Hakuna Matata."*

"Shh," said Una, holding a finger up, enraptured.

Pretentious Jerome, pierced nipple clearly visible through black wet-look vest, was standing in front of the cut-glass dish collection, bellowing belligerently: "I watch his hard, bony, horny, hams. I watch, I want, I grab," at a semicircle of appalled Jaeger-be-two-pieced Lifeboat Luncheon Book Club ladies on reproduction Regency dining chairs. Across the room I saw Mark Darcy's mum, Elaine, sporting an expression of suppressed amusement.

"I want," Jerome bellowed on. "I seize his horny, hairy, hams. I have to have. I heave, I hump, I . . ."

"Well! I think that's been absolutely smashing!" said Mum, jumping to her feet. "Does anyone fancy a vol-au-vent?"

Is amazing the way the world of middle-class ladies manages to smooth everything into its own, turning all the chaos and complication of the world into a lovely secure mummy stream, rather as lavatory cleaner turns everything in the toilet pink.

"Oh, I love the spoken and written word! It makes me feel so free!" Una was gushing to Elaine as Penny Husbands-Bosworth and Mavis Enderbury fussed over Pretentious Jerome as if he were T. S. Eliot.

"But I hadn't finished," whined Jerome. "I wanted to do 'Fister Contemplations' and 'The Hollow Men-Holes.'"

Just then there was a roar.

"*If you can keep your head when all about you are losing theirs and blaming it on you.*" It was Dad, and Admiral Darcy. Both paralytic. Oh God. Every time I see Dad these days, he seems to be completely pissed, in bizarre father-daughter role-reversal scenario.

"*If you can trust yourself when all men doubt you,*" Admiral Darcy bellowed, leaping on to a chair to a flutter from the assembled ladies.

"*And make allowance for their doubting too,*" added Dad, almost tearfully, leaning against the admiral for support.

The pissed duo proceeded to recite the whole of Rudyard Kipling's "If" in manner of Sir Laurence Olivier and John Gielgud to the fury of Mum and Pretentious Jerome who started throwing simultaneous hissy fits.

"It's typical, typical, typical," hissed Mum as Admiral Darcy, on his knees, beating his breast, intoned, "Or being lied about, don't deal in lies."

"It's regressive, colonialist doggerel," hissed Jerome.

"*If you can force your heart, and nerve and sinew.*"

"I mean it fucking rhymes," rehissed Jerome.

"Jerome, I will not have that word in my house," also rehissed Mum.

"*To serve their turn long after they are gone*," said Dad, then flung himself on the swirly carpet in mock death.

"Well, why did you invite me then?" hissed Jerome really hissily.

"*And so keep on, when there is nothing in you*," roared the admiral.

"*Except your nerve*," growled Dad from the carpet. "*Which says to you*"—he leapt to his knees and raised his arms—"*hold on!*"

There was a huge cheer and round of applause from the ladies as Jerome flounced out slamming the door and Tom rushed after him. I looked despairingly back at the room straight into the eyes of Mark Darcy.

"Well! That was interesting!" said Elaine Darcy, coming to stand by me as I bent my head, trying to recover my composure. "Poetry uniting the old and young."

"The pissed and sober," I added.

At this Admiral Darcy lurched over, clutching his poem.

"My dear, my dear, my darling!" he said, lunging at Elaine. "Oh here's what's-her-name," he said, peering at me. "Lovely! Mark's arrived, that's my boy! Come to pick us up, sober as a judge. All on his own. I don't know!" he said.

They both turned to look at Mark who was sitting at Una's three-penny-bit occasional table, scribbling something, watched over by a blue-glass dolphin.

"Writing my will for me at a party! I don't know. Work, work, work!" roared the admiral. "Brought this bit of totty along, what was 'er name, m'dear, Rachel, was it? Betty?"

"Rebecca," Elaine said tartly.

"And the next thing she's nowhere to be seen. Ask him what's happened to her, and he mumbles! Can't stand a mumbler! Never could."

"Well, I don't think she was really . . ." murmured Elaine.

"Why not! Why not! Perfectly good! I don't know! Fussing about this, that and the other! I hope you young ladies are not always flitting hither and thither like these young fellers seem to be!"

"No," I said ruefully. "In fact if we love someone it's pretty hard to get them out of our system when they bugger off."

There was a crash behind. I turned to see that Mark Darcy had knocked over the blue-glass dolphin, which in turn had dislodged a vase of chrysanthemums and a photo frame, creating a melee of shattered glass, flowers and bits of paper, the hideous dolphin itself remaining miraculously intact.

There was a commotion as Mum and Elaine and Admiral Darcy all rushed at the scene, the admiral striding around and bellowing, Dad trying to bounce the dolphin on to the floor saying, "Get rid of the bloody thing," and Mark grabbing at his papers and offering to pay for everything.

"Are you ready to go, Dad?" muttered Mark, looking deeply embarrassed.

"No, no, in your own time, I've been in very good company, with Brenda here. Get me another port, will you, son?"

There was an awkward pause as Mark and I looked at each other.

"Hello, Bridget," Mark said abruptly. "Come on, Dad, I really think we should go."

"Yes, come along, Malcolm," said Elaine, taking his arm affectionately. "Or you'll be widdling on the carpet."

"Oh, widdling, widdling, I don't know."

The three of them made their good-byes, Mark and Elaine easing the admiral out of the door. I watched, feeling empty and flat, then suddenly Mark reappeared and headed towards me.

"Ah, forgot my pen," he said, picking up his Mont Blanc from the occasional table. "When are you going to Thailand?"

"Tomorrow morning." For a split second I could swear he looked disappointed. "How did you know I was going to Thailand?"

"Grafton Underwood speaks of nothing else. Have you packed?"

"What do you think?"

"Not a single pant," he said wryly.

"Mark," bellowed his father. "Come on, boy, thought it was you who was keen to be off."

"Coming," said Mark, glancing over his shoulder. "This is for

you." He handed me a scrumpled piece of paper, flashed me a . . .
er . . . penetrating look, then left.

I waited till no one was watching then unfolded the sheet with
shaking hands. It was just a copy of Dad and Admiral Darcy's poem.
What did he give me that for?

*128 lbs. (huh, total preholiday diet failure), alcohol units 5, cigarettes 42,
calories 4,457 (total despair), items packed 0, ideas as to whereabouts of
passport 6, passport whereabout ideas proved to have any substance whatsoever 0.*

5 a.m. Why oh why am I going on holiday? I will spend the entire
holiday wishing Sharon were Mark Darcy, and she that I were
Simon. It's five o'clock in the morning. My entire bedroom is covered in wet washing, ballpoints, and polythene bags. I do not know
how many bras to take, I cannot find my little black Jigsaw dress
without which I cannot go or my other pink jelly mule, I haven't
got any traveler's checks yet and do not think my credit card is working. There are now only 1.5 hours left till I have to leave the house
and everything will not fit into the suitcase. Maybe will have cigarette and look at brochure for calming few minutes.

Mmm. Will be lovely just to lie and sunbathe to get all brown on
beach. Sunshine and swimming and . . . Oooh. Answerphone light
is flashing. How come did not notice?

5:10 a.m. Pressed ANSWER PLAY.

"Oh Bridget, it's Mark. Just wondered. You do realize it's the rainy
season in Thailand? Maybe you should pack an umbrella."

1 1

Thai Takeaway

Weightless (in air), alcohol units 8 (but in-flight so canceled out by altitude), cigarettes 0 (desperate: no-smoking seat), calories 1 million (entirely made up of things would never have dreamt of putting in self's mouth were they not on in-flight tray), farts from traveling companion 38 (so far), variations in fart aroma 0.

4 p.m. English time. In airplane in sky. Having to pretend to be very busy wearing Walkman and writing as ghastly man next to self in pale brown synthetic-type suit keeps trying to talk to me in between silent but deadly farting. Tried pretending to have fallen asleep whilst holding nose but after a few minutes ghastly man tapped me on the shoulder and said, "Do you have any hobbies?"

"Yes, napping," I replied but even that didn't put him off and within seconds I was plunged into the murky world of early Etruscan coinage.

Sharon and I are separated as we were so late for plane that there were only separate seats left and Shazzer was in complete grump with me. She seems, however, to have unaccountably got over it, which has clearly nothing to do with fact that she is sitting next to Harrison Ford–style stranger with jeans and crumpled khaki shirt, laughing like drain (weird expression, surely?) at everything he says. This, in spite of the fact that Shaz hates all men for losing their roles and turning to pashmina-ism and mindless violence. I, meanwhile, am stuck to Mr. Synthetic Fabric Fart Machine, and cannot have cigarette for twelve hours. Thank God have got Nicorette.

Non-v.g. start but still v. excited re: Thailand trip. Sharon and I are going to be *travelers* rather than tourists i.e. not stay in hermetically sealed tourist enclaves but really experience the religion and culture.

Holiday Aims:

1. Be hippie-style traveler.
2. Lose weight through mild, ideally not life-threatening dysentery.
3. Get subtle biscuit-style suntan—not bright orange in manner of George Hamilton, or melanoma- or wrinkle-inducing.
4. Have nice time.
5. Find self, also sunglasses. (Hopefully are in suitcase.)
6. Swim and sunbathe (sure only rains in short tropical bursts).
7. See temples (not too many, though, hope).
8. Have spiritual epiphany.

~ **MONDAY 4 AUGUST**

119 lbs. (weighing no longer possible, so can select weight according to mood: excellent advantage of travel), calories 0, minutes not spent on toilet 12 (feels like).

2 a.m. local time. Bangkok. Shazzer and I are trying to get to sleep in worst place I have ever been in. Think am going to suffocate and stop breathing. When we flew in over Bangkok there was thick gray cloud and it was pissing rain. The Sin Sane (Sin Sae) Guest House has no toilets, just hideous stinking holes in ground in cubicles. Open window and fan make no difference whatsoever since air is nearest possible thing to warm water without actually being it. There is disco underneath (hotel, not toilet) and in pauses can hear everyone in entire street moaning and not able to get to sleep either.

Feel like great white flobbering bloated thing. Hair has first turned into feathers then become plastered down on face. Worst of it is, Sharon is wittering on about Harrison Ford–style airline stranger.

". . . So well traveled . . . was on Sudan Airways when the pilot and co-pilot decided to shake hands with all the passengers and the cockpit door shut behind them! They had to hack it down with an ax. So witty. He's staying at the Oriental—he said to come over."

"I thought we didn't want anything to do with men," I said grumpily.

"No, no, I just think if we're in a strange place it's useful to talk to someone really well traveled."

6 a.m. Finally got to sleep at 4:30 only to be woken at 5:45 by Sharon bouncing on the bed saying we should go to a temple and watch the sunrise (through three hundred ft. of cloud?). Cannot go on. Gaah! Something v. horrible seems to be going on in stomach. Keep having little eggy burps.

11 a.m. Sharon and I have been up for five hours, four and a half of which have been spent taking it in turns to go to the "toilet." Sharon says suffering and simple life is part of spiritual epiphany. Physical comfort is not only unnecessary but an impediment to spirituality. We are going to meditate.

Noon. Hurrah! We have checked into the Oriental Hotel! Realize will cost more for one night than week in Corfu but is emergency and what are credit cards for? (Shazzer's is still working and she says I can pay her back. Wonder if is all right to have spiritual epiphany on someone else's credit card?)

Both agreed hotel marvelous and changed immediately into powder-blue bathrobes and played with bubble bath etc. Also Shazzer says it is not necessary to completely rough it all the time in order to be a traveler since it is the contrast between worlds and lifestyles that makes one have a spiritual epiphany. Could not agree more. Greatly appreciate, for example, simultaneous presence of toilet and bidet in view of current stomach scenario.

8 p.m. Shazzer was asleep (or dead from dysentery), so decided to go out for walk on terrace of hotel. Was just beautiful. Stood in inky darkness with soft warm breezes lifting plastered-down feathers off face, looking over bend in Chao Phraya river—and all twinkly lights and lurking Oriental-style boats. Flying is marvelous thing—only twenty-four hours ago was sitting on bed at home surrounded by wet washing—now all is unbelievably exotic and romantic. Was just about to light cigarette when suddenly posh gold lighter appeared under nose. Glanced at the face in the matchlight and made odd noise. Was the airline Harrison Ford! Waiter brought gin and tonics that seemed quite strong. Harrison Ford, or "Jed," explained was v. important to take quinine in tropics. Could quite see why Shaz was going on about him. He asked what our plans were. Told him we had decided to go to hippie island of Koh Samui to stay in hut and have spiritual epiphany. He said he might come too. I said Sharon would like that (as obviously he was hers though did not say that to Harrison Ford), and maybe I should go wake her up. By this time was feeling rather woozy what with all the quinine then panicked as he brushed one finger gently down the side of my cheek and leaned towards me.

"Bridget," hissed a voice, "call yourself a bloody friend."

Oh no, oh no. Was Shazzer.

⌒ THURSDAY 7 AUGUST

118 lbs. or maybe 114?, cigarettes 10, appearances by the sun 0.

Koh Samui Island, Thailand. (Hmm: rhymes in manner of rap song or similar.)

Have arrived at v. idyllic—apart from teeming rain—hippie beach: lovely crescent of sand and little huts on stilts and restaurants all along it. The huts are made of bamboo with balconies overlooking the sea. Things are still rather frosty between me and Shaz and she has developed an irrational aversion to "Boys Who Have Huts Near One" with the result that even though we have not yet been here eighteen hours we have had to move huts three times in rain. The first time it was fair enough as after three minutes the boys came over and tried to sell us something that was either heroin, opium, or fudge. Then we moved to a new hut hotel where the boys in the next hut looked v. clean-cut in manner of biochemists or similar. Unfortunately, however, the biochemists came over and told us someone had hanged himself in our hut three days ago at which Shazzer insisted we leave. By this time it was pitch-black. The biochemists had offered to help with our bags but Shaz would have none of it and we had to tramp along the beach with rucksacks for ages. The upshot of it was, having traveled about twenty thousand miles to wake up by the sea, we ended up in a hut overlooking the back of a restaurant and a ditch. So now we have to go up and down the beach looking for another hut that is on the sea but does not have the wrong sort of boys near it, or posthanging karma. Bloody Shazzer.

11:30 p.m. Hurrah! Es wor blurry brill in ganja restaurant, Shazz blurry fantastic. Bessfrien.

~ **FRIDAY 8 AUGUST**

112 lbs. (marvelous by-product of stomach explosion), alcohol units 0, ciga-rettes 0 (v.g.), magic mushrooms 12 (mmmmm wooooo weeeeee).

11:30 a.m. When woke up, admittedly quite late, found myself alone. Could not find Shaz anywhere in the hut, so came out on the balcony and looked around. Worryingly, the frightening Swedish girls next door seemed to have been replaced by a Boy Who Has Hut Near One but clearly this could not be my fault as travelers constantly coming and going. Put on prescription sunglasses as lenses not in yet and on closer inspection, Boy Who Newly Had Hut Near One turned out to be airline Harrison Ford lookalike—Oriental Hotel snogger. As I watched he turned round and smiled at some-one coming out of his hut. It was Shazzer, revealing whole "be careful while traveling, avoid Boys Who Have Huts Near One" philosophy to contain gigantic "unless they're really attractive" caveat.

1 p.m. Jed is taking us both to the café for a magic mushroom omelette! Initially we were doubtful as strictly against classified substances but Jed explained magic mushrooms are not drugs but natural and will provide a gateway to our spiritual epiphany. V. excited.

2 p.m. I am beautiful in a striking, exotic way, beautiful and part of all colors and life with its laws. When lie on the sand and look at the sky through my army hat pinpricks of light shine through and it is the most beautiful, beautiful, precious thing in imagery. Shazzer is beautiful. I will take my hat into the sea so the beauty of the sea will combine with the precious pinpricks of light like jewels.

5 p.m. In ganja restaurant on own. Shazzer is not speaking to me. After the magic mushroom omelette, nothing happened initially but on the way back to our hut everything suddenly began to seem most amusing and I unfortunately began to giggle uncontrollably. Shaz, however, did not seem to be joining in the joke. On arrival at our latest hut I decided to put my hammock up outside, using thin string, which broke, so that I landed on the sand. This seemed at the time so very amusing I immediately wanted to do it again and, Shazzer is claiming, reperformed amusing hammock crash repeatedly for forty-five minutes finding the amusingness undiminished by repetition. Jed had been in the hut with Shaz but gone off for a swim so I decided to go in to find her. She was lying on the bed moaning, "I'm ugly, ugly, ugly, ugly." Alarmed by Shazzer's contrasting-with-own-mood self-loathing, hurried towards her to cheer her up. On the way, however, caught sight of self in the mirror and had never seen a more beautiful or entrancing creature in entire life.

Shaz alleges that for the next forty minutes kept attempting to rouse her spirits but I became repeatedly distracted by sight of self in the mirror, striking poses and beseeching Shaz to admire me. Shaz, meanwhile, was suffering total trauma believing her entire face and body to be grievously deformed. I went off to get her some food and returned giggling with a banana and Bloody Mary, telling her the waitress in the restaurant had a lampshade on her head, then returned besottedly to my station at the mirror. Following this, Shaz claims, I lay on the beach for two and a half hours staring up at army hat and waving fingers softly in the air while she contemplated suicide.

All can remember was being in midst of happiest time of life, sure that had understood deep, permanent laws of life and that all that was necessary was to get into deep Flow state—as fully described in *Emotional Intelligence*—thereby to go along with Laws in Zen-like fashion, then suddenly it was as if a switch had been turned off. Returned to hut and instead of radiant Buddha/Yasmin Le Bon–type female incarnation in mirror it was just me, bright red and sweating in the face, one side of hair plastered down my head and the other side sticking out in peaks and horns, and Shaz on the bed looking at me with the expression of an ax murderer. V. sad and ashamed of behavior but it was not me, it was the mushrooms.

Maybe if I go back to the hut and talk about spiritual epiphanies she will not be so grumpy.

~ **FRIDAY 15 AUGUST**

113 lbs. (in slightly rounder mood today), alcohol units 5, cigarettes 25, spiritual epiphanies 0, disasters 1.

9 a.m. We have had a fantastic holiday though not a spiritual epiphany. Felt a bit left out because Shaz was often with Jed, but the sun made really quite a few appearances so swam and sunbathed when they were shagging, and at night the three of us had dinner. Shaz is a bit heartbroken because Jed left last night to go on to some other islands. We are going to have cheer-up breakfast (though not magic mushrooms) and then can be just the two of us again and have fun. Hurrah!

11:30 a.m. Oh my bloody God and fuck. Sharon and I have just got back to our hut to find our padlock was open and our rucksacks have gone missing. Definitely left it locked but they must have broken in. Fortunately we had our passports and not all the stuff was actually in the bags but our air tickets and traveler's checks appear to be no longer there. Shazzer's card is not working after Bangkok with all shopping etc. We only have $38 between us and the flight to London from Bangkok is on Tuesday and we are hundreds of miles away on an island. Sharon is crying and I keep trying to cheer her up to little effect.

Whole scenario reminiscent of *Thelma and Louise* when Thelma sleeps with Brad Pitt who steals all their money and Geena Davis is saying it's all right and Susan Sarandon is crying and saying, "It is not all right. Thelma, it is definitely not all right."

Even to fly to Bangkok in time for the plane will cost us $100 each, and then who knows if they would believe us at Bangkok airport about lost tickets or whether we could . . . Oh God. Must keep head and spirits up. Just suggested to Shazzer that we go back to the ganja restaurant and have a couple of Bloody Marys and sleep on it and she went mental.

The trouble is part of me is frantic and part of me thinks it is brilliant to have a crisis and adventure and it is such a change from worrying about the circumference of my thighs. Think I will just sneak out and get the Bloody Marys. Might as well cheer ourselves up. Can't do anything about it till Monday anyway as everything closed: short of going to a bar and raising money by doing exotic dances with Ping-Pong balls coming out of us but somehow do not think we would stand up to the competition.

1 p.m. Hurrah! Shazzza I going tor live in KohSamui like hippies off bananas sell shells onsbeach. IIs y spiritual epiphany. Blurry brilli. Nothing but selves to re on. Spirtal.

5 p.m. Hmm. Shaz is still asleep, which I am glad about as she seems to be taking things rather hard. This, I feel, is an opportunity to test our self-reliance. I know. Am going to go to the big hotel and enquire at reception as to what facilities are available to deal with a crisis. For example I could ring the traveler's check company. But then we'll never get the refund in time. No, no. Keep positive.

7 p.m. You see. As long as you keep your spirits up something always comes along to get you out of a hole. Who should I bump into in the hotel foyer but Jed! He said his trip to the other islands had been rained off, he was going back to Bangkok later tonight and was just about to come to see us to say hi before he goes. (Think Shaz might be a bit upset he didn't come to find her straight away, but still. Maybe he thought we'd already gone or . . . Look, I am *not* going to start obsessing on behalf of Sharon.)

Anyway, Jed was really sympathetic, though did say we should never have left anything valuable in the hut, even if it was padlocked. He gave me a bit of a lecture (bloody sexy, sort of father/priest figure) then said we'd be pushing it to get to Bangkok in time for Tuesday's flight, as all the flights from here today and tomorrow were full, but he would try to get us tickets for the overnight train tomorrow, which should make the connection. Also offered to give us some money for taxis and to pay the hotel here. He thought if we rang the travel agent in London first thing Monday they would definitely reissue the tickets to pick up at the airport.

"We'll pay you back," I said gratefully.

"Hey, don't worry," he said. "It's not very much."

"No, we will," I insisted.

"Well, when you can afford it." He laughed.

He is a generous, wealthy dreamgod, though obviously money not important. Except when missing in crisis.

⁓ **MONDAY 18 AUGUST**

On train from Surat Thani Koh Samui to Bangkok. Is quite nice on the train, watching all the paddy fields and people with triangular hats go by. Every time it stops, people come up to the windows offering us chicken saté, which is delicious. Cannot stop thinking about Jed. He was so kind and there for us in way that reminded self of Mark Darcy when not gone off with Rebecca. He even gave us one of his bags to put our stuff in that wasn't nicked and all his little shampoos and soaps from his various hotels. Shaz is happy because they've swapped numbers and addresses and are going to see each other as soon as she gets back. In fact, to be perfectly honest about it, Shazzer is smug to the point of insufferability. Is good though, as she had horrible time with Simon. Always suspected she did not hate all men, just crap ones. Oh God. Hope we get the plane in time.

~ **TUESDAY 19 AUGUST**

11 a.m. Bangkok airport. A terrible nightmare seems to be happening. Blood all seems to be racing through my head and I can hardly see. Shaz went on ahead of me to hold up the plane while I brought the luggage. Had to walk past an official with a dog on a leash, which was straining at my bag and barking. The airline officials all started jabbering, and then an army woman took me and the bag away to a separate room. They emptied the holdall, then took a knife and slashed open the lining, and inside was a polythene bag full of white powder. And then . . . Oh God. Oh God. Someone help me.

~ **WEDNESDAY 20 AUGUST**

84 lbs., alcohol units 0, cigarettes 0, calories 0, likelihood of ever eating Thai takeaway again 0.

11 a.m. Police custody, Bangkok. Calm. Calm. Calm. Calm.

11:01 a.m. Calm.

11:02 a.m. Am wearing leg irons. Am wearing LEG IRONS. Am in stinking Third World cell with eight Thai prostitutes and a potty in the corner. Feel like am going to faint in heat. This cannot be happening.

11:05 a.m. Oh God. It's all falling into place what has happened. Cannot believe anyone could be so callous, to sleep with someone then nick all their things and dupe their friend into being a pigeon. Is unbelievable. Anyway, I expect the British ambassador will be here soon to explain everything and get me out.

Noon. Becoming slightly anxious about whereabouts of British ambassador.

1 p.m. Sure the British ambassador will be along after his lunch break.

2 p.m. Maybe the British ambassador has been held up, perhaps by a more pressing case of real drug trafficking as opposed to an innocent dupe.

3 p.m. Oh my bloody God and fuck. I hope they have bloody well *told* the British ambassador. Surely Shazzer will have raised the alert. Maybe they have got Shazzer as well. But where is she?

3:30 p.m. Look, have got to, got to keep myself together. All I have got now is myself. Fucking Jed. Must not hold on to resentment . . . Oh God, I'm so hungry.

4 p.m. Guard just came by with some disgusting rice and some personal effects was allowed to keep—one pair of knickers, a photo of Mark Darcy and another of Jude showing Shazzer how to have an orgasm and a screwed-up bit of paper from jeans pocket. Tried to ask guard about British ambassador but he just nodded and said something I couldn't understand.

4:30 p.m. You see. Even when things seem bad, still enlightening things happen. Screwed-up paper was Dad's poem from book club that Mark gave me. Is literature. Am going to read it and think of finer things.

"If" by Rudyard Kipling
If you can keep your head when all about you
Are losing theirs and . . .

Oh my God. Oh my GOD. Do they still have beheading in Thailand?

⁓ **THURSDAY 21 AUGUST**

70 lbs. (v.g. but imaginary), alcohol units 14 (but also imaginary), cigarettes 0, calories 12 (rice), no. of times wish had gone to Mallorca instead 55.

5 a.m. Hideous night huddled on flea-infested old sack stuffed with socks masquerading as mattress. Funny how quickly you get used to being dirty and uncomfortable. Is the smell that is the worst. Managed to sleep for a couple of hours, which was great except for moment when woke up and remembered what happened. Still no sign of British ambassador. Sure it is just a mistake and will all be OK. Must keep spirits up.

10 a.m. A guard just appeared at the door with a Sloaney-looking chap in a pink shirt.

"Are you the British ambassador?" I yelled, practically flinging myself on him.

"Ah. No. Assistant to the consul. Charlie Palmer-Thompson. Jolly good to meet you." He shook my hand in a manner that would have been reassuringly British had he not involuntarily wiped it on his trousers afterwards.

He asked me what happened and took down the details in a Mulberry posh leather-bound notebook, saying things like "Yar, yar. Oh Christ, how frightful," as if I were telling him a polo anecdote. Started to panic as (a) did not seem quite to grasp the gravity of the situation, (b) did not seem—not to be snobbish or anything—exactly brain of Britain and (c) did not seem nearly as certain as I would have liked that this was all a mistake and I was about to be released any second.

"But why?" I said, having told him the whole story again. Explained how Jed must have broken into the hut himself and planned the whole thing.

"Well, you see the bore is"—Charlie leaned forward confidentially—"everyone who comes in here has some sort of story, usually pretty much along the lines of yours. So unless this bloody Jed character makes a full confession it's a bit of a sticky wicket."

"Am I going to get the death penalty?"

"Good God, no. Bloody hell. Shouldn't think so. Worst you'd be looking at is about ten years."

"TEN YEARS? But I haven't done anything."

"Yar, yar, it's a bastard, I know," he said, nodding earnestly.

"But I didn't know it was there!"

"Sure, sure," he said, looking as if he'd got himself into a slightly awkward situation at a drinks party.

"Will you do everything you can?"

"Absolutely," he said, getting up. "Yar."

He said he would bring me a list of lawyers to choose from and he could make two calls on my behalf, just to give the details of what had happened. Was in quite a quandary. Best person, practically speaking, would be Mark Darcy but really did not like idea of admitting have got into mess again, especially after he sorted out all the Mum and Julio stuff last year. In the end I plumped for Shazzer and Jude.

Feel like my fate is now in the hands of some fresh-out-of-Oxbridge Sloane. God, it is so awful in here. So hot and stinking and weird. I feel like nothing's real.

4 p.m. Very black. All my life I have had the feeling something terrible was about to happen and now it has.

5 p.m. Mustn't get down. Must keep my mind off it all. Maybe will read poem, and try to ignore first two lines:

"If" by Rudyard Kipling

If you can keep your head when all about you
 Are losing theirs and blaming it on you;
If you can trust yourself when all men doubt you,
 But make allowance for their doubting too;
If you can wait, and not be tired by waiting,
 Or, being lied about, don't deal in lies,
Or, being hated, don't give way to hating,
 And yet don't look too good, nor talk too wise;

If you can dream—and not make dreams your master;
 If you can think—and not make thoughts your aim;
If you can meet with Triumph and Disaster
 And treat those two impostors just the same;
If you can bear to hear the truth you've spoken
 Twisted by knaves to make a trap for fools,
Or watch the things you gave your life to broken,
 And stoop and build 'em up with worn-out tools;

If you can make one heap of all your winnings
 And risk it on one turn of pitch-and-toss,
And lose, and start again at your beginnings
 And never breathe a word about your loss;
If you can force your heart and nerve and sinew
 To serve your turn long after they are gone,
And so hold on when there is nothing in you
 Except the Will which says to them: "Hold on!"

If you can talk with crowds and keep your virtue,
 Or walk with Kings—not lose the common touch;
If neither foes nor loving friends can hurt you;
 If all men count with you, but none too much;
If you can fill the unforgiving minute
 With sixty seconds' worth of distance run—
Yours is the Earth and everything that's in it,
 And—which is more—you'll be a Man, my son!

Poem is good. Very good, almost like self-help book. Maybe that is why Mark Darcy gave it to me! Maybe he sensed I might get into danger! Or maybe he was just trying to tell me something about my attitude. Bloody cheek. Not sure about sixty seconds' worth of distance run anyway, or if actually want to be man. Also is a bit hard to treat this disaster the same as triumphs as have not had any triumphs that can think of, but still. Will force heart and nerve and sinew to serve turn etc. in manner of First World War or jungle soldier or whatever Rudyard Kipling was and just hold on. At least am not being shot at or having to go over top. And also am not spending any money in jail so actually helping financial crisis. Yes, must look on positive side.

Good things about being in jail:
1. Not spending any money.
2. Thighs have really gone down and have probably lost at least seven pounds without even trying.
3. Will be good for hair to leave it without washing such as have never been able to do before as hair too mad-looking to go outside.

So when go home will be thin, with shiny hair and less broke. But when will I go home? When? I'll be old. I'll be dead. If I am here for ten years I will never be able to have any children. Unless I take a fertility drug when I get out and have eight. I'll be a lonely, broken old woman shaking my fist at street urchins who put turds through the letter box. But maybe I could have a child while in prison? I could get the assistant to the British consul somehow to impregnate me. But where would I get hold of folic acid in jail? The baby would grow up stunted. Must stop this. Stoppit. Stoppit. Am catastrophizing.

But it is a catastrophe.

Will read poem again.

Calories 22, unforgiving minutes filled with distance run 0.

8 p.m. Women's Correctional Institute, Bangkok. This morning they came and moved me from police custody to proper prison. In despair. Feel as if this means they have given up on me and accepted I'm done for. Cell is big filthy room with at least sixty women squeezed in. Seems that any power or individuality is being relentlessly peeled away as get filthier and filthier and more exhausted. Cried today for first time in four days. I feel like I'm slipping through the net. I feel like I'm going to get forgotten now and just languish here, a wasted life. Will try to sleep. Would be so great to sleep.

11 p.m. Aargh. Had just got off to sleep when was woken by something sucking my neck. It was the Lesbian Ring who had got me. They all started kissing and groping bits of me. I could not bribe them to stop because I had already given away my Wonderbra and no way was I going round with no knickers. I could not scream for the guard as that is the worst thing you can do here. So I had to swap my jeans for a filthy old sarong. Although obviously I felt violated, part of me could not help but feel it was so nice just to be touched. Gaaah! Maybe I am a lesbian? No. Don't think so.

Minutes spent crying 0 (hurrah!).

Much more cheerful since sleep. Think will find Phrao. Phrao is my friend as she was transferred at same time as me and I lent her my Wonderbra. Even though she has no breasts to put in it she seems to like it—she is always walking around in it saying "Madonna." Cannot help thinking it is cupboard love or underwear drawer love but beggars can't be choosers and it is nice to have a friend. Also do not want it to be like when Beirut hostages got out and it was obvious no one really liked Terry Waite.

You see, you can get used to anything if you try. Am not going to give in to being all mopey. Sure they must be doing something at home. Shazzer and Jude will be organizing newspaper campaigns like for John McCarthy and standing outside the House of Commons with banners with my head on, holding up torches.

There must be something I can do. It seems to me if getting out depends on catching Jed and extracting a confession then there ought to be a bit more bloody effort put into catching and extracting.

2 p.m. Hurrah! Am suddenly most popular girl in cell. Was quietly teaching Phrao words to Madonna songs as she is obsessed with Madonna, when a little group started forming round us. Seemed to be considered some kind of goddess as knew words to *Immaculate Collection* all the way through. Ended up being forced by popular demand to perform "Like a Virgin" standing on a pile of mattresses wearing the Wonderbra and sarong and using a Tampax as a microphone at which point the guard started shouting in a high-pitched voice. Looked up to see the representative to the British consul had just been let in.

"Ah, Charlie," I said graciously, getting down off the mattress and hurrying towards him, whilst trying to pull the sarong up over the bra and retain my dignity. "So glad you've come! We've got lots to talk about!"

Charlie did not appear to know which way to look but seemed to keep plumping for the Wonderbra direction. He brought me a kit from the British Embassy with water, biscuits, sandwiches, insect repellent, some more pens and paper and, best of all, soap.

Was completely overcome. Was the best present I had ever had in life.

"Thank you, thank you, I can't thank you enough," I said emotionally, on the verge of flinging my arms round him, and taking him roughly against the bars.

"No problem, standard issue, actually. Would have brought you one before but all the bloody totty in the office kept woofing the sandwiches."

"I see," I said. "Now, Charlie. Jed."

Blank stare.

"You remember Jed?" I said in a Listen-with-Mother voice. "The guy who gave me the bag? It's very important that we catch him. I'd like you to take down lots more details about him and then send me someone from the Drug Squad who can spearhead the search."

"Right," said Charlie seriously yet at the same time deeply unconvincingly. "Right."

"Now come along," I said, turning into a Peggy Ashcroft–style figure from the last days of the Raj who was about to rap him over the head with an umbrella. "If the Thai authorities are so keen to set an example over drugs that they're locking up innocent Westerners without trial, they've got to at least show an interest in catching the drug traffickers."

Charlie stared up at me thickly. "Yar, right, right," he said, furrowing his brows and nodding heartily, not the faintest glimmer of understanding illuminating his gaze.

After had explained it a few more times Charlie suddenly saw the light.

"Yar, yar. See what you mean. Yar. They've got to go after the guy that put you in here because otherwise it looks as though they're not making an effort."

"Exactly!" I said, beaming, delighted at my handiwork.

"Right, right," said Charlie, getting to his feet, still wearing his very earnest expression. "I'm going to get them to get moving on this right now."

Was watching him leave, marveling at how such a creature could have risen through the ranks of the British diplomatic service. I suddenly had a brain wave.

"Charlie?" I said.

"Yar," he said, looking down to check that his flies weren't undone.

"What does your father do?"

"Dad?" Charlie's face brightened. "Oh, he works in the Foreign Office. Bloody old fart."

"Is he a politician?"

"No, civil servant actually: Foreign Office."

Checking swiftly that the guards weren't looking, I leaned forward.

"How's your career going here?"

"Bit bloody static, to be perfectly honest," he said cheerily. "Black bloody hole of Calcutta, unless you get down to the islands of course. Oh sorry."

"Wouldn't it be really good for you if you pulled off a diplomatic coup?" I began temptingly. "Why don't you just give your dad a little call . . ."

~ **MONDAY 25 AUGUST**

100 lbs. (attention-seeking thinness), no. of—oh fuck it, brain has dissolved. Good for slimming, surely.

Noon. Bad, low day. Must have been mad to think I could influence anything. Am bitten to death by mosquitoes and fleas. Am nauseous and feeble with constant diarrhea, which is difficult in view of potty situation. In a way is quite good, though, as light-headedness makes everything unreal: much better than reality. Wish could sleep. So hot. Maybe have got malaria.

2 p.m. Bloody Jed. I mean how could anyone be so . . . ? But mustn't hold on to resentments or will harm self. Detach. I do not wish him ill, I do not wish him well. I detach.

2:01 p.m. Bloody fucking dog pig black-livered bastard from hell. I hope his face gets put on a porcupine.

6 p.m. Result! Result! An hour ago the guard came in and hustled me out of the cell. Fantastic to get out and away from the stink. Was taken to a small interview room with a wood-effect Formica table, a gray metal filing cabinet and a copy of a Japanese gay porn magazine, which the guard hurriedly removed as a short, distinguished middle-aged Thai man entered and introduced himself as Dudwani.

He turned out to be Drug Squad and a pretty hard nut. Good old Charlie.

I started on the details of the story, the flights Jed had arrived on and probably left on, the bag, the description of Jed.

"So surely you can trace him from this?" I concluded. "There must be his fingerprints on the bag."

"Oh, we know where he is," he said dismissively. "And he has no fingerprints." Ieuw. No fingerprints. Like having no nipples or something.

"So why haven't you captured him?"

"He is in Dubai," he said dispassionately.

Suddenly I felt really quite annoyed.

"Oh, he's in Dubai, is he?" I said. "And you know all about him. And you know he did it. And you know I didn't do it and he made it look as though I did and I didn't. But you go home to your lovely saté sticks and wife and family in the evening and I'm stuck here for the rest of my childbearing years for something I didn't do just because you can't be bothered to get someone to confess to something I didn't do."

He looked at me in consternation.

"Why don't you get him to confess?" I said.

"He is in Dubai."

"Well, get somebody else to confess, then."

"Miss Jones, in Thailand, we . . ."

"Someone must have seen him break into the hut or broke in for him. Someone must have sewn the drugs into the lining. It was done with a sewing machine. Go investigate it like you're supposed to do."

"We are doing everything we can," he said coldly. "Our government takes any breach of the drug codes very seriously."

"And my government takes the protection of its citizens very seriously," I said, thinking for a moment of Tony Blair and imagining him striding in and coshing the Thai official on the head.

The Thai man cleared his throat to speak. "We . . ."

"And I am a journalist," I interrupted him. "On one of Great Britain's top television current affairs programs," I said, trying to fight back a vision of Richard Finch going "I'm thinking beer-drinking snails, I'm thinking skateboarding ducks, I'm thinking . . ."

"They are planning a vigorous campaign on my behalf."

Mental cut to Richard Finch: "Oh, Bridget droopy bikini hasn't come back from her holiday, has she? Snogging on the beach, forgot to get the plane."

"I have connections in the highest ranks of government and I *think*, given the current climate"—I paused to give him a meaning-ful stare, I mean the current climate's always *something*, isn't it?—"it would look very bad indeed in our media if I were imprisoned in these frankly appalling conditions for a crime I plainly and by your own admission did not commit, while the police force here are fail-ing to enforce their own laws with their own people and properly investigate the crime."

Gathering my sarong around me with tremendous dignity, I sat back and gave him a cool stare.

The official shuffled in his seat, looked at his papers. Then he looked up, pen poised.

"Miss Jones, can we go back to the moment at which you real-ized your hut had been broken into?"

Hah!

~ **WEDNESDAY 27 AUGUST**

112 lbs., cigarettes 2 (but at hideous price), fantasies involving Mark Darcy/Colin Firth/Prince William bursting in saying: "In the name of God and England, release my future wife!": constant.

Worrying two days with nothing. No word, no visits, just constant requests to perform Madonna songs. Repeated reading of "If" only means of keeping nerve. Then this morning Charlie appeared—in a new mood! Extremely earnest, top level and overconfident, with another kit containing cream cheese sandwiches that—given earlier flight of fantasy about in-jail impregnation—found self not really wanting to eat.

"Yar. Things are starting to move," said Charlie with the heavy air of a government agent burdened with explosive MI5 secrets. "Bloody good actually. We've had movements from the Foreign Office."

Trying not to think about tiny top-level turds in boxes, I said, "Did you speak to your dad?"

"Yar, yar," he said. "They know all about it."

"Has it been in the papers?" I said excitedly.

"No, no. Hush-hush. Don't want to rock the boat. Anyway. There's some mail for you. Your friends got it to Dad. Bloody attractive actually, Dad says."

I opened the big brown Foreign Office envelope, hands shaking. First was a letter from Jude and Shaz, rather carefully written almost in code, as if they thought spies might read it.

> Bridge,
>   Don't worry, we love you. We're gonna get you out of there. Jed tracked down. Mark Darcy helping (!).

Heart leaped. Was best news possible (apart, obviously, from ten-year jail sentence being lifted).

> Remember Inner Poise and diet potential of jail. 192 soon. Repeat do not worry. Girls on top.
>
> All our love,
> Jude and Shaz

Looked at letter, blinking with emotion, then tore eagerly at the other envelope. Maybe from Mark?

Was written on reverse of long concertina of views of Lake Windermere and said:

> Visiting Granny in St. Anne's and touring the Lakes. Weather a bit mixed but super factory shops. Daddy has

bought a sheepskin gilet! Could you call Una and check
that she's put the timer on?

Love,

Mum

∿ SATURDAY 30 AUGUST

112 lbs. (hope), alcohol units 6 (hurrah!), cigarettes 0, calories 8,755 (hurrah!), no. of times checked bag to make sure no drugs in same 24.

6 a.m. On plane. Going home! Free! Thin! Clean! Shiny-haired! In own clean clothes! Hurrah! Have got tabloids and *Marie Claire* and *Hello!* All is marvelous.

6:30 a.m. Unaccountable plummet. Is disorientating being squashed on plane again in darkness with everyone asleep. Feel huge pressure to be euphoric but feel really freaked out. Guards came last night and called me out. Was taken to room and given clothes back, met by a different embassy official called Brian with strange short-sleeved nylon shirt and wire specs. He said there'd been a "development" in Dubai and pressure from the highest level in the Foreign Office and they had to get me out of the country immediately before the climate changed.

Was all strange in the Embassy. No one there except Brian who showed me straight to a very bare old-fashioned bathroom where there was a little pile of all my things and said to have a shower and change, but be really quick.

Couldn't believe how thin I had got, but there was no hair dryer so hair was still pretty mad. Obviously not important but would have been good to look nice on return. Was starting with makeup when Brian knocked on the door saying that we really had to leave.

Was all a blur, rushed out in steamy night to car, rushing through streets full of goats and tuk-tuks and honking and people with entire families on one bicycle.

Couldn't believe cleanliness of airport. Did not have to go

through normal channel but some special Embassy route, everything all stamped and cleared. When got to the gate, whole area was empty, plane ready to leave with just one guy in a luminous yellow jacket waiting for us.

"Thank you," I said to Brian. "Thank Charlie for me."

"I will," he said wryly. "Or his dad anyway." Then he handed me my passport and shook my hand in really quite a respectful way such as was not at all used to even before incarceration.

"You did very well," he said. "Well done, Miss Jones."

10 a.m. Just been to sleep. Really excited about return. Have actually had spiritual epiphany. Everything is going to be different now.

New post–spiritual epiphany life resolutions:

1. Not start smoking or drinking again as have not had drink for eleven days and only two cigarettes (do not want to go into what had to do to get them). Though may just have small bottle of wine now. As obviously need to celebrate. Yes.

2. Not rely on men but on self. (Unless Mark Darcy wants to go back out with me. Oh God, hope so. Hope he realizes still love him. Hope it was him who got me out. Hope he is there at airport.)

3. Not bother about stupid things e.g. weight, mad hair, who Jude invited to wedding.

4. Not discard advice of self-help books, poems etc. but limit it to key things e.g. optimism, not freaking out, forgiving (though maybe not Fucking Jed as shall now be known).

5. Be more careful about men as are plainly—if evidence of Fucking Jed not to mention Daniel anything to go by—dangerous.

6. Not take shit from people i.e. Richard Finch, but have confidence in self-reliance.

7. Be more spiritual and stick to spiritual principles.

Goody, now can look at *Hello!* and tabloids.

11:15 a.m. Does not seem to be anything in papers about me— though as Charlie said, it was all hush-hush and kept under wraps by government so as not to interfere with Thai relations, imports of peanut sauce etc.

11:45 a.m. Mmm. Wine delicious after so long. Really goes to head.

12:30 p.m. Yuk. Feel slightly sick after tabloid gorging. Had forgotten depressed, ashamed feeling you get afterwards like hangover—and sense of world being turned into same horrible tale over and over again where people get set up as good then turn out to be evil and bad.

Particularly enjoyed, at time, priest-turned-shagging-fuckwit story. Is always so enjoyable when other people behave badly. Feel, however, that founders of support group for victims of shagging priest (because "women who have relationships with priests often have no one to turn to") are being rather partisan. What about others who have no one to turn to? Should surely also be support groups for women who have been victims of shagging Tory ministers, members of British national sporting teams who have slept with members of the Royal family, Roman Catholic clergy who have slept with celebrities or members of the Royal family, and celebrities who have slept with members of the public who have confessed their story to members of the Roman Catholic clergy who have then sold the story to the Sunday papers. Maybe I will sell story to Sunday papers and that is where money will come from. No, that is wrong, you see spirituality has already been infested by tabloid mentality.

Maybe will write book though. Maybe will get hero's return in England like Beirut hostage John McCarthy and write a book called *Some Other Cloud Formation* or other meteorological phenomenon. Maybe will get hero's welcome with Mark, Jude, Shazzer, Tom, and parents and crowds of waiting photographers and Richard Finch grovelingly begging for exclusive interview. Had better not get too pissed. Hope am not going to go all mad. Feel like I should be met by police or counselors or something and taken to a secret base for debriefing. Think will have little sleep.

9 p.m. (UK time now.) Arrived at Heathrow with clouting post-flight hangover trying to purge clothes of remnants of bread and pink toothpaste fraudulently offered as airline dessert, rehearsing lines, in preparation for waiting press phalanx—"It was a nightmare. A living nightmare. A thunderbolt out of the blue. I feel no hatred (bitterness?) for if others are warned of the dangers of one's friends sleeping with strange men, my incarceration will not have been wasted (in vain?)." Whole time, however, did not think waiting phalanx would actually be there. Passed through customs without incident and looked around excitedly for familiar faces, only to be engulfed by—well, press phalanx. Crowd of photographers and journalists with flashguns. Mind went completely blank and could not think what to say or do except parrot "No comment," in manner of government minister who has been caught shagging prostitute, and keep walking, pushing the trolley, thinking my legs were going to collapse under me. Then suddenly the trolley was taken away, and someone put their arm round me saying, "It's all right, Bridge, we're here, we've got you, it's all right."

It was Jude and Shazzer.

⌢ **SUNDAY 31 AUGUST**

114 lbs. (Yess! Yess! Triumphant culmination of 18-year diet, though perhaps at unwarranted cost), alcohol units 4, calories 8,995 (deserved, surely), progress on hole in wall made by Gary the Builder 0.

2 a.m. My flat. So nice to be home. So nice to see Jude and Shazzer again. At airport, policeman took us through the crowd to an interview room where there were Drug Squad people and a man from the Foreign Office who started asking lots of questions.

"Look, can't this bloody well wait?" burst out Shaz indignantly after about a minute. "Can't you see the state she's in?"

Men seemed to think it was necessary to carry on but eventually became so terrified of Shazzer's growls of "Are you men or monsters?" and threats to report them to Amnesty International that they gave us a policeman to take us back to London.

"Just be careful who you get mixed up with next time, ladies," said the Foreign Office man.

"Oh please," said Shaz, just as Jude was saying, "Oh quite right, Officer," and launching into a professional woman vote-of-thanks-style speech.

Back in my flat, the fridge was full of food, there were pizzas waiting to go in the oven, Milk Tray and Dairy Box, smoked salmon pinwheels, packets of Minstrels, and bottles of Chardonnay. There was a big sign on the polythene hole in the wall saying "Welcome back, Bridget." And a fax from Tom—who has *moved in* with the customs guy he flirted with in San Francisco—saying:

> DARLING, DRUGS ARE POWDER OF SATAN. JUST SAY NO!
> ASSUME YOU WILL NOW BE THINNEST EVER. GIVE UP ALL
> MEN IMMEDIATELY AND BECOME GAY. COME HERE AND
> LIVE WITH US IN CALIFORNIAN GAY SEX-SANDWICH THREE-
> SOME. HAVE BROKEN JEROME'S HEART! HAHAHAHA.
> CALL ME. LOVE YOU. WELCOME BACK.

Also Jude and Shaz had cleaned all the packing mess up from the bedroom floor and put clean sheets on the bed and fresh flowers and Silk Cut on the bedside table. Love the lovely girls. And the lovely self-obsessed Tom.

They ran me a bath and brought me in a glass of champagne and I showed them my flea bites. Then I got into my pajamas and we all sat on the bed with cigarettes, champagne and Cadbury's Milk Tray and started going through everything that had happened.

"I knew something was wrong when I got to the gate," Shaz was saying. "But the airline people wouldn't tell me what had happened and insisted I got on the plane, then they wouldn't let me get off again, and the next thing we were taxiing along the runway."

"So when did you find out?" I said, polishing off my Chardonnay, at which Jude immediately held out the bottle to pour me another. Was marvelous, marvelous.

"Not till we landed," said Shaz. "It was just the most terrible flight. I was hoping you'd just missed it, but they were being really odd and sniffy with me. Then the second I got off the plane . . ."

"She got arrested!" said Jude gleefully. "Pissed as a fart."

"Oh, no," I said. "And you were hoping Jed would be there."

"That bastard," said Shaz, coloring.

Somehow thought I'd better not mention Jed again.

"He had someone behind you in the queue at Bangkok," Jude explained. "Apparently he was waiting at Heathrow for a call and immediately got on a plane to Dubai."

Turned out Shaz called Jude from the police station and they quickly got on to the Foreign Office.

"Then nothing happened," said Jude. "They started talking about you being in for ten years."

"I remember." I shuddered.

"We called Mark on the Wednesday night and he immediately got on to all his contacts in Amnesty and Interpol. We tried to get hold of your mum but the answerphone said she was touring the Lakes. We thought about ringing Geoffrey and Una but we decided everyone would just get hysterical and it wouldn't help."

"Very wise," I said.

"On the first Friday we heard you'd been transferred to proper jail . . ." said Shaz.

"And Mark got on a plane to Dubai."

"He went to Dubai? For me?"

"He was fantastic," said Shaz.

"And where is he? I left him a message but he hasn't rung back."

"He's still there," said Jude. "Then on Monday we got a call from the Foreign Office and everything seemed to have changed."

"That must have been when Charlie talked to his dad!" I said excitedly.

"They let us send out your mail . . ."

"And then on Tuesday we heard they'd got Jed . . ."

"And Mark called on Friday and said they'd got a confession . . ."

"Then the call came out of the blue on Saturday that you were on the plane!"

"Hurrah!" we all said, clinking glasses. Was desperate to get on to subject of Mark but did not want to appear shallow and ungrateful for all the girls had done.

"So is he still going out with Rebecca?" I burst out.

"No!" said Jude. "He's not! He's not!"

"But what happened?"

"We don't really know," said Jude. "One minute it was all on, next thing Mark wasn't going to Tuscany and—"

"You'll never guess who Rebecca's going out with now," interrupted Shaz.

"Who?"

"It's someone you know."

"Not Daniel?" I said, feeling an odd mixture of emotions.

"No."

"Colin Firth?"

"No."

"Phew. Tom?"

"No. Think of someone else you know quite well. Married."

"My dad? Magda's Jeremy?"

"Now you're getting warm."

"What? It's not Geoffrey Alconbury, is it?"

"No." Shaz giggled. "He's married to Una and he's gay."

"Giles Benwick," said Jude suddenly.

"Who?" I gibbered.

"Giles Benwick," confirmed Shaz. "You know Giles, for God's sake, the one who works with Mark, who you rescued from suicide at Rebecca's."

"He had that thing about you."

"He and Rebecca both stayed holed up in Gloucestershire

after their accidents reading self-help books and now—they are together."

"They are as one," added Jude.

"They are joined in the act of love," expanded Shaz.

There was a pause while we all looked at each other, stunned at this strange act of the heavens.

"The world has gone mad," I burst out with a mixture of wonderment and fear. "Giles Benwick isn't handsome, he isn't rich."

"Well, actually he is," murmured Jude.

"But he isn't someone else's boyfriend. He isn't a status symbol in any normal Rebecca way."

"Apart from being very rich," said Jude.

"Yet Rebecca has chosen him."

"That's right, that's exactly right," said Shaz, excitedly. "Strange times! Strange times indeed!"

"Soon Prince Philip will ask me to be his girlfriend, and Tom will be going out with the queen," I cried.

"Not Pretentious Jerome, but our own, dear queen," clarified Shaz.

"Bats will start eating the sun," I expanded. "Horses will be born with tails on their heads, and cubes of frozen urine will land on our roof terraces offering us cigarettes."

"Strange times," pronounced Shaz, shaking her head with heavy portentousness. "Strange times indeed."

Think I must have just fallen asleep because now it is all dark, Jude and Shaz are not here but have left a note on my pillow saying to call them when I wake up. They are both staying at Shazzer's because Jude's flat is being done up so she and Vile Richard can live together after the wedding. Hope she has got a better builder than me. Hole in wall entirely unchanged.

1 2

Strange Times

115 lbs. (will definitely stop gorging tomorrow), alcohol units 6 (must not start drinking too much), cigarettes 27 (must not start smoking too much), calories 6,285 (must not start eating too much).

8 a.m. My flat. Determined now not to sink back into old ways, spending entire life checking answerphone and waiting for Mark to ring, but to be calm and centered.

8:05 a.m. But why did Mark split up with Rebecca? Why is she going out with speccy Giles Benwick? WHY? WHY? Did he go to Dubai because he still loves me? But why hasn't he rung me back? Why? Why?

Anyway. All that is irrelevant to me now. I am working on myself. I am going to get my legs waxed.

10 a.m. Returned to flat to find answerphone flashing.

Was Mark! He sounded very faint and crackly. "Bridget . . . only just got the news. I'm delighted you're free. Delighted. I'll be back later in the . . ." There was a loud hiss on the line, then it clicked off.

Ten minutes later, the phone rang.

"Oh, hello, darling, guess what?"

My mother. My own mother! Felt great overwhelming rush of love.

"What?" I said, feeling tears welling up.

"'Go quietly amidst the noise and haste and remember what peace there may be in silence.'"

There was a long pause.

"Mum?" I said eventually.

"Shhh, darling, silence." (More pause.) "'Remember what peace there may be in silence.'"

I took a big breath, tucked the phone under my chin, and carried on making the coffee. You see what I have learned is the importance of detaching from other people's lunacy as one has enough to worry about keeping oneself on course. Just then the mobile started ringing.

Trying to ignore the first phone, which had started vibrating and yelling: "Bridget, you'll never find equilibrium if you don't learn to work with silence," I pressed OK on the mobile. It was my dad.

"Ah, Bridget," he said in a stiff, military-style voice. "Will you speak to your mother on the land line? Seems to have got herself worked up into a bit of a state."

She was in a state? Didn't they care about me at all? Their own flesh and blood?

There was a series of sobs, shrieks and unexplained crashes on the "land line." "OK, Dad, bye," I said, and picked up the real phone again.

"Darling," croaked Mum, in a hoarse, self-pitying whisper. "There's something I have to tell you. I cannot keep it from my family and loved ones any longer."

Trying not to dwell on the distinction between "family" and "loved ones," I said brightly, "Well! Don't feel you have to tell me if you don't want to."

"What would you have me do?" she yelled histrionically. "Live a lie? I'm an addict, darling, an addict!"

I racked my brains as to what she could have decided she's addicted to. My mum has never drunk more than a single glass of cream sherry since Mavis Enderbury got drunk at her twenty-first birthday party in 1952 and had to be taken home on the crossbar of a bicycle belonging to someone called "Peewee." Her drug intake is limited to the occasional Fisherman's Friend in response to a tickly cough triggered during the biannual performances of Kettering Amateur Dramatic Society.

"I'm an addict," she said again, then paused dramatically.

"Right," I said. "An addict. And what exactly are you addicted to?"

"Relationships," she said. "I'm a relationship addict, darling. I'm co-dependent."

I crashed my head straight down on to the table in front of me.

"Thirty-six years with Daddy!" she said. "And I never understood."

"But, Mum, being married to someone doesn't mean—"

"Oh no, I'm not co-dependent on Daddy," she said. "I'm co-dependent on fun. I've told Daddy I . . . Ooh, must whizz. It's time for my affirmations."

I sat staring at the cafetière, mind reeling. Didn't they know what had happened to me? Had she finally gone over the edge?

The phone rang again. It was my dad.

"Sorry about that."

"What's going on? Are you with Mum now?"

"Well, yes, in a manner of . . . She's gone off to some class or other."

"Where are you?"

"We're in a . . . well, it's a sort of . . . well . . . It's called 'Rainbows.'"

Moonies? I thought. Scientologists? Est?

"It's, um, it's a rehab."

Oh my God. It turns out it wasn't just me who was starting to worry about Dad's drinking. Mum said he went off into Blackpool one night when they were visiting Granny in St. Anne's and turned up at the old people's home completely plastered holding a bottle of Famous Grouse, and a plastic model of Scary Spice with a pair of wind-up false teeth attached to her breast. Doctors were called and they went straight from Granny in St. Anne's last week to this rehab place, where Mum, as ever it seems, was determined not to be up-staged.

"They don't seem to think it's a major problem with the old Scotch. They said I've been masking my pain or some such about all these Julios and Wellingtons. Plan is we're supposed to indulge her addiction to 'fun' together."

Oh God.

Think it is best not to tell Mum and Dad about Thailand, just for the time being.

10 p.m. Still my flat. There, you see. Hurrah! Have spent all day tidying up and sorting out and everything is under control. All the mail is done (well, put in pile anyway). Also Jude is right. Is ridiculous to have bloody great hole in the wall after four months and a miracle no one has climbed up the back wall and broken in. Am not going to engage with Gary the Builder's nonsensical excuses anymore. Have got lawyer friend of Jude's to write him a letter. You see what one can do when one is empowered new person. Is marvelous . . .

Dear Sir,

We act for Ms. Bridget Jones.

We are instructed that our client entered into a verbal contract with you on or about 5 March 1997 further to which you agreed to construct an extension to our client's flat (consisting of a second study/bedroom and a roof terrace) for a (quoted) price of £7,000. Our client paid £3,500 to you on 21 April 1997 in advance of work being commenced. It was an express term of the contract that work would be completed within six weeks of this first payment being made.

You commenced work on 25 April 1997 by knocking a large 5 ft. x 8 ft. hole in the exterior wall of our client's flat. You then failed to progress the work for a period of some weeks. Our client attempted to contact you by telephone on a number of occasions leaving messages, which you did not return. You eventually returned to our client's flat on 30 April 1997 while she was out at work. However, rather than continuing with the work you had agreed to do, you simply covered the hole you had made in her exterior wall with thick polythene. Since then, you have failed to return to finish the work and have failed to respond to any of our client's numerous telephone messages requesting you to do so.

The hole you have left in the exterior wall of our client's flat renders it cold, insecure and uninsured against burglary. Your failure to carry out and complete the work you agreed to undertake constitutes the clearest possible breach of your contract with our client. You have therefore repudiated the contract, which repudiation is accepted by our client . . .

Blah, blah, rudiate woodiate gibberish gibberish . . . entitled to recover costs . . . directly responsible for any losses . . . unless we hear from you within seven days of this letter with confirmation that you will compensate our client for the losses suffered . . . as a result we are instructed to issue proceedings for breach of contract against you without further notice.

Ha. Ahahahaha! That will teach him a lesson he won't forget. Has gone in post so he will get it tomorrow. That will show him I mean business and am not going to be pushed around and disrespected anymore.

Right. Now, am going to take half an hour to think up some ideas for morning meeting.

10:15 p.m. Hmmm. Maybe need to get newspapers in order to get ideas. Bit late, though.

10:30 p.m. Actually, am not going to bother about Mark Darcy. One does not need a man. Whole thing used to be that men and women got together because women could not survive without them but now—hah! Have own flat (even if hole-filled), friends, income and job (at least till tomorrow) so hah! Hahahahaha!

10:40 p.m. Right. Ideas.

10:41 p.m. Oh God. Really feel like having sex, though. Have not had sex for ages.

10:45 p.m. Maybe something on New Labour New Britain? Like after the honeymoon, when you've been going out with someone for six months and start getting annoyed with them for not doing the washing up? Scrapping student grants already? Hmm. Was so easy to have sex and go out with people when one was a student. Maybe they do not deserve bloody grants when they are just having sex all the time.

> Number of months have not had sex: 6
> Number of seconds have not had sex:
> *(How many seconds are there in a day?)*
> $60 \times 60 = 3{,}600 \times 24 =$
> *(Maybe will get calculator.)*
> $86{,}400 \times 28 = 2{,}419{,}200$
> $\times 6$ months $= 14{,}515{,}200$
> *Fourteen million five hundred and fifteen thousand two hundred seconds have not had sex in.*

11 p.m. Maybe I will just, like, NEVER HAVE SEX AGAIN.

11:05 p.m. Wonder what happens if you do not have sex? Is it good for you or bad?

11:06 p.m. Maybe you just, like, *seal up*.

11:07 p.m. Look, am not supposed to be thinking about sex. Am spiritual.

11:08 p.m. And then surely it is good for one to procreate.

11:10 p.m. Germaine Greer did not have children. But then what does that prove?

11:15 p.m. Right. New Labour, New . . .
Oh God. Have become a celibate.
Celibacy! The New Celibates! I mean if it's happening to me, chances are it's happening to lots of other people as well. Isn't that the whole point about zeitgeist?

"Suddenly there is less sex everywhere." Hate, though, this about popular news coverage. Reminds me of when there was an article in *The Times* that started: "Suddenly there are more Dining Rooms everywhere," the same day as there was one in the *Telegraph* on "Whatever Happened to the Dining Room?"

Right, must go to bed. Determined to be very early on first day of new me at work.

~ **WEDNESDAY 3 SEPTEMBER**

117 lbs. (gaah, gaah), calories 4,955, no. of seconds since had sex 14,601,600 (yesterday's figure + 86,400—a day's worth).

7 p.m. Got into office early, first day back since Thailand, expecting new concern and respect to find Richard Finch in traditional foul mood: petulant, obsessively chain-smoking and chewing with crazed look in his eye.

"Ho!" he said as I walked in. "Ho! Ahahahahaha! What've we got in that bag, then? Opium, is it? Skunk? Have we got crack in the lining? Have we brought in some Purple Hearts? Some E for the class? Is it poppers? Is it some nice speedy speed? Hasheeeesh? Some Rokeycokey cokey? *OHHHHH okeecokeycokeeee*," he started to sing maniacally. "*Oooh okeecokeycokeeee. Ooooh! okeecokeycokeeee!*" An idiotic gleam in his eye, he grabbed the two researchers next to him and started rushing forward, yelling, "Knees bent, arms stretched, it's all in Brid-get's bag, Ra-Ra!"

Realizing our executive producer was coming down from some drug-induced frenzy, I smiled beatifically and ignored him.

"Oh, little Miss Hoity-toity today, are we? Oooh! Come on, everybody. Bridget Hoity-bottom-just-out-of-prison's here. Let's start. Let's startitdeedoodaa."

Really, this was not at all what I had in mind. Everyone began to converge on the table, looking from the clock to me resentfully. I mean it was only twenty bloody past nine: the meeting wasn't supposed to start till half past. Just because I start coming in early doesn't mean the meeting has to start early instead of late.

"Right then, Brrrrrridget! Ideas. What ideas have we got today to delight the breathless nation? Ten Top Smuggling Tips from the Laydee in the Know? Britain's Best Bras for stashing Charlie in the booster pads?"

If you can trust yourself when all men doubt you, I thought. Oh fuck it, I'm just going to sock him in the mouth.

He looked at me, chewing, grinning expectantly. Funnily enough the usual sniggers round the table weren't happening. In fact the whole Thailand interlude seemed to have brought a new respect from my colleagues that I was naturally delighted by.

"What about New Labour—after the honeymoon?"

Richard Finch crashed his head down on to the table and started snoring.

"Actually, I have got another idea," I said, after a casual pause. "About sex," I added, at which Richard sprang to attention. (I mean just his head. At least I hope.)

"Well? Are you going to share it with us—or save it, for your chummies in the Drug Squad?"

"Celibacy," I said.

There was an impressed silence.

Richard Finch was staring at me bulgy-eyed as if he couldn't believe it.

"Celibacy?"

"Celibacy." I nodded smugly. "The new celibacy."

"What—you mean monks and nuns?" said Richard Finch.

"No. Celibacy."

"Ordinary people not having sex," Patchouli cut in, looking at him insolently.

Really there was a very changed atmosphere around the table. Maybe Richard had begun to go so far over the edge that no one was sucking up to him anymore.

"What, because of some Tantric, Buddhist thing?" said Richard sniggering, one leg twitching convulsively as he chewed.

"No," said sexy Matt, carefully looking down at his notebook. "Ordinary people, like us, who don't have sex for long periods of time."

I shot a look at Matt, just as he was doing the same to me.

"What? You lot?" said Richard, looking at us incredulously. "You're all in the first flush of youth—well, except Bridget."

"Thanks," I muttered.

"You're all at it like rabbits every night! Aren't you? *In, out, in, out and shake it all about,*" he sang. "*You do the Okeekokee and you turn her round, and do it to her from—be-hind! Aren't* you?"

There was a certain degree of shuffling round the table.

"Aren't you?"

More pause.

"Who here hasn't had sex in the last week?"

Everyone stared hard at their notepads.

"OK. Who *has* had sex in the last week?"

No one raised their hand.

"I don't believe this. All right. Which one of you has had sex in the last month?"

Patchouli raised her hand. As did Harold, who beamed at us all smugly from behind his spectacles. Probably lying. Or maybe just puppy-love-type shagging.

"So the rest of you . . . Jesus. You're a bunch of freaks. It can't be because you're working too hard. Celibacy. Pah! Talk about bums off seats. You lot had better come up with something better than this for the rest of the season. None of this limp no-sex bollocks."

118 lbs. (this must stop or jail sentence will have been wasted), no. of ways imagined killing Richard Finch 32 (this too must stop otherwise deterrent value of jail sentences annihilated), no. of black jackets considered buying 23, no. of seconds not had sex 14,688,000.

6 p.m. V. happy about return-to-school-autumnal-style feel of world. Going to go late-night shopping on way home: not to buy anything as financial crisis, just to try on new autumn wardrobe. V. excited and determined this year to be better at shopping i.e. (a) not panic and find only thing able to buy is black jacket as only so many black jackets one girl needs and (b) get money from somewhere. Maybe Buddha?

8 p.m. Angus Steak House, Oxford Street. Uncontrollable panic attack. Shops all seem to have just slightly different versions of each thing. Throws self into thought fug with mind unable to settle until has encompassed and catalogued all, for example, available black nylon jackets: French Connection one at £129 or high-class Michael Kors (tiny, square quilted one) at £400. Black nylon jackets in Hennes are only £39.99. Could for example buy ten Hennes black nylon jackets for price of one Michael Kors one but then wardrobe would be more riddled with more black jackets than ever and cannot buy any of them anyway.

Maybe whole image is at fault. Maybe should start wearing brightly colored pantomime outfits in manner of Zandra Rhodes or Su Pollard. Or have a capsule wardrobe and just buy three very classy pieces and wear them all the time. (But what if spill or throw up on them?)

Right. Calm, calm. This is what need to buy:

Black nylon jacket (1 only).
Torque. Or maybe Tong or Tonk? Anyway, choker thing
    to go round neck.

"Boot leg" brown trousers (depending what "boot leg"
should turn out to mean).
Brown suit for work (or similar).
Shoes.

Was nightmare in shoe shop. Just trying on brown square-toed high-
heeled '70s-style shoes in Office feeling v. déjà-vu-esque for all those
back-to-school times buying new shoes and fighting with bloody
Mum about what they were allowed to be like. Then suddenly had
horrifying realization: was not freaky sense of déjà vu—they were
exactly the same shoes I had in Six Lower from Freeman Hardy
Willis.

Suddenly felt like innocent dupe or stooge of fashion designers
who cannot be arsed to think of new things. Worse, am now so old
that young fashion buying generation no longer remember wearing
things I wore as teenager. At last realize point at which ladies start
going to Jaeger for two-pieces—when do not want to be reminded
of lost youth by high-street fashion anymore. Have now reached
said point. Am going to abandon Kookaï, Agnès B, Whistles etc. in
favor of Country Casuals and spirituality. Also cheaper. Am going
home.

9 p.m. My flat. Feel very strange and empty. Is all very well thinking everything is going to be different when you come back but
then it is all the same. Suppose I have to make it different. But what
am I going to do with my life?

I know. Will eat some cheese.

The thing is, as it says in *Buddhism: The Drama of the Moneyed Monk*,
the atmosphere and events around you are created by the atmosphere within you. So it is no wonder all that bad stuff—Thailand,
Daniel, Rebecca etc.—happened. Must start being more inner-
poised and spiritual epiphanied, then will start attracting peaceful
things and kind, loving, well-balanced people. Like Mark Darcy.

Mark Darcy—when he returns—is going to see the new me, calm
and centered, attracting peace and order all around me.

119 lbs., cigarettes 0 (triumph), no. of seconds since had sex 14,774,400 (disaster), (must treat both impostors just the same).

8:15 a.m. Right. Up bright and early. You see, this is important: steal a march on the day!

8:20 a.m. Ooh, a package has come for me. Maybe a gift!

8:30 a.m. Mmm. Is in gift box with roses on. Maybe from Mark Darcy! Maybe he's back.

8:40 a.m. Is a lovely little gold truncated ballpoint with my name on it. Maybe from Tiffany's! With red tip. Maybe is lipstick.

8:45 a.m. That is weird. Is no note in there. Maybe promotional lipstick from PR company.

8:50 a.m. But is not lipstick as is solid. Maybe is ballpoint. With my name on it! Maybe invitation to party in manner of forward-thinking PR firm—perhaps launch of new magazine called *Lipstick!*, maybe product of Tina Brown!—and the invitation to glittering party will follow.

Yes, you see. Think will go to Coins and have cappuccino. Though not, of course, chocolate croissant.

9 a.m. In café now. Hmm. Delighted with the little gift but not sure is ballpoint either. Or at least if is, is very obscurely functioning one.

Later. Oh my God. Had just sat down with cappuccino and chocolate croissant when Mark Darcy came in, just like that, as if not away at all: in his work suit, newly shaved, a little cut on his chin with toilet paper on, as traditional in the mornings. He walked to the takeaway counter and put his briefcase down as if looking around for something or someone. He saw me. There was a long moment when his eyes softened (though not, obviously, melting like goo). He turned to deal with the cappuccino. Quickly made myself even more calm and centered seeming. Then he came towards my table, looking much more businesslike. Felt like throwing my arms round him.

"Hello," he said brusquely. "What have you got there?"—nodding at the gift.

Hardly able to speak with love and happiness, I handed him the box.

"I don't know what it is. I think it might be a ballpoint."

He took the little ballpoint out of the box, turned it round, put it back like, well, a shot, and said, "Bridget, this isn't a promotional pen, it's a fucking bullet."

Later still. OhmyChristalive. Was no time to discuss Thailand, Rebecca, love, anything.

Mark grabbed a napkin, took hold of the lid of the box and replaced it.

"*If you can keep your head when all about you . . .*" I whispered to myself.

"What?"

"Nothing."

"Stay here. Don't touch it. It's a live bullet," said Mark. He slipped out into the street, and glanced up and down in manner of TV detective. Interesting how everything in real-life police drama reminds one of TV, rather in same way picturesque holiday scenes remind one of postcards or . . .

He was back. "Bridget? Have you paid up? What are you doing? Come on."

"Where?"

"The police station."

In the car started to gabble, thanking him for everything he'd done and saying how much the poem had helped me in jail.

"Poem? What poem?" he said, swinging into Kensington Park Road.

"The 'If' poem—you know—*force your heart and nerve and* . . . oh God I'm really sorry you had to go all the way to Dubai, I'm so grateful, I . . ."

He stopped at the lights and turned to me.

"That's absolutely fine," he said gently. "Now stop autowittering gibberish. You've had a big shock. You need to calm down."

Humph. Whole idea was he was supposed to notice how calm and centered I am, not be telling me to calm down. Tried to calm down, but was very difficult when all could think was: someone wants to kill me.

When we got to the police station it was slightly less like a TV drama because everything was tatty and dirty and nobody seemed the slightest bit interested in us. The police officer on the desk tried to make us wait in the waiting room but Mark insisted we were taken upstairs. We ended up sitting in a great big dingy office with nobody in it.

Mark made me tell him everything that had happened in Thailand, asking me if Jed had mentioned anyone he knew in the UK, if the packet had come with the normal post, if I'd noticed anyone strange hanging around since I got back.

Felt a bit stupid telling him about how trusting we'd been with Jed, thinking he was going to tell me off, but he was really sweet.

"The worst you and Shaz could be accused of was breathtaking stupidity," he said. "You did very well in jail, I heard."

Although he was being sweet, he wasn't being . . . well it all seemed on a very businesslike footing, not like he wanted to get back together or talk about anything emotional.

"Do you think you'd better call work?" he said, looking at his watch.

My hand shot to my mouth. Tried to tell self it would not matter whether I still had a job or not if I was dead but it was twenty past ten!

"Don't look like you've just accidentally eaten a child," said Mark laughing. "For once you've got a decent excuse for your pathological lateness."

I picked up the phone and dialed Richard Finch's direct line. He answered straight away.

"Oooh, it's Bridget, is it? Little Miss Celibacy? Two days back and she's playing truant. Where are you, then? Shopping, are we?"

If you can trust yourself when all men doubt you, I thought. *If you can . . .*

"Playing with a candle, are we? Candles out, girls!" He made a loud popping noise.

Stared at phone in horror. Could not work out whether Richard Finch has always been like this and I was different, or whether he was getting into some terrible drug-induced downward spiral.

"Give it to me," said Mark.

"No!" I said, grabbing the phone back and hissing, "I'm a person in my own right."

"Of course you are, darling, just not in your own right mind," murmured Mark.

Darling! He called me darling!

"Bridget? Fallen asleep again, have we? Where are you?" chortled Richard Finch.

"I'm in the police station."

"Ooh, back on the rokeekoke cokee? Jolly good. Got some for me?" he chuckled.

"I've had a death threat."

"Oooh! That's a good one. You'll get a death threat from me in a minute. Hahahaha. Police station, eh? That's what I like to see. Nice stable drug-free respectable employees on my team."

That was it. That was just about enough. I took a big breath.

"Richard," I said grandly. "That, I'm afraid, is like the kettle calling the frying pan dirty bottom. Except that I haven't got a dirty bottom because I don't take drugs. Not like you. Anyway, I'm not coming back. Bye." And I put the phone down. Hah! Hahahaha! I thought briefly before remembering the overdraft. And the magic mushrooms. Except not strictly drugs, as natural mushrooms.

Just then, a policeman appeared, rushing by and completely ignoring us. "Look!" said Mark banging his fist down on the desk.

"We've got a girl with a live bullet with her name on it here. Can we see some action?"

The policeman stopped in his tracks. "Ooh, sorry," he said huffily. "We've had a knifing in Notting Hill. I'm afraid we're very busy with people who've already been murdered." He tossed his head and flounced out.

Ten minutes later the detective who was supposed to be dealing with us came in with a computer printout.

"Hello. I'm DI Kirby," he said without looking at us. He stared at the printout for a while, then up at me, raising his eyebrows.

"This is the Thailand file, I take it?" said Mark, looking over his shoulder. "Oh I see . . . that incident in . . ."

"Well, yes," said the detective.

"No, no, that was just a piece of fillet steak," said Mark.

Had forgotten about that. Six months ago my only contact with the police was to do with traffic offenses and since then I'd been up for suspected harboring of body parts, drug smuggling and now this.

The policeman was looking at Mark oddly.

"It was left in a shopping bag by my mother," I explained, "and was starting to decay."

"You see? There? And this is the Thai report," Mark said, leaning over the form.

The detective put his arm around the form protectively, as if Mark was trying to copy his homework. Just then the phone rang. DI Kirby picked it up.

"I want to be next to the touchline," he said in an exasperated voice. "What's DI fucking Rogers doing there? OK, well, behind the goal then. What?" Could not believe it. They were talking about a football match.

"What did it say about Jed?" I whispered.

"'Jed,' he said his name was, did he?" scoffed Mark. "Roger Dwight, actually."

"OK then, but I want to be behind the Arsenal goal in both halves. Well, I'll switch. No, in front of the crowd. Sorry about that," said DI Kirby, putting the phone down and assuming the sort of overcompensatory efficient air I identified totally with from when I

284

am late for work. "Roger Dwight," the detective said. "It's kind of pointing that way, isn't it?"

"I'd be very surprised if he's managed to organize anything himself," said Mark. "Not from Arabian custody."

"Well, there are ways and means."

Was absolutely infuriating the way Mark was talking to the policeman over my head. Almost as if I was some kind of bimbo or half-wit.

"Excuse me," I said, bristling. "Could I possibly participate in this conversation?"

"Of course," said Mark. "As long as you don't bring up any kettles or frying pans."

Saw the detective looking from one of us to the other with a puzzled expression.

"He could, I guess, have organized someone else to send," said Mark, turning to the detective. "But it seems somewhat unlikely, foolhardy even, given . . ."

"Well, yes, in cases of this kind— Excuse me." DI Kirby picked up the phone. "Right. Well, tell Harrow Road they've already *got* two detective inspectors at the game!" he said petulantly. "Yes. Well, tell DI Rimmington to eff off. Sorry, sir." He put the phone down again and smiled masterfully.

"In cases of this kind . . . ?" I said.

"Yes, it's unlikely that a person with serious intentions would advertise his—"

"You mean they'd just shoot her, right?" said Mark.

Oh *God*.

An hour later the package had gone off to be fingerprinted and DNA'd and I was still being questioned.

"Is there anyone outside from the Thai connection who has a grudge against you, young lady?" said DI Kirby. "An ex-lover perhaps, a rejected suitor?"

Was delighted by being called "young lady." You see may not be in first flush of youth but . . .

"Bridget!" said Mark. "Pay attention! Is there anyone who might want to hurt you?"

"There are lots of people who have hurt me," I said, looking at Mark and racking my brains. "Richard Finch. Daniel—but I don't think either of them would do this," I said uncertainly.

Did Daniel think I'd been talking about that night we were supposed to have dinner? Was he so annoyed about being rejected? Surely that would be a bit of an overreaction? But then maybe Sharon was right about fin-de-millennium males losing their roles.

"Bridget?" said Mark gently. "Whatever you're thinking, I think you should tell DI Kirby."

Was so embarrassing. Ended up going into whole Daniel lingerie and jacket evening while DI Kirby took down details with a poker face. Mark didn't say anything when I was talking but he looked really angry. Noticed the detective kept looking hard at him.

"Have you been involved with any low-life characters at all?" said DI Kirby.

The only person I could think of was Uncle Geoffrey's possible rent boy, but that was ridiculous because the rent boy didn't know me from Adam.

"You're going to have to move out of your flat. Is there anywhere you can go?"

"You can stay with me," Mark said suddenly. My heart leapt. "In one of the spare rooms," he added quickly.

"Could you give me a moment, sir," said the detective inspector. Mark looked dropped on, then said, "Of course," and abruptly left the room.

"I'm not sure staying with Mr. Darcy would be wise, miss," said the detective, glancing at the door.

"Yeah, you might be right," I said, thinking he was taking a fatherly interest and suggesting, as a man, that I should keep the air of mystery and unavailability and let Mark be the pursuer, but then I remembered was not supposed to be thinking like that anymore.

"What exactly is your past relationship with Mr. Darcy?"

"Well!" I said and started the story.

DI Kirby seemed oddly suspicious about the whole thing. The door opened again at the moment he was saying, "So Mr. Darcy *just happened* to be in the coffee bar, did he? On the morning you got the bullet?"

Mark came and stood in front of us.

"OK," he said wearily, looking at me as if to say, "You are the source of all that is opposite to serene." "Print me, DNA me, let's get this out of the way."

"Oh, I'm not saying it was you, sir," said the detective hurriedly. "It's just we have to eliminate the—"

"All right, all right," said Mark. "Let's go get on with it."

1 3

Gaaah!

120 lbs., no. seconds since had sex: no longer care, no. of minutes stayed alive since death threat 34,800 (v.g.).

6 p.m. Shazzer's flat. Looking out of window. It can't be Mark Darcy. That's ridiculous. It can't be. It must be something to do with Jed. I mean, he's probably got a whole ring of contacts here, desperate for drugs whom I have deprived of their livelihood. Or Daniel? But surely he wouldn't do something like that. Maybe it's just some nut. But a nut who knows my name and address? Someone wants to kill me. Someone has bothered to get a live bullet and engrave my name on it.

Must keep calm. Calm, calm. Yes. Must keep head when all around you . . . Wonder if they have bulletproof vests in Kookaï?

Wish Shaz would come back. Am all disorientated. Shazzer's flat is tiny, and messy at the best of times, especially as all open-plan, but with two of them here the floor and every surface seems completely covered with Agent Provocateur bras, leopardskin ankle boots, Gucci carrier bags, faux Prada handbags, tiny Voyage cardigans and odd strappy shoes. V. confused. Maybe will find space somewhere and lie down.

After they took Mark away DI Kirby repeated that I mustn't stay in my flat and took me back there to collect some things, but trouble was did not have anywhere to stay. Mum and Dad were still in rehab. Tom's flat would have been ideal but couldn't find his San Francisco number anywhere. Tried both Jude and Shaz at work but they were both out at lunch.

Was awful really. Was leaving messages everywhere while the police stamped around getting things to fingerprint and looking for clues.

"What's this hole doing in the wall, miss?" said one of the policemen, as they wandered around, dusting things.

"Oh, it, um, got left," I said vaguely. Just then the phone rang. Was Shaz who said I could stay and told me where spare key was hidden.

Think will have little sleep.

11:45 p.m. Wish did not keep waking up in night, though is v. comforting having Jude and Shaz asleep in the room too like babies. Was v. nice when they came home from work. Had pizzas and I went to sleep really early. No word from or about Mark Darcy. At least have got panic button. Is nice. Is remote control operated by a little suitcase. Just think if I press it lithe young policemen will come round in uniform to save me!!!! Mmm. Delicious thought . . . v. sleepy . . .

〜 **SATURDAY 6 SEPTEMBER**

121 lbs., cigarettes 10, alcohol units 3, calories 4,255 (might as well enjoy life while still lucky enough to have it), minutes since had sex 16,005,124 (must, therefore do something about this).

6 p.m. Bit lonely now. Jude and Shaz went out shopping as said they had cabin fever. We tried ringing the police station, as am not allowed out without a policeman, but eventually, after forty-five minutes, we got through to a woman on central switchboard who said everyone was busy. Told Jude and Shaz definitely did not mind if they went out without me as long as they brought back a pizza. Ah. Telephone.

"Oh, hello, darling, it's Mummy here."

Mummy! Anyone would think I was about to do a poo-poo in her hand.

"Where are you, Mother?" I said.

"Oh, I've come out, darling."

For a second I thought she was telling me she was a lesbian and was going to set up home with Uncle Geoffrey in a gay, sexless marriage of convenience.

"We're back home. Everything's sorted out and Daddy's going to be fine. I don't know! Drinking all that time in his shed when I thought it was the tomatoes. Mind you, Gordon Gomersall had exactly the same thing, you know, and Joy had no idea. It's a disease, they say now."

"What's going on?" I said.

"Well, darling . . ." she began, then there was a kerfuffle and Dad came on the phone.

"It's all right, love. I've just got to stay off the booze," he said. "And they were trying to get Pam out of there from day one."

"Why?" I said, a lurid vision of my mother seducing a procession of eighteen-year-old drug addicts loomed up before my eyes.

He chuckled. "They said she was too normal. Let me give you back."

"Honestly, darling. It was all complete silly-daft nonsense charging these celebrity type of people loads of money to tell them things everybody knows already!"

"What kind of things?"

"Oooh, hang on. I'll just turn the chicken over."

I held the phone away from my ear, trying not to think about what kind of bizarre dish would involve an upside-down chicken.

"Oof. There we go."

"What things did they tell you?"

"Well, in the mornings we all had to sit in a circle and say all kinds of silly things."

"Like . . . ?"

"Oh, durrr! You know. My name's Pam and I'm a whatever!"

What? I wondered . . . ever? Madly overconfident nightmare? Lump-free gravy obsessive? Girl-child torturess?

"The things they were coming out with! 'Today I will be confident in myself, I will not worry about other people's opinions of me.' On and on and on. I mean, honestly, darling. If someone isn't confident in themselves they're not going to get anywhere, are they?" she said, roaring with laughter. "Durrr! Not confident in yourself! I don't know! Why would anyone go around worrying about what anyone else is thinking about them?"

I looked worriedly from side to side. "So what did you say for your affirmations?"

"Oh, I wasn't allowed to say anything. Well, actually I was, darling."

"What? What did you have to say?"

Heard my dad laughing in the background. He sounded on good form, anyway. "Tell her, Pam."

"Ufff. Well, I was supposed to say, 'I will not allow overconfidence to blind me to reality' and, 'Today I will recognize my faults as well as my assets.' I mean, it was completely ridiculous, darling. Anyway, must whizz, there's the buzzer. So I'll see you on Monday."

"What?" I said.

"Don't say what, say pardon, darling. I've made an appointment for you to have your colors done in Debenhams. I told you! Four o'clock."

"But . . ." I mean, she didn't. When did she tell me? January?

"Got to go, darling. The Enderburys are at the door."

~ **SUNDAY 7 SEPTEMBER**

122 lbs., sq. feet of floor space not covered by bras, shoes, food, bottles or lipstick 0.

10 a.m. Hurrah! Another day, and still not dead. Hideous night, though. Felt really tired after I'd been talking to Mum, so checked all the doors were locked, climbed under confusion of Shazzer's pants, camisoles and leopardskin throws and went to sleep. Didn't hear them come in, then woke up at midnight to find them asleep.

Is really starting to stink in here. Also, trouble is if wake up in night all can do is lie staring quietly at ceiling so as not to wake them up by knocking things over.

Ooh. Telephone. Best pick it up so as not to wake them.

"Well, they've realized I'm not a homicidal ex-lover."

Hurrah! Was Mark Darcy.

"How are you?" he said considerately, given that, thanks to me, it turned out, he'd been at the police station for seven hours. "I'd have called but they wouldn't tell me where you were till they'd cleared me."

Tried to be cheerful but ended up telling him in a whisper that it was a bit of a squash at Shazzer's.

"Well, the offer's still open to come and stay with me," he said off-handedly. "Plenty of bedrooms."

Wished he wouldn't keep rubbing it in so much that he didn't want to sleep with me. Seems to be turning into pashmina scenario and know from Shazzer and Simon how impossible that is to get out of once you start because at the merest hint of sex everyone starts panicking about "spoiling the friendship."

Just then, Jude yawned and turned over, dislodging a pile of shoe boxes with her foot, which crashed to the ground spilling beads, earrings, makeup and a cup of coffee into my handbag. I took a big breath.

"Thanks," I whispered into the phone. "I'd love to come."

11:45 p.m. Mark Darcy's house. Oh dear. Is not going very well. Am just lying alone in strange white room with nothing in it except white bed, white blind and worrying white chair which is twice as high as it should be. Is scary here: great big empty palace with not even any food in house. Cannot seem to find or do anything without colossal mental effort as every light switch, toilet flush, etc. disguised as something else. Also is freezing cold in manner of fridge.

Strange, twilight day, drifting in and out of sleep. Keep finding self going along as normal then hitting Sleepy Pocket, almost like when airplanes plunge down fifty feet as if from nowhere. Cannot decide if it is still jet lag or just trying to escape from everything.

Mark had to go into work today, even though Sunday, because of missing whole day on Friday. Shaz and Jude came round about four with the *Pride and Prejudice* video but could not face watching lake scene after Colin Firth debacle so we just talked and read magazines. Then Jude and Shaz started looking round the house, giggling. I fell asleep and when I woke up they'd gone.

Mark came home about nine with a takeaway for us both. Had high hopes for romantic reconciliation but was concentrating so hard on not giving the impression that I wanted to sleep with him, or in any way think staying at his house is anything other than police-type legal arrangement, that we ended up being all stiff and formal with each other in manner of doctor and patient.

Wish he would come in now. Is very frustrating being so close to him, and wanting to touch him. Maybe I should say something. But it seems too scary a can of worms to open, because if I tell him how I feel, and he doesn't want to get back together, it will just be hideously humiliating, given that we're living together. Also is middle of night.

Oh my God, though, maybe Mark did do it. Maybe he's going to come into the room and just, like, shoot me, and then there'll be blood all over the virgin white room in manner of virgin's blood except am not virgin. Just bloody celibate.

Must not think like that. Of course he didn't. At least have got panic button. Is so awful not being able to sleep and Mark downstairs, naked probably. Mmmm. Mmm. Wish could go downstairs and, like, ravish him. Have not had sex for . . . v. difficult sum.

Maybe he will come up! Will hear footsteps on stairs, door will open softly and he will come and sit on the bed—naked!—and . . . oh God, am so frustrated.

If only could be like Mum and just have confidence in self and not worry what anyone else is thinking, but that is very hard when you know that someone else *is* thinking about you. They're thinking how to kill you.

123 lbs. (serious crisis now), no. of death threateners captured by police 0 (non-v.g.), no. of seconds since had sex 15,033,600 (cataclysmic crisis).

1:30 p.m. Mark Darcy's kitchen. Have just eaten huge lump of cheese for no reason. Will check calories.

Oh fuck. One hundred calories an ounce. So pack is eight oz. and had already eaten a bit—maybe two oz.—and little bit left, so have eaten five hundred calories in thirty seconds. Oh well, might as well eat the rest of it as if to draw a line under whole sorry episode.

Think may be forced to accept truth of doctors saying diets don't work because your body just thinks it's being starved, and the minute it so much as sees any food again it gorges like a Fergie. Awake every morning now to find fat in bizarre and horrifying new places. Would not be in least surprised to find pizza dough–like strand of fat suspended between ear and shoulder or curving out at the side of one knee, rippling slightly in the wind like an elephant's ear.

Is still awkward and unresolved with Mark. When I went down this morning he'd already gone to work (not surprising as was lunchtime) but he had left a note saying to "make myself at home" and ask anyone I want to round. Like who? Everyone is at work. It's so quiet here. Am scared.

1:45 p.m. Look, it's all fine. Definitely. Realize have no job, no money, no boyfriend, flat with hole in which cannot go to, and am living with man I love in bizarre, platonic housekeeper-style capacity in giant fridge and someone wants to kill me, but this, surely, is temporary state.

2 p.m. Really want my mum.

2:15 p.m. Have rung police and asked them to take me to Debenhams.

Later. Mum was fantastic. Well, sort of. Eventually.

She turned up ten minutes late in top-to-toe cerise, hair all bouncy and coiffed with about fifteen John Lewis carrier bags.

"You'll never guess what, darling," she was saying as she sat down, dismaying the other shoppers with the carrier-bag spread.

"What?" I said shakily, gripping my coffee cup with both hands.

"Geoffrey's told Una he's one of these 'homos,' though actually he's not, darling, he's a 'bi,' otherwise they'd never have had Guy and Alison. Anyway, Una says she isn't the least bit bothered now he's come out with it. Gillian Robertson up at Saffron Waldhurst was married to one for years and it was a very good marriage. Mind you, in the end they had to stop because he was hanging round these hamburger vans in lay-bys and Norman Middleton's wife died— you know, who was head of the governors at the boys' school? So in the end, Gillian . . . Oh, Bridget, Bridget. What's the matter?"

Once she realized how upset I was she turned freakishly kind, led me out of the coffee shop, leaving the bags with the waiter, got a great mass of tissues out of her handbag, took us out to the back staircase, sat us down, and told me to tell her all about it.

For once in her life she actually listened. When I'd finished she put her arms round me like a mum and gave me a big hug, engulfing me in a cloud of strangely comforting Givenchy III. "You've been very brave, darling," she whispered. "I'm proud of you."

It felt so good. Eventually, she straightened up and dusted her hands.

"Now come along. We've got to think what we're going to do next. I'm going to talk to this detective chappie and sort him out. It's ridiculous that this person's been at large since Friday. They've had plenty of time to catch him. What have they been doing? Messing around? Oh, don't worry. I've got a way with the police. You can stay with us if you want. But I think you should stay with Mark."

"But I'm hopeless with men."

"Nonsense, darling. Honestly, no wonder you girls haven't got boyfriends if you're going out pretending to be superdooper whizz kids who don't need anybody unless he's James Bond, then sitting at home gibbering that you're no good with men. Oh, look at the time. Come on, we're late for your colors!"

Ten minutes later I was sitting in a Mark Darcy–esque white room in a white robe with a white towel on my head surrounded by Mum, a swathe of colored swatches and somebody called Mary.

"I don't know," tutted Mum. "Wandering round on your own worrying about all these theories. Try it with the crushed cerise, Mary."

"It's not me it's a social trend," I said indignantly. "Women are staying single because they can support themselves and want to do their careers, then when they get older all the men think they're desperate retreads with sell-by dates and just want someone younger."

"Honestly, darling. Sell-by dates! Anyone would think you were a tub of cottage cheese in ASDA! All that silly-daft nonsense is just in films, darling."

"No, it's not."

"Durrr! Sell-by date. They might pretend they want one of these bimbas but they don't really. They want a nice friend. What about Roger what's-his-name that left Audrey for his secretary? Of course she was thick. Six months later he was begging Audrey to come back and she wouldn't have him!"

"But . . ."

"Samantha she was called. Thick as two short planks. And Jean Dawson, who used to be married to Bill—you know Dawson's the butchers?—after Bill died she married a boy half her age and he's devoted to her, absolutely devoted and Bill didn't leave much of a fortune you know, because there isn't a lot of money in meat."

"But if you're a feminist, you shouldn't need a—"

"That's what's so silly about feminism, darling. Anyone with an ounce of sense knows we're the superior race. The only problem is when they think they can sit around when they retire and not do any housework. Now look at that, Mary."

"I preferred the coral," said Mary huffily.

"Well, exactly," I said, through a large square of aquamarine. "You don't want to go to work and then do all the shopping if they don't."

"I don't know! You all seem to have some silly idea about getting Indiana Jones in your house loading the dishwasher. You have to train them. When I was first married Daddy went to the Bridge Club every night! Every night! *And* he used to smoke."

Blimey. Poor Dad, I thought, as Mary held a pale pink swatch up against my face in the mirror and Mum shoved a purple one in front of it.

"Men don't want to be bossed around," I said. "They want you to be unavailable so they can pursue you and—"

Mum gave a big sigh. "What was the point of Daddy and me taking you to Sunday school week after week if you don't know what you think about things. You just stick to what you think's right and go back to Mark and—"

"It's not going to work, Pam. She's a Winter."

"She's a Spring or I'm a tin of pears. I'm telling you. Now you go back to Mark's house—"

"But it's awful. We're all polite and formal and I look like a dishrag . . ."

"Well, we're sorting that out, darling, aren't we, with your colors. But actually it doesn't make any difference what you look like, does it, Mary? You just have to be real."

"That's right," beamed Mary, who was the size of a holly bush.

"Real?" I said.

"Oh, you know, darling, like the Velveteen Rabbit. You remember! It was your favorite book Una used to read you when Daddy and I were having that trouble with the septic tank. There now, look at that."

"D'you know, I think you're right, Pam," said Mary, standing back in marvelment. "She is a Spring."

"Didn't I tell you?"

"Well, you did, Pam, and there was me with her down for a Winter! It just shows you, doesn't it?"

2 a.m. In bed, alone, Mark Darcy's house still. Seem to be spending entire life in entirely white rooms now. Got lost with policeman on way back from Debenhams. Was ridiculous. As said to policeman, was always taught as a child, when lost, to ask a policeman, but somehow he failed to see the humor of the situation. When eventually got back, hit another Sleepy Pocket and woke up at midnight to find house in darkness and Mark's bedroom door closed.

Maybe will go downstairs, make myself a cup of tea and watch TV in the kitchen. But what if Mark isn't back and is going out with someone and brings her home and I am like the mad aunt or Mrs. Rochester drinking tea?

Keep thinking back about what Mum said about being real and the Velveteen Rabbit book (though frankly have had enough trouble with rabbits in this particular house). My favorite book, she claims—of which I have no memory—was about how little kids get one toy that they love more than all the others, and even when its fur has been rubbed off, and it's gone saggy with bits missing, the little child still thinks it's the most beautiful toy in the world, and can't bear to be parted from it.

"That's how it works, when people really love each other," Mum whispered on the way out in the Debenhams lift, as if she was confessing some hideous and embarrassing secret. "But, the thing is, darling, it doesn't happen to ones who have sharp edges, or break if they get dropped, or ones made of silly synthetic stuff that doesn't last. You have to be brave and let the other person know who you are and what you feel." The lift was now stopping at Bathroom Fittings and Fixtures. "Oof! Well, that was fun, wasn't it!" she trilled with an abrupt change of tone, as three ladies in brightly colored blazers squeezed themselves and their ninety-two carrier bags each in alongside us. "You see, I knew you were a Spring."

It's all very well for her to say. If I told a man what I really feel they would run a mile. This—just to pluck an example out of the air—is what I feel at this precise moment.

1. Lonely, tired, frightened, sad, confused and extremely sexually frustrated.
2. Ugly, as hair sticking up in imaginative peaks and shapes and face all puffy from tiredness.
3. Confused and sad as no idea if Mark still likes me or not and scared to ask.
4. V. lovingful of Mark.
5. Tired of going to bed on my own and trying to deal with everything on own.
6. Alarmed by horrifying thought that have not had sex for fifteen million, one hundred and twenty thousand seconds.

So. To sum up what I really am is a lonely, ugly, sad act gagging for sex. Mmmm: attractive, inviting. Oh, I don't bloody well know what to do. Really fancy a glass of wine. Think will go downstairs. Will not have wine but probably tea. Unless there's some open. I mean it might actually help me sleep.

8 a.m. Crept down towards kitchen. Could not turn on lights as impossible to find designer light switches. Half hoped Mark would wake up when went past his door, but he didn't. Carried on creeping down the stairs, then froze. Was big shadow ahead like man. Shadow moved towards me. Realized it was man—great big man—and started screaming. By time had realized man was Mark—naked!—realized he was also screaming. But screaming much more than me. Screaming in complete, abandoned terror. Screaming—in a half-asleep way—as if he had just come across the most horrifying terrible scenario of his life.

Great, I thought: "Real." Then this is what happens when he sees me with mad hair and no makeup.

"It's me," I said. "It's Bridget."

For a second I thought he was going to start screaming even more, but then he sank down on the stairs, shaking uncontrollably. "Oh," he said, trying to breathe deeply. "Oh, oh."

He looked so vulnerable and cuddly sitting there that could not resist sitting down next to him, putting arms round him and pulling him close to me.

"Oh God," he said, nestling against my pajamas. "I feel such an arse."

It suddenly struck me as really funny—I mean it was really funny being terrified out of your wits by your own ex-girlfriend. He started laughing too.

"Oh Christ," he said. "It's not very manly, is it, getting scared at night. I thought you were the bullet man."

I stroked his hair, I kissed his bald patch where his fur had been loved off. And then I told him what I felt, what I really, really felt. And the miracle was, when I had finished, he told me he felt pretty much the same.

Hand in hand like the Campbell's Soup Kids, we made our way down to the kitchen and, with extreme difficulty, located Horlicks and milk from behind the baffling walls of stainless steel.

"You see, the thing is," said Mark, as we huddled round the oven, clutching our mugs trying to keep warm, "when you didn't reply to my note, I thought that was it, so I didn't want you to feel I was putting any pressure on. I—"

"Wait, wait," I said. "What note?"

"The note I gave you at the poetry reading, just before I left."

"But it was just your dad's 'If' poem."

Was unbelievable. Turns out when Mark knocked the blue dolphin over he wasn't writing a will he was writing me a note.

"It was my mother who said the only thing to do was to be honest about my feelings," he said.

Tribal elders—hurrah! The note was telling me that he still loved me, and he wasn't with Rebecca, and that I should ring him that night if I felt the same and otherwise he'd never bother me with it again but just be my friend.

"So why did you leave me and go off with her?" I said.

"I didn't! It was you who left me! And I didn't even bloody realize I was supposed to be going out with Rebecca till I got to her summer house party and found myself in the same room as her."

"But . . . so you didn't ever sleep with her?"

Was really, really relieved he had not been so callous as to wear my Newcastle United underpants gift for prearranged shag with Rebecca.

"Well." He looked down and smirked. "That night."

"What?" I exploded.

"I mean one's only human. I was a guest. It seemed only polite."

I started trying to hit him around the head.

"As Shazzer says, men have these desires eating away at them *all* the time," he went on dodging the blows. "She just kept inviting me to things: dinner parties, children's parties with barnyard animals, holidays—"

"Yur, right. And you didn't fancy her at all!"

"Well, she's a very attractive girl, it would have been odd if . . ." He stopped laughing, took hold of my hands and pulled me to him.

"Every time," he whispered urgently, "every time I hoped you'd be there. And that night in Gloucestershire, knowing you were fifty feet away."

"Two hundred yards in the servants' quarters."

"Exactly where you belong and where I intend to keep you till the end of your days."

Fortunately he was still holding me tight, so could not hit him anymore. Then he said the house was big, cold and lonely without me. And he really liked it best in my flat where it was cozy. And he said that he loved me, he wasn't exactly sure why, but nothing was any fun without me. And then . . . God, that stone floor was cold.

When we got up to his bedroom noticed a little pile of books beside his bed. "What are these?" I said, not believing my eyes. "*How to Love and Lose but Keep Your Self-Esteem? How to Win Back the Woman You Love? What Women Want? Mars and Venus on a Date?*"

"Oh," he said sheepishly.

"You bastard!" I said. "I threw all mine away." Fistfight broke out again, then one thing led to another and we just shagged, like, *all night!!!*

8:30 a.m. Mmm. Love looking at him when he's asleep.

8:45 a.m. Wish he would wake up now, though.

9 a.m. Will not actually *wake* him up, but maybe he will wake up himself just through thought vibes.

10 a.m. Suddenly Mark sat bolt upright and looked at me. Thought he was going to tell me off or start screaming again. But he smiled sleepily, sank back down and pulled me roughly to him.

"Sorry," I said afterwards.

"Yes, you should be," he murmured hornily. "What for?"

"Waking you up by staring."

"You know what?" he said. "I kind of missed it."

Ended up staying in bed quite a long time after that, which was fine because Mark didn't have any appointments that couldn't wait and I didn't have any appointments ever again for the rest of life. Just at a crucial moment, though, the phone rang.

"Leave it," gasped Mark, carrying on. The answerphone boomed out.

"Bridget, Richard Finch here. We're doing an item on the New Celibacy. We were trying to find a personable young woman who hadn't had sex for six months. Didn't have any joy. So I thought we'd settle just for any old woman who can't get laid and try you. Bridget? Pick up the phone. I know you're there, your loopy mate Shazzer told me. Bridget. Bridguuuuuuuurt. BRIDGURRRRRRRRRRRRT!"

Mark paused in his activities, raised one eyebrow in manner of Roger Moore, picked up the phone, murmured, "She's just coming, sir," and dropped it into a glass of water.

~ **FRIDAY 12 SEPTEMBER**

Minutes since had sex 0 (hurrah!).

Dreamy day, highlight of which was going to Tesco Metro with Mark Darcy. There was no stopping him putting things into the shopping cart: raspberries, tubs of Pralines and Cream Häagen-Dazs, and a chicken with a label on saying "extra fat thighs."

When we got to the checkout it was £98.70.

"That's incredible," he said, taking out his credit card, shaking his head in disbelief.

"I know," I said ruefully, "do you want me to chip in?"

"God, no. This is amazing. How long will this food last for?"

I looked at it doubtfully. "About a week?"

"But that's incredible. That's extraordinary."

"What?"

"Well, it cost less than a hundred quid. That's less than dinner at Le Pont de la Tour!"

Cooked the chicken with Mark and he was really quite carried away, pacing around the room expansively, in between chopping.

"I mean it's been such a great week. This must be what people do all the time! They go to work, and then they come home and the other person's there, and then they just chat and watch the television and they *cook food*. It's amazing."

"Yes," I said, looking from side to side wondering if actually he might be mad.

"I mean, I haven't rushed to the answerphone once to see if anyone's aware of my existence in the world!" he said. "I don't have to go sit in some restaurant with a book, and think I could end up dying alone and . . ."

". . . Being found three weeks later half eaten by an Alsatian?" I finished for him.

"Exactly, exactly!" he said, looking at me as if we had just discovered electricity simultaneously.

"Will you excuse me a minute?" I said.

"Of course. Er, why?"

"I'll just be a moment."

Was just rushing upstairs to call Shazzer with the groundbreaking news that maybe they are not the unattainable strategic adversary aliens after all, but just like us, when the phone rang downstairs.

Could hear Mark talking. He seemed to be on for ages, so could not ring Shazzer and eventually, thinking, "bloody inconsiderate," went down to the kitchen.

"It's for you," he said, holding out the phone. "They've got him."

Felt as if I'd been hit in the stomach. Mark held my hand as I took the phone, shaking.

"Hello, Bridget, DI Kirby here. We're holding a suspect over the bullet. We've obtained a DNA match with the stamp on the envelope it came in and the cups in your flat."

"Who is it?" I whispered.

"Does the name Gary Wilshaw mean anything to you?"

Gary! Oh my God. "He's my builder."

Turned out Gary was wanted for a number of petty thefts from houses he'd been doing up, and was arrested and fingerprinted early this afternoon.

"We have him in custody," said DI Kirby. "We haven't obtained a confession as yet but now we can go ahead on the connection, I'm pretty confident. We'll let you know and then you'll be safe to go back to your flat."

Midnight. My flat. Oh blimey. DI Kirby called back half an hour later and said Gary had made a tearful confession, and we could go back to the flat, not to worry about anything, and remember there was a panic button in the bedroom.

We finished the chicken then went over to my place, lit the fire, and watched *Friends*, then Mark decided to have a bath. The doorbell rang when he was in there.

"Hello?"

"Bridget, it's Daniel."

"Um."

"Can you let me in? It's important."

"Hang on, I'll come down," I said, glancing towards the bathroom. Thought I'd better sort things out with Daniel but did not want to risk incensing Mark. The minute I opened the front door I knew I'd done the wrong thing. Daniel was drunk.

"So you put the police on me, did you?" he slurred.

I started inching backwards away from him while maintaining eye contact, as if he were a rattlesnake.

"You were naked under that coat. You . . ."

Suddenly there was a great bounding of footsteps on the stairs, Daniel looked up and—*wham*—Mark Darcy had socked him in the mouth, and he was slumped against the front door, blood coming out of his nose.

Mark looked rather startled. "Sorry," he said. "Um . . ." Daniel started trying to get up and Mark rushed over and helped him up. "Sorry about that," he said again politely. "Are you all right, can I get you, um . . . ?"

Daniel just rubbed his nose and looked dazed.

"I'll be off then," he mumbled resentfully.

"Yes," said Mark. "I think that's best. Just make sure you leave her alone. Or, um, I'll have to, you know, do it again."

"Yup. Right," said Daniel obediently.

Once back in the flat, doors barred, it got pretty wild on the bedroom front. Could not bloody believe it when the doorbell rang again.

"I'll go," said Mark with a heavy air of manly responsibility, wrapping a towel round him. "It'll be Cleaver again. You stay here."

Three minutes later there was bounding of feet outside and the bedroom door burst open. Nearly screamed when DI Kirby put his head round. Pulled the blankets up to my chin, and followed his eye, scarlet with embarrassment, along the trail of clothes and underwear leading to the bed. He closed the door behind him.

"You're all right now," DI Kirby said in a calm, reassuring voice as if I were about to jump off a tall building. "You can tell me, you're safe, I've got people holding him outside."

"Who—Daniel?"

"No, Mark Darcy."

"Why?" I said, completely confused.

He glanced back at the door. "Miss Jones, you pressed the panic button."

"When?"

"About five minutes ago. We got a repeated, increasingly frantic signal."

I looked up to where I'd hung the panic button on the bedpost.

Not there. I fumbled sheepishly in the bedclothes beneath it, and produced the orange device.

DI Kirby looked from the button, to me, to the clothes on the floor, then grinned.

"Right, right. I see." He opened the door. "You can come back in, Mr. Darcy, if you still have the, er, energy."

There was much smirking amongst the policemen as the situation was euphemistically explained.

"OK. We're off. Enjoy yourselves," said DI Kirby as the policemen trundled back down the stairs. "Oh, just one thing. The original suspect, Mr. Cleaver."

"I didn't know Daniel was the original suspect!" I said.

"Well. We've attempted to question him on a couple of occasions and he did seem quite angrily resistant. It might be worth a call to smooth things over."

"Oh, thanks," said Mark sarcastically, trying to be dignified in spite of the fact that his towel was slipping. "Thanks for telling us now."

He saw DI Kirby out and could hear him explaining about the punch-up and DI Kirby saying to keep him informed of any problems and all stuff about deciding whether to press charges against Gary.

When Mark came back in I was sobbing. I'd just suddenly started and once I'd started for some reason I couldn't stop.

"It's all right," said Mark, holding me tight, stroking my hair. "It's all over. It's all right. Everything's going to be all right."

14

For Better or Worse?

11:15 a.m. Claridge's Hotel. Gaaah! Gaaah! GAAAAAAAAAH! Wedding is in forty-five minutes and have just spilt enormous splodge of Rouge Noir nail varnish down front of dress.

What am I doing? Weddings are insane torture concept. Torture-victim guests (though not, obviously, on same scale as Amnesty International clients) dressed up to nines in weird things such would never wear normally e.g. white tights, having to get out of bed practically in middle of night on Saturday morning, run round house shouting "Fuck! fuck! fuck!" trying to find old bits of wrapping paper with silver on, wrap up bizarre unnecessary gifts in manner of ice cream– or bread-makers (destined for endless recycling amongst Smug Marrieds, as who wants to lurch home at the end of the evening and spend an hour sieving ingredients into giant plastic machine, so when wake up in morning can consume entire giant loaf of bread on way to work instead of buying chocolate croissant when get cappuccino?), then drive four hundred miles, eating petrol-station wine gums, vomit in car and be unable to find church? Look at me! Why me, Lord? Why? Looks as if have started period in weird backwards-way-round way on dress.

11:20 a.m. Thank God. Shazzer just came back to room and we have decided best thing is to *cut out* the nail varnish patch from the dress as material so stiff, shiny and sticky-outy that has not gone through to lining underneath, which is same color and can hold bouquet in front.

Yes, sure that will be fine. No one will notice. Might even think it part of design. As if whole dress is part of extremely large piece of lace.

Good. Calm and poised. Inner poise. Presence or otherwise of hole in dress is not point of occasion, which is to do with other things. Fortunately. Sure it will all be serene and fine. Shaz was really far gone last night. Hope she is going to get through it today.

Later. Blimey! Arrived at church only twenty minutes late and immediately looked for Mark. Could tell he was tense just from back of head. Then the organ started up and he turned round, saw me and, unfortunately, looked as if he were going to burst out laughing. Could not blame him really as dressed not as sofa but as giant puffball.

We set off in stately procession down the aisle. God, Shaz looked rough. Had that air of intense concentration to prevent anyone noticing hangover. Walk seemed to go on forever to the tune of:

> *Here comes the bride*
> *Sixty inches wide.*
> *See how she wa-ddles from side unto side.*

I mean, why oh why?

"Bridget. Your foot," hissed Shaz.

Looked down. Shazzer's Agent Provocateur lilac bra with fur on was attached to the heel of my satin kitten-heel shoe. Considered kicking it off but then bra would be left lying tellingly in aisle throughout ceremony. Instead tried unsuccessfully to flip it under my dress causing brief interlude of awkward leaping gait with little result. Was blessed relief when got to front and could pick bra up and stuff it behind bouquet during hymn. Vile Richard looked great, really confident. He was just wearing an ordinary suit which was nice—not all dressed up in some insane morning suit–style outfit as if one of the extras from the film *Oliver* singing "Who Will Buy This Wonderful Morning?" and doing a high-kicking formation dance.

Unfortunately, Jude had made the—it was already beginning to seem—crucial mistake of not excluding tiny children from the wedding. Just as the actual wedding ceremony began, a baby started crying at the back of the church. It was top-level crying, of the sort when they start it off, then there's a pause while they draw breath like waiting for the thunder to come after the lightning, then a huge primal scream follows. Cannot believe middle-class modern mothers. Looked round to see this woman was jigging the baby up and down, rolling her eyes smugly at everyone as if to say "Durrrr!" It didn't seem to enter her head that it might be nice to take the baby out so the audience could hear Jude and Vile Richard pledge their souls together for a lifetime as one. A swish of long shiny hair at the back of the church caught my eye: Rebecca. She was wearing an immaculate soft gray suit and craning her neck in the direction of Mark. Beside her was a glum-looking Giles Benwick, holding a present with a bow on top.

"Richard Wilfred Albert Paul . . ." said the vicar in a resounding tone. Had no idea Vile Richard had so many Vile names. What were his parents thinking of?

". . . Wilt thou love her, cherish her . . ."

Mmmm. Love the wedding ceremony. V. heartwarming.

". . . Comfort and keep her . . ."

Dumph. A football crashed down the aisle into the back of Jude's dress.

". . . For better, for worse . . ."

Two tiny boys, wearing, I swear, tap-dancing shoes, broke free from their pews and tore after the ball.

". . . So long as you both shall live?"

There was a muffled noise, then the two boys started having an increasingly loud whispered gibberish conversation while the baby started crying again.

Above the din could faintly hear Vile Richard say "I will," though could possibly have been "I won't" apart from the fact that he and Jude were beaming at each other gooily.

"Judith Caroline Jonquil . . ."

How come I have only got two names? Has everyone except me got great long lists of gibberish after their name?

". . . Wilt thou take Richard Wilfred Albert Paul . . ."

Was vaguely aware of Sharon's prayer book starting to sway out of the corner of my left eye.

". . . Hapag . . ."

Shazzer's prayer book was definitely swaying now. Looked round in alarm, just in time to see Simon, in full morning dress, rush forward. Shazzer's legs started to fold under her in a slow-motion-type curtsy and she collapsed in a heap, straight into Simon's arms.

". . . Wilt thou love him, cherish him . . ."

Simon was now dragging Shazzer shiftily towards the vestry, her feet trailing along the ground out of the lilac puffball as if she were a dead body.

". . . Honor and obey . . ."

Obey Vile Richard? Briefly considered following Shazzer into the vestry to see if she was OK but what would Jude think if she turned round now in her worst hour of need, to find Shazzer and I had buggered off?

". . . So long as you both shall live?"

There was a series of bumps as Simon manhandled Shazzer into the vestry.

"I will."

The vestry door slammed shut behind them.

"I now declare you . . ."

The two little boys emerged from the font area and set off back down the aisle. God, the baby was really yelling now.

The vicar paused and cleared his throat. Turned round to see the boys kicking the football against the pews. Caught Mark's eye. Suddenly he put down his prayer book, stepped out of the pew, picked one of the boys up under each arm and marched them out of the church.

"I now declare you man and wife."

The whole church burst into applause and Jude and Richard beamed happily.

By the time we emerged from signing the register the atmosphere amongst the under-fives was positively festive. There was, effectively, a children's party going on in front of the altar and we walked back down the aisle behind a furious Magda carrying a screaming Constance out of the church going "Mummy will smack, she will smack, she will smack."

As we emerged into freezing rain and high winds, I overheard the mother of the footballing boys saying nastily to a bemused Mark, "But it's wonderful having children just being themselves at a wedding. I mean that's what a wedding is all about, isn't it?"

"I wouldn't know," said Mark cheerfully. "Couldn't hear a bloody thing."

Returned to Claridge's to find Jude's parents had unbridledly pushed the boat out and the ballroom was festooned with bronzed, beleaved and be-fruited streamer things and copper-colored pyramids of fruit and cherubs the size of donkeys.

All you could hear, when walked in, was people going:

"Two hundred and fifty grand."

"Oh come on. It must have been at least three hundred thousand."

"Are you kidding? Claridge's? Half a million."

Caught sight of Rebecca, looking frantically round the room with a fixed smile like a toy with a head on a stick. Giles was nervously following her, his hand hovering round her waist.

Jude's father, Sir Ralph Russell, a booming "don't worry, everyone, I'm a fantastically rich and successful businessman," was shaking Sharon's hand in the line.

"Ah, Sarah," he roared. "Feeling better?"

"Sharon," corrected Jude, radiantly.

"Oh yes, thank you," said Shaz, a hand delicately fluttering to her throat. "It was just the heat . . ."

Nearly spurted out laughing considering it was so fridgelike that everyone was wearing thermal underwear.

"Are you sure it wasn't the tightness of your stays against the Chardonnay, Shaz?" said Mark, at which she stuck a finger up at him, laughing.

Jude's mother smiled icily. She was stick-thin in some sort of encrusted Escada nightmare with unexplained fins sticking out around the hips, presumably to make it look as if she had some. (Oh joyous deception to be in need of!)

"Giles, don't put your wallet in your trouser pocket, darling, it makes your thighs look big," snapped Rebecca.

"Now you're being co-dependent, darling," said Giles, putting his hand towards her waist.

"I'm not!" said Rebecca, brushing his hand away crossly, then putting back the smile. "Mark!" she cried. She looked at him as if she thought the crowd had parted, time had stopped still and the Glenn Miller Band was going to strike up with "It Had to Be You."

"Oh hi," said Mark, casually. "Giles, old boy! Never thought I'd see you in a waistcoat!"

"Hello, Bridget," said Giles, giving me a smacking kiss. "Lovely dress."

"Apart from the hole," said Rebecca.

I looked away in exasperation and spotted Magda at the edge of the room looking agonized, obsessively pushing a nonexistent strand of hair from her face.

"Oh that's part of the design," Mark was saying, smiling proudly. "It's a Yurdish fertility symbol."

"Excuse me," I said. Then reached up and whispered in Mark's ear, "There's something wrong with Magda."

Found Magda so upset she could hardly speak. "Stop it, darling, stop it," she was saying vaguely as Constance tried messily to push a chocolate lolly into the pocket of her pistachio suit.

"What's wrong?"

"That . . . that . . . witch who had the affair with Jeremy last year. She's here! If he so much as dares fucking speak to her . . ."

"Hey, Constance? Did you enjoy the wedding?" It was Mark, holding out a glass of champagne for Magda.

"What?" said Constance, looking up at Mark with round eyes.

"The wedding? In the church?"

"The parpy?"

"Yes," he said laughing, "the party in the church."

"Well, Mummy took me out," she said, looking at him as if he were an imbecile.

"Fucking bitch!" said Magda.

"It was supposed to be a parpy," Constance said darkly.

"Can you take her away?" I whispered to Mark.

"Come on, Constance, let's go find the football."

To my surprise, Constance took his hand and happily pottered off with him.

"Fucking bitch. I'm gonna kill 'er, I'm gonna . . ."

I followed Magda's gaze to where a young girl, dressed in pink, was in animated conversation with Jude. It was the same girl I'd seen Jeremy with last year in a restaurant in Portobello and again outside The Ivy one night, getting into a taxi.

"What's Jude doing inviting her?" said Magda, furiously.

"Well, how would Jude know it was her?" I said, watching them. "Maybe she works with her or something."

"Weddings! Keep you only to her! Oh God, Bridge." Magda started crying and trying to fumble for a tissue. "I'm sorry."

Saw Shaz spot the crisis and start hurrying towards us.

"Come on, girls, come on!" Jude, oblivious, surrounded by enraptured friends of her parents, was about to chuck the bouquet. She started ploughing her way loudly towards us, followed by the entourage. "Here we go. Ready now, Bridget."

As if in slow motion, I saw the bouquet fly through the air towards me, half caught it, took one look at Magda's tear-stained face and chucked it at Shazzer, who dropped it on the floor.

"Ladies and gentlemen." A ludicrous be-knickerbockered butler was banging a cherub-shaped hammer on a bronze flower-decked lectern. "Will you please be silent and upstanding as the wedding party makes its way to the top table."

Fuck! Top table! Where was *my* bouquet? I bent down, picked up Jude's from Shazzer's feet and, with a gay fixed grin, held it up in front of the hole in my dress.

"It was when we moved to Great Missenden that Judith's outstanding gifts in the freestyle and butterfly strokes . . ."

By five o'clock Sir Ralph had already been talking for twenty-five minutes.

". . . Became *strongly* apparent not only to us, her admittedly *biased*"—he looked up to elicit a dutiful faint ripple of pretend laughter—"parents, but to the entire South Buckinghamshire region. It was a year in which Judith not only attained *first place* for the butterfly and freestyle sections in three consecutive tournaments in the South Buckinghamshire Under-Twelves Dolphin League but obtained her Gold Personal Survival Medal just three weeks before her first-year exams! . . ."

"What's going on with you and Simon?" I hissed to Shaz.

"Nothing," she hissed back, staring straight ahead at the audience.

". . . In that same very busy year Judith obtained a distinction in her Grade II Associated Board Examinations on the clarinet—an early indication of the rounded 'Famma Universale' she was to become . . ."

"But he must have been watching you in church otherwise he wouldn't have rushed up in time to catch you."

"I know, but I was sick in his hand in the vestry."

". . . Keen and accomplished swimmer, deputy head girl—and frankly this, as the headmistress privately admitted to me, was an error of judgment since Karen Jenkins's performance as head girl was . . . well. This is a day for celebration, not for regret, and I know Karen's, er, *father* is with us today . . ."

Caught Mark's eye and thought was going to explode. Jude was a model of detachment, beaming at everyone, stroking Vile Richard's knee and giving him little kisses for all the world as if the cauchemarish cacophony were not happening and she had not, on so many occasions, slumped drunkenly on my floor incanting

"Commitment-phobic bastard. Vile by name, and Vile by nature, 'ere, 'ave we run out of wine?"

". . . Second lead clarinetist in the school orchestra, keen trapezer, Judith was and is a prize *beyond rubies . . .*"

Could see where all this was leading. Unfortunately it took a further thirty-five-minute trawl through Jude's year off, Cambridge triumph, and meteoric rise through the corridors of the financial world to get there.

". . . And finally, it only remains for me to hope that, er . . ."

Everyone held their breath as Sir Ralph looked down at his notes for really beyond all sense, beyond all reason, beyond all decorum and good English manners, too long.

"Richard!" he said finally, "is suitably grateful for this priceless gift, this jewel, which has today been so graciously bestowed upon him."

Richard, rather wittily, rolled his eyes, and the room broke into relieved applause. Sir Ralph seemed inclined to continue with another forty pages, but mercifully gave up when the applause didn't.

Vile Richard then gave a short and rather endearing speech, and read out a selection of telegrams, which were all as dull as bricks apart from one from Tom in San Francisco, which unfortunately read: "CONGRATULATIONS: MAY IT BE THE FIRST OF MANY."

Then Jude got to her feet. She said a few very nice words of thanks and then—hurrah!—started reading out the bit that me and Shaz had done with her last night. This is what she said. As follows. Hurrah.

"Today I bade farewell to being a Singleton. But although I am now a Married I promise not to be a Smug one. I promise never to torment any Singletons in the world by asking them why they're still not married, or ever say 'How's your love life?' Instead, I will always respect that that is as much their private business as whether I am still having sex with my husband."

"I promise she will still be having sex with her husband," said Vile Richard and everyone laughed.

"I promise never to suggest that Singletondom is a mistake, or that because someone is a Singleton there is anything wrong with them. For, as we all know, Singletondom is a normal state in the modern world, all of us are single at different times in our lives and the state is every bit as worthy of respect as Holy Wedlock."

There was a ripple of appreciation. (At least I think that's what it was.)

"I promise also to keep in constant contact with my best friends, Bridget and Sharon, who are living proof that the Urban Singleton Family is just as strong and supportive, just as there for you, as anyone's blood family."

I grinned sheepishly as Shazzer dug her toe into mine under the table. Jude looked round at us and raised her glass.

"And now I'd like to raise a toast to Bridget and Shazzer: the best friends a girl could have in the whole world."

(I wrote that bit.)

"Ladies and gentlemen—the bridesmaids."

There was a huge roar of applause. Love Jude, love Shaz, I thought as everyone rose to their feet.

"The bridesmaids," said everyone. Was marvelous having all the attention. Saw Simon beaming at Shaz and looked across at Mark to see him beaming at me too.

Was all a bit hazy after that, but remember seeing Magda and Jeremy laughing together in a corner and catching her afterwards.

"What's going on?"

Turned out the trollop works in Jude's company. Jude told Magda all she knew was that the girl had had this distraught affair with a man who was still in love with his wife. She nearly died when Magda told her it was Jeremy, but all agreed we should not be horrible to the girl because it was really Jeremy who had been the fuckwit.

"Bloody old bugger. Anyway, he's learned his lesson now. Nobody's perfect and I love the old fart really."

"Well, look at Jackie Onassis," I said encouragingly.

"Well, exactly," said Magda.

"Or Hillary Clinton."

We both looked at each other uncertainly then started laughing.

Best bit was when I went out to the loo. Simon was snogging Shazzer with his hand up her bridesmaid dress!

There are sometimes those relationships that once you see them starting you just know, click: that's it, it's perfect, it's going to work, they'll go for the long haul—usually the sort of relationships you see starting between your immediate ex, who you were hoping to get back with, and somebody else.

I slipped back into the reception before Sharon and Simon saw me, and smiled. Good old Shaz. She deserves it, I thought, then stopped in my tracks. Rebecca was clutching Mark's lapel, talking passionately to him. I darted behind a pillar and listened.

"Don't you think," she was saying. "Don't you think it's perfectly possible for two people who ought to be together, a perfect match in every way—in intellect, in physique, in education, in position—to be kept apart, through misunderstanding, through defensiveness, through pride, through . . ." She paused, then rasped darkly, "the interference of others and end up with the wrong partners. Don't you?"

"Well yes," murmured Mark. "Though I'm not quite sure about your list of . . ."

"Do you? Do you?" She sounded drunk.

"It so nearly happened with Bridget and me."

"I know! I know. She's wrong for you, darling, as Giles is for me. . . . Oh, Mark. I only went to Giles to make you realize what you feel for me. Perhaps it was wrong but . . . they're not our equals!"

"Um . . ." said Mark.

"I know, I know. I can sense how trapped you feel. But it's your life! You can't live it with someone who thinks Rimbaud was played by Sylvester Stallone, you need stimulus, you need—"

"Rebecca," said Mark quietly, "I need Bridget."

At this, Rebecca let out a horrifying noise, which was something between a pissed wail and an angry bellow.

Gently determined not to feel any shallow sense of triumph, nor gloating, unspiritual glee that the two-faced, stick-insect-legged snooty bitch from Bogoffland had got her comeuppance, I glided away, beaming smugly all over my face.

Ended up leaning against a pillar by the dance floor, watching Magda and Jeremy locked in an embrace, bodies moving together in a ten-year-old practiced dance, Magda's head on Jeremy's shoulder, eyes closed, peaceful, Jeremy's hand roaming idly over her bottom. He whispered something to her and she laughed without opening her eyes.

Felt a hand slip round my waist. It was Mark, looking at Magda and Jeremy too. "Want to dance?" he said.

15

Excess Christmas Spirit

129 lbs. (seems, alas to be true that weight finds own level), cards sent 0, presents purchased 0, improvement in hole in wall since originally made: single holly sprig.

6:30 p.m. Everything is lovely. Usually, week before Christmas, am hung over and hysterical, furious with self for not escaping to tiny woodman's cottage deep in forest to sit quietly by fire; instead of waking up in huge, throbbing, mountingly hysterical city with population gnawing off entire fists at thought of work/cards/present deadlines, getting trussed up like chickens in order to sit in gridlocked streets bellowing like bears at newly employed minicab drivers for trying to locate Soho Square using a map of central Addis Ababa, then arrive at parties to be greeted by same group of people have seen for last three nights only three times more drunk and hung over and want to shout "WILL YOU ALL JUST SOD OFF!" and go home.

That attitude is both negative and wrong. At last have found way to live peaceful, pure and good life, hardly smoking at all and only a bit pissed once at Jude's wedding. Even drunk man at party on Friday did not really disturb equilibrium when called me and Sharon "glib media whores."

Also got brilliant mail today, including postcard from Mum and Dad in Kenya saying Dad has been having a whale of a time on

Wellington's jet ski and did the limbo with a Masai girl on buffet night and they hoped Mark and I won't be too lonely without them at Christmas. Then a PS from Dad saying, "We haven't got twins (beds, not gigolos), it's well over six foot and more than satisfactory on the bouncy front! *Hakuna Matata.*"

Hurrah! Everyone is happy and at peace. Tonight, for example, am going to write Christmas cards not with reluctance but with joy!—for as it says in *Buddhism: The Drama of the Moneyed Monk*, the secret of spiritual happiness is not doing the washing up in order to get the washing up done but to do the washing up. Is exactly the same with Christmas cards.

6:40 p.m. Bit of a boring idea though, just sitting in all evening writing Christmas cards when is Christmas.

6:45 p.m. Maybe will have one of chocolate tree decorations.

6:46 p.m. Maybe—too—will just have little festive glass of wine to celebrate Christmas.

6:50 p.m. Mmm. Wine is delicious. Maybe will have one cigarette also. Just one.

6:51 p.m. Mmm. Cigarette is lovely. I mean self-discipline isn't everything. Look at Pol Pot.

6:55 p.m. Will start cards in a minute when have finished wine. Maybe will just read letter again.

• **CINNAMON PRODUCTIONS** •
Sit Up Britain   FiveAlive   Blind Snog

FROM THE DESK OF GRANT D. PIKE, CHIEF EXECUTIVE

Dear Bridget,

As you may have been aware, a Staf-trak program has been under way during the last year monitoring staff performance and the flow of ideas throughout Cinnamon Productions.

You will be delighted to hear that 68 percent of the fun "And finally" end of program items on Sit Up Britain have originated with you. Congratulations!

We understand that your resignation in September arose through disagreements with Sit Up Britain's executive producer Richard Finch. Richard, as I'm sure you have heard, was suspended from his position in October due to "personal difficulties."

We are currently reorganizing the staffing on the show and would like to invite you to rejoin the team, either promoted to assistant producer or in consultatory capacity, providing a flow of ideas on a freelance basis. The period since your resignation would be considered as paid leave.

We believe that—injected with new positive energy and get up and go—Sit Up, as the flagship of Cinnamon Productions, has a great future in the twenty-first century. We hope that you will be a major creative force in our new revamped team. If you will telephone my secretary to arrange an appointment I will be delighted to discuss revised terms and conditions with you.

Yours,
Grant D. Pike
Chief Executive, Cinnamon Productions

You see! You see! Also Michael from the *Independent* says I can have another go at a celebrity interview as they got quite a few letters after the Mr. Darcy interview. As he said, anything that gets letters is good no matter how bad it is. So I can be a freelance. Hurrah! And then I never have to be late. Think will have a top up to celebrate. Ooh goody, doorbell!

Goody, goody. Is arrival of Christmas tree. You see! *Really* on top of Christmas. Mark is coming round tomorrow and will find Christmas Casbah!

8 p.m. As tree men staggered upstairs, grunting and gasping, feared may have underestimated largeness of tree, especially when terrifyingly filled entire doorway then burst through, branches flapping like invasion of Macduff in woods of Dunsinane. A spray of soil and two youths followed going, "It's a fucking big 'un, where do you wan' it?"

"By the fire," I said. Unfortunately, however, tree would no way fit, some branches poking into flames, others forced up vertically by sofa and rest burgeoning into middle of room while top of tree bent at odd angle against ceiling.

"Can you try it over there?" I said. "What's that smell by the way?"

Claiming it was some Finnish invention to stop the needles dropping, rather than the obvious fact that the tree had gone off, the boys struggled to place tree between bedroom and bathroom doors at which branches sprang out totally blocking both.

"Try the middle of the room?" I said with tremendous dignity.

The boys sniggered at each other and manhandled tree monster into the center of the room. At this point I couldn't see either of them anymore. "That's fine, thank you," I said in a high, strangled voice, and they departed giggling all the way down the stairs.

8:05 p.m. Hmm.

8:10 p.m. Well, is no problem. Will simply detach from issue of tree and write cards.

8:20 p.m. Mmm. Love the lovely wine. Question is, does it matter if you don't send Christmas cards? Sure there are people from whom have never in my life received a Christmas card. Is this rude? Always seems faintly ridiculous to send e.g. Jude or Shazzer a Christmas card when see them every other day. But then how can one expect cards in return? Except that, of course, sending cards never yields fruit until following year, unless send cards in first week of December but would be unthinkable, Bored-Married-style behavior. Hmm. Maybe should do list of pros and cons of sending cards.

8:25 p.m. Think will just have little look at Christmas *Vogue* first.

8:40 p.m. Attracted yet massively undermined by *Vogue* world of Christmas. Realize own fashion look and gift ideas grimly outdated and ought to be cycling, wearing slippy Dosa petticoat with eiderdown on top and puppy slung over shoulder, posing at parties with prepubescent model daughter and planning to buy friends pashmina hot-water bottle covers, fragrant stuff to put in laundry instead of usual stench from service wash, silver flashlights from Asprey—with Christmas tree lights meanwhile reflecting sparklingly off teeth.

Am not going to take any notice. Is v. unspiritual. Just imagine if Pompeii-style volcano erupted south of Slough, and everyone was preserved in stone on bicycles wearing puppies, eiderdowns and daughters, future generations would come and laugh at spiritual emptiness of it. Also reject mindless luxury gifts, which say more about showy-offiness of giver than thought for receiver.

9 p.m. Would quite like pashmina hot-water bottle for self though.

9:15 p.m. Christmas gift list:

> Mum—pashmina hot-water bottle cover.
> Dad—pashmina hot-water bottle cover.

Oh God. Cannot ignore tree pong any longer: is pungent and repulsively reminiscent of pine-scented shoe insole that has been worn for several months penetrating walls and solid hardwood door. Bloody tree. Only way to traverse room now would be to snuffle under tree in manner of wild boar. Think will read Christmas card from Gary again. Was great. Card was rolled up in shape of bullet and "Sorry!" on it. Inside it said:

> Dear Bridget,
>
> Sorry about the bullet. I do not know what come over me but things have not gone good for me with money and the fishing incident. Bridget, it was special between us. It really meant something. I was going to finish the infill when the money came through. When that solicitor's

letter come it was that wanky I was gutted and lost a grip on myself.

Then there was a copy of *Angler's Mail* opened at page 10. Opposite a page headed "Carp World" with an article on "Pick of the Pellet Feeds" were six pictures of fishermen all holding big slimy gray fish, including one of Gary with a pretend stamp across saying "Disqualified" and a column underneath headed:

BOILING MAD

THREE TIMES EAST HENDON CHAMPION GARY WILSHAW HAS BEEN SUSPENDED FROM EAST HENDON AA AFTER A FISH SWITCHING INCIDENT. WILSHAW, 37, OF WEST ELM DRIVE, TOOK FIRST PLACE WITH THIS 32 LB. 12 OZ. COMMON CARP ALLEGEDLY ON A SIZE 4 HOOK TO A 15 LB. SNAKE-BITE HOOK LINK AND 14 MM. BOILIE.

IT LATER EMERGED, THROUGH A TIP-OFF, THAT THE CARP WAS A FARMED FISH FROM EAST SHEEN, PROBABLY PLANTED ON THE SIZE 4 OVERNIGHT.

A SPOKESMAN FOR EAST HENDON AA SAID, "THIS KIND OF PRACTICE BRINGS THE ENTIRE SPORT OF RESERVOIR COARSE FISHING INTO DISREPUTE AND CANNOT BE TOLERATED BY THE EAST HENDON AA."

9:25 p.m. You see, felt powerless like Daniel. Poor Gary with his fish. Humiliated. He loves fish. Poor Daniel. Men at risk.

9:30 p.m. Mmm. Wine's delicious. Is festive party on own. Think of all lovely people who have been in life syear, even ones who did bad things. Feel nothing but love and forgiveness. Holding on to resentment juss eesaway at one.

9:45 p.m. Swil write carsnow. Will do liss.

11:20 p.m. Dunnit. Off to postssbox now.

11:30 p.m. Backinfla. Blurry tree. I know. Wllget scissors.

Midnight. Yurs. Berrer. Oof. Sleepynow. Oops. Tumbled over.

138 lbs., alcohol units 6, cigarettes 45, calories 5,732, chocolate tree deco-rations 132, cards sent—oh God, hell, beelzebub and all his subpoltergeists.

8:30 a.m. Bit confused. Has just taken an hour and seven minutes to get dressed and am still not dressed, having realized there is splodge on front of skirt.

8:45 a.m. Have got skirt off now. Will put gray one on instead, but where the fuck is it? Oof. Head hurts. Right, am not going to drink again for . . . Oh, maybe skirt is in living room.

9 a.m. In living room now, but everything is such a mess. Think will have some toast. Cigarettes are evil poison.

9:15 a.m. Gaah! Have just seen tree.

9:30 a.m. Gaah! Gaah! Have just found card that got missed. This is what says:

> Happy Christmas to my dearest, dearest Ken. I have so ap-preciated all your kindness this year. You are a wonderful, wonderful person, so strong, and clear-sighted and good with figures. Although we have had our ups and downs, it is so important not to hold on to resentment if one is to grow. I feel very close to you now, both as a professional, and as a man.
>
> With real love,
> Bridget

Who is Ken? Gaaah! Ken is accountant. Have only met him once and then we had row about sending my VAT in late. Oh my God. Must find list.

Gaaah! As well as Jude, Shazzer, Magda, Tom etc. list includes:

The assistant to the British Consul, Bangkok
The British ambassador to Thailand
Rt. Hon. Sir Hugo Boynton
Admiral Darcy
DI Kirby
Colin Firth
Richard Finch
The foreign secretary
Jed
Michael at the *Independent*
Grant D. Pike
Tony Blair

Cards are at large in the world and do not know what have put in them.

~ **WEDNESDAY 17 DECEMBER**

No feedback from cards. Maybe the others were fine actually and Ken's was throwback freak.

~ **THURSDAY 18 DECEMBER**

9:30 a.m. Was just on way out when phone rang.

"Bridget, it's Gary!"

"Oh hi!" I trilled hysterically. "Where are you?"

"In the nick, aren't I? Thanks for the card. That was sweet. Sweet. It really means the world."

"Oh, hahahaha," I laughed nervously.

"So are you going to come to see me today?"

"What?"

"You know . . . the card."

"Uuuum?" I said in a high, strangled voice. "I can't quite remember what I put. Do you . . . ?"

"I'll read it to you, shall I?" he said shyly. Then proceeded to read, stumbling over the words.

> Dearest Gary,
>
> I know that your job as a builder is very different from mine. But I totally respect that, because it is a real craft. You make things with your hands and get up very early in the mornings and together—even though the infill extension isn't finished—we have built something great and beautiful, as a team. Two very different people, and even though the hole in the wall is still there—after nearly eight months!—I can see the growth of the project through it. Which is wonderful. I know that you are in prison, serving your dues, but soon the time of that will be over. Thank you for your card about the bullet and the fishing and I really, really forgive you.
>
> I feel very close to you now, both as a craftsman, and as a man. And if anyone deserves joy and a real creative charge in the coming year—even in prison—it is you.
>
> > With love,
> > Bridget

"Creative charge," he said in a throaty voice. Managed to get away by explaining was late for work but . . . Oh God. Who have I sent them to?

7 p.m. Back home. Went in for first consultancy meeting in office, which went really quite well, actually—especially since Horrible Harold has been demoted to fact checker for being boring—until

Patchouli yelled that she'd got a call from Richard Finch in the Priory, she was putting it on speakerphone and everyone had to listen.

"Hello team!" he said. "Just called to spread a little festive spirit as it's the only sort I'm allowed. I'd like to read you something." He cleared his throat. "'A merry, merry Christmas, dearest Richard.' Isn't that nice?" There was a spurt of laughter. "'I know our relationship has had its ups and downs. But now it is Christmas I realize it is very strong—challenging, vigorous, honest and true. You are a fascinating, fascinating man, full of vigor and contradiction. I feel very close to you now it is Christmas—both as a producer and as a man. With love, Bridget.'"

Oh, oh, it was just . . . Gaah! Doorbell.

11 p.m. It was Mark. With a very odd expression on his face. He came into the flat and looked around in consternation. "What's that strange smell? What in the name of arse is that?"

I followed his gaze. Christmas tree in truth did not look as good as remembered. Had chopped off top and tried to trim rest into traditional triangular shape but now, in middle of room, was tall thin shorn thing with blunt edges like very bad cheap pretend tree from discount store.

"It was a bit—" I started to explain.

"A bit what?" he said with a mixture of amusement and incredulity.

"Big," I said lamely.

"Big, eh? I see. Well, never mind that for now. Can I read something to you?" he said, taking a card out of his pocket.

"OK," I said resignedly, sinking down on the sofa. Mark cleared his throat.

"'My dear, dear Nigel,'" he began. "You remember my colleague, Nigel, do you, Bridget? Senior partner in the company. The fat one who isn't Giles?" He cleared his throat again. "'My dear, dear Nigel. I know we have only met once at Rebecca's when you pulled her out of the lake. But now it is Christmas, I realize, through being Mark's closest colleague, you have in a strange way been close to me

336

all year too. I feel' "—Mark paused and gave me a look—" 'very close to you now. You are a wonderful man: fit, attractive'—this, I remind you, is Fat Nigel we're talking about—'vigorous' "—he paused and raised his eyebrows—" 'brilliant creatively, because being a lawyer is actually a very creative job, I will always think fondly of you, glistening' "—he was laughing now—" 'glistening . . . glistening *bravely* in the sunlight and the water. Merry Christmas to my dear, dear Nigel. Bridget.' "

I slumped on the sofa.

"Now come on." Mark grinned. "Everyone will know you were pissed. It's funny."

"I'm going to have to go away," I said sorrowfully. "I'm going to have to leave the country."

"Well, actually," he said, kneeling in front of me and taking my hands, "it's interesting you should say that. I've been asked to go to LA for five months. To work on the Mexican Calabreras case."

"What?" It was all getting worse and worse.

"Don't look so traumatized. I was going to ask you . . . Will you come with me?"

I thought hard. I thought about Jude and Shazzer, and Agnès B on Westbourne Grove, and cappuccinos in Coins, and Oxford Street.

"Bridget?" he said gently. "It's very warm and sunny there and they have swimming pools."

"Oh," I said, eyes darting interestedly from one side to the other.

"I'll wash up," he promised.

I thought about bullets and fish, and drug smugglers and Richard Finch and my mum and the hole in the wall and the Christmas cards.

"You can smoke in the house."

I looked at him, so earnest and solemn and sweet and thought that wherever he was, I didn't want to be without him.

"Yes," I said happily, "I'd love to come."

11 a.m. Hurrah! Am going to America to start again, like the early pioneers. The land of the free. Was really good fun last night. Mark and me got out scissors again and did festive topiary turning tree into tiny Xmas cracker. Also we have made list and are going to do shopping tomorrow. Love Christmas. Celebration of good fun life, surely not perfection. Hurrah! Will be fantastic in California with sunshine and millions of self-help books—though will eschew all dating books—and Zen and sushi and all healthy stuff like green . . . Ooh goody, telephone!

"Er, Bridget. It's Mark." His voice did not sound good. "There's been a bit of a change of plan. The Calabreras case has been put back till June. But there is another job I quite fancy taking on and, er, I was wondering . . ."

"Yes?" I said suspiciously.

"How would you feel about . . ."

"About what?"

"Thailand?"

Think will just have a little glass of wine and a cigarette.